PRAISE FOR

when
patty
went
away

"A remarkably moving novel, heartbreaking and hopeful; there are scenes of great power; but what strikes me most about this novel is that it is true, and real."

—**Molly Gloss**, author of *The Jump-Off Creek* and
The Hearts of Horses

"Jeannie Burt's important debut signals that another powerful voice has joined the chorus of outstanding women writing about the West."

—**Craig Lesley**, author of *The Sky Fisherman* and
Winterkill

"Jeannie Burt writes like a dream. Her nuanced tale of a quiet man who confronts his weaknesses to become a hero resonates with grace, depth, and humanity."

—**Lisa Alber**, author of *Kilmoon, A County Clare Mystery*

"Engaging, hypnotic . . . a wonderful read from a debut novelist."

—**Michael Bigham**, author of *Harkness* and
Thunderhead

Also by Jeannie Burt

LYMPHEDEMA:
A BREAST CANCER PATIENT'S GUIDE
TO PREVENTION AND HEALING

WHAT YOU NEED TO KNOW
TO SHOW YOUR DOG

when patty went away

Muskrat Press • Portland

when patty went away

A NOVEL

JEANNIE BURT

Muskrat Press, LLC
Portland, Oregon
info@muskratpress.com or publicity@muskratpress.com

Publisher's Cataloging-in-Publication Data
Burt, Jeannie.
  When Patty went away / Jeannie Burt.
    pages cm
  ISBN: 978-0-9895446-3-4 (pbk.)
  ISBN: 978-0-9895446-4-1 (e-book)
    1. Missing persons—Fiction. 2. Teenage prostitution—Fiction. 3. Life change events—Fiction. 4. Oregon—Fiction. I. Title.
PS3602.U7691 W56 2014
813—dc23
                              2013915865

Book design: Jennifer Omner
Book cover: Kimberly Glyder
Cover photo (table): Horiyan © (landscape): Roger Burt
Author photo: Manuel Cobarrubias

Printed in the United States of America
First Edition

For Roger

chapter 1

I USED TO think if you didn't take a breath, or didn't blink, or didn't make any other kind of move, nothing would ever change, and you could hold onto that moment and that day, and you could count on it. But I came to learn you could hold your breath forever and it wouldn't make one inch of difference.

Looking back, I could blame everything on the storm. Only it wasn't the storm, it was the times, and the way we lived, and the way we looked away when things weren't what we wanted them to be.

The summer had been sweet. Our crop, durum wheat, with heads as blond as Marilyn Monroe, whistled in the dry wind, calling out. In spite of three years of dry so bad it went on record, we were counting on a good year, even putting a dollar or two in the bank. The way the prices were going, it could have been gold for us. We'd guessed we were heading for fifty, sixty bushels to the acre, poor yields in the best years, but the wife had been saying, "Praise the Lord if the prices stay up," and I let myself believe she had some kind of link that pulled strings up there.

The day of the storm, my Molly was at the doctor's again, trying something new to get pregnant. Edie, our only child, was spending the afternoon in town at the swimming pool. It was the first time she'd had courage enough to go in for swimming since the shame of the past few months when we all, everyone but my daughter, shut our eyes to what was right before us.

We had planted sixteen hundred acres and, when the storm was done with it, all that stood of our crop was fifty. Prices had been good since the start of the drought three years before, but after the storm, it didn't matter how the prices went. A ruined crop wasn't worth a dime.

The storm came up toward Milton-Freewater, fifteen miles away. Lee and I were in the shop inside the old barn I'd split in half for a repair shop. My brother and I had been working on one of the two threshers for nearly a week, changing sickle sections, checking bearings. A bearing in the scythe had gone out as we were winding up the year before, and we had limped along the rest of harvest, finishing up with the old International. People joked that farmers could do anything with a little string and haywire, and Lee and I pretty much proved them right.

The day had started out with a soft kind of warm that made you want to gulp it down and swallow the clear blue of it, the sky so deep you could just flop over and lie there in it forever. Lee had come out about seven fifteen, the same time he showed up every morning at the school, where during the rest of the year he taught history and coached basketball. He must have felt like I did about the day, because he had pulled the barn doors open to let in as much of it as he could. It was near noon. Pretty soon, we'd hear Molly drive in from her doctor's appointment in Pendleton, and a little while later she would bang a spoon on a pot from the house and call us in for something to eat.

Sometimes I felt like Lee and I only pretended we knew what we were doing in the shop. We were farmers, or at least I was. Lee had moved on after he went to college, married Helen a year after he'd started teaching school. He always joked it took him nine months' teaching school to get the grit out of his ears from helping me during summer harvest.

The way farming had been going the past three years, with the hopelessness a drought could leave with you, I'd started to think maybe younger brothers were smarter than their older ones, that my little brother had it right when he passed up farming to go on to Oregon State for his teaching degree. But I had always pictured myself farming, doing what my dad did, and his dad, and his granddad before him. No matter, I looked forward to summers with my little brother, and I think he did, too.

We'd taken the header off the John Deere, had parts spread all over the place, some soaking in a pail of gasoline outside the doors, out of the reach of sparks we might have thrown up from the welder. Now and then a little breeze wafted in and carried the smell of gas with it. I liked that smell. Two of the cats, Tom, the yellow striped, and Queer, the long-haired white, were asleep in the seat of the thresher, paying no attention to our pounding or to the fizz of the welder.

We might have noticed the clouds sooner, but the light didn't go out of the sky until the thunderhead was almost on us. We heard it first, a whack so loud Lee heard it over the welder and pushed up his helmet. Then it went dark, and everything outside the barn started hissing and popping as hail hit it.

I unknotted myself from the innards of the John Deere as another crack let loose, so loud it made me duck. The dogs started barking, came running from somewhere out around the pigpens. One of the pigs squealed, another made a deep sound like it was clearing its throat.

"Jack!" Lee yelled. He dropped the welding helmet. His mouth moved, but another clap hit with so much noise I couldn't hear him.

3

Everything outside the barn went dark as coal. Lee and I stumbled out the door as the sky belched ice balls. The whole world made noise, the balls sizzling like bacon in a frying pan, on every piece of metal they hit—the gas tanks, the oil drums, the silo, the hood of my pickup, the roofs of the wheat trucks. The hail beat Lee and me on the head, hammered our shoulders. It blew into the pan of gas, and the gas splattered like it was alive, white balls bobbing back up again, dark with grease.

The hills disappeared. We couldn't see any farther than the pigpen in one direction and the house in the other. All but one pig had hidden inside the sty, but that one pig was running around the pen squealing, shaking its head, flapping its ears, its back beginning to bleed, taking on the color of hamburger from the pounding of hail.

All my life I'd believed a farm was a solid thing, something to keep hold of like my wife, like my daughter. A farm was not something that was supposed to lie open, vulnerable to anything that came along. You learned a farm like you learned your face when you shaved it, or the way you knew onions were going to sit in your stomach, or the way your wife would scold when you tracked mud into the house. You learned the cant of every hill, how to set a drill to work it, where a crop would prosper and where you had to coddle it. You learned the creatures on it, the pigs, the calves in the feeding pen, the crows that lived with the rust of machines in the junkyard, the pheasants that flushed up every year and startled you all over again. You learned the frogs that croaked in the ditch like a hundred wood screws too tight for their holes. You learned which cow would come in first every year and bellow for the bull. You learned it all, down to when to shave the dogs because their haunches were sore from the mess of cockle burrs caught in their fur.

But you couldn't learn sleet, or smut, or drought. And you couldn't learn hail.

chapter 2

LEE STAYED OUT at my place long after the noise and the blackness blew over. When the sun blasted out from behind the thunderhead, the world went quiet. A branch from one of the big poplars lay on the ground, the barn roof dripped with ice melt. Steam rose from the beds of the trucks, from the hood of the tractor, from the chicken house and the pig shed.

I tried to concentrate, tried to think what came next. Two hours ago, I would have known. Sections of the scythe were still strewn all over the shop floor.

Lee and I climbed into the pickup and drove, saying nothing until we came to the one corner of a quarter section that had been spared. And there we sat, the truck running, our palms set on our thighs as if waiting for the wheat to pop right back up for the headers and scythes. It was geometric, the damage, the break between the tattered wheat and the fifty acres that hadn't been touched, straight as a knife blade.

It was Lee who spoke first. "There's some you could probably still get up." He was always the one to look at the lighter side.

"Yeah," I said, hearing the bitterness. "Maybe bring in eighty, ninety clods to the bushel." The stalks had snapped so low, the heads of the wheat had shattered, so their bounty of grain lay like a gold foil on the damp ground. All of it was down, so flat no thresher could get it.

In silence, Lee and I drove back to the house, stumbled into the barn. Molly and Edie pulled in not long after that. I watched as the station wagon edged into the garage, slowly, carefully, a little too close to the wall. Edie was driving more since she got her permit. For five years, I'd had her driving truck. A truck she could handle. But a car, on the road, with her mother sitting beside her, seemed to make her lose the little bit of confidence she had.

Molly and Edie approached the barn door together, Edie holding the roll of her damp towel from swimming, Molly in her flowered tent of a dress clutching two grocery bags in her large, tanned arms. Her mouth was pinched in, and I knew she had seen some of the damage from the road.

Molly nodded at Lee, her expression formal, keeping him at arm's length. Then she came over and stood by me, her breath coming shallow and raspy. "When did it happen?"

"A couple hours ago," I said.

"What's the damage?"

"All," I said.

A WEEK LATER, the light-headedness still hadn't left. I couldn't sleep, yet in spite of that, I didn't feel sleepy. I ate, did chores, cleaned the watering trough, but it was dizzy in my head, like I was watching someone else. I felt breathless, clouded, a feeling that made grade school teachers put paper bags over students' mouths and tell them to breathe five times. The world vibrated and spun and all I had was years of habit to hang onto.

I walked nearly every acre I'd planted. The fields crackled under my feet. Fifty acres. That was it. We'd have to make do with fifty acres. I should have been thankful for it, but the fifty acres that were still standing might give us enough to live on for a month, *if* we didn't pay any bills, or buy school clothes for Edie.

Molly and I farmed nearly ten sections, 3,253 acres of dryland crop. Every year, after harvest, land without irrigation has to lie fallow, unplanted, left to breathe, to collect, and store up what you hope will be enough moisture to support a crop the next year. Every year we, Lee, Molly, Edie, and me, brought in crop from half of our land. And from it I had to pay my mother her share, had to pay Lee for the work he did, had to buy fertilizer and diesel for the equipment, had to buy clothes, and braces for my daughter's teeth. On a good year, it took every inch of every acre to do it.

On the surface, our lives had not changed a whole lot. The summer appeared no different from any of the rest, though I was getting more and more light-headed by the day. Mornings I milked. At noon I sat down with my wife and daughter to dinner. Evenings my daughter and I traipsed out to the barn and did chores again, and we came back into the house, sat down to a supper my wife laid out. Afterward I sat in front of the television chewing handfuls of Rolaids before stumbling up the back stairs to bed. After an hour or two in bed, I came back down, turned the TV on to a whisper, and sat with the antacid bottle in my hand.

Johnny Carson, the evening *East Oregonian*, the TV news were all shouting about America's birthday until I was sick of it. The bicentennial, history, the signing of the Declaration of Independence, Thomas Jefferson, George Washington, Philadelphia—all that went on two hundred years ago, until I was so fed up with it I could puke. I wanted it to be over, and I switched to the second of the two channels that made it down through the canyons, hoping for something else. The Olympics were coming up in a few weeks, in Montreal, Canada, athletes all cherry-cheeked and pumped up, another celebration.

Everywhere, people were getting all jacked up for the Fourth. In Philpott, the town council—Bob and Roy Jenkins and Mildred Ferligee—spent a hundred dollars of the town budget for decorations. It took Roy and Bob two days' working on ladders to hang red, white, and blue streamers off the streetlights and tie bows around the "Entering Philpott pop. 211" sign. Edie seemed to pick up on the way I was feeling and stayed home, in her room mostly. Molly, though, was making herself busy. She spent a good part of the week after the storm in the rec room of the church with the four other women who made up the First Christian Fellowship Church Aid. The Ladies' Aid was organizing the Fourth of July picnic in the park. Molly had been cooking for it for a week.

I needed somebody to talk to and I wanted it to be Molly, but I didn't have the courage to interrupt her life, didn't have the backbone to take her away from it and bring up one more of my disappointments to her. I wanted to confess the decision I had made late last year, a decision which had turned out to be a catastrophe, I knew that now, but I'd made it on my own, without her counsel. Sooner or later, she'd find out, like she found out everything else.

With the bicentennial Fourth, Molly's life and the town's had spun into overdrive. She was on the telephone several times a day, running back and forth into town, cooking us our meals between dishes she made especially for the picnic. In her rare moments of peace, she had her nose stuck in a Bible or was turning down corners in a copy of *Guideposts*, or *Christian Home and School*, or the *Word*. It seemed like the rest of the world was still going around, only I had been whirled off the day the storm hit, and was left wandering around, lost in a season that should have been the busiest of the whole year.

For the first couple of days after the storm, Lee had showed up as he usually did in a regular year. Maybe I could have talked to him, confessed what I'd done, but whenever I thought of it, I compared myself to him and Helen, and their two kids, and the way they never seemed to worry about things, how they could afford a new addition onto their house, how he was going to coach the men's basketball team at Whitman College come fall, how Helen's real estate business was starting to take off.

We worked on repairs, but the push was gone, the need to get it done, and Lee took time off to drive his family to Lake Chelan. With any luck, we'd need both threshers again, but not for another year. I hadn't seen him in three weeks when the letter arrived from First National Bank.

The bank was calling a meeting, wanting us to bring in our books for the year. Molly had picked up the mail that afternoon while I was puttering out in the shop. When I came into the house that night, she was sitting at her desk, running figures on her adding machine, rolls of paper strips winding along the back of her desk. She looked up at me and said that interest on our operating loan would eat up five times what that fifty acres could bring. She thought the totality—that's the word she used, *totality*—of the loss would assure that the insurance would cover the whole crop, and asked me if I knew where the insurance policy was we took out at the end of last year.

I shrugged. There was no policy, and I still didn't have the guts to tell her. There were no papers. Last year, after we had decided to take out a policy that covered hail, I'd written a check for cash, told her I'd paid Blanton's for the insurance with the check. But I hadn't done that at all. I had decided to risk it, and I bought a four-year-old used Massey Ferguson tractor Molly had said we didn't have money for. I bought it anyway, hauled it home one day when I knew she was not there. The tractor looked enough like my old one; I figured she wouldn't notice. She hadn't.

We went to bed that night, and as she settled back her blanket, she said, "I need those insurance papers in the morning, Jack." Then she leaned over, gave me a peck on the cheek, and turned out the light. And I laid there listening to her lips tick as she whispered through her prayers.

chapter 3

AT SOME TIME or other, every farmer in the county experienced mishaps, but the realization didn't make bad luck any easier. You wanted to shut up about things, let your dirty laundry hide in a pile. But you couldn't hide from anything in a place like Philpott. You saw one another at the post office, at the gas station, maybe even occasionally on the street in Pendleton. The knowing, the gossip glued all of you together. You shared the bits about the new two-ton truck somebody just got, about wheat prices, maybe some oddity like someone had bought a Santa Gertrudis bull to breed with his Hereford cows. And all of us, everyone in the county, knew the feeling of mishap, the clutch of a stomach, the gas, the smell of armpits under stress. The Farmers' Brotherhood of Mishap.

We were alike in a lot of ways. We drove Fords and Chevrolets. What was going on at the school brought us together—football in the fall, the grade school Christmas play, winter basketball. We even felt like we were together when we were in our own homes, knowing everybody else was watching the same games on TV, in the dead of winter. Every year, we worked on the same broken-down machinery. We ate what we raised—beef and pork—and potatoes, corn, and beans from garden rows the women kept out back of our houses. But that year, the hailstorm was a mishap not many of us shared. The Jensens lost a little of their crop to it, and the Haskells, and Tropshills. But no one but Molly and me had been so totally wiped out.

The night the letter from First National came, she cooked a roast and laid the table with string beans soaked in butter, a plate of pineapple slices, her fresh-baked bread, cinnamon rolls, corn with butter melting on it, Bundt cake with a topping of strawberries and whipped cream. The three of us, Molly, Edie, and me, sat at the same table we had sat at for a good part of our lives. It was like Molly determined that if she cooked for the six kids she always wanted, it might make the little mouths appear. A couple of years ago, in bed at night, she finally gave up and sighed down in her stomach and said, "Praise the Lord we at least had Edith."

But lately, Dr. Vingerud had started telling her there was some new treatment she might be able to take to have another baby, but she was going to have to lose a little weight. All of a sudden her hopes went right back up, and she fixed piles of food for Edie and me but ate almost none of it and threw herself into one more diet.

Between reading the Bible and cooking and doing her usual chores, Molly was spending more time at the desk in the little nook off the kitchen, hammering away at her adding machine. She'd asked me for more information than she had ever wanted before, estimates as to what everything on the place was worth, how much diesel and gas we had in the tanks, how much I thought I would need to run essential equipment, the rod weeder, the hay baler, threshers, whatever she could think of. How was I supposed to know how much stuff was worth, stuff like the water truck left over from the war, the tractor sitting on blocks, the welder, the hoist, the compressor? How could we put a value on our lives?

Molly was cold about the figures, distant, unsentimental. She should have been an accountant. She could have gone to school, but she hadn't, she married me, and we settled down to starting our family and working the farm together with my dad. Now and then she assigned me a duty like picking up a new check register in town or paying a bill in person, like she had with the insurance. But most everything else—the taxes, the bills, all of it—she always took care of herself.

She brought out a hot apple pie from the oven, set it on the last open space on the table. "I need that policy from Blanton's," she said, her voice sure and direct. She licked her thumb, fanned her face, then sat in her chair across from Edie's place. Edie hadn't said a word since she came in from helping with chores. She sat down and started sipping a drink of water through her braces. Dr. Cavalcanti had adjusted them the day before and the adjustments always gave her a sore mouth. She lifted the ice water in her spidery fingers. She was thin like me and was going to end up tall, like me, and probably skinny, her arms sharp as tree branches, her wrists flat as school rulers, her knees seeming to poke hurtfully at her skin.

But she was beginning to bud a little bit, her T-shirts revealing the beginning of breasts, and she held in her shoulders as if embarrassed or wanting to hide that soon she wouldn't be a girl any more, though Molly said she was late getting her curse and the doctor said not to worry about it. She was turning sixteen in September.

Molly put the triangle pie cutter beside the pie, sat down at the table and bent her head. She reached for our hands to start grace. The adding machine hummed on the desk. It was like she had grown so used to the sound, she didn't hear it anymore, but to me it was like a growl, a hunger, and it filled the room with its demands.

Molly said in her clear, clean voice, "Lord, thank you for the blessings we are about to receive, and for your care and protection in this time. In Jesus's name we pray. Amen."

She let go of my hand, and when she did, I said, "Don't you ever turn that thing off?"

The noise from the adding machine took over, set up a grind in the walls, the beams, in my molars. Molly quietly got up. The extra weight she had put on over the years made her sway from side to side when she walked, so she grabbed at counters, the backs of chairs for stability. She clicked off the machine. She was the smart one of the two of us. She belonged where I was sitting, at the head of the table. But it had been my place since we had lived in the house, like it had been my dad's, and his dad's, and great-granddad's before him. The room was large enough that the table could have been turned sideways, but had always been turned long way around, so the man of the house could peer out the window at his hills, at his crop, at his fields rolling away into the sun as it set.

Four generations of McIntyres had sat right there looking out that window at the calm brown summer-fallow in the years the fields rested, and at the gentle velvet of green that came up in the spring like fuzz on a newborn's head. Then, almost without notice, each one watched as the fields waved thick with green, then turned gold as the weeks turned over into summer. I never could quite listen to "America the Beautiful" without getting a catch in my throat when it came to "amber waves of grain."

Molly made it back to the table, let herself down onto her chair. The weight had started to come on her twelve years before, the same year she took to church and to her Bible. We'd been married five or six years then, and Edie was three. It was a year I did something I had tried to take back ever since.

She reached out, took up a bowl of buttered string beans, shoved it my way. "Beans, Jack," she said. It was not a question like *Would you like some string beans, Jack?* More of a statement so that I had no choice but to take the beans because she was passing them up because of her diet. All she had on her plate was a peeled carrot and a mug of chicken broth.

For years she dieted, off and on, limiting her meals to one type of food for as long as she could stand it; like baked potatoes. She'd eat baked potatoes for breakfast, lunch, and dinner or maybe it was a celery-with-peanut-butter diet, or cheddar cheese, or sweet corn, or eggs, or whole wheat rolls. One of the last diets she was on was one where she could eat only bananas. It was the banana diet I remembered most, because of what happened one night when she was on it. I thought Edie probably would remember it too, not for the gas-ups it gave her mother, or the stink of old peels blackening in the garbage, but for the way it twisted us all up that one night at dinner.

Patty Pugh was staying the night with Edie. The kids were in seventh grade. It wasn't more than a few months after Patty's dad had died, and she was spending more and more of her time with us. I remembered thinking it seemed sort of strange that Larry's death didn't seem to affect her much.

Patty and Edie had turned thirteen that year. Both Patty's father and her grandmother had recently died in the car wreck, yet I hadn't seen her cry, hadn't seen her withdraw or be sad at all. She seemed sharper, maybe, and angrier, but that was it. Her mother took up with a fellow named Murcheson a few weeks after the funeral, and I thought maybe Murcheson filled the sad gap her dad left. I didn't know. She had often slept over with Edie, but she began staying at our place several nights a week after her dad died.

I don't remember the season when that dinner with the banana diet took place, only that it was the time of year when bananas were on special at Safeway in Pendleton, and Molly had several baskets of them sitting around getting black specks.

The girls had come down from Edie's room a few minutes before dinner, had helped set the table, pour the drinks. It was a regular night, I remember, routine: Patty getting milk from the fridge, Edie clattering the silverware from the drawer, one of the thousands of our dinners, the radio on the shelf playing Charlie Pride and Hank Williams, a little bit of Emmy Lou Harris.

Edie's plate and Patty's and mine were heaped with fried chicken and corn on the cob, so it must have been summer. Only a banana lay on Molly's plate, and another sat beside her fork, as if it was supposed to be dessert. Patty passed Molly the chicken, held the plate for Molly to take some. Molly shook her head.

"You don't want any?" Patty said.

Molly looked at the platter for a moment, then passed it over her banana and on to me. "Special diet," she said.

"Bananas?" Patty said and flipped a hank of red hair away from her face, over her shoulder.

Molly squinted at all of us, at our plates full of food. She sighed in a pathetic, resigned way. Then her eyes lit on Patty, sitting there in a cloud of red hair, slim as a cotton swab. Patty pulled her shoulders back, sat taller. It was a braggy posture aimed right at Molly. It said she could eat all that was on her plate and still keep the trim of her ribs. Molly's eyes locked on Patty's. Patty's eyes locked right back. This eye-locking was becoming some kind of activity between them, a challenge that thickened the air, an exchange with Molly neither Edie nor I dared; Patty never seemed to get a handle on the danger that lurked behind it.

She sat there straight as an icicle and grinned. I could see a thought welling up in her brain. She had a way of taking a discussion, shrugging into it like she might put on a dress covered with spangles and lights. It made everyone around pay attention to her, and her only. Molly was used to having that attention for herself with us. I could see Patty winding up to provoke Molly. I missed the chance to say something.

"Well," Patty said, "you might not lose any weight." Her eyes were still locked on Molly's. "But you could sure climb trees."

Edie tittered. It *was* funny. But Molly's face pinched in and she sat on the pillowy form of her own backside like some queen over the rest of us. Though Molly didn't say anything in rebuttal right then, it would not be the last of it.

chapter 4

AS THE FOURTH approached, weeds gave the days some shape. I had not answered Molly's questions about the insurance, and I waited until one morning to tell her, when she was flush with peace from her morning Bible reading. Waiting was the chicken's way out, I knew, when would have read her passage out loud to Edie and salved herself with righteousness for the day.

I waited around in the house until they were finished and Edie had gone outside. "Mol," I said, "I have something to . . . ," and my throat clenched so, for a moment, I could not say more. "About those insurance papers."

"Yes?" she said and her eyes lightened.

"There aren't any papers."

"There have to be. Blanton's gives them to you when you pay the policy."

"That's just it," I said. "There is no policy."

"There is a policy. We always have insurance," she said with such certainty I could almost believe it was true.

"Not this time," I said.

"Not this time," she repeated. And she looked up toward the ceiling which stood in for heaven. "Where did the money go I gave you for it?"

"I spent it on equipment."

Her eyes welled and she closed them as her lips made their way through some prayer, her expression pinched as if ready to hear worse. "Is that the truth, Jack?" she said. "Or did you spend it on something else?"

She meant some*one* else. "I swear."

She took up a clean apron, slung it over her head and let it lie, untied, down her front. "Well," she said. That was all. "Well." And I felt struck with that one word, like I had been slapped.

THERE WAS NOTHING much to distract from the misery I felt, the farm was becoming more of a mess than it ever had been. Cheatgrass, ugly green-black patches of pretenders that sucked the ground of water and food, and tarweed, tall hairy stick-weeds that hid out along fence rows and took root in pastures and fields. A patch of morning glory was setting up shop on the north side of the Jackson quarter. It had claimed a half dozen fence posts, stretching along the barbed wire, and was beginning to spill into the field. The tarweed and cheatgrass screamed out, and I could at least do something about them. The morning glory I had to turn away from and leave because morning glory could take root from the smallest pieces of vine or stem. Caught in the axle of a tractor or truck, or in the mechanism of a drill, you could spread it hell to breakfast. Morning glory required spray. I had no money for herbicides. So I had to leave it alone to string its pretty little white flowers into a hedge, the only thing green in the fallow section. I still had a few gallons of diesel in the tanks, and I still had a tractor and a rod weeder. I could mangle the tarweed and cheatgrass. That I could do. That I could do.

The rodding took up the days, dragging the weeder round and round, leaving behind the satisfaction of a mulch of uprooted weeds. I did it in the mornings, in the afternoons, only breaking to go to the house midday and then for dinner at night. It occupied my life, gave me something to do like the Bible and the festivities for the Fourth were taking up Molly's days, giving them shape.

Over the past few months, since an incident with Patty and Kenny Muffin at school, Molly and her scriptures had clamped down on Edie more than ever. Edie had grown even quieter, more drawn into herself than ever. She rarely looked up from her feet, she did whatever her mother asked. As the school year wound down, she plodded through her homework, set the table, cleaned the bathroom, did four loads of laundry every week, slogged through evening chores with me. Molly had heaped Edie with requirements that she said had to be met for her soul's redemption. Molly seemed to take a particular glee in cleansing Edie's soul, and had set out dozens of ports to redemption: she had to bring up her grades, had to average at least Bs. She had to come directly home every evening after school, start immediately into doing her homework. She could have no distractions, no influences from the outside world, no telephone calls, no overnights, no company. She had to stand for her mother's daily inspections of her room. And, in order to learn the ways she had sinned against the Lord, Molly ordered her to start memorizing Matthew, Mark, Luke, and John, all because the kids had been caught skipping school and smoking, and Molly seemed to think the answer and antidote was the Bible.

She made demands for Patty as well, if the girls were ever going to be able to see each other ever again in their lives. She spelled her requirements for Patty out to Mr. Norton, the high school principal. He agreed she would have to bring up her grades from last year, and he agreed with Molly's requirement that she behave like a lady.

Edie had done what her mother demanded and the school year had closed. Edie had passed, made her B average. Though she got only a B minus in social studies, it was still a B. She got an A plus in gym. It was at dinnertime that the weight of change in her spoke loudest, when everything was quiet, she sat in a gray kind of silence that had no color whatever. If it hadn't been for the radio, there would have been no noise at all. Obediently, Edie set the table, dished up her food, ate, cleaned up the table and went back up to her room, sometimes without saying more than "Amen" after grace.

THE LETTER FROM First National bank was sitting on the desk where Molly had put it, under rolls of adding machine tape and piles of receipts from purchases of supplies and equipment. The storm had rolled over us two weeks ago, but the thunder of it still pounded our lives.

We were at dinner again. As wonderful as Molly's cooking was, meals had long ago quit being comfortable, and that evening Edie was sitting with her hands in her lap, looking down at her fingers twisting and untwisting the edge of her napkin. Her nose and her lips were swollen as if she had a cold. To me, and I knew to Molly, our daughter was lovely, but would likely never be what somebody would call a looker. Molly did not allow lipstick nor face coloring, even though our daughter's color was often sallow. Molly called Edie's hair color light brown, but in truth it was rat-colored from the McIntyre side—*my* side—was her tree-branch build. She had once fussed about her hair. She hated it, she said, and Molly countered that she hated the Lord, then, because who but the Lord made Edie's hair. But Edie wanted red hair, like Patty's. I had to admit it was something, Patty's hair, full, a rage of a red bush. Edie begged her mother to give her permanents and to use the smallest curlers and to let the potion sit for hours, way beyond the time on the box. And still the brown stuff hung limp as a tattered rag on her head.

Edie snuffed. Molly held a spoon of the string beans midway over Edie's plate. "You look like you don't feel well. Do you have hay fever?" she asked.

Edie shook her head. Molly plopped the beans on Edie's plate. "Edith," she said, "eat."

I took a bit of my own food before Molly could come back at me. I could barely breathe. The letter with the blue First National on the letterhead was taking every breath of air in the world. The letter said we had to meet with the bank to discuss "a few matters." It didn't say anything about sucking air. It didn't say anything about swallowing Molly's string beans.

Edie put her hand over her mouth as if she was about to throw up.

"Slice the roast, Jack," Molly said. Molly was like a conductor when it came to meals. "Edith's waiting for the meat." I started slicing the roast. Edie sniffed again.

"Do you have a Kleenex, Edie?" I said. It sounded pushy, somehow, like her mother did when she was pushing the string beans. Something about my question made Edie heave in a huge gulp of air and then erupt into tears.

"Edith?" Molly said. She was as surprised as I was.

Edie began to blubber, out of control. I was beginning to think we'd burdened her with too much worry about the troubles with the ranch, that she was too young for it. I said, "Edie?"

Molly said, "Give unto the Lord thy worries, Edith." It was times like this, when things weren't going too smoothly, that Molly pulled out the *untos* and *thees*, like nobody would get the gist if she spoke regular.

Edie flopped back into her chair, her stomach collapsed toward her backbone. She gulped in another painful breath and let loose with a little squeak.

"Don't worry, Edie," I found myself saying, "we're going to be all right. It's a setback." I wished I believed it. But I was starting to think we should watch what we said in front of her, that all our talk about the farm since the storm, the finances, the letter from First National were too much for a girl to take in. "It's going to be all right," I said again and I found saying it made *me* feel better for a second or two.

But it didn't perk Edie up at all. She shook her head, her short bangs swinging side to side. "No it's not," she said.

Molly gulped a big breath that rattled the little flap in the back of her throat. "The Lord will provide," she said.

"True," I said, but I could hear my own bitterness.

"He will, Jack." Molly's voice commanded me to believe.

I couldn't take it anymore, sometimes could hardly swallow any part of this Lord of hers. What God had done this to us anyway? It was like the pressure of the past few weeks uncorked something inside me. "So, why," I said, "doesn't your Lord take back this storm?" It shot right out of my mouth. "Why doesn't Jesus do whatever you want, huh, Molly? Why, for instance, why doesn't he pop up another kid you want so bad? Huh, Molly? Tell me that."

Molly was sitting there, speechless, her mouth opening and closing like a guppy's.

I should have shut up, and I couldn't. "Why doesn't he wave his wand and peel off a couple hundred of those pounds you're packing, Molly?"

"Don't think I don't pray on it."

"Jesus," I said.

"Jack!"

"It's not Jesus, Molly, it's not a goddamned diet. It's us. You. Me. Edie. We are the ones in trouble here. I have to get us out of it. And I don't know how. I don't know how."

I wished she'd comfort me, I wished she'd come over and grab my head and hold it against her soft stomach. But she didn't. She slapped her stomach. It set to rippling like a water balloon. "I pray for strength, Jack." Her face grew tomato red. It was like she was blaming her fat, her stomach, for everything that had happened. She started pounding on herself with her fist like she hated herself. "You don't know how I pray." She kept pounding. Pounding. Pounding.

"Well, apparently it hasn't been enough," I said.

And then she stopped and she looked up at me like she did when we had started struggling over the Patty issue. It had been the first time in our marriage we fought. "I told you to take out insurance," she said. "We could have been covered."

Edie was starting to whimper. I'd almost forgotten she was there. Her whimpering got louder and louder until she sounded like a pig squealing. She was winding up something awful, her stomach heaving, her lips drawing back to show every brace in her mouth.

I realized her mother and I had probably gone way too far. I stood up. God why couldn't I have shut up? Edie was a teenager, for Christ's sake. "We'll make it, Edie," I said.

But what I was saying wasn't helping. Edie made more of those noises, tears and snot running down her face.

Molly heaved herself out of her chair, lumbered over to stand behind Edie. When she raised her face to the ceiling, I knew a prayer was on the way. "God heal thy child," she said. She watched too much Oral Roberts.

"Mooooom," Edie said. She drug out the word, made it three sentences long and rippling with tears.

"Pray, my child."

Molly pulled out a tissue from the pocket of her smock, handed it to Edie. Edie tooted into it.

"Pray to almighty God to see us through."

Edie hiccuped. "God won't help," she said. Then she wailed into the tissue again. "It's not what you think."

"What is it then, Edie?" I said.

Molly's thick fingers dug into Edie's shoulders, gathered up her T-shirt. But having her mother stand with her seemed to buck Edie up a little. She blew again into the tissue, which was nothing more than a little wet ball. "It's Patty," she said. She dabbed the ball on her nose.

"Patty!" Molly blared.

Oh God, I thought, here we go again.

Molly's voice was back out of the heavens, right there in the kitchen with us, it said, *not her again*, loud and clear as a thunderclap. "Have you been talking to *Patty* again?"

"No," Edie said and burst into the pig wail again.

"Who then?"

"Kenny," Edie said.

"So you have been talking to Kenny behind my back," Molly said. "Oh Lord above," she added, in her best Oral Roberts.

Edie sniffed, but she was not crying. It was like she'd been relieved of something. "Mom," she said, "you don't understand."

"Understand? Understand? You bet I understand. I understand you have been keeping the company of sinners." She was winding up like she did when this all started. "Be not unequally yoked with unbelievers," she said. "My daughter running with the godless and unchurched." She let out a huge, mournful sigh. "Lord knows I tried."

"Molly," I said. "They are kids." When Edie skipped school, I stood with Edie then, taking up against the force of Molly's voice from the Lord. I looked down at my daughter. "What about Patty?" I said. Edie had something to say, something that was eating into her.

Both of Edie's hands lay unmoving and limp on her thighs. She sniffed again and her head gave a little jerk like it was about to shake out a no. But she only lifted her hands in a helpless, accusing way. I had been so stupid, so blind to the signs, it was not until Patty was about to slip from our hands that I would understand why Edie was so upset.

chapter 5

I HAD NOT set foot off the place since the storm. I didn't want to
see, or face, anybody. But a couple of days before the Fourth, Molly
asked if I'd go into town and pick up the mail.

She was in the kitchen when I came in from morning chores.
Bacon was frying on the stove. She'd laid out three eggs, ready to
crack into the grease. The room was still hot from the oven. Four
pans of brownies were cooling on the counter. She leaned over the
pans, squeezed a cake decorator, laying down stripes of red frost-
ing between wavering white ones she had already put on the sheets.
Her apron slipped off her shoulder. She stood up straight, pulled
the strap back up high, near her neck. "Jack," she licked her thumb,
snapped it away from her lips. "I'm not going to have time to go to
town this morning to get the mail."

I started to say I didn't have time, either, because I didn't feel up
to seeing anyone. By now the whole town would know what the
hail had done to us.

"I'm expecting a package," she said. "Wicker baskets for the picnic tables that the Ladies' Aid ordered from Sears. They should be at the post office today."

THE STEEPLE OF the Philpott First Christian Fellowship Church rose above every other building in town, higher even than the locusts in the park or the Farmers' Mutual grain elevator. The church's oak doors watched over Maple, Birch, and Main streets. Its dark front windows frowned over the two teachers' houses, the grade school, the post office, the hardware store, and the boarded-up Pugh Market. The steps, the steeple, the clanking bell anchored one end of Main Street, the high school the other end. They had been in a standoff for nearly eighty years, since the new brick school building replaced the wooden one that had had only two rooms.

To the rear, behind the pulpit, the church looked out over the town park and the bright water of the swimming pool. Every town around our parts, no matter how big or small, took on some element that made it special. For Philpott, it was the pool. The pool gave the town the right to brag that no other town around had a pool, not Athena, not Adams, not Weston, though all of them were bigger, and by the looks of them richer.

There wasn't anything like an official building in Philpott, other than the cinder-block fire station; there was no need for it. The church took up where a city hall might do, or a police station. A few years ago, the room that used to have a rod and hangers for parishioners' coats was refurbished. The rod was taken out, and Edmund Swearingen cut a hole in the side wall and put in a window that still leaked, no matter how much caulk the Ladies' Aid smeared on. And Whitey Smith cleaned the pigeon shit from a desk that had been in his hayloft since his granddad died and donated the desk for the new room. The closet became the office for Rusty Cousins who was the town manager, sheriff, and fireman, though I wasn't sure he ever used the office.

Most nights a handful of cars and pickups were parked at the curb in front of the church. The church's community room provided space for the monthly city council meetings, and for the weekly 4-H sewing club, and for bingo on second and fourth Thursdays. The Ladies' Aid met there on Mondays at three. Two or three times a year the LA hung crepe paper and decorated with vases of cut flowers, pulled out the tables and chairs and shuffled them around for a wedding, or a golden anniversary, or a funeral. The LA—Mildred Coxen, Rena Olmstead, May Rae Burnbaum, Sissy Misczek, and Molly—saw to the cleaning, the upkeep, the polishing of the arched window, the sanding of the old pews, and they saw to the kitchen, the cleanup after a reception, the arrangements for the food.

The LA organized the Fourth in the park, like they did every year. The picnic wasn't until tomorrow, Sunday, yet they had already folded and stacked picnic chairs against the church pews and had collapsed metal tables and leaned them by the front door. Reverend Acheson was having services at seven o'clock so everybody could get out early for the picnic. Every year the men moved the chairs and the tables from inside the church and set them up in prescribed settings in the park, so the women could decorate and make room for the food. This year, they had to make room for the band as well. It was our country's two hundredth birthday and that meant the tables had to be pushed back for the high school band, which was going to blat the "Star Spangled Banner." At one time Edie played trumpet, and Patty played the drums. But after Patty's mother latched up with the Murcheson fellow, Patty quit the band, then our Edie did as well. Looking back, the girls' dropping out of band seemed to signal the start of what was beginning to go wrong in their lives.

Any other time I would have been looking forward to the picnic. It was important, our country would be two hundred years old that very day. The *East Oregonian* was full of stories on Abe Lincoln, and the television showed hour after hour of life in Williamsburg and Philadelphia and reported the progress of the Freedom Train puffing all around the country. All that stuff any other time would have given me some pride.

I picked up the baskets and heaved a sigh that I'd only had to speak with Sissy Misczek, the postmaster, and she was too busy sorting mail to say anything more to me than, "Morning Jack." It left no need to hear her sympathy about the hail.

chapter 6

EDMUND NORTON, THE principal at Philpott High, called the house that night as I was coming in from chores. Edie was in the basement separating the milk. I heard the phone ring as I was toeing off my chore boots at the back door. It was Saturday evening. From the living room came the sounds of Donny and Marie on the television, the tinkle of a piano, their harmonies, now and then, an explosion of fake laughter. Someone had turned on the TV—Edie probably—then abandoned it when it came time for chores.

Molly yelled at me to come to the phone. "Ed Norton wants to talk with you," she said.

Why him? Why then? It was summer. Why didn't he just talk with Molly like always? "Can you take a message?" I shouted back. She'd handled the stuff with him and the girls at school, so much that she was calling him Ed.

"He wants both of us," she said.

God, I thought, what now? I plopped the boots in their place, picked one up to flick a slick of manure and straw in the tread. I was dawdling away the moments. Whatever Mr. Norton was calling for, it couldn't be good.

Edie clattered separator parts in the basement sink, probably unaware the principal was on the line. In one of Molly's phone calls with Mr. Norton, she learned Patty had returned to school for a couple of weeks after the kids had all gotten in trouble. Then she dropped out again, came back and left two more times before the year ended. After that, she didn't return for the rest of the year. This off-and-on seemed to be the way she was turning out, now that her dad wasn't around to keep her feet on the ground. Mr. Norton had said he'd tried to find her, so he could convince her to get back into school. He'd even gone to the apartment where Patty and her mother lived with that guy. He said the Murcheson fellow had answered the door, said he didn't know where Patty was. All around town there was gossip. There *always* was gossip when it came to Patty. We heard that she stayed in Pendleton sometimes, was "sleeping around with anybody she could get her hands on." At least that was the gossip. People talked about Patty in tones frosted over, described how she was going to the dogs, how they'd seen her running around, almost nude, in shorts "up to here," and dragging Main with guys she picked up in Pendleton and Walla Walla, speeding around with them, smoking cigarettes, windows open, radios blaring, and all that red hair whipping in the wind. They talked about how Rusty Cousins caught her and Richie Steiner parked in Richie's folks' Thunderbird convertible out at the dump in the broad light of day, slouched out of sight so nobody could see them drinking beer and doing stuff she did with every other guy in town.

It seemed Patty was the mark for everything that went wrong. Everybody was convinced nobody but Patty Pugh could have orchestrated the wave of corruption that hit town right before the holidays last year. It had to be her who stole the presents from the back seats of Ev Blakley's Dodge and Melvin and Edna

Rothwalker's Malibu on Christmas Eve, *right in front of their houses*. No one ever proved it was Patty, but everyone knew—proof positive—it was her. Who else could it be? For weeks, Molly prayed on it, out loud and in tones so accusing it made Edie cringe.

Philpott had started girls' track the year before. At first, Edie had turned out for sprints then lost interest in it. I thought the whole idea of track wasn't anything more than a convenient excuse, something that Molly approved of that allowed Edie to delay coming home to her mother's new rules and pinched demands and all the chores her mother required of her. Edie didn't seem to have much heart for anything any longer, never seemed to be able to get herself out of first gear. But then she picked up a pole vault and, somehow, that stick did something for her. She was the only girl to enter the event, and with that stick in her hand, she sailed past every one of the four Philpott boys who turned out and I was happy my sad daughter had, at least for a few seconds, something in her life that lifted her.

Then, from nowhere, with no more than a couple of weeks left in the school year, Patty appeared for class again one morning. The day we found out Patty had showed up again, we'd watched Edie clear almost eight feet eleven inches. I'd happily banged my hand on her back when she took first place and she was hot, the green jersey sticking to the small of her back, her hair limp, glued to her temples. But it seemed like even that small victory couldn't bring her to look up at me, her posture slumped as if she were ashamed or something. I said, "Congratulations, Ede."

She muttered, "Thanks," then shuffled off to the showers.

When the meet was done, Mr. Norton had sauntered over to the treats table. Molly was putting the last of the leftover candy bars away. Mr. Norton was young, small, wiry as a shortstop, his hair trimmed in a dishwater crew cut. The day was warm enough that all he wore were slacks and a button-down shirt with the sleeves rolled up. He was not more than twenty-seven or twenty-eight.

Most everybody in town liked him. He spoke straight out in a way that made you glad he was entrusted with your kids' care. We all knew he'd be going somewhere else in his life. He wasn't the kind to hang around a small place like Philpott for long. Philpott was merely a way for him to earn some stripes, then move on to somewhere bigger, better.

He had shaken my hand that day, then turned to Molly and said that he had begun working with Patty, had laid out a plan for her to catch up with the rest of the class. It was going to take most of the summer, he said. And as he walked away, I realized we were the only grown-ups, besides Patty's addled mother, he could tell that news to. Patty had no one else.

This was what I thought of as I dragged my feet to the phone that night before the Fourth, and I knew, for sure, he was calling to tell us Patty had failed, or worse, had dropped out of sight again.

I said, "Hello, Mr. . . . Ed."

"Jack," he said, clear, open, "I'm calling to talk with you about Patty Pugh."

I took a breath. "Let me get Molly," I said.

"No," he cleared his throat. "She asked me to call and tell *you* she passed. She's moving up to her junior year when school starts in the fall."

My breath blew out in a burst.

From the kitchen doorway, Molly said, "Jack?"

"It's good news, isn't it?" I said.

"Yes," Mr. Norton said.

EVERYBODY AT THE picnic would be aware of the pickle Molly and I were in after the storm, since nothing in Philpott ever went unobserved or unspoken. I knew everyone would start out being tactful. Conversations would begin innocent enough, discussing the chances for the Cardinals at a pennant, the price of GMC trucks these days, the pinkish color Homer Sparks painted his barn. Then curiosity would get the best of things and the conversation would turn to the hailstorm, and after a while somebody would start looking at their boots and ask, "How's it going, Jack?" and I'd know he'd want me to tell him how bad it was so he'd feel better about his own dry crops, thinned out and stunted from the drought.

Picnic morning, I drew out chores as long as I could. I hosed out the barn, took sheep dip to the years of spit slime in the mangers, set a dozen mouse traps around the bin with the cows' grain, stuff I hadn't done in years, as if all of my flurry could hold off facing the picnic. The cows would know, right away that I'd been messing with their places, they'd blow at the stink of disinfectant in their feedboxes and turn white and accusing eyes at me. But I knew that eventually the pile of oats and beet pulp would win out, and they'd eat and let down their milk.

I was the only one in my family who wasn't looking forward to the picnic. Molly whirred into action the minute she got up in the mornings, then didn't quit until night. The First National letter still sat in its place on the desk, unmoved, with all the activity of the Fourth taking Molly's mind from it. I envied her. I wished I could forget.

Edie was so revved up to see Patty that all through breakfast she talked so fast and with her mouth so full she spit food crumbs. After months of being apart, the girls had earned permission.

I couldn't drag out the stalling any longer. I made my way into the house after nearly two hours' dinking. It was not yet eight a.m., but already the kitchen smelled of Molly's fried chicken and dish soap. "There's a couple boxes that need loading," she said over her shoulder. I traipsed upstairs, got the keys to her car out of her purse and passed by Edie's room. Her room, which Molly made her keep neat, was a mess of clothes heaped on the floor, on the bed, hanging from the doorknob as if she had tried on everything she owned, then had shed it as not right for the day. Since her mother's decision to let her see Patty, she had turned back to her old self overnight.

At breakfast she had chattered, at dinner she babbled. In fact she hadn't shut up for twenty-four hours. She was holding up a purple shirt, side-to-siding in the mirror. She saw me in the door. "You better pick up," I said, "before you mother sees your room." She took in the room. There was color in her face for a change, even a little bounce to her short hair. "Guess so," she said.

I got the keys, carried two boxes out the back door, put them into Molly's car. I backed the station wagon up to the porch. Molly came out, laid two more cardboard boxes on the tailgate, and the red, white, and blue brownies, then lumbered back into the kitchen. The smell of fried chicken and the aroma of maple bars lingered around her.

We were about ready to go. Molly brought out one more box, handed it to me to add to those I'd already put in the car. That last box had no food in it at all. It was a box of Patty's folded clothes, shirts and a couple of pairs of jeans she'd left in Edie's room the last time she'd stayed with us. Molly had washed and dried them and had patched the shirt where the knit of the neck was tearing away. The clothes smelled fresh, like bleach.

ON THE SURFACE of it, the day turned out to be great for a picnic. It was dry, the sun glaring, there was even a little breeze to chase away any threat of heat. Not two miles from the house though, the luck of the day started to change. The car started to cough. "Shit," I said. "Jack!" Molly said.

The car bucked, sputtered. I pumped the gas, and the motor smoothed out before we got into town. But right in the middle of Main, three blocks from the park, it acted up again. A cloud of black smoke shot out of the tailpipe, and the car bucked the rest of the way like a Round-Up bronc. We coughed by the church. Molly grabbed the armrest. I turned, finally found a spot a few spaces from the steps of the church.

The doors of the church were chocked open with river rocks.

Mildred Coxen was bringing out an armload of folded blue plastic tablecloth material, starting down the steps with it. It was the material that the LA set out every Sunday for after-service reception, a shade of blue that turned the community room dark as a thunderstorm. Mildred stopped and watched as we bucked into the space and the engine died. Molly opened the car door on her side, flapped her hand at a cloud of fumes.

Cars were filling up any spaces near the park, had even filled up the vacant lot by the parsonage. The picnic would start at eleven. It was just past ten o'clock, and already the ladies had filled three of the six tables with pies, barbecued ribs, coolers with pop, biscuits, marshmallow-and-whipped-cream salad, angel food cakes six inches high, gravy, noodle casserole, stuffed cabbage.

A handful of men stood commiserating around a pit, situated near the tables. Some of them had dug the pit last week. It was heaped now with ashes and coals that covered the whole beef they'd been roasting for nearly two days and nights.

Molly wandered off toward the tables, carrying a couple of boxes. Over her shoulder she said, "Edie, grab one of the brownie boxes. Jack, see if there's more tables to set up."

I went into the church, found it empty but for the sounds of a couple of women knocking and banging pans in the kitchen. I busied myself unloading the last boxes from the car. Elmer Hutchinson, Boone Ellis, George Schnauble, and Henry Akins were standing around the roasting pit drinking beer. A dozen elm and locust trees shaded the rough grass. A breeze whipped at the red, white, and blue streamers tied onto the link fence by the pool and at the bows hanging from the trunks of the locust trees. I should have been happy. It was a beautiful day.

The wind shifted, carrying smoke up from the pit. Roasting a steer for the Fourth was a tradition. Farmers donated the beef. It used to be Larry Pugh who organized the roasting, along with the men who lived in town. Two nights, they would set up shop in the women's side of the bathhouse by the pool and drink beer and smoke cigars and play poker all night long while they checked on the coals. Every year, around sunrise, they'd swing open the bathhouse windows and open the doors to air out the smoke, then brag what a chore it was to dig the pit, then spend the night shoveling coals.

Dad and Lee and I had donated a whiteface yearling a few years back. Pretty soon it was going to be my turn again, and I didn't know if we were even going to have animals to donate.

I shuffled over to the bunch of guys I'd known all my life. As I walked up, Elmer Swearingen flapped his hand in front of his face. "Whew," he said, "when are you getting rid of that beater, Jack? It nearly fumigated us."

The guys laughed, and I laughed with them. I shoved my hands in my pockets. "It's getting traded," I said, "for the Lincoln Continental I ordered from Portland."

"Fat chance," Elmer said.

"Fat chance," I repeated.

I left them and ambled over to Raunch Boletti, who was holding a beer and standing next to Boone Ellis. If Raunch hadn't been there, I would never have gotten close to Boone. Raunch, somehow, made Boone safe. They were standing watching George Schnauble and Henry Akins poking a pitchfork into the roasting pit and arguing who was going to start shoveling the coals into the two drums they'd set out for cooling barrels. And they were discussing how they were going to lift the calf out when it was ready.

Raunch said, "'Lo, Jack." He was guzzling the last of a bottle of Bud and reaching into the cooler for another when I came up. When we were in school, Raunch and Larry Pugh and I ran together.

Raunch popped the cap with his thumb. "How's tricks?" he said. We'd known each other since we were kids. We took Philpott to Class B basketball championships in 1953, our senior year. A framed black-and-white photograph still sat in a display case inside the front door of the high school. We lost, but we made it to the playoffs, something no team from Philpott had ever done before or since.

Boone Ellis still hadn't spoken to me. He stood there holding in his gut and sipping from the Bud he held with the tips of his fingers.

I could count on Raunch not to bring up what I didn't want brought up. He knew, from experience himself, how it was when personal gossip was let out for everyone to see flapping in the breeze like laundry on a clothesline. Raunch and I didn't see much of each other anymore. After school we sort of went our separate ways, him to work at the cannery in Weston, and me to farm.

Boone jabbed me in the shoulder with the hand that held the bottle. "Heard what the storm did to you," he said. Then he took back his Bud and grinned with half his mouth. No "sorry," no sympathy, no "tough luck."

I didn't say anything. I should have known not to get near him, even if it did give me a chance to say hello to Raunch. I should have known Boone would try to rub my nose in my misfortune. Boone's farm, down by Sage Canyon, had missed the storm. "Our place missed the hail altogether." He chuckled like I needed to know it and it was just the dearest thing in the world.

"I see Molly brought her fried chicken," Raunch said, changing the subject.

But Boone didn't let up. "We're going to have a hundred-bushel year," he said. A hundred-bushel year was a farmer's dream. You might be able to manage it in a patch or two on a good year, but the *average?* The whole crop? Nobody was getting a hundred bushels, even in patches in this kind of dry, not even Boone Ellis. A hundred-bushel year happened only once in a lifetime, and we still spoke of the last one fifty-two years ago, like we spoke of John Glenn or Johnny Unitas.

Boone was short, maybe that was what made him so sour. I didn't know. They said short men needed to buck themselves up to feel important. It seemed like it was true with Boone Ellis.

Like the rest of us, Boone had lived around Philpott all of his life. He married a girl from Tollgate, Francie Nutbrock, who was shorter than him by two inches, and who plucked her eyebrows until there were no hairs left to pluck, and who was so quiet some people said they'd never heard her speak. It was like Francie didn't seem to exist anymore than her eyebrows did. They had two children, a boy and a girl who were younger than Edie and who both had eczema on their faces and up into their hair.

I looked at Raunch. He shuffled from one foot to another as if he was trying to think up something to say. I wasn't doing too well in that department, myself.

"We saw the storm coming," Boone said, "and we knew it was going to blow right by us."

I never thought I hated Boone, but right then I was beginning to. He was a couple of years ahead of Raunch and Larry and me in school. He'd quit growing about the end of middle school, the age the rest of us were beginning to catch up with the girls. He'd tried out for sports—baseball, track, football—but what he really wanted to play was basketball. All four years he'd tried out for it. He even made the team during his sophomore year because there weren't enough boys to make a five-man team without him. The next year, he expected to be right back out there on the court, but that was the year our class made it into high school. Coach didn't pick him, even for second string because he had Raunch and Larry and me to choose from and he had Teddy La Rosa and Jim Doss and Doug Stewards for second string. We made up the biggest class since Philpott High opened in 1913—six boys and one girl. The girl was Jackie Simington Pugh, Patty's mom.

Boone looked up at me. "I hear you're taking it in the shorts," he said, unrelenting.

"Guess so," I said.

"Maybe going to lose everything." He clicked his tongue.

I looked away from Boone. "How you doing, Raunch?" I said.

"Up and taking nourishment," he said. He was still the best-looking guy around.

Even as far back as in school, Boone seemed to choose Raunch to hang onto. He hovered around Raunch as if the nearness would rub off on him, make him taller, make him handsome like Raunch, make him collect cheerleaders and majorettes, right along with Raunch. Maybe it did, to a point. I didn't know. No matter, Boone never yapped at Raunch like he did the rest of us, not once, that I ever heard.

Raunch was sporting a moustache now, and it made his teeth look whiter, like he bleached them. He had married Esther Browning, the homecoming queen, the year after we graduated. He stayed married to her for nearly two years. A year after the divorce he and Vicky de Santo tied the knot. That lasted five years. After Vicky it seemed like the women around Philpott were already taken. He never married again, and he started going to Walla Walla for what he said were real good times.

Raunch took another bottle from the ice chest near his knee, popped the cap, and tipped it back. "You think we're going to see the Reds again in the fall?" he said to me.

"We were talking about that," Boone said. "The Yank's are going to do it, man." He clicked his tongue, a most irritating sound. "Munson's going to trim Rose, or if he doesn't do it, it's going to be Chambliss. Get old Charlie Hustle where it hurts." He elbowed Raunch's ribs.

Raunch flipped his brows like something was expected from him. "Boone thinks Cincy's going to tank," he said.

Boone folded his arms across his chest, held his beer against his shoulder like some kind of weapon. He looked at me. "So," he said, "your mother planning to bail you out?"

Apparently Cincy, Pete Rose, the distraction was done. Boone was like a little rat terrier attacking anything bigger than it was. He still blamed me, I guessed, but for what? For having six inches of height on him? For having a voice that wasn't as high as a girl's? For being Raunch's best friend in high school? He wasn't going to let go now that he had something to grab onto, something he could use to take me down a peg or two. He didn't need to do that. I already felt like I was carved into a groove as small as he was.

"Let it go," Raunch said. I didn't know if he meant it for me or for Boone.

Boone ignored Raunch. "I mean," he went on, "how you going to make it? I hear you already been borrowing every year to operate."

Raunch popped his arm over my shoulder. "Hey, Jack, you going hunting after harvest?" Then he frowned, like he knew he'd left another opening for Boone and he rushed along fast so as not to give Boone a chance to work that comment against me. "I been thinking it looks like there might be a good chance for a buck or two up near Tollgate."

"What you hunt now on your place, Jack?" Boone said. "Rats?"

"Chuck it, Boone," Raunch said, then gave my shoulder another pop. "Beer's good and cold," he said. He bent down, scrambled through the ice in the cooler with his hand, pulled out a bottle. "Got a minute?" he said.

I had more minutes than I knew what to do with. He handed me the beer. "I got something to run by you," he said.

I started to shake my head no to the beer, then surveyed the picnic area for Molly. She was cutting a pie over at one of the tables, her back to me. I took the beer from Raunch. It was the first beer I'd held in my hands for a dozen years, and it was Raunch I'd been with the last time I'd had a drink, at least one anyone knew about.

"I didn't think Molly let you drink anymore," Boone said. "I thought she made you stop that years ago."

Raunch pulled me away from Boone. I wished I knew how to come back at that little son of a bitch, but sometimes the words never came until years later.

THE WIND WHIPPED up about eleven thirty, sent the red, white, and blue bows thrashing on the trees and the plastic cloths popping on the tables. Dust headed straight for our eyes.

It wasn't just Philpott that was throwing itself into the Fourth, the whole country was doing it. It seemed like a kind of salve for the exhaustion all of us felt over the way the world was changing since we got into Vietnam. Because of it, we knew a part of the world we didn't think we wanted to know about, but the TV and the newspapers shoved it down our throats. We knew about Saigon, we knew about Ho Chi Minh. It was over a year since the whole thing was done with and the bicentennial was meant to put the whole thing into history and bring back what made America great in the first place. Even the word *Vietnam* was slipping from our talk, from our news, from our lives as if it no longer had any more meaning than the words *and* or *the*. But it left a taint in our mouths that we all seemed to hope the carcass in the pit or the high school band playing the "Star Spangled Banner" could take away.

A dust devil kicked up the blue tablecloths, sent grit toward the pies. The women held down their skirts, put rocks along the edges of the tables, and they licked their thumbs and swiped their hands on paper napkins. Elmer and Henry, with the help of some of the others, had managed to clear the coals from the calf and to shovel them into one of the oil drums to cool. They had started cutting the crisped fat into sections, and laying pieces of roast, chunk by chunk, onto platters the women held out. Now and then another whirl of dust kicked up and crackled between our teeth.

Raunch took the beers over to my station wagon, stood by the car as I lifted the hood. I stuck my head underneath, out of sight, and I slugged down some of the beer. The taste of cold, the carbonated sting brought back—what? It brought back *then*, it brought back *before*. I swallowed against the shame.

I fiddled a little with the choke. Raunch went back to the ice chest, came back with his fingers stuck between four more bottles. The cool brew took away the storm, took away the struggles over Edie, took away the distance between Molly and me the past twelve years.

From a distance, I heard Molly's voice saying to somebody, "I'll ask Jack," and I set the bottle on the engine block. I stood up, my back to the motor and to the bottle. Molly was holding down her skirts against the wind. Her short permed hair shifted on her head like a hat. I wiped my hands on my jeans. Raunch moved to stand by me, between Molly and the engine block and my bottle of beer. "'Lo Molly," he said, then gave her a shy grin that showed his white teeth.

"Randall," she said. She was the only one I knew who called him by his true name. I stepped back, put her upwind of my breath. Then she looked at me. "Did we put in a spatula?" she said.

I said, "I saw that spatula in the back of the car and wondered if you might want it. Just a minute." I went around the station wagon, opened the back door. The spatula had fallen into the crack by the wheel well. I picked it up, wiped it on my Levi's, and handed it to her with a flourish. And when she took it, I smiled, sucked in my breath, and gave her a peck on the cheek.

SOMETIME NEAR NOON, Patty Pugh came riding up on a bicycle. I was wiping oil off my hands. I had finished fiddling with the choke, had cranked the car over a time or two. It ran somewhat better. Patty was bent over the handlebars like a racer, like she had come from somewhere farther than five blocks away, where she lived. She skidded the bike onto the gravel at the edge of the park, leaned it against one of the trees. I looked for Edie. She was standing by her mother fussing with something on one of the tables. Mable had banged a pan and people were starting to pick up their paper plates and to form lines around the salads and meat. For a minute, neither Molly nor Edie saw Patty.

Patty looked like a different girl. She was totally covered up with clothes, no skin showed, no curve of her behind under tight shorts, no line of her narrow waist under a shirt slit to show off her shape. Now, she was wearing a baggy T-shirt big enough for a pregnant woman, her hair tied back in a knot. And she wore ragged jeans that were unraveling at the ankles. She wore no makeup, no lipstick, no black smears around her eyes. Her face was clear but for a thick serving of freckles.

Molly saw Patty then. She stood there, her hands on her hips, her skirts shifting. Edie saw her then, too. She tipped her head toward her mother, jutted her chin, saying nothing yet asking permission. Molly didn't speak, only turned back to the table and began cutting one of the pies. I let out a breath. For the moment, Patty had passed inspection.

The two girls turned to walk away together. The wind carried Molly's voice. "I don't want either of you out of my sight," she said and her voice was tough as twine.

chapter 7

IT ALWAYS FELT like maybe if Molly hadn't been so strict, or if I'd had more backbone to speak out, Patty might not have dropped so far out of reach. But her presence at the picnic, her passing grades made me think maybe, maybe, it was going to work out after all. I wanted it to, not just for Edie, but because Patty had a pluck, the same kind of stubbornness and courage Molly had, something I never felt in myself, nor saw in Edie. When the girls were little, Patty's certainty seemed to give Edie something, a solid sense of her own self, that neither her mother nor I could give her. The memory of the girls when they were young broke open how it used to be for all of us, how child-Patty came and stayed with Molly and me and Edie when Patty's mother was the sickest, how Edie's room always had two twin beds, and we all referred to one of them as Patty's.

I could not remember how old they were one summer when I saw them in the backyard. The sun was strong, the girls were probably seven or eight. Edie's skin had already turned the color of tea, and Patty's was pink under the freckles.

They had spread an old blanket on the grass, Edie was sitting like an Indian chief with her back to Patty. Patty was kneeling behind her, a line of hairpins in her mouth, a hairbrush and comb, and a mirror and canister of Molly's hairspray laid out on the blanket. One by one, Patty twirled pieces of Edie's hair around a finger and pinned it, then combed out another hank which she twirled and pinned. I left, then, came back some time later. And when I looked out again, Patty was taking out the pins, and I watched as she whisked the comb through my daughter's hair and fluffed it. She took up the hairspray and Edie closed her eyes. And when she was done with the spray, she handed the mirror to Edie and Edie eyed herself side to side and I could see a change come on her, a beautiful thing, a sense of something. Patty waddle-kneeled around to the front and tipped her head one way, then the other, like a real hairdresser. And for a moment, while the hairspray held, and the breeze was still, my daughter's hair was no longer thin and lank and she sat there still as a statue, in the sun, on the blanket, with her best friend, as if moving would take it all away.

But things did move, times were blown away as if by the wind, and I would have given anything for them to be back in our hands once again. I knew things would never return to what they were that day, though hope poked me in the rib.

AS THINGS WITH Patty turned to trouble, the sweet child in her disappeared and a new tough one took her place. Molly seemed to think the new Patty was some kind of assault against Jesus, and events began to look like Molly was right.

One day, Molly discovered a pin missing from her jewel box. She had been making the bed. She kept the room clean and practical, the bed made, her slippers by her side, her housecoat hung over the corner of the closet door, which never stayed shut, her Bible, on the bedside table, with its leather marker where she left off the night before. I knew all this, though I was outside, because it was the routine she kept every day.

When she was through patting down the green quilt on our bed, she would take one last look back, then start her day, in earnest. It would be then she would have seen something askew: the jewelry box she kept on the dresser. Its little tray inside, covered with blue velvet, was pulled out. She had never been one for jewelry, wore only the band I gave her, and at Christmas the pearl necklace her grandmother gave her when she was baptized as a girl. There never was much to speak of in the box—the pearl necklace, a pair of cuff-links I'd worn in the days when we still dressed for one of Mother's Sunday dinners, and a diamond pin my mother gave Molly for our wedding.

Molly kept the pin wrapped in toilet paper in the space under the tray. I guessed that space was supposed to be a secret place, but it turned out it wasn't. At noon, she'd warned me I'd better come into the house when I heard the bus come to drop the girls from school, because she had something she needed to handle and it concerned the girls, Patty most specifically.

I was waiting at the edge of the road as the bus wheezed up. The summer had held well into the start of the school year, though the heat had gone out of it that morning. When the bus doors popped open, out came the full spectacle of Patty, the fluorescent green of her pants, the bush of her hair, the thump of her feet as she hopped the last step onto the gravel. By then, Patty had started turning "cheap," her gaudiness catching attention, the blazing red of her hair, the slick of tomato red on her mouth, the swipe of blue over her eyelids. Molly groused about the way Patty was beginning to display herself, then threatened Edie with the eternal evils of "that kind" of taste.

Patty was carrying her books in a belt slung over her shoulder. Her Levi's jacket was flapping open, declaring the new fullness of her chest. Edie hugged her books tight to herself as if covering up her own budding. Our daughter seemed to swallow light and color, Patty to pulse with it.

I said, "Your mother wants to talk with you."

The girls shot looks at each other, then followed me into the house. Molly was standing at the entrance of the stairs, her arms crossed, her face pinched in. She said nothing, only turned and left no doubt we were all supposed to follow as she made her way up the stairs and into our room.

The jewelry box was sitting on the bureau where it always sat, but the lid was propped open and resting on its little ribbon hinges. The velvet shelf lay beside it and the stretched-out crinkle of toilet paper. The toilet paper was empty.

As the girls came into the room, Molly patted smooth the front of her apron and folded her arms again. She stood there, then, and waited. Her eyes stuck on Patty. Edie crunched her books tighter into herself, her knuckles glowing white, her hair hiding her face. Patty tucked her books under one arm, twitched out one hip and said, "So, Molly, hello to you, too."

Molly stood for three centuries beside the open box. The floor moaned as I shifted one foot to the other.

Finally Molly took a breath, said, "Do you have something to tell me?"

Patty didn't wait a beat. "Looks like it's *you* who's got something to say."

Molly picked up the sections of the wrinkled toilet paper, dangled them in the air. She'd worn the pin maybe twice. It was delicate, a burst of a jewelry tumbleweed, gold with fifteen small stones that set it on fire. Mother had had it made special for Molly. As our marriage went on, Molly never wore it. It was as if it represented something Molly spurned in the same way she spurned Mother.

"What's missing?" Molly said.

Patty said, "You're holding up toilet paper and asking what's missing." She started to snicker. Edie looked like she was about to bawl.

Molly began to fold the paper into halves lengthwise, then again widthwise, lengthwise, until it was a little square the size of her thumbnail. Her eyes still riveted on Patty. "Wherever it is," she said, "get it out now and we'll be done with it."

Patty turned to Edie, made a face that said, *I don't know what she's talking about, how about you?* and shrugged.

"Don't look at me like that," Molly said.

Patty shrugged again, a shrug that might as well have been right in Molly's face. "Like what?" she said.

"Like a harlot."

"*Har*-lot?" she said. "Harlot?" She slapped her chest with her hand. "You mean me? You mean *whore*? I'm a *whore*?"

"And a thief."

Patty bellowed, "Oh, *that's* good."

Molly's face flared. "What *is* someone supposed to think?"

"I don't know," Patty said, "you tell me."

"When Judah saw her," Molly said, her voice going wavy and high like it did when she brought out the Bible to quote, "when Judah saw her, he thought her to be a harlot, because she had covered her face."

Patty's face was glowing redder than Molly's then, with anger, I thought, but also with the makeup she'd plastered on it. "Ah," she said, "so somehow that little square of toilet paper's making me Judah."

"Tamar," Molly spit out.

"I don't get it," Patty said. She wasn't backing down, wasn't cowering. It was Edie who was cowering, and me stepping back. Patty was the only one who could get Molly worked up in this very way. Her nose turned purple.

"'Pride goeth before destruction, and a haughty spirit before a fall,'" Molly said.

Patty put one finger in front of her face as if she was going to share some big secret. "Oh, the Bible again," she said. "OK, OK, here's the Bible. What about gluttony, Molly, huh? What about that? It says hold a knife at your throat if you're a glutton. Glutton. That means eat too much." She was leaning so far into Molly I thought she was going to fall over. "You're fat. What's the Bible say about that, huh, Molly? Tell me that."

"Me," Edie whispered, her voice so quiet I could barely hear it.

Molly's eyeballs flittered to Edie, did not linger long enough to inquire about Edie's single word, but went back to Patty, accusing. "How many times must I make you swear to tell me the truth? In the name of the Lord, tell ... me ... the ... truth."

"You wouldn't know the truth if it took a chomp out of that gut of yours," Patty said.

Edie worked her mouth like a guppy. I took a gulp of air.

Molly closed her eyes, mouthed a conversation toward the ceiling. When her silent discussion was done she looked straight at Patty again. "We'll see about this."

Two days later the girls and Kenny Muffin were caught smoking and skipping school.

chapter 8

THERE WAS A red scribble on Molly's calendar marking our appointment with First National at two o'clock, today, July 8. I'd come into the house early to get ready. Water was running in the upstairs bathroom Molly and I put in a couple of years ago.

Patty had ridden out on her bike a little over an hour ago. Because things had gone OK at the picnic, the girls had permission to see each other again, but Patty was not allowed to stay overnight. The girls were cooped up in Edie's room. If the girls were ever allowed to spend days and nights together again, they were going to have to earn it in steps, and Molly and I were the ones to determine the steps. As it was, Patty was allowed to stay only through lunch. When the water shut off I could hear them talking behind Edie's closed door.

Patty had given Molly or me no excuse but to approve what she made of herself now; she dressed as plain as Edie and I saw maybe a little spark of disappointment come on Molly's face when she saw that the girls intended to follow her rules. It would have been easier if Patty acted up again and gave Molly an excuse to be done with the problem of her. But so far there had been no excuses. She had knocked on the back door before she came into the house, she had greeted Molly and me in a cordial tone, and she had been dressed conservatively, wearing the same drab T-shirt and frayed jeans as she had worn to the picnic, her tumbleweed hair pulled back in a knot as plain as Olive Oyl's. She was as dull as our daughter.

When I came down from the bathroom after shaving for the meeting, the second shave in one day, Molly was standing at the stove, turning a pan full of round steak. She forked over the meat, her breath coming loud and thick as if she had just run a mile or two. A carton of brown eggs from our hens sat on the counter. She was wearing a dress that had no fit to it at all, only yards of material patterned with little purple flowers. The sleeves flared out from her arms like butterfly wings. She'd tied on a pink apron with a knot in the back.

I came up behind her, kissed her on the cheek.

She turned to me, gave me a glance up and down, then forked over another one of the steaks that were sizzling in a quarter-inch of fat. "Jack," she said into the pan, "You've got to get dressed before we go to the bank."

I looked down at myself, shrugged her a look like *isn't this dressed?* A joke. I was still wearing coveralls and boots. Looking at me, no one would think this was anything but a normal, calm day in our lives, Molly getting us lunch, the girls' feet thumping on the floors upstairs, the rush of the shower one of the girls was taking, the kitchen radio playing Brenda Lee.

Molly licked her thumb, then wiped her hands on the apron. "I laid out slacks and a shirt," she said, "on the bed." The First National letter sat in a folder, with half an inch of documents we would take in with us for the meeting. She slapped her fingers on the apron, left streaks of grease on the pink ruffle. "The way Patty looked when she came, I don't think she had bathed since the last time she was here," Molly said. "Filthy."

The ties of Molly's apron shimmied as she turned to stir the corn boiling on the back of the stove. I knew, like me, she was concentrating on everything but the red mark on the calendar, concentrating on my clothes, on the steak, on the corn to shove out thoughts of the importance of the two o'clock meeting. "I laid out socks and your oxfords, too," she said, her breath puffing from somewhere back in her throat. A bowl of dipping flour and a sheet of wax paper sat where she had powdered the steaks.

"Girls are upstairs," I said like it was news.

She grunted, then bent over and opened the oven door. Lately, the thickness of her waist made it difficult for her to move. Two years ago in a fit of anger at herself, she went to a doctor who specialized in nutrition. He weighed her, gave her a book with food groups and calories. She said his scale must have been off, because he told her she was two hundred and eighty-five pounds. She had gained more since then and was starting to complain about her knees. She opened the oven door, took out cookie sheets filled with two dozen biscuits, set them on the breadboard.

"That's enough for a harvest crew," I said.

Molly slammed the oven door a little harder than necessary. The comment was a slipup on my part. I'd learned to stop talking about food around her. The mention of it made her think I was pestering her about her weight. I'd learned long ago she did that well enough on her own.

Eight chairs sat around our kitchen table, as if we still would fill them with four more kids. We had lost one baby, a little boy who came early. He would have been twelve now, four years younger than Edie. In our scrapbook there was a picture from that time. Lee took it at Christmas. Edie was three and we didn't know Molly was pregnant, though she didn't feel too well and wondered if she was getting a bug. That morning she'd said her stomach was a little

JEANNIE BURT

bit queasy. I thought then it was probably nerves, from what happened that year and I was the cause of it. Later, I took the blame for the miscarriage.

Lee's Christmas picture caught Molly and me standing in front of the tree with Edie sitting at our feet holding on to her new doll. I had put my arm around Molly. In the picture she was wearing a dark red dress. It had a sparkling pin on it in the shape of a Christmas tree and her middle was drawn in by a wide belt. The night of my mistake had happened only a couple of months before the picture. You could see the start of distance between us. She was leaning away from me, and the Christmas tree lights sparkled between us.

Losing the baby had set us back, Molly particularly, and after a year of dark days, Molly and I began trying to have another baby. We tried for two years, and finally we went to the doctor for tests. Molly had gained some weight by then, and he couldn't find anything wrong but suggested it wouldn't hurt Molly to trim down a little.

I left Molly turning out those steaks onto a paper towel on the counter. We'd eat, so we had something "in us," Molly said, before the meeting with the bank. Upstairs, I started to put on the slacks and shirt Molly had laid out for me. Edie's door was closed. I could smell the damp from the bathroom, but the door was open and no one in the room. I could hear the girls still mumbling, whispering, making no noise otherwise.

THE GIRLS CAME downstairs, took their places at the table. Patty pulled out the chair at the place she had sat all those years she used to stay over. It was her place when the girls used to do homework together, where she blew out candles for her eighth birthday, and her tenth, and whatever other birthdays she celebrated with us.

Molly had stacked biscuits in a pile on a big platter. I reached for one. "Jack," Molly said, a rebuke. With Patty back at the table, things seemed so mixed up, I'd forgotten grace.

Molly bowed her head. "Lord," she said. The rest of us dipped after her. "Thank you for the blessings of this day."

Edie slumped in her chair, her hands folded in front of her face in the same pious way her mother folded hers. Patty merely lowered her chin. Her hair was damp and the thick of it slicked back off her face, but it was clean and she smelled of shampoo. She held her fingers at the ready over her plate. Her hands were clean but rimmed with dark stains at the edges of her nails. In her thinness, she had grown narrow-faced. She was still pretty, but in the last half year, she had grown older than Edie, older somehow, than even Molly or me. Her eyes were circled underneath with color as dark as her fingernails.

Molly squeezed her eyes shut. "Lord," she said again, "we thank Thee for the blessing of the food we are about to receive."

Edie's hands twitched slightly then went still.

"And Jack and I ask your blessings, Oh Lord, we ask you to be with us, Lord, as we meet with the bank this afternoon. In Jesus' name we pray. Amen. Jack," she said, and nodded it was time to eat.

I took a biscuit, set it on my plate, passed the biscuits to Molly, who took one in her cracked fingers and passed them to Patty. Patty took two. Patty didn't look up. As she cut into one of the biscuits, her mouth made little expectant motions until she caught it and pulled it in so it cut straight across her face. Without butter, or jam, or honey, Patty began shoveling the biscuit into her mouth. Our Edie sat watching with her hands in her lap, not saying a word.

"Don't you want butter and jam?" Molly said.

Patty nodded but still didn't utter a sound. It wasn't right having her so quiet.

Molly passed the butter, then the jam.

Patty took a pat of the butter nearly the size of her biscuit. "Thank you," she said.

Molly set her hand beside Edie's, nodded once. "Aren't you hungry?"

Edie moved her shoulders up a little bit, almost a shrug. A strand of her thin hair jutted out from her right ear. Sitting there at the table where we had all spent a good deal of our lives, our Edie had grown so soft and unprotected, and Patty so tired.

Life on a farm doesn't change much. Most of us lived in the same houses passed down from one generation to the next, never changing over the years but for maybe a slathering of a new color of paint, the same barns and sheds scattered around under clusters of locusts, and elms, cottonwoods and Russian olives, trees that had taken root from seeds planted a century before and that had since grown old and split by the strikes of lightning, bits of them dying, their limbs dull and riddled by ants and beetles. It seemed like only a day ago Patty had been staying with us for the night or the week, bubbling with talk, her hair flying into her face, her eyes snapping like lamps.

Now, her eyes dodged us, would not look at any of us, only at the food on her plate.

I looked away from her, down at the comfort of the clutter in the middle of the table—the cup of toothpicks, the spindly brown donkey salt and pepper, the napkin rack I'd made from wood shingles. Patty had given Molly the salt and pepper for Christmas years ago. The donkeys, the napkins, the toothpicks sat there where they always were, and I could find a little comfort in it. It was as if that little arrangement represented the core of our family, and that core of our family was forged by Molly three times a day with her food and her graces. And that core had been broken up for months, ever since Patty had been out of our lives. She'd brought light to the table, light we didn't seem to be able to conjure without her.

By the time they were ten, the girls had gone through a series of ideas about what they were going to be when they grew up. Patty came up with the schemes, and the whirl she stirred sucked Edie and Molly and me up with her. The first big idea was to become ballet dancers. They spent a few days posing their arms and pointing their legs and leaping around until they shook a lamp off the living room table. Next was singers. We'd made the mistake of buying Edie a record player for her birthday, and they stayed in Edie's room screaming out tunes from Donny and Marie Osmond, the only record Edie had so far. We could hear the music all the way down to the basement, could even hear it vibrate the living room window when the low notes or the drums hit. Why, Molly asked, did everything have to be so *loud* anymore?

Then it was making money. Patty thought they needed some money one summer. It was hot, the girls out of school. I had been fertilizing, doing the last bit of fieldwork before finishing up equipment repairs for harvest. At noon, as I drove in from working on the Vancycle section, Molly was out banging a wood spoon on a pan, calling us in for supper.

Outside the back door, I had shrugged out of my coveralls, and for a moment the breeze swept over the sweat trapped under the coveralls and I was cool. Lee was planning to start coming out to work with me in mid-July. He had finished up that year's teaching, and he and Helen were taking the two kids to Disneyland for a couple of weeks before he started harvest work with me. I laid the coveralls by the back door as the girls ran past and into the house. I hoped Inkie, one of the dogs, wouldn't lift his leg on my coveralls, which he did sometimes when I didn't hang them out of his reach. I never figured out what it was with my coveralls, only that they must have smelled of something I'd brought in from the fields, coyote, maybe, or badger. I never knew.

That day, the girls had been doing something in the barnyard and had brought the whiff of the pigpen into the house with them. They clattered up the back porch stairs three at a time. We'd had Patty with us a lot that summer. Jackie Pugh's mind had started going screwy again, and Larry was about to take her to the hospital again for treatments. We would later learn Jackie had schizophrenia, but then we only knew Patty said her mother wasn't eating again and she was up wandering the house at nights, smoking cigarettes. Larry had found her sitting in her nightgown out on the curb in front of the house at three a.m., blinking her eyes at a streetlight. He had his hands full, too, with his own mother, who lived eight miles away in Athena and whose heart was starting to act up.

As the girls clomped into the house, Molly was in the kitchen slicing beef from a roast for sandwiches. She always felt guilty, she said, when she didn't have anything hot ready to serve. But none of us wanted hot. It was 102 already, and barely noon. She'd laid out fresh bread she'd baked at sunrise and had put the jar of mayonnaise on the table in a bowl filled with ice, and had filled the pitcher with pink lemonade.

The girls were in such a hurry, they hadn't even noticed I was there. "Molly," Patty shouted as soon as they were inside the door. From the kitchen, Molly shouted back, "Do you have to shout?"

The girls stood shoulder to shoulder behind Molly. She had not conceded to turn around. Patty stood there. "Molly," she demanded, "we got to talk."

Molly turned on the tap, high. Water came rushing out loud, hitting on a pan or something in the sink I couldn't see.

Patty tapped Molly on the back. "Molly," Patty said, pushing herself next to Molly. It was becoming a test of wills.

I said, "What's the hurry?"

The girls turned to me at the same time like they had no idea I was there until then. Their faces were red with heat, sunburned and sweaty from running from the barn.

"We got an idea," Patty said, "me and Edie."

"Wash up," Molly said.

Patty seemed to ignore Molly. "It's gonna," she sputtered, breathing hard, "I mean . . . take . . . the . . . place . . . by *storm*," she said.

They stood there panting, waiting for some response, not from me, but from Molly, but it wasn't coming. I turned them around, gave them a little push toward the bathroom to wash up.

Molly licked her thumb. "We can talk about it after we eat."

After saying grace, Edie sat there in her place, hiccuping and leaning forward on her hands, her elbows jutting out behind, looking at Patty now and then but never at her mother. It turned out the big idea was to put on a pet show. They had come up with it that morning. One of the sows had farrowed a week before, and the girls had been spending a lot of time with the piglets. They had even named one of them Wilbur from a book we gave Patty one Christmas. Wilbur, it turned out, was the reason for this pet show.

Molly took a bite of her sandwich, chewed. Patty looked straight at her, her eyes narrowed down as if in a dare. Edie's eyes flicked at Patty, then came to rest on her own hands folded in her lap.

Molly swallowed, took a slow drink of lemonade, calmly wiped her napkin across her mouth. "Edie, who's going to come to this show?"

Edie looked to Patty for an answer.

"*Everybody*," Patty said, "we're going to be famous." Her hair pounced down on her head like a huge red animal. She flung her arms back like she was taking in the whole world. Her hair flew up then settled again.

"You need a haircut," Molly said. "I don't know why Larry doesn't cut some of that bush." It was a damper, the kind Molly was good at.

Patty didn't take the bait. "We could *charge*," she said.

Molly wheezed an accusation. "Just where do you think you are going to have this circus?"

"Pet show," Patty said. "We don't have any elephants."

"So?" Molly said, "where?" Her voice was low, satisfied as if she felt she'd finally stumped Patty, shut her up.

Edie sat between them watching back and forth like she'd watch a ball tossed from one to the other.

"The barn," Patty said. It was not a question. There was no asking of permission in it.

"*Here?*" I said.

"We could clean it out," Patty said.

"I'm not," Molly said, "having half the county traipsing out here for a circus."

Patty's jaw shot out.

Molly flapped her hands away from herself as if the game with Patty was done. "Eat."

"In town," Patty said.

Edie sprang forward, leaning over her sandwich, her elbows on the table. "We could have it at the school."

"Sit up straight, Edith!" Edie sat up. "Eat the sandwich I fixed for you. Now." She let her eyes slide back over to Patty. "Who in their right mind would let you kids have a half-baked pet show at the school?"

"Or in the park," Patty said, like Molly hadn't interfered at all.

Edie spoke up, her face red again, excited. "Or maybe we could have it on Main Street." Edie was out of control now, in spite of Molly's efforts.

Molly *tsked*, puffed out a disgusted little breath. "Not so fast, Edith. Who said you're getting involved with this harebrained idea?"

Edie slid back in her chair, drowned out finally by her mother.

Molly pushed away from the table as if she had won. She went to the refrigerator, turned her back on us, her motions controlled, righteous. She brought back a tray of ice, which she cracked into the lemonade pitcher.

It turned out that Patty's idea didn't die. Three weeks later Patty got Rusty Cousins to agree to move the fire truck out of the station for an afternoon. And, at her dad's store, Pugh Market, after swimming at the park one day, she and Edie hand drew posters and taped them to light posts in town. And Patty got her dad to put up a banner announcing the show in the front window of the market. All of this without Molly knowing.

The day after the banner went up, at the meeting of the Ladies' Aid, Sissy Misczek proposed that the LA donate cookies and packets of punch for the show and they voted in the idea while Molly had to sit there and agree to supporting the first-ever Philpott Pet Preview.

But that was then. Where had that Patty gone? A sort of ghost of her sat at the table with us. The biscuits, the creamed corn, the slices of roast, the potatoes and honeyed carrots, the peanut butter cookies had been passed around. We each took some and began quietly to eat, no chatter, no laughing. Molly and Edie and I were all watching Patty eat. Patty didn't look up, didn't make a sound, kept on putting fork after fork of food into her mouth.

chapter 9

A MEETING, LIKE the one marked on the calendar, had no place in a farmer's life. A meeting like the one at the bank didn't come with the seasons, did not find a place in one year after another. I should have been thankful for that. One of the blessings of a farmer's life was in the regularity of it, the sense of a start and a finish, year after year. I always felt the year began toward the end of July, when I walked the fields, imagining, hoping the crops would put out eighty-, hundred-bushel yields, and driving the roads from one end of a crop to another watching for the heads to plump up, waiting for the last little bit of the green to bleach out, and then counting days that never seemed to end before it was dry enough to be cut.

When there was a crop, you made "busy," you fiddled with the last repairs, you greased every bearing that ever existed, you tricked up old equipment to do what it was never intended to do. And at night you tried to sleep, tried to think of anything but the possibility the price would sink before you sold, or that it would rain and the crops would mold, or that it would test out with so much rye they'd drop the grade. And you'd crave to get it over with, do away with the suspense. You'd want to be on the other end of harvest, the end where you knew where you stood, the end that let you know whether you would have enough to replace the old Ford, or whether your wife could set up that appointment to get your kid braces and fix her bite so she could say an *S* the way it was supposed to be said.

That was, *when* there was a crop.

"YOU OWE PENDLETON Grain Growers $3,252," the bank manager said. "You owe Dr. Vingerud . . . ,"

"For Molly's checkups," I said, like it would make some difference.

"You owe Dr. Vingerud," he continued as if I'd said nothing, "nearly fifteen hundred. Then there's the gas company, electric, Pioneer Implement." He swiped the list of our debts with the back of his fingernails, disgusted, then picked up another entry.

Molly and I were sitting in the conference room of First National, the second door to the left, down a hall behind the tellers' counters. Mr. Sturgis sat at the head of the table reviewing the state of our lives and fingering a droop of slick hair out of his face. His forehead wrinkled. "You have an entry for Dr. Cavalcanti for Edith's dental work." He looked up. "Who's Edith?"

"Our daughter," Molly said.

He waggled his head side to side. "Dr. Cavalcanti goes to our church."

"Methodists," Molly muttered.

When we'd come into the bank, a girl not much older than our Edie had showed us back to the conference room. She was dressed in a navy blue skirt that made little whispers when she walked. She had shaken hands with us and said her name was Jennifer something, then added, "Mr. Sturgis is on the telephone with Philadelphia," and led us down the hall.

When we were seated, Jennifer had offered us coffee and Molly pulled a sour face and said no for the both of us. Coffee drinking was not allowed in Molly's church. "You can have a seat," the girl said. "Mr. Sturgis will just be a few minutes." Then she left the room and pulled the door closed behind her.

As we waited, Molly had laid our folders on the table, and then we sat, the two of us, side by side in the metal and leather chairs. It was quiet in there, muffled like you feel when a loud noise suddenly shuts off. It was like the bank had swallowed up the world. The click of the door, when the manager came in, made both of us jump.

Molly patted the folders she'd laid out in front of herself as he shuffled through our list of debts. His eyeglasses were fashionable ones that enlarged his eyes and filled his face like a windshield. No bifocals, he was too young for that.

Molly gave out a sigh like she was getting impatient, then leaned over the arm of her chair and pulled her purse up from the floor, set it on the table. He continued to review our papers and she began digging around inside the purse. The purse was dull, becoming worn at the corners. She'd made it herself out of squares of material she'd pieced together in little square puffs, printed with brown flowers and stripes in a checkerboard arrangement. It had squatted on our bureau for two or three years and it looked like Molly in a way, squat, plain, puffy. She rustled her hand around in the purse and came up with a Payday candy bar. She peeled back the paper and took a bite.

"It looks like you owe nearly ninety thousand dollars," Sturgis said. He was slim, with a white shirt so starchy it crackled when he moved. He ran his finger down a column, reading items one by one. He looked up at me, then at Molly with an expression like he'd stepped in dog poop. He must have been just out of college, half my age.

The amount of money we owed wound around in my head, *ninety thousand, ninety thousand, ninety thousand,* and I was beginning to see where he was going. With the crop a total loss, there was no way to make the ranch give us a living and pay back what we owed.

"Who is Mrs. John McIntyre?" he said.

Molly turned to me.

"My mother," I said. It was also Molly, but Molly never went by Mrs. John anything.

"I see you owe her sixty thousand dollars."

Neither Molly nor I spoke. If there had been any crop to sell, we would also have owed a good part of it to Mom, forty percent—her share. I shuffled in my chair. I hadn't told her yet about the extent of damage, though I'd gone to her place a couple of weeks ago, intending to.

I'd driven into Pendleton that day and had stopped at her apartment, planning to ask her if she could give us some room on her loan. She had heard about the storm, we'd talked about it on the telephone, but I hadn't admitted the whole thing.

Her apartment was filled with light. She'd painted it white, then put up drapes as wispy as summer clouds. Her air conditioner clattered all summer, but still she didn't close the blinds, said she didn't have the heart to make it dark after all those years living in the dim light of the house at the farm. "I could never get enough light out there," she said. Molly had never complained.

When Mother opened the door, she gave me a light hug, pipped a little kiss at my ear, then said, "Are your feet clean?"

I swiped my feet on the welcome mat that was a miniature Oriental rug. The feet-wiping was more for effect, more for the tradition, the ritual greeting she'd given all of us, Dad, Lee, me, every time we walked into the house.

She said I looked pale and fed me a piece of angel food cake from the crystal dish sitting on the kitchen counter. Since Dad died, Mother seemed to have brought her life into herself, tidied it, culled out what she no longer wanted. It was like all those years we were growing up, she'd wanted to carve out some place that was all hers but she'd had to wait to do it. And now she could, and her place now included a Cadillac sedan, a wig, and a trip on an ocean liner she was taking in two months. It was the trip she had always wanted to take with Dad, and he'd always come up with some excuse not to go. And now that Ethel Langsdorf's and Mildred Piotowski's husbands had died, Mom and Ethel and Mildred were taking that trip. Her life these days seemed to fit her like a custom-made dress.

She kept her apartment neat, but a mess of brochures littered the table, in the little living room, by her tapestry chair. And a book from the Umatilla Library sat open to a page with a picture of the pope and the Vatican on the table by her davenport. They were flying from Portland to New York. They were sailing from New York on the *Rotterdam V.* The details made my head whirl. We talked a few minutes, mostly about the trip. They'd be gone over a month to Greece, Italy, and France. They were taking in England as well, where Mother's great-greats came from and she, on her own, was taking a train to County Cork, Ireland, to visit the town where Dad's people came from. She spoke of Ireland in a wistful way, like it was something of Dad to hold onto. Though she'd arranged her life and her apartment in ways I always thought she wanted, I don't think she ever got used to being without him.

She closed the booklet that the Holland America lines had sent, laid it beside the sterling candy dish on the coffee table. "Have some pecan clusters, sweetie?"

I patted my belt, shook my head no. "Thanks, though," I said.

She set the dish back down without taking one for herself. Molly would have managed to eat them until only one or two were left, and those would be gone too but for the sake of appearances.

"The paper," Mother said, "said your storm did some damage in the Walla Walla valley," and she patted a wisp of hair over her temple without looking at me. In her own way, she was asking how

Molly and I were doing. The opening was there for me to blurt out every bit of my trouble, but I couldn't find the guts.

Now the bank manager was about to make me come clean. "What's the status of that loan," he said, "to your mother?"

Molly crinkled the candy wrapper, waited for me to answer. I leaned back in my chair, putting her between me and sight of the manager. "I've taken care of it," I said.

"What's 'taken care of it' mean?" he said. "It shows you still owe it."

Molly's breath came out heavier. Insurance would have covered Mom's loan and the bank's as well. Dad always took out insurance; Mother would have assumed I had, too. Without my payment every year, I didn't know how Mom would manage, with only her Social Security. Would she cancel the trip, maybe, or dig into the savings accounts she had started for the kids' college? I didn't know. I only knew I was the one who was responsible.

"What's the status of the loan from Mrs. McIntyre?" he insisted.

"Excused," I said almost below my breath.

"What?" the manager said.

Molly turned toward me and gave me a look that pierced the side of my head. I wanted to duck and hide. I held my stomach waiting for her to bring out her Bible and exclaim my lie to the Lord. But she sat quiet except for the rumble of her breath.

I couldn't bring myself to let my lie sit there like a rotting body. I thumped my chest and cleared my throat. "Excuse me," I said, and Molly turned her flat face away and set her gaze back on the manager. "I plan to speak to her about the loan."

It was at that point that Molly wheezed and folded her arms under her breasts. For a minute, the room was quiet but for her breathing. Then suddenly her lips gave a little smack. "Do you pray?"

The manager blinked twice and looked at me like he was asking me to answer Molly's question.

She lifted her chin high, stretched out the flesh of her neck. "Are you at peace with the Lord?" She was winding up, I could see it, the way she did to me and Edie. I had learned to let her and her Lord roll together. They knew things I never seemed to be able to get my hands on. "Are you a Christian?" she said and the room filled up with *good* as though she'd said it.

Mr. Sturgis leaned back. His chair let out a groan. And he looked down his nose at Molly. "Yes. For what it's worth."

"For what it's worth?" Molly said. "For what it's *worth?*" She pulled her purse onto the tiny space her stomach left for a lap. Mr. Sturgis began twirling the ring on his finger. It was not a wedding band, but a heavy, inscribed ring with a blue stone—a fraternity ring similar to the one Lee had from college.

Molly rummaged in her purse, sent the brown calico flowers this way and that as she wrestled with candy wrappers, pens, packets of tissue. Mr. Sturgis's ring flickered blue, gold, blue, gold, round and round. Molly finally yanked her white Bible from her purse, set it on the table in front of her. She thumped her hand on it. "What do you mean, 'for what it's worth'?"

Mr. Sturgis quit twirling the ring, leaned back. His white shirt crackled. "You're taking what I said out of context," he said. "Now, about the loan."

"No," Molly said, "now back to 'what it's worth.'"

His mouth drew in and I could see he knew what Molly was doing, where she was taking the conversation, and that he didn't like it.

"A good Christian believes," Molly said. "A good Christian claims the Lord. A good Christian never has to ask what it's worth."

"I didn't mean anything by that," he said. His face went red, and a vein popped up along his temple, blue as a worm. "We need to get back to the business at hand."

"Isn't the *Lord* the business at hand?" Molly said, her voice loud, horrified.

"I meant it's not the business today."

"The Lord is always our business," she said. "The Lord knows what you meant."

She was starting to make Jell-O out of him like she made Jell-O out of me. It was her gift to have the Lord always on her side. "'The Lord lifteth up the meek,'" she said, "'He casteth the wicked down to the ground.' Do you refute the Lord? Do you want to do the Lord's work with us?" She didn't wait for an answer. "Or will you blaspheme the name of the Lord?"

He said, "I don't know how you could say I was blaspheming," trying to put smugness into his tone.

"Jack and me, we are not wicked."

"I didn't say you were wicked."

"You are about to cast us down to the ground," she said.

"The bank sets parameters," he said.

She thrust her finger into the air. "Nehemiah, said, 'I beseech thee, O Lord God of heaven,'" her voice quivering like Oral Roberts, "'the great and terrible God, that keepeth the covenant and have mercy for them that observe His commandments.'"

"Mrs. McIntyre."

"It is the will of God," she said.

He was beginning to look exasperated, like he couldn't grasp what had happened. "So," he said, putting some pressure behind his word, "I am supposed to forgive all this?"

"It is not in your hands." She sat back, like it was up to him see things her way, to figure out whose hands it was in.

He shook his head. "There is no way I can see of making this work."

Molly held up three fingers. "Three months," she said. "Give us time to do the Lord's work. Three months."

His face had broken out in shining beads. Molly patted her Bible again, poked a finger toward the ceiling like she was about to launch into more of the Lord.

"Two," he said.

chapter 10

WE WERE BARELY into summer and already knew how the year would end. Usually you had *something* come September. September made the year concrete. September put the suspense behind us. Well, we were going to know the end way before September.

I tried to take some consolation in the news. We weren't the only ones with trouble that year. South Dakota was in the worst drought in over forty years, and farmers in the Midwest had gone so long on dry they were about at the end of their credit lines. It should have been some comfort knowing that Molly and I weren't the only ones in trouble, but it didn't help, somehow.

I didn't recall Dad's ever having to face anything like Molly and I were. While I was growing up, Septembers always seemed to be good times for Dad. Only once did we miss getting the crops in before we tore August off the calendar, and it was because it had been too wet that year. Hah. Wet.

Looking back, those years when the responsibility of life was still on Dad and Mom's shoulders, were the happiest of my life. I remembered Dad teasing me, before my first year of high school started, that I was going to be in for it, the juniors and seniors would see to that. But it didn't happen that way. I sort of fell in line with Raunch and Larry Pugh and took on some of the shine that went with them. Things were expected of them, even as freshmen. It was like the whole of Philpott knew they were going to be someone.

Raunch became what we thought was a *man* first. By junior high, he was almost six feet tall and had been laid—twice—by the end of seventh grade. But he stopped growing, and by the time we were in high school, I'd caught up, even passed him an inch or so. I was bone-skinny, but he was long and lean, and white-toothed and combed his hair high off his face like Elvis would five years later. Larry was shorter than we were, but his reputation for athletics followed him into high school. In a game—any kind of game—he was everywhere, fast as a quarter horse, grabby as a monkey.

The three of us walked Philpott High's halls, three abreast. We filled the school with ourselves. The juniors and seniors tried to bull their way around, tried to hold onto their rightful places, but couldn't when Larry and Raunch and I were the ones the whole town was watching like heroes for the games we had started winning right from the start. By high school, it was like we had caught our breath, like the six inches or the eight inches we'd grown, or the size twelve shoes were some kind of badges that gave us power to run and throw and shoot better than anybody who ever lived before. It was, I recalled, the first time I felt like I belonged. It was Larry and Raunch and me.

I remember only one year when I might have been aware of a cloud over Dad and Mom's life. It had rained most of May and June that year and had been cool enough through July that you could wear a jacket. Dad was growing sullen, getting angry at everything, at Lee and me for nothing, at the prices of calves, the paint peeling on the barn, the Dodgers, the Ford truck he'd been so proud of the year before. He'd go all quiet and his jaw muscle would shiver and jerk in his cheek. Nothing could make him happy.

Because of the cool and the damp, harvest had been real late. It wasn't until the last part of August that the moisture in the crops came down to a level where we could start to run machines. School started a week late that year, to allow kids to work the late harvest. Finally, by the second week of September, we had the crop in. Dad sold some of it, but a good part of it was sitting in the silo out back of the barn.

Not more than a couple of weeks later, the wheat in the bin started smoldering. Dad had never had a fire, but now and then you'd hear where somebody lost everything they had stored and you might drive by and see the empty air where there'd been a grain elevator or a silo and where there was nothing left but a pad of cement and ash the dull color of death. And so you kept an eye out, you measured the temperature, and you rotated and stirred the bins to let the moisture out or it might go up in a blaze.

We didn't usually store much grain. Maybe that was why Dad hadn't kept an eye on it, maybe he was too preoccupied, I don't know. Most years Dad sold grain right away and the silo sat empty but for mice track. Other years, like that one, when he thought the price would go up later in the season, or when he wanted to wait to sell because of taxes, the grain sat there and worried him until it was augured away.

But by the luck, on a Saturday, I discovered the grain was heating up. Grandpa had built a little lean-to against one side of the silo. He'd done a fancy carpenter's job of it, had curved the little roof, had caulked against leaks, and he'd bolted it tight. It was the kind of project you could only get to in the middle of winter, when the ground had been frozen for weeks, and you'd been shut in the house or in the draft of the shop. You'd feel trapped until the day when, all of a sudden, the wind would die and the sun would come out and you'd be walking on ground frozen hard as stone. You could pile your coat on a fencepost and the sun would sit on your head, and on the tops of your shoulders and you couldn't bear to stay anywhere but right out there in the light.

For years, Grandpa stacked wood for the woodstove in the lean-to beside the silo, but there was no need for wood anymore, since Mom had Dad put in a furnace and took out the woodstove. She said the wood stove was too ugly to live with and was messy and took up too much room and she had Dad take it out. Without the wood in it, the lean-to started accumulating odd stuff—worn tires that fit a truck Dad sold years ago, halters and bridles hung on nails out of reach of rats and mice.

That day, the day I found the silo heating up, it was cold and damp, with the wind whining through the blades of the harrow. I'd gone out to the lean-to where I could smoke a cigarette without Mom finding out, and where I could sit and rifle through the little wood box where Dad kept old *Playboy* magazines.

I didn't know if Lee ever came out there. I doubted it. He was more interested in reading and drawing and spending time with Timmy Smart.

Things never seemed to change much out there in the lean-to, except for the shifting of the dry little pile of dirt where I hid my cigarette butts, and the addition, now and then, of another *Playboy* in the box.

I'd stacked two of the tires against the silo wall, one on the other. I had sat down on the tires, my knees poked into the air, my butt in the tire hole, and I felt the sensation I was sitting on the seat of a toilet. I leaned my back against the ridges of the silo and felt the warmth bleeding through my jacket. I turned, put my hand on the metal. It was almost too warm to touch. I could smell the heat coming off the grain. It smelled like bread baking.

I ran to the house, yelling for Dad, and together, Dad and I and

Lee augured the grain out of the bin onto the dry ground, where it lay like a huge mound of sand open and vulnerable to wind, and rats and rain. It couldn't stay there. Dad sold it that week. And he patted my back a couple of times and thanked me for saving his bacon. If he ever saw my cigarette butts he never squeaked, and I never squeaked about the *Playboys*.

AFTER OUR MEETING at the bank, Molly was quieter than usual. When she spoke, she talked like she knew everything was going to be all right. "We're in God's hands," she'd say time and time again, but after a while it seemed like she wasn't so sure. She was reading her Bible day and night and attending church services in the middle of the week. The Philpott First Christian Fellowship Church had only one sermon a week, at ten o'clock on Sundays, so Molly was dragging herself and Edie all the way into Pendleton for Wednesday night services at the First Congregational Church. When she came back home, sometimes after nine o'clock at night, she carried sacks of candy and gallons of ice cream from Safeway into the house. Several times, I found empty maple bar boxes, still smelling of sugar and maple, under the seat of her car where I guess she thought nobody would see.

We had sent in the revised statement of assets Mr. Sturgis had asked for. It was not to include some of the equipment Molly had put on, equipment he said was of too little value. Molly marked the calendar for the next meeting, and I couldn't see, for the life of me, what two months was going to buy us.

As I look back on that time, we didn't talk about much of anything at all. It was Edie who was doing all the talking. It was like she had been asleep for over half a year and now that she could see Patty again, she was awake, pink-cheeked and happy. She did things in a fever, setting the table, doing chores without either of us asking her and without a breath of complaint. I didn't know what to make of it. In contrast, the one day of the week she was allowed to visit, Patty seemed all puckered up, quiet, humble even. It wasn't like her. And it made me worried.

I hadn't seen Edie so eager for the start of school since she was little. I knew the reason was that she was going to be able to see Patty every day. We allowed the girls to see each other one day a week, on Saturday. Saturday mornings Patty would ride out on her bike and stay the day. The girls followed the rules, but they still were not allowed to be alone together, without one of us—either Molly or me—in the house. We had not moved to allowing them overnights yet, though Edie was beginning to hint at it. When it was time to go, I'd put Patty's bike in the back of my pickup and the girls would sit beside me as I took her and her bike back into town, the girls not saying a word as I parked in front of the Masonic Hall and unloaded the bike from the back. Patty would wait there in front of the hall and watch as Edie and I pulled away to go home. I never saw her go up the side stairs to the apartment where she and her mother and her mother's boyfriend lived.

Finally Edie asked outright if Patty could stay overnight.

Molly shook her head.

"Please," Edie said.

And Molly said, "No," with a firmness that sounded mean.

"I don't see why not," I said.

"Jack," Molly said low, warning me to butt out.

Edie looked down at her hands, sucked on her braces.

Then, as if Molly realized the harshness in her voice, she said, "Do you think you learned the Lord's lesson?"

"Yeah," Edie said.

"Yeah?" Molly said and poked up an eyebrow in judgment.

"Yes," Edie said and gave another slurp at her braces.

Molly stood there, her hands thrust into the depths of her waist, facing Edie, staring her down. I could see Edie begin to give in, begin to melt, but she didn't flinch, didn't look away from her mother. "I need to pray over it," Molly said, and she looked at me accusing, like she did a lot of the time, like maybe I could do with a prayer or two myself.

That space, that divide that came between us so many years ago, still weighed on Molly, and I felt she always blamed Patty over it, though Patty and Edie were only young children at the time. Molly and I never spoke of it again, but it laid there between us like something rotting. After it happened, she started losing herself in the Bible, talking to the Lord and shutting me out. A thousand times over the years I must have envisioned what life would have been like if I hadn't done what I did. Maybe I could have patched it a little between us by taking up Jesus with her and by going to church and by studying the scriptures every waking minute of the day. But it was like Jesus, and the scriptures, rubbed my nose in my mistake, like someone would rub a puppy's nose in its crap.

For two days, Molly mulled whether Edie would be safe if Patty stayed over one night. Her decision involved a lot of praying and asking the Lord to tell her what to do. She finally came up with the Lord's answer one night, and she came out to the barn to talk to me while I was cleaning up after chores. Edie had already finished her part of chores and had gone into the house to separate the milk. It startled me, Molly coming out there, out of nowhere. She showed up in the barn maybe every couple of years. The barn—and the shop—were my place, mine and Edie's.

Molly pulled herself up the step onto the wood floor where the cows came in to be milked, grabbing onto the barn door for assistance. I was shoveling up a pile Henrietta had left on the floor. The whine of Molly's breath startled me and I whirled around. It was cool that afternoon, the days becoming shorter, the evenings a little crisper. The leaves of the maple trees were dry like they got before they started to turn.

Molly's face was red, with purpose and with the effort of walking from the house to the barn—she was pretty, lit up, her expression round and warm. In her rolling walk, she went to one of the bales of straw by the calves' pen, let herself down onto it. Her lap spread across the bale, the flesh of her thighs rippling a moment, then becoming still. When Edie was real small, sometimes she would sit on the bale where her mother was now, her narrow legs dangling over the edge, and she would play with one of the cats, dragging a long piece of straw and watching the cat chase it.

Molly took a rattling breath. "Jack," she said.

I had the urge to go over to her and to squeeze myself next to her and to feel the warmth of her arm against mine. She took another breath before she went on, "We need to talk about what to do about Patty."

God.

I took the shovel, scooped up the manure. I threw the pile out the door into the corral.

Molly spread the skirt of her dress over the edges of the bale. I kept a small stack there for bedding for bummer calves, but we hadn't had one for a while. Molly looked down at her lap, spread more of her dress as if trying to make it look like it was her dress, instead of herself, that was taking up the bale. "Patty," she said.

I braced myself on the handle of the shovel. "She's a kid," I said.

"She gave herself to the devil," Molly said, her back rigid and straight. The sweet redness drained out of her face.

"And Edie didn't?"

"Edith has repented, as the children of Israel repented. Edie is no longer cut off from the chosen."

Often enough I had learned not to quibble, not to confront her with reason, not to counter, but I tried to now. "Patty made up her schoolwork," I said.

"She will not go to services," Molly said. "She has not repented."

"She did everything we asked."

And for the first time in a long time, her posture loosened a little. It was as if she gave up a little of the steel the Lord put in her spine. "I know," she said. "I know."

chapter 11

OUR PLACE LIES in a draw off Sandhollow Road. If you take Sand-hollow north, you'd weave in and out of the canyons and end up in the spot where, in 1847 across the border into Washington, the Cayuse massacred Marcus Whitman and his wife and others of his group at the mission. The Indians killed Marcus Whitman because they thought he was poisoning them. The massacre took place less than twenty miles from our farm.

Sandhollow Road takes you through hills that fold one into another like dinner rolls. Here and there a lane leads off the main road and juts straight up over the hills, out of sight. Even if you didn't know the family who lived where the road ends, you could imagine their place. It wouldn't be much different from ours, though maybe not quite as eye-catching.

The seeds of beauty of our place were planted by Jasper and Adelaide McIntyre, my great-greats. Our place had sat there in that same draw since thirty years after the Whitman massacre. By the time Jasper and Adelaide settled, the Cayuse had ambushed more people but were finally put down, leaving the rich hills to settlers.

Jasper knew to build the house out of the wind, but it was Adelaide who had the eye for making it something other than plain. A grove of her seedlings still sheltered our house and the barn. There is an old photo of her, out in her garden, bent over in a long dress and straw hat, her hand on the handle of a hoe. She used to put her garden where Dad had since built the shed, a few feet from where Molly planted her own garden. In the photo, behind Adelaide, there was a tiny shoot of an oak tree sitting in a ring of dark earth that had been watered.

A ditch meandered between the house and Sandhollow Road. There had once been a little wood bridge over the ditch, but I knew that only from pictures. The bridge had been replaced by a cattle guard that kept the cows from straying too far if they got out. From a distance, there was still enough paint on the barn to call it red and the house white. But the magic of the place really came from Adelaide's trees. Two huge oaks framed the house on the west. In the summer they cooled the house and the barn, and in winter they sat there in their perfect roundness, open as two splayed hands. There are still a couple of slats nailed to the trunk of one of them that Lee and I hammered in when we were kids. We had climbed the slats to a platform Dad put up that we used as a lookout. The platform was gone, rotted and fallen years ago, but there were still those two slats and a half dozen nails, and the stains of rust where we'd hammered more of the steps.

Adelaide also planted a couple of maples for balance, and three cottonwoods that poked at the sky and made a sort of texture of green. In the late summer every year, the cottonwoods blew fuzz-seed that stuck to your hair and drifted everywhere like snow.

Down by the ditch Adelaide planted a weeping willow. On a hot evening, Mother would set up a table and lawn chairs and serve us dinner under the whisper of Adelaide's willow branches. She'd put on a summer dress and the skirt of it would blow in the breeze, and she would drift across the expanse of lawn she'd had Dad plant, carrying out platters from the house. And she would set the table with a vase filled with cosmos and daisies and gladiolas, and we would eat her endive salads and asparagus with sauce and roasted chicken and boiled potatoes. And for the mosquitoes, she'd slather our legs and our arms with Skeeter Scoot.

One summer when Lee was home from college, he had sat on the edge of the road with a sketch pad and canvas and oils, and had painted a picture of the place. He'd met Helen by then, and Mom suspected they were getting to be an item. His painting had captured the place on a hot day. Mother's golden retriever, Matilda, was lying stretched out in the front lawn. It was near sunset, the light a peach-orange, the slow sort of light that will bleed darker so gradually you can't see it, but could feel it turn to purple, then to gray, then to night. Mother had set Lee's painting in a thick gold frame, which she displayed on the dining room wall. Once, over Sunday dinner, she'd said to Lee, "I wish you would concentrate more on your art." He had decided to become a history teacher by then, and a coach.

I remember Dad had groaned at the mere thought of Lee becoming an artist, and I remember Lee's eyes flickered Dad's way. I remember Lee saying, "Well, art's not going to pay the bills."

Dad had answered, "You better believe it."

And Mother tipped her head and said, "Pity."

IT SEEMED LIKE Molly and Edie and I were spending our whole lives sitting around the kitchen table. Between meals, we went through our days poring over Molly's books, clearing away dishes after dinner so Edie could spread out her homework. It seemed like the only comfort we had was the comfort of habits, milking, me puttering in the shop, Molly bringing in the last of the beets and turnips from her garden, Edie going, then coming from school,

Molly spreading the dinner table with enough food to feed an army. Little things held us together, shutting off the lights at night, treading upstairs to bed, turning on the fan in our room, me giving Molly a kiss, then listening as she whispered her prayers and lulled herself to sleep. For me, sleep didn't usually come until near dawn.

Molly and I hadn't spoken of Patty since two evenings ago in the barn. At dinner, Molly said grace, and we passed the fried potatoes, and the whipped cream salad, and the squash swimming in brown sugar and butter, and a plate of her new pickled beets. "Edith," she said.

Edie's shoulders jerked, startled.

"Your dad and I have decided something about you and Patty."

God, I thought, what had we decided? It seemed like nothing in any part of our lives was decided.

Molly passed Edie a bowl of homemade peaches in butter and syrup. "Edith," she said, "get the bread from the box." She snapped her fingers twice. "We forgot the bread."

I could see on Edie's face that she was as worried as I was what her mother and I had supposedly decided. She got up out of her chair, tiptoed to the breadbox. She brought the bread in its plastic sack to the table.

"And where," her mother said, "is the plate?"

Edie shuffled to the cupboard, took up a plate, laid a few slices on it. After she'd set the bread on the table, Edie stood by her mother, her hands folded in front of herself.

Molly said, "Sit down."

Edie sat with her hands in her lap. It was a humble posture, like she had no right to move or prompt her mother to continue.

"Patty can stay one night." She held up one finger, wagged it. "One night." She picked up the fried squash, dished a plop of it onto Edie's plate. "For a try."

Edie sucked in her lips, said nothing. I thought she should have been elated, happy. But Edie sat there holding herself in, looking down at her hands in her lap, keeping them quiet, noncommittal.

"Isn't that good news?" I said.

She didn't look up, only wove her fingers together so tightly they turned white. "Dad," she finally said, "could you take me into town?"

"Why?" I said.

"To tell her she can stay."

"Why don't you call her on the phone?" Molly said.

Edie didn't answer.

I said, "You still know how to use the phone, don't you?" and right away I regretted my sarcasm.

Edie managed a bare little smile but didn't say anything.

"It wasn't so long ago," I teased, "that you and Patty were on the telephone so much neither Mom nor I had a chance."

"I can't," Edie said.

"You can't what?" I said.

"Call Patty on the phone."

"Why?"

"Because Bill Murcheson ripped out their phone."

chapter 12

AFTER A COUPLE of days of sputtering rain late in September, the weather turned back to the dry of summer. The wind sucked any hint of moisture out of the hills. The ground turned to powder, thirsty, helpless, dust lifting up with every whim the wind chose to make.

Saturday came. In three days, we had another meeting at the bank. For weeks, acid had been shooting into my gut all day and all night.

Patty was supposed to be coming out sometime after breakfast. She would be riding her bike. Molly was in the dining room sewing quilts for Helen and Lee's kids for Christmas. The last time Mother was out at the place—for Edie's sixteenth birthday a few days ago— Molly had shown her the colors she'd chosen for the quilts. She had told Mother she had enough of the calicos to make a quilt for Mother as well if she wanted. Mother stood there in her slim skirt and her low pump shoes and said, "My," surprised. "You don't have to go to all that trouble, Molly."

"Oh," Molly said, "It's no trouble."

"But it is," Mother said. I could tell she was gathering her thoughts on the quilts. They didn't seem to me to be the sort of thing, tiny brown and green flowers, dull yellows and tans, that Mother would choose. Mother idly ran her finger through the gold charms on the bracelet on her wrist. It tinkled. It was an old bracelet, an assortment of real gold coins that Molly called extravagant. Mother had worn the bracelet for many years. "And I don't know where I would keep it," she said, blending a sort of disappointment into her voice.

"On the bed, of course," Molly said.

Mother reached out, laid her hand on a length of uncut brown material. I'd heard Lee and Mother chuckle about Molly's tastes one time, when they didn't know I was listening, but Mother had never said anything to me. She wouldn't. "But then," Mother said, "come summer what would I do? Where would I store all your wonderful effort?" She took back her hand, set the coins jingling. "My apartment's so small. I'm afraid something as nice as one of your quilts must find a more comfortable home. The church, maybe," she said. "One of your quilts would bring a ransom." And Molly smiled.

Molly had spent two days cutting the fabric, concentrating on tiny pieces she cut into triangles and squares and odd flower-petal shapes she'd stacked in neat little piles of tan and brown and seaweed green. The mahogany dining table where Mother had gathered us all for her linen-and-chinaware dinners was Molly's sewing table now. Gone were the centerpieces of flowers in crystal bowls Mother kept on it and gone were the candlesticks and tapered candles. Mother had left the table to us when she moved to her apartment. At one end, now, sat a box of patterns, at the other, Molly's Singer, and in between, stacks and stacks of assorted fabrics arranged by color.

The house was quiet, the kitchen neatened from breakfast. Molly's desk in the nook was cleared but for the documents and sheets of columned paper with row after row of figures, papers we'd be taking with us to the bank on Tuesday. A load of laundry was sloshing in the washer in the basement.

Edie had been upstairs in her room ever since breakfast. Now and then, there would be a rush of water as she flushed the toilet. I never knew what she did all those hours she spent in her room. She might as well have been in school, as much company as she was.

Molly shuffled fabric and made little snips with her scissors. I'd read the entire *East Oregonian* and was thumbing through back issues of the *Farm Journal*. The house had an expectant feel about it, as if we were waiting for Patty to give us all focus, give us something worthwhile to think about.

About ten thirty, the gravel popped in the driveway and Edie came slamming down the stairs. Without a word to her mother or me, she thumped out the door and down the back steps. The girls talked for a minute outside before they came in. Finally the back screen slapped shut and the girls were in the living room.

Patty's hair was blown, one leg of her Levi's was rolled up to her knee, and her face flared red. She greeted both Molly and me as she passed through the house. And as she passed, she left the tart stink of her sweat.

AT NOON, WE were all sitting at the kitchen table, Patty at the end, in her old place. Her hair was wet from the shower. Molly had told Patty she needed a bath and Patty had said the water heater was broken at her mom's and asked if she could use ours. Molly had responded, "Please do." The glare of light from the window behind Patty seemed to sizzle the fine fuzz over her forehead.

Molly had roasted a haunch of one of the pigs we took in to butcher that spring. The roast sat on a platter in front of my place, surrounded by roasted potatoes and carrots. A variety of other dishes were out as well, peas Molly had gotten a week before at the LA's garden exchange, some fried zucchini that had taken over her garden, a loaf of sweet bread suspiciously flecked with more of the squash, and half an apple pie from the LA bake sale the day before.

Molly was on another diet—this time squash only—and she was suffering alone again in her efforts to lose. Not more than a couple of years back, Molly had spearheaded the LA plan to put together a TOPS club, Take Off Pounds Sensibly, and she started eating what looked like a more regular diet. She ordered booklets and handouts and set the tone for donations for members. And Tuesdays at ten o'clock in the morning, a handful of women met in the Community Room. They weighed in and talked about their diets and read hints from their pamphlets. Several of them, Molly included, started to lose a pound here and there. But it was Mildred Coxen who became sort of the star. When TOPS started, Mildred was stocky as a railroad car. Mildred and her husband, Ernie, lived at the edge of town. Ernie was going to retire from the railroad in a year or two. All her life, Mildred had taken a backseat to her family, five boys, and it looked like she was going to be in the seat for a while longer when Ernie's mother moved into their house. But, as the club continued to meet, Mildred took up TOPS like a convert.

The first couple of months, Molly was feeling good. With the loss of her first ten, then fifteen, then twenty pounds, she was beginning to hope maybe she could get down to where she once was. I knew she was already thinking maybe, maybe, she could get pregnant again. And, for the first couple of months, she was holding her stomach in and sticking her thumbs in the waist of her pants and flapping the waistband around as if bragging how loose everything was getting. About that time, I remember Inkie and Sarge—both dogs—started to gain weight, and I didn't let myself wonder where the trim of meat fat and grease had gone before TOPS came along.

In the next eleven months, Mildred Coxen lost over a hundred pounds, and it was as if Mildred's success doused Molly's. I could see she wasn't losing weight any more, and we stopped hearing Molly mention Mildred's name around the house. Molly dropped out of the club after she gained back all twenty of the pounds she'd lost.

Now, Molly's plate was piled with strips of steamed zucchini. Her eyes took in the food on the table, then went to Patty. The girls were both sitting still, quiet, Edie peering at Patty from the sides of her eyes. Patty's wet hair was springing loose from her head as it dried, and in the backlight from the window it blazed red as a halo.

Molly wheezed in one breath, then two. She bowed her head, and she reached out for my hand, then for Patty's. For a moment, Patty hesitated, then touched Molly's hand with the tips of her fingers, and I hoped the warmth of Molly's hand might soften whatever had grown so hard deep inside her.

chapter 13

THE BROWN BUILDING in Pendleton, where my mother lived, was built long before anyone considered elevators. The sagging wood stairs shone from wax that had yellowed and crackled. When elevators finally came around, one had been carved out of a niche in the lobby. Mother lived in apartment 409 on the top floor. I teased her she should have bought a Formula 409, instead of her first Cadillac, to go with her new digs. I'd been in a teasing mood, happy that year, since Molly and I were moving to the farm and I was going to live in the house I'd grown up in.

"Funny," Mother had said about the car, "real funny."

That had been only a few years ago. How could everything seem so much different now? I stood at the elevator waiting for the door to clatter open and let me in. When it did, I poked 4 and the narrow door closed. The motor began to whir and I got heavy on my feet.

Molly wasn't with me. I hadn't told her I was coming to town to see Mother that day. I didn't want her with me, didn't want her listening to me spill out my story, didn't want her clucking with her tongue and remarking how the things in Mother's china cabinet alone could support Philpott First Christian for three years. I imagined Molly wheezing out, "Think of the Lord's work we could do with that silver pitcher."

The elevator whirred up to the fourth floor, the door drummed open. I stood there a minute while I tucked in my shirttail. I was going to have to tell Mom stuff I didn't want her to know, stuff like how I really didn't know my ass from a hole in the ground anymore, that she'd trusted the farm to me and I wasn't man enough to handle it. I was coming to beg like a kid.

I never figured out how the word *bumper* got to be associated with a crop, but with prices up the way they were, if we'd had any crop at all, it would have been bumper enough to make a decent year of it. Instead of coming to beg, I could have been coming to Mother's place to exercise my rights to brag a little, to stand straight like Dad used to at the end of a year. But it wasn't working out that way.

All spring, the fields had looked good. By the beginning of June, Mom was catching our enthusiasm, showing us shiny brochures of Rome, London, and Paris. In the last year she had traded her first Cadillac and had bought the new one with money from her share of last year's crop. And this month she was leaving on the trip of her lifetime, a trip Dad never wanted to take because it meant leaving what was familiar and regular; it meant leaving home. Molly never wanted to travel, and I was glad, because if I had my way, I'd never set foot off the farm, either.

In private one day, I mentioned to Molly that if Mother ever wanted to get rid of any of her nice things, I thought her china cabinet might look good in the dark corner of the living room where, hanging from the ceiling, Molly kept a wandering Jew. The stringy plant had been in that corner of the room for years. Molly had recently knotted string into a sort of macramé sock for it and had tried to brighten the pot with a piece of green ribbon that hung among the vines like kelp.

In answer to my suggestion about Mother's china cabinet, Molly said, "We don't have her sort of," she paused for a little too long, "things." She looked me in the eye and said, "He that is greedy of gain, troubleth his own house; but he that hateth gifts shall live.'" Her refusal was one more way of laying judgment on my family, and her summary of them always came up short.

The fourth-floor hall of the Brown Building smelled like salad dressing, vinegary and tart, and like scorched toast. I started toward 409 but heard a door open behind me. Mrs. Engles lived right across from the elevator. She ducked her head and her thin blue hair out her door.

I waved, said, "Mrs. Engles."

"Jack," she said, disappointed, like I could have been one of her family coming for a visit. She must have spent her days listening for the elevator to thunk to a stop because only once had she missed peeking out when I came and that was when she had taken ill with pneumonia and spent nearly a month in the hospital.

Mom's door was open wide, waiting for me to let myself in. I looked around at the small kitchen, with its tiny counters and at the spread of her Oriental carpets in the living room at the end of the entry.

"Mom?" I said.

"Jack? Come in," she said, "I'll be right there." Water ran in the bathroom, at the end of the narrow hallway to the back bedrooms. Outside, a horn honked twice, two little *bip-bips*. It was a sound Mother never would have heard in the years living on the farm. One summer evening when Lee and I were still in school, I saw her standing in the window beside the table in the kitchen, looking out over the fields to the west. Harvest was done. The grain was in, and Dad, Lee, and I had spent the day burning stubble. Cinders flickered in the dark, glowing brighter, then dimming again in the movement of air. Mother took a little breath, and she sighed and said, "Every year when we burn, I pretend those embers are the lights of a city."

Her tapestry chair and footstool were placed beside the window from where she could oversee whatever went on in the street. The Oriental rug that had been on our living room floor while Lee and I were growing up was laid out, too big for the apartment. She'd rolled one end of it under and had positioned two French tapestry chairs to cover the roll.

From her back hallway, she said, "I'll be right out."

A couple of minutes later, she whooshed into the living room. She never dressed in a showy way but always had an air about her that she somehow came from good stock, rich even. She was wearing a navy blue dress with a full skirt that scooped in at her waist. And she wore a blond wig she had bought in Portland earlier that year, "Because after seventy years, I don't want to fiddle with hair one more day."

Molly had been appalled at the wig. "Blond?" she had said, and her tone implied *who does your mother think she is?* And, she had added, "She must have paid two hundred dollars for that wig."

Two china cups and saucers were sitting on the counter beside a couple of dessert plates. The little table in the nook that Mother called the dining room was set for two with forks and napkins.

"Jack," she said, "there are strawberries in a bowl in the refrigerator."

I went to the tiny kitchen, happy to delay what I'd come to town to do. While she poured coffee into a silver urn, I opened the refrigerator and found the berries in their crystal bowl.

OUR TEACUPS WERE empty; juice from the berries puddled in our china bowls. I still hadn't managed to tell her about the business I'd come for. We'd talked, so far, about her trip.

"I think we've timed it just right," she said, "for Paris." She held her hands to her chest, batted her eyes at the ceiling, "Paree," she said, "before the weather turns cold." She chattered on about the tour. She and Ethel Langsdorf and Mildred Piotowski had been planning the trip for a year, ever since Mildred's husband collapsed with a stroke on the golf course. Among them, it seemed like death had cleared their lives of distractions; Mildred sold her house in Reith Canyon and moved to McCall in Idaho. After Ernie died, Ethel moved to Florida. Mother had traveled to see both of them in the past year or two. She had driven to Mildred's in May. And the year before, in the cold of winter, she had flown to visit Ethel in her condominium on the beach in Miami. It was like they had spent their lives pent up, waiting, and they were free once and for all.

For a while, after the funeral, Mother had been swallowed up in the cloud of Dad's death. She had stayed put in the house for a year, keeping everything the way it had been before he died. She kept his clothes in their closet, his shoes and his work shirt on the chair in their bedroom. She kept all of the furniture like it was the last day he was in the house. And she went about her days setting the table in the evening for the two of them, pouring toddies in two glasses before bed, rumpling the bed as if he'd slept in it. The only change she made all that year was to throw away the shotgun that he had kept in the cupboard by the back door.

Then, one day, as if a storm had cleared, it seemed her mourning was over. She started to clean the house, to shuffle things around, to box up what she wanted to give to the Salvation Army and display what she wanted to give us, if we wanted. She was ready to move on. It bothered me, a little, her getting on with her life without Dad around, like it was somehow a betrayal, though I never would have said it out loud.

Now, a set of canvas luggage, covered with clasps and zippers, sat expectantly off to one side of the livingroom, the price tags still on them.

Mother looked up like she was waiting for me to launch into the real reason I'd come. "More coffee, honey?" she said.

"A little," I said and pushed my cup closer to her.

She stood up, brushed at a wrinkle in her skirt. "Let me," she said, "get a little something from the cabinet." She went to the tiny French Louis-the-something-or-other cabinet where she kept her liquor. She took out a bottle, and I suspected she knew what I'd come for. She straightened up, holding a bottle of Courvoisier over her head. Her gesture was triumphant. She nodded, took the bottle into the kitchen. I heard the pop of the cork.

I sat, fingering the saucer under my cup, listening as she moved around the kitchen. She came out carrying a silver tray on which she had set a small pitcher of cream, a carafe with the brandy, and two crystal snifters. She set down the tray. Her hands had never been a farm wife's hands. They were not thick and strong, not cracked and callused and burned from mishaps with the oven. Her nails were painted a deep red to go with the buttons down the front of her dress. They had never been Molly's hands, hands that would put in a truck garden or hammer up studs for a new closet in the laundry or pluck pinfeathers from the skin of a chicken she'd wrung the neck of.

She poured a shot of brandy into each of our cups, filled them with coffee, then a teaspoon of sugar. She topped them with thick cream she poured from a creamer. She gathered her skirts behind her, sat down again at her place. She scooted the cup and saucer toward me. "Talk," she said.

WE SIPPED AT the brandied coffee. And, as we dabbed the cream from our mouths, I let go the story I'd held in for months, told her about the bank, my debt, my failings all around.

Finally I said, "There's not going to be anything to sell this year."

"I knew that," she said, "the day the storm hit."

"You did?" I said.

She held the cup in her long thin hands. "What do you think your dad and I were doing all the years you kids were growing up?" She set the cup down on the saucer without a sound. "It wasn't always easy, honey," she said.

"It seemed like it when you and Dad were in charge."

"We didn't think you kids needed to know everything. But your father was a businessman. He always made good decisions in the hard times as well as the good." She looked away, made a little knot in her napkin, dabbed her eyes. "There's never going to be anyone like him. He was," she said, "he was . . . ," and she didn't continue.

All I could do was feel the implication lie between us that Dad would have known how to pull us out of trouble, that maybe I wasn't up to the challenge. I don't know why the realization sat there so damned heavy, it was always what I'd believed anyway. Stupid. Slow. Gutless.

Mother tapped the side of her head. "Listen to Molly," she said. "I can't say I understand her, or what's happened to change her in the past few years, but Molly's got a head on her shoulders." She leaned toward me, set her hand with its red nails on my arm. "Are you happy, Jack?' she said. "I've wondered sometimes if you're happy together." As if she didn't expect me to comment, she didn't pause long. "Don't worry," she said. "It won't be the first time I've pulled in my belt." She laid her hand on her slim stomach. "But there's nothing in the world, *nothing*, that'll keep me from going on my trip."

chapter 14

MORNING, BEFORE THE meeting with the bank, Molly laid out the pants and the shirt I was supposed to wear. "It's not until *tomorrow*," I said. My mother's generosity still rang shame in my head. I should have been more thankful she was the way she was, but still I felt small and like a boy, something I conjured all on my own.

Edie had already stumbled down the drive carrying an armful of books to wait for the school bus. Inkie and Major had sniffed the ditch in the same places they did every morning as they waited for the bus to come. The bus came, picked her up, and the dogs ambled back to the house, tails limp, bored until they trotted out again in the afternoon to wait for the bus to bring her back.

I had dawdled away the morning, gathered branches fallen from the summer, sawed them into lengths for the burning barrel in the shop. I piled the twigs in a heap at the end of the drive, doused them with gas, set them on fire. When I walked into the house again at noontime, Molly said, "You smell like smoke."

Now the things we were to wear were lying on the bed, pressed smooth. I picked up the slacks and the belt. Molly bent over. Her blue and green dressy caftan pulled high over the backs of her thighs as she pawed around the closet for her slip-on shoes. She slid her feet in the shoes, and as she stood, she said, "You want your jacket?"

It was going to be warm, the forecast said, in the mid-70s. "Don't think I'll need it," I said. It was the small things, the focus on a belt, a jacket, on Molly's shoes, that seemed to be holding us together.

It had been three days since Patty stayed the night. And, for a while, Patty and Edie had been sufficient distraction. All Saturday their movements upstairs had been something else to think about, their voices mumbling from Edie's room, the clicking of her bedroom door, the running of water. They'd spent the whole afternoon closed up in Edie's room.

Finally, at chore time, they had emerged when it was time to feed and milk. Patty tried to help with milking like she used to in the old days, but she'd lost the stride of Edie's and my habits and she got underfoot. I told her to take a scoop full of grain out to the trough for the bull, and when she was done feeding him, she waited around holding one of the cats in her arms, rubbing her cheek on its head as Edie and I finished up. It was strange, having her so silent. I had no idea where the old Patty had gone, but I was beginning to think I wanted her back, trouble and all. The next morning when she'd gotten on her bike and headed home again, Edie slid back into her own form of tight-wadded silence, waiting.

Molly took the jacket off the hanger. "I think you want to wear the jacket, anyway." She held it for me to get into. "For the bank."

I slipped it on, buttoned it closed.

Molly's purse sat on the bureau, packed with the papers that read like a diary of our lives: the promissory note from Mom, a list of liens for machinery and land, documents showing the payments we'd made over the years to the bank, to grain growers, and lately to Dr. Cavalcanti, Edie's dentist. It was all there, everything we owed, everything we owned.

Molly kept saying, "It'll be all right."

Since the first First National meeting, Molly had been working overtime on the books. She had tried to come up with cash, had even made a few phone calls to creditors to try to string out our payments and to see about selling some of the equipment we could do without. I had tried to spiff up some of the machinery earmarked to sell, had spent days on the old Ford fuel wagon to get it into some kind of shape, had taken the tanks off the back and had oiled, greased and tuned it up as well as I could. Even with work, the compression on one valve was almost nonexistent. The truck had been running on a valve with no compression for twenty years. That I couldn't fix. But the floorboard had rusted through. You could see straw and plow furrows through it. I'd lost a wrench down that hole, and didn't find it until the next year when the header of the thresher scooped it up and the wrench bent the reel and half of the blades. That wrench had stopped us cold for a couple of days while Lee and I cobbled together a repair. I had done the best I could to patch the hole in the floor, and Molly put an ad in the *East Oregonian* offering the truck and one of the tractors for sale.

On the surface of it, our lives didn't look much different. At night, after dinner while I watched television, Molly sat at the kitchen table knitting as Edie finished her schoolwork. When the schoolwork was done, they read scripture together and Molly gave Edie her Bible lesson. Finally we'd all go to bed, and I'd listen to the rumble of Molly's snores. Some nights, after we had turned off the lights, I'd reach over and touch Molly's shoulder. She would mumble something in her sleep, and I would take back my hand. One night she woke up, pulled herself over, laid her hand on my stomach. "Take Jesus Christ as your Lord and Savior, Jack."

"I do the best I can," I said.

It was the nights I dreaded most, the wind howling around the eaves, the house shuddering and groaning in the low tone the cows moaned before birth or when they were calling for the bull. Sometimes it seemed like the wind howled every night of my life.

Long ago she had given up trying to nudge me to go to church with her, but she'd never given up on my salvation at home. I had tried to pray, knew the words to pray, but they left me only the burden of judgment for my sins. I had learned to rely on her and her Lord. The longer I lived with Molly, the more I realized my life without her would be as directionless as a truck without a steering wheel. But I could never take in her Lord, could never make myself believe the way she did; the tone of the scriptures, their judgment, always got in the way.

Since I'd blurted everything to Mother, I felt some better, but not a whole hell of a lot. But it seemed Edie was chewing on worries as well. I could see the tightness pucker around her mouth, could see her shoulders pull forward in a posture that came with worries. She seemed restless. In the darkest part of the nights, while I tried to force sleep to come, I'd hear her door squeak open around midnight, and I'd listen as the floor in the hallway moaned under her feet. I was beginning to think my daughter had developed some of my nighttime habits as well, and for that I was sorry. She would go into the bathroom, and I'd wait for the few seconds for the rush of water from the toilet to come, then lie there listening as she clicked the light off in the bathroom and, every night, I would hear the creak of the stairs as she put her toe down on a step, then the ball of her foot, then the heel on the next, and the next tread carefully as if she didn't want to wake us.

After fifteen or twenty minutes, she would creep back up the stairs and slip back into her bedroom and close the door until morning. All the while, I'd still be searching the ceiling I knew every crack of.

chapter 15

NEITHER MOLLY NOR I felt like talking as we drove into town. We leaned away from each other as the hills rolled by, me wearing my wedding slacks, her in an ocean of blue and green she called a caftan. I could not get a picture on the next year. No matter how hard we tried to make it work, we did not have enough money. Buying seed, paying for fuel, tires for the trucks seemed as impossible as flying to Jupiter.

Molly sat quiet with her purse in her lap. Now and then she would reach into it and pull out a bag of chips, or another candy bar, and she would eat them with her face turned toward the window, away from me. It was mechanical, the way she ate, shoving the paper back into her purse, popping the candy into her mouth, chewing without pleasure. Once, after she had opened a Baby Ruth, she sat with the bumpy bar in her hand, its crumpled-back paper resting on her thigh like maybe she didn't have energy to put it in her mouth. "Slow down, Jack," she said. "You're making me dizzy."

She finished the Baby Ruth and put the wadded paper in a side pocket of her purse. "It's too bright today," she said, her eyes squinting nearly shut. We were passing Woodpecker Trucking, about to hit the long slope into Pendleton. She pushed the paper down deeper into her purse and squinted ahead, and she zipped the purse closed.

There was a parking space right in front of the bank. Less than three months ago America had celebrated its two hundredth birthday and Pendleton had filled up with flags and parades. But there was no sign of the celebration left anywhere. The windows of the Bon and the Curio Shop were plastered with end-of-season sales, neon orange signs saying 50–60% off, a few with paper jack-o'-lanterns and witches on brooms. There wasn't an American flag flying anywhere up the street, except on the pole at the First National. I was glad the hoo-hah was over.

I parked in front of the bank. Molly gathered her purse and the folders with the papers. I went around to her side of the car, opened the door. She swung out her thighs, set both feet on the ground. I grabbed her arm to help her out, but she didn't come right away. "Remember, Jack, we're going to do whatever the Lord wants us to do." She looked me in the eye. "Aren't we?" she said. I couldn't get a handle on the meaning of it. "You won't refuse the Lord's word, will you?"

I must have looked puzzled.

"Jack?"

"Sure," I said.

MR. STURGIS HELD the sheet of paper with Molly's revised figures. The sheet was typed, laid out in two columns detailing the items that could produce cash and the value of them. The sheet listed the three milk cows, the John Deere combine, the water wagon, the four pigs, the bull and our ten head of Hereford cows, Molly's station wagon. She'd even listed a few dollars on the sheet for selling furniture; the couch, and dining room table where she sewed, and the twelve chairs, which had been my mother's wedding gift from her family. I had challenged Molly on the dining room set. It had been there since before I was born. I couldn't imagine the room bare of it, stripped of the memories of Christmas dinners and of the parties Mom threw. But Molly listed it anyway.

Sturgis turned the sheet toward us, held it beside his face. With one hand, he shoved his windshield eyeglasses higher, gave a sniff with his nose. "This doesn't add up to more than fifteen, sixteen thousand dollars, and that, I'd say, is wishful."

He laid the page down in front of himself. Without saying another word, he took up the bank's papers and covered Molly's sheet with his own papers. And then he sat back, barred an ankle over his knee. It was arrogant, the way he sat, like he was bored with everything about us. He leaned back in his chair with his knee higher than the edge of the table. He twirled a pen between his fingers. "Truthfully, I know, and you know, this isn't going to fly." His voice took on a low, friendly quality like he was not our loan officer anymore, or the bank manager, but our friend in mourning. "There's nothing the bank can do," he said, and then he added, "with your situation." The word *foreclosure* smoked up the room as if he had already said it.

"Just a minute," Molly said.

He set his mouth and made an expression like he was ready for Molly this time, like he wasn't going to let her slide out from under him again. But he quit twirling the pen.

"We are God-fearing people," she said. "We've always paid our bills."

He leaned up, hovered over his figures. "1971," he said, the year Molly and I took over the farm, "late payment to Pendleton Grain Growers, late on your operating loan with us. 1973, late again." He thumbed up a couple of pages. "1974, loan extended. Last year late. What about the amount you owe Francine McIntyre?" He looked at me, now. "Last month you mentioned you would speak with her. Did you?"

"Yes," I said.

He wagged his hand in front of himself, prompting me to go on. "Is she forgiving your payment to her?"

"No," I said. "She isn't."

Molly heaved in a rasping breath. "The Lord will provide"

Mr. Sturgis sat up, laid his pen on the desk. "Heaven doesn't tend to pay bills," he said. "The bank is, unfortunately, unable to wait for heaven to keep it afloat. Mr. and Mrs. McIntyre, I'm afraid we are going to have to initiate an unfortunate action."

"You're going to start foreclosure," I said. I knew it, had known it all the time. Because I was not the man my father was, I was losing the farm that had prospered ever since Jasper J. McIntyre settled on it. I looked at Molly. Her eyes weren't on me or on Sturgis, but on her own fingers kneading the Bible she'd set on the table beside her folder.

The manager patted his chest. "The decision is not up to me. Policy dictates we move forward." He stood up, smiled like he'd finally made it through a situation no more unpleasant than wading through puddles in the rain. He came around, reached out for my hand to shake it, "I'm sorry, Mr. McIntyre," he said as though he was consoling me on a death in my family. My hand went out to him in reflex, and before I knew it, I was shaking the hand that was going to yank my life out from under me. How had we come to this in a few short years?

I heard the manager say, "Mrs. McIntyre, I am so sorry." His voice went all soft, a voice he'd use to put his children to sleep at bedtime. "I understand how hard this is."

He reached down to shake Molly's hand, but she didn't take it. Her hand was making petting motions on her Bible.

"Have you ever lost anything you love?" she said. She waited a few seconds.

He crossed his arms.

Her hand on the Bible went quiet. She looked straight at him, jerked her fingers away like the book had burned her. She held her hand up, the palm was bright red. "It's expensive for the bank to take a farm, isn't it?" Her eyes had gone black, dilated.

Sturgis took a step back as Molly went on.

"The bank isn't in the business of farming, right?"

Sturgis managed to look away from her. "Right," he said, trying for the sound of boredom again.

"The bank sells what it forecloses on," Molly said, almost to herself. She patted her chest, and it set her boson in motion. "We could sell." She looked up at me.

Sell the farm?

She was still holding up her hand. It flamed red. "We own the Vancycle quarter outright," she said. "We could sell it."

ON A PARTICULARLY windy day toward the beginning of fall, Mother, Ethel Langsdorf, and Mildred Piotowski left on the train for Portland. I loaded Mother's suitcases in the back of my truck and drove her the five blocks from her apartment to the train station. She was wearing the beaver coat Dad had given her on their twenty-fifth anniversary. As we were leaving her apartment, I told her we'd gotten a six-month extension from the bank. Sturgis had said he wasn't hopeful, but he had agreed to allow us time to put some of our land on the market. I'd waited for Mom to protest, but she hadn't.

chapter 16

FALL WINDS STARTED whipping in before Molly turned the page from the October calendar. A couple of weeks after the meeting at First National, someone called and made an offer on the tractor. The fellow was from Boardman, and it was two hundred dollars less than we'd advertised. That night I found myself knotted under the covers, wound so tight Molly woke briefly and muttered, "Jack, lie still." I had to force myself to do that, but worries didn't take a break.

We had to raise money. The only thing we had of any value was the Vancycle acreage. In better times, while Dad was alive and I worked for him, Molly and I had managed to buy the Vancycle's one hundred and twenty-five acres. The rest of the land we farmed had been put in my name, but Mother still held title to it. It would be mine only when she died, or if I could buy her out. If I lost it in bankruptcy, I would take my mother down with me.

I watched the light of the night shuffle the patterns of cracks on the ceiling, and listened to the last frogs of the season singing in the ditches, listened to a killdeer spew its lonesome story. There had been no rain—none—for weeks, though temperatures were beginning to freeze at night.

I heard Edie's door crack open, heard her go into the bathroom and then listened as she eased herself down the stairs. She was predictable. I'd hear her door open at 12:15 every night, the same time. It seemed this listening to her at night was the only piece of her I had left. I had grown lonesome for the way we used to be, for her girl's giggle at my stupid jokes, lonesome for her to beg to ride with me on the tractor like she once did, lonesome for the days we would bump along the fence lines in the pickup looking for breaks in the barbed wire or for the encroachment of morning glory and mustard, talking—just us—about the kids at school, the doll or the blouse she wanted for her birthday, me teasing her about her boyfriends when she was only ten years old. I wanted her to look at me fake-disgusted again and to drag out, "Daaaaad," one more time.

Downstairs, the pipes from the kitchen sink wheezed water. Maybe she went to the kitchen for a snack every night to help her get back to sleep. I wanted to join her, envisioned sitting with her in the middle of the night, snacking on a cookie and milk, or on a sandwich with mayo and maybe talking again, like we used to. I pulled back the covers, put on the slippers Molly gave me for my birthday.

The house had already cooled. I followed the light coming through the doorway. The kitchen still smelled of dinner's roast.

Edie's back was to me. She had a pot on the stove that had already started to steam, and was rummaging around in the refrigerator. The basket Molly used to collect eggs sat on the counter by the stove. There was half a loaf of bread in the basket, a banana, and a quart bottle of milk. Edie was wearing her coat over her nightgown, and socks and shoes on her feet.

I stood back and watched as she put one apple in the basket, then considered for a moment and added another. I had expected her to be getting a cookie and a glass of milk. I had expected to find her huddled at the table in her housecoat dunking that cookie into that milk.

She had seemed to lighten up somewhat this summer when we let her see Patty again. But when school started, she had grown quiet again. Every day, she was changing. She went about her days in a kind of trance, like she'd set something inside herself in gear and it was running her. Her grades had returned to her usual Bs, but she had dropped band and she wasn't trying out for cheerleading like she'd always planned for her junior year, and she had no calves in the pen because she'd dropped out of 4-H.

The day before, Molly had asked Edie how school was going.

"Fine," Edie said.

Molly hadn't let it drop. "How's Patty doing?"

"Fine."

"Is she coming to school every day?"

"Yes."

"We might check on it," Molly said to me. I was getting suspicious, too.

Edie's eyes jittered down to her papers spread out on the kitchen table.

Molly crammed her fists into the sides of her waist. "*Is* she going to school?"

And Edie turned around, grabbed the back of her chair. "I said 'yes,'" she said.

"Don't you speak to me like that, young lady," Molly said.

Now I watched as Edie turned to stir the pot once, then washed the spoon clean and put it in the drawer. She took something I couldn't see from the refrigerator and put it in the egg basket. She worked in a mechanical way, like this was all habit, a routine she had gotten down pat.

She turned toward the table and I pulled back behind the jamb. But she was concentrating so hard on getting a handful of those napkins out of the holder on the table, she didn't even look up.

She took the basket by the handle and shuffled out the back door, into the night.

For a moment, I thought to go back upstairs and get Molly, but I didn't. I needed to see what was going on, and somehow I knew Molly should stay ignorant, at least for a while. Whatever Edie was up to, it was something Molly would disapprove of.

I got my coat from the closet, went out the back door, was careful to be quiet. Edie pulled her coat tighter. As she passed under the flood light of the driveway, the wind whipped her hair off to one side, exposed the pink of her ear. The napkins fluttered out of the basket like white butterflies and she put her arm over the basket to hold the rest of the stuff tight. The dogs came out from under the chicken house and nosed her thighs like they'd been expecting her. She didn't pat them. She didn't look anywhere but straight ahead. Her shoulders were drooped, her gait like an old lady's. She yawned and stumbled ahead, not looking right or left.

She rounded the corner of the shed, followed by the dun-colored plume of Sarge's tail. Gravel poked at my feet through the soles of my birthday slippers. From the back corral, Whinny's eyes flashed white and he nickered at me over the fence. He nickered again, then blew at me. He hadn't made a sound when Edie passed, hadn't even seemed to notice her. He stomped, and I worried Edie would hear and come back to see me limping along after her.

Until last year, we had had two horses. Whinny might have been quiet if we still had Sabrina, but she had died. She had been one of my mother's whims years ago, a beautiful bay who cropped gracefully in the front pasture, but if ridden, was lame from founder, which had happened sometime before Mother ever saw the ad in the paper. "Mare," the ad had said, "purebred Arabian, eight years old, bay, out of Smithie's Rigors."

Sabrina had a narrow, refined white blaze and four white socks that she never seemed to get dirty. In the end, she died as gracefully as she'd lived. We found her stretched out one sunset evening in the summer, her coat still glossy. She had fallen over in a heap with a heart attack. Edie had cried and cried. Sabrina had been Edie's starter horse, gentle, slow, too gimpy to run or cause trouble. Whinny had been Dad's farm horse for times he had to move cattle. His roan coat was dull and patchy, and even though it was well into fall, it was still as thin as it was in the heat of summer. Edie had been too afraid of his personality, too scared of the way he sidled and threw his head, so whenever she rode, she saddled up gentle Sabrina. When the girls used to ride only Patty risked riding Whinny. One day, when Molly was gone into town, Patty haltered him up and was showing off to Edie by riding him bareback. I was in the shop and didn't see what happened. I heard Patty screech and Edie shout, "Daddy!" Patty said he bucked, but you never knew from her stories. At any rate, Whinny dumped her and her ring finger got tangled in the lead. When the fracas was done, the lead had torn off the tip of her finger. When I got to her, Patty was holding her bloody hand and stooping over the ground trying to find the tip of her finger. She didn't cry, she didn't make a peep, only kept looking for it so the doctor could sew it back on. We never found it. When we took her in to the house to wash up her hand and see what was done, there was a little stub of a nail left. But her nail never grew right again.

Looking back, I should have had some hint why my daughter was out in the cold at midnight, but I did not. Whinny blew again, and I whispered, "Shut up." Finally I made it past his corral and he grew quiet.

Light from the flood bleached one side of everything it hit—the diesel and gas tanks stilted high on their crossbeams, the corral fences, the steel shed. But where the light didn't hit, everything was sucked dry of light, left with nothing but black, not even a silhouette. I crept into the shadow of the chicken house. The chickens murmured a low warning, then went quiet.

Looking back, I wished I could have enjoyed what I saw, the stars sitting in a bright smear across the sky, the moon leaving traces on the backs of my eyes. Looking back, I realized how much you take your everyday life, the beauty and specialness of it for granted and when you do that, you don't really see what God might see. You see the work of it, you see the dirt, you see the plow needing repair, or the cows needing to be fed. It wasn't anything near God I was seeing right then. I was waiting like some kind of rodent listening while I heard my daughter grunt, as she shuffled the basket to her arm, as she pulled open the barn door.

I waited, glued into the shadow of the chicken house, and when I didn't hear anything more from the barn, I stepped back out into the light of the flood. I was humped over, hiding in my overcoat, mincing like Inspector Clouseau in my slippers.

In the barn, the light turned on. Edie had not bothered to close the door. I expected to see Edie as I stepped up onto the wood floor, but I could see no part of my daughter until I looked up and saw the backs of her legs disappearing up the ladder into the mow. Her foot pulled up from the last rung, disappeared in the hole, and left the twenty-foot ladder shimmying.

I hadn't been up in the mow for years. We didn't use it to store hay any more, instead stacked it outside. But I remembered Grandpa and Dad winching hay, bale by bale up through the outside door, hay they'd baled and bucked together onto the old cart that now sat rotting in the junkyard. I remembered the screech of the pulley as it hefted the bales up and up, and I remembered the whip of the chain after Dad grabbed the bale and lumbered back into the dark with it. I remembered the owls flying out and sitting in the cottonwood trees until the loading was done and they could go back to their hayloft and to their young.

The ladder quit whipping. The loft's floorboards creaked. Through the hole came the mumble of voices, muffled from the chaff and straw and old dust up there. One of the voices was my daughter's.

IT WAS STRANGE to be in the barn that time of night. At the far end in the shop, tools, the workbench, the transmission from one of the tractors seemed to lurk in the dark. A barn is for living, and at night there was no living in it. The bummers' pen was empty, the mangers bare of grain, the cats tucked away somewhere sleeping or out mousing. A moment later the dogs followed me in, thrusting their noses into my thighs.

I went to the ladder, took hold of the uprights. I could hear the low mumble of Edie's voice, could see dust motes in the splintered glow of the barn light. The ladder steps, which were broad and stable enough when you climbed them with boots, seemed flimsy and dangerous with slippers. The slippers had no tread, the soles were of slick, black leather that flapped against my heels. The ladder shifted, and the voices went quiet. I stopped and I waited there, holding my breath, like a thief in my own barn. Finally Edie started mumbling something again.

The wind whistled through the hole in the floor and down my neck, carrying bits of chaff with it. The chaff worked itself down the neck of my pajamas and poked slivers against my back. I heard the other voice then, saying something sleepy and distant. Edie must have set down the basket because I heard the shuffle of paper and the rustle of plastic bags. Another gust of wind whipped through, blasted me on the head. It carried the smell of Molly's roast with it. A light went on, dim and far away in the back of the loft. I didn't remember the mow having electricity.

I climbed the last few steps and must have gotten careless because as I was about to make the last step, I lost a slipper. It slapped once against the next step, then flew down, flopping on the floor. I waited once more to be caught, but they must not have heard, the voices didn't go quiet.

I pulled myself up the last step.

THE TROUBLE LIGHT, which usually hung over my workbench, was plugged into an orange extension cord that had been poked up through a hole in the floor directly over the only plug in the barn. The orange cord ran over to a scatter of blankets. Edie kneeled by the blankets, her back to me. A stockinged foot came out from under the makeshift bed. Edie's back blocked my view of everything but the blankets and the foot. I recognized the blanket, a moth-holed army blanket from Molly's linen closet, and I recognized the yellow-and-red quilt she had made some years ago for Helen. After a few months, Helen had given the quilt back. Helen had made some excuses, said she didn't think it went with the things in her house and knew Molly surely could use it, or give it to someone with a yellow-and-red color scheme. It was clear she didn't like the quilt. Molly tried to be charitable about the return, put on a show of understanding, but had been hurt, I knew. She had stuffed the quilt away in the cedar chest and never brought it out again.

Edie kneeled in the dust, unwrapping stuff from the basket. There was a stack of books and paper tablets by the head of the makeshift bed, and shoes and clothes tossed at the foot. Whoever was lying on it turned toward Edie and for a moment I worried I'd be seen, but Edie's kneeling form blocked me. I stood on the ladder, only the top of my head poking into the loft. If Edie had turned around and looked my way, she would have seen only a lump with two eyes.

Edie leaned away for a moment, and the other person sat up. I saw her face then.

Patty Pugh.

Patty reached up, turned the trouble light around, settled it so the glare illuminated the rafters. The light swung on its cord, the shadows came alive, the rafters moved, the divots in the chaff started to dance. The girls didn't seem to notice.

Edie's shoulders worked as she brought more food out of the basket. Her posture gave the impression she might have been saying her bedtime prayers, kneeling as she was, her head bowed and the soles of her boots under her bottom. "It was roast tonight," she said.

How long had this been going on? Surely Molly would have noticed things disappearing from the kitchen. Or would she? I didn't know. The trouble light lit up Patty's hair like a haze but her face was lost in it, bits of straw dangled from it.

"And cherry crisp," Edie said.

"Mom will like that," Patty said.

Edie spread out a newspaper she pulled from the basket and laid out a paper plate while Patty searched around behind the pile of books and tablets, came up with one of the drinking glasses from our kitchen. It was milky with ick and needed to be washed.

Patty's bike leaned against the timbers near the foot of her bed. I could not imagine how much effort it must have taken to get it up there or how she could have been here without my seeing her come and go. And then I realized there had been a couple of times when Patty came out on the days we allowed her to visit and she'd surprised me. I hadn't seen her roll down the driveway from town, and she seemed to appear all of a sudden. She had acted surprised and made quick excuses, but now I knew; she had been living up here for God knows how long. She was not living in town; it was why she stank and why she used our shower.

With one hand, Patty started eating some of the roast, with the other she poured milk into the glass. The girls worked in a drill, neither of them speaking, a team that had practiced for a long, long time. Edie pulled a Red Delicious apple from the basket and set it on the paper plate. "You need fruit."

"Who are you, my mother now?"

It was a joke that could have been funny, but neither of the girls laughed.

Edie set out a couple of the dinner rolls we'd had at dinner. Patty shook her head. I don't think so," she said, "Mom's not eating anything with yeast. She says anything with yeast is poison."

"She back to eating fruit?"

"Only if it's red. I think I can get the apple down her."

Edie wrapped up what was left of the roast in a plastic bag. In another bag she put an apple. She held up one of the rolls, tipped her head. Patty shook her head no. Edie left the roll on Patty's plate. "Cherry crisp?" Edie said.

"I don't know. Maybe give it a try."

Edie grunted, then stood up. Straw stuck to the skirt of her nightgown. She took the bags she'd packed over to Patty's bike and put them in the wire basket.

When my daughter had settled the stuff onto the bike, I pulled myself up the last steps of the ladder. "What's going on here?" I said.

"Dad!" Edie screamed.

"Fuck," Patty said.

chapter 17

WE LIVED IN our own world around Philpott. We fashioned our beliefs from traditions, and stories, and safeties that let in what we wanted to believe. I think some place in me, in my gut or my heart, I knew things my head would not accept, and I think that was the way with everyone in Philpott's world. Later, I would wonder why couldn't I see.

If there was ever a place I could straighten out the bent stuff in my head, it had always been the barn. The barn was our place, Dad's and mine, the dogs milling around, the cows clomping in, bringing with them the warmth of their flanks, their full hard udders, and their jaws grinding grain. I could understand the barn. It was the only place where I felt free to mumble a few words with my dad, about a cow coming in, maybe, wanting the bull, or about the last game Philpott High played against Heppner. In the barn one night, I admitted I had my eye on Molly. And he said, "Well, I'm not surprised, she's a pretty cute little flicker," and then he popped me on the shoulder and said, "You sure could do worse than Molly Magruder."

Everything about the farm—the fields, the crops, even the machine-shop section of the barn—meant responsibility. But the stanchions, the bummer pen, the places where my dad, my daughter, and the animals and I gathered was the one place in my life where things drifted right. And now, even that had turned heavy, like something wrong. A thing like a barn should never be taken away.

The night had turned even colder, the wind whipping this way and that in gusts from the east, then the north, the south like it couldn't get a grip on where it was supposed to be going. Edie and I shuffled across the gravel of the drive, her following a half-step behind me. Neither of us spoke, her arms were wrapped around the empty egg basket, her shoulders humped in what looked like shame. A gust billowed out the skirt of her nightgown. Before I left the mow, I'd told Patty to come into the house where it was warm. She refused. She had merely stood up, leaned toward me, so close I could smell the roast on her breath. She was fully dressed in a sweater and jeans and wool socks. A piece of straw dangled from her hair. She had started to say something, something that flamed in her face and turned her eyes into a rage. But she held onto herself, slammed herself back down on the litter of blankets, and didn't say a word.

Edie's nose was plugged from crying. She grabbed the basket tighter into her coat. She shuffled along, looking at her feet.

"Why can't you two *behave*?" I said. "Why can't Patty stay in town with her mother?" And as I said it, I realized how that didn't make much sense. It was Larry who had kept that family together. With Larry gone, there was no one to take care of Jackie any more, no one to hold in and steer all of the energy stored up in his daughter. It was Larry who had taken care of everything, taken Jackie to the hospital when she had her episodes, it was Larry who had run the store, rebuilt that shack of a house on Maple and painted it red.

The summer a few years back, when Larry painted the house, the doctors gave Jackie a holiday from her medication and took her off it for a few weeks. There were things, they said, the medications did that were hard on her. Off and on, she needed a rest from the effects. With the tail-end of medication still in her and the bad effects of it gone, she had some good times that carried a lot of hope they would last. She'd bounce back normal, for a while, and you'd see her smiling, her hair curled, fixed high on her head, making change at the counter at the store, and she'd be talking about the dinners she cooked at night and the afghan she was making to put over the back of the couch. Jackie was doing well, then, and actually helped with part of the work. I saw her out on the front porch painting yellow on the trim. She was concentrating like anyone else, loading her brush and wiping it on the edge of the can, ever so carefully, moving the brush up and down. She was wearing an old pair of jeans and a scarf and one of Larry's old shirts. Even with the bandana tied around her hair, and a drip of yellow paint along her cheek, she was someone you'd turn to look at. She never lost her looks, even with everything that went on inside her. After a few weeks though, her mind began slipping again and Larry had to take her in for her medications.

Sooner or later, the schizophrenia always came back, and her mind would throw itself into thinking things none of us could understand. It was then that Molly and I would see a lot more of Patty around our house. After a few days back on her Haldol, Jackie's mind would level out again and she'd get an expression as blank and flat as paper and we'd see her making her strange movements again, walking like she had things to step over, moving her mouth in chewing motions, even when she had nothing in it to chew. But for those medicine holidays, anyway, Larry always held out hope that Jackie's mind would stay clear, that by some miracle she'd be OK that time, like she used to be.

When Jackie took up with a new guy, everybody in town including me, made ourselves believe he would step into Larry's shoes and take care of things. We just didn't want to see that was not what was happening.

It was Jackie, Patty's only family, I thought of as my daughter and I made our way toward the house on a cold, blown midnight. A year after they painted the house, Larry died, taking his mother to her doctor's appointment because her heart had started acting up. They didn't make the turn at Hendersons' Corner. The wreck was a total, Mrs. Pugh thrown into the ditch, forty feet away. They found Larry pinned to the seat by the shaft of the steering column. The only part of the car left whole was a hubcap that had flown off when the car rolled.

Not more than a couple of months later, Jackie found some guy to live with her in the red-and-yellow house on Maple. Pugh Market never reopened. There had been a sale of what was left in the store. The front window still had a paper sign in it, "Fresh Sausage, 89¢/lb." The shelves were bare, the bread rack empty, and the butcher tables sold to de Soto's Meat Market in Walla Walla. Clive Hutchinson, who owned the building, opened the back of the store for one day after the funeral, to let any of us with meat in the lockers to take out what was ours.

Stumbling along in the light of the flood now, I finally realized Patty didn't have anywhere to call home. The wind whipped grit into Edie's face. My slippers flapped against the heels of my feet. "How long has this been going on?" I said.

"What going on?" Edie said, her nose stuffed closed.

"You tell me," I said. I made my tone strong, although I wasn't feeling strong about any of this. At all.

"I don't know," she mumbled.

"A month?"

Edie shrugged.

"Two months? Three months?"

She only clung tighter to the basket.

"I don't know what gets into you two," I said.

I held the back door for her. She slipped through with her egg basket. "You better get to bed," I whispered.

She stood there hugging the handle of the egg basket and looking up at me. "What's going to happen?"

"Go to bed. Your mother and I will talk in the morning."

"Do you have to tell her?" Edie said.

"What do you think?" I answered.

"Oh, Daddy," she said, and she started a bitter, silent crying.

chapter 18

MOLLY WAS GETTING up when I left the house in the morning. She'd been sound asleep when Edie and I came back. I hadn't woken her nor talked to her yet.

It had peppered rain in the night. Around three thirty it had started to thunder and crack lightning. I was still awake when the first bolt of it broke. Molly had jerked in her sleep, then began the slow crawl she always made to get herself turned over, flopping one arm aside, then twisting the weight of her chest after it, then her hips and her legs until she'd made it. The bed groaned, another bolt struck and set the ceiling flickering. The storm and Molly's snores were comforting.

By the time the chores were done, and by the time I came back into the house, Molly would be dressed, her hair would still be wet from the shower and she would be setting the bacon and eggs on the table. Edie wouldn't get up until her mother called to her up the stairs. It was our habit. We'd done it for years. But since yesterday everything I counted on had shifted, flickered like the light in the thunderstorm.

When I went out in the morning, the three cows, Bossy, High-Pocket, and Henrietta, were waiting at the barn door, where they waited for me every morning. The ground was pitted from the bit of rain we'd had, the cows' backs damp and steaming under the floodlight. It was pitch dark, still, getting darker earlier every day, as the nights took up more of the clock.

My hand wavered over the hatch of the barn door and I stood there a moment. Henrietta grumbled behind me in her cow's complaint that I was taking too long. Finally, I managed to open the door. Henrietta stepped up and into the barn, High Pockets and Bossy following behind. Each of them went to her own stanchion, waited for me to scoop a coffee can's worth of grain at her place. I kept thinking that every morning—for how long?—Patty had been up there stone quiet, sleeping maybe or listening while I went through morning chores. The ladder rose up to the mow, its feet buried in a litter of chaff. She was up there, lying in the old straw under the old blankets all night long. I couldn't quit thinking of my daughter kneeling beside her, giving her food.

I milked, set the full buckets by the door. One of the cats was braced on it, dipping a paw into the foam. How could I have not known Patty Pugh was up there, sensed it or something? It made my insides quiver. The cows streamed out the door. It was getting light by then, the sun smearing the sky over Athena, setting what few clouds were left from the storm a gypsy's colors of orange and purple. It was a beautiful morning, and somewhere way down in my gut, I realized it.

THE LADDER RATTLED against the timbers. I was not trying to be quiet any longer. I did not stop climbing when the whipping ladder shook bits of old hay from the mow. God, how did the girls get that bike up and down? Dust and chaff rained down on my head. When

I got to the top, I hesitated, giving Patty a minute to cover up—or whatever—then continued on. "Patty?" I said. I finally poked my head through the hole and let my eyes adjust to the dark up there.

Patty was gone.

The bike was gone, the bags of food, and the pile of clothes, the jeans, T-shirts and socks, all gone. I turned on the trouble light. All the books and the tablets and the two pencils were still laid where they had been when I saw them last night. The blankets were cold, thrown back in a tumble. There still lingered the thinnest aroma of Molly's cherry crisp.

A lined sheet of tablet paper, folded in quarters, lay on the blankets. "Edie" was written in pencil on the top quarter of it in Patty's scrawling hand. My knees cracked as I knelt in the same spot my daughter had kneeled last night. I felt like a spy, like this loft was no longer mine, that I had no right to see the paper meant for my daughter, or be there in that private place where Patty had slept.

I pulled open the note. It said:

> E,
>
> I guess this is it. I'm out of here. All I'm really worried about is Mom. I can't go back there. You know why. I wonder if you could look in on her sometimes, maybe take her something if Molly and Jack will let you. Something to eat I mean. It's eating we have a problem with. She won't eat bread now, or anything she thinks has yeast in it. And she'll only eat fruit if it's red. Pretty much anything red still goes down, so tomatoes and beets and she liked your mom's radishes this summer. I don't have time to list more, get whatever you can down her.
>
> But watch out for the son of a bitch's truck. If it's there, he's there. If it's gone, you're ok. He's

usually gone by about 3 in the PM. If you hear the truck pull in when you're up there, GET OUT QUICK. You can get out through the window in my room (which I guess you never saw). It's the room way in the back on the right. You can jump down on the roof of the shed. Don't be scared, I did it millions of times.

I wish I knew where I was going to be, but I don't. I'll stop at K's, see if he's home. Guess I'll know where I'll be when I get there.

Adios, sayonara, good-bye.

Love, P

chapter 19

THE BLACKTOP TO Elsie Standinghorse's place petered out four or five miles out of town. You were on gravel after that, then on bare dirt. Patty's note was folded in the pocket of my shirt. I could feel it against my chest, the awful, hot responsibility of it. It was early yet, breakfast just finished, Edie off to school.

Edie had sat in her chair at the breakfast table, picking at pieces of bacon. Her eyes shifted toward me, now and then, then toward her mother as if she knew the wrath of Molly's Jesus was about to come down on her. Edie was dressed for school in a loose brown sweater and a blouse with a high collar. Her face was puffy and she didn't look like she'd slept any more than I had.

All through breakfast, I didn't say anything I'd planned to say, didn't tell Molly, didn't open my mouth to my daughter. The note Patty left changed everything, at least for a while.

After the bus came and Edie got on it, I left the house. I told

Molly I was going into town to run an errand and was out the door before she had a chance to ask what kind of errand.

I hadn't been out Sagebrush Canyon for years. It ran through the west hills, traveling the opposite direction of our place. Here and there land had been seeded and harvested on the tops of the knolls, but where they dropped off into the canyons that washed out most years, the knolls were too steep to farm, leaving sage and juniper to mottle the ravines. The narrow gravel road rippled along ditches that ran with water in the spring, then sat dry the rest of the year, growing cheatgrass and foxtails. Sagebrush Canyon was the poorest land in the area. Unless we got more rain soon, there wouldn't be enough moisture for anything to sprout.

The turnoff up the draw to Elsie's house had washed out some years back and the dirt road took a little turn. Elsie's shack was over the hill, out of sight from the road.

Elsie's husband, Homer, killed himself rodeoing—bull-riding drunk, they said— and left Elsie to raise their daughter alone. The daughter's name was Smoke. She quit school early, maybe even before she got to high school, I couldn't remember for sure. Smoke followed her dad, in the dying department, and killed herself drinking, but not before she had Kenny.

Dust from the track up the hill rose like a rooster's tail behind my pickup. Two bike tracks went over the hill, intersecting here and there. I knew that if anybody was home, the dust I was kicking up would let them know somebody was coming. Out here, a plume of dust meant company.

Pieces of Elsie's place lay like a scatter of garbage deep in the shadows of the draw. There was the house with the black tarpaper roof, a tub from an old wringer washer, a Ford truck with no door and the hood propped up, and two milk cows with their heads in a scramble of dried foxtails and curled wire. I searched among the stuff for some sign of Patty, her bike—or her.

Kenny came out of the lean-to hauling a bale of hay in his hands. I waited to see if Patty was going to come out with him, but she didn't. Kenny didn't look up.

The cows started nosing the hay while Kenny popped the twine. Kenny must have been too busy to see my dust. I watched, and I wondered if Elsie was somewhere inside the shack watching me watch, and I wanted to tuck tail and run back home, away from the poverty of Elsie's place, away from what had happened last night, run back to my daughter and to Molly, and to the times when everything was right.

Kenny ambled over to the Ford truck, sat with one hip on the driver's seat, his leg out the door. A cloud of exhaust began coughing out the back of it, then quit, then blew out again, sooty and black. As I drove closer, Kenny got out and began banging on something in the engine, the carburetor probably. I'd done it myself.

The Ford was a '37, nearly as old as I was. It had lost a good bunch of its parts; the driver's door was gone and one fender was lying beside the wringer washer looking like it had dropped off right there in the front yard. Kenny stepped out of the truck, went around and ducked under the hood. He had lost weight since the last time I'd seen him. His pelvis bones poked at his Levi's, sharp as the Holstein's. He hadn't looked up when I drove in, didn't hear my truck over the noise of the engine. The smell of exhaust, pure raw oil and gas, was thick enough to make you gag. Kenny was probably fussing with a bad carburetor. From the smell of it he had a long way to go, if he wanted to fix it.

The Shorthorn looked up, and the Holstein's ears flicked and she shook her head. Her bell clanged like church. A white shepherd dog ran out from a hole under the house and barked. Hearing the barking, Kenny raised up, slammed his head against the hood. He rubbed the back of his skull, coughed at a cloud of exhaust. "Blackie," he shouted in a *shut up* tone.

Kenny was a nice kid, no matter what Molly said, no matter that he was part of the kids' troubles last fall. There was a time Kenny had held out a lot of promise. He was a natural runner. Until he dropped out of school, nobody in the state had beaten his times in the 220 or the 440, and Philpott had begun hoping for a bicentennial trophy this year to put in the glass trophy cabinet, but it didn't come.

Last fall, before the kids were caught skipping, Kenny had missed a meet against Weston. Right after that meet, he dropped out of school altogether. Then came the trouble with Patty and Edie, and nobody had seen him run since.

He stood there rubbing the back of his head. His black hair had grown past his shoulders, and the wind blew it into the wet of his lips. I shut off the pickup. All I could hear then was the bad running of Kenny's Ford and the banging of the cow's bell as she ate her hay.

Kenny reached into the truck. The ignition wires were together with a loose twist. He pulled the wires apart and the Ford went quiet.

"How long ago you steal that thing?" I said.

He smiled. "Never had a key." He reached out to shake my hand. "'Lo Jack." His hand was bristly with calluses and filthy with grease. "Sight for sore eyes."

I let go his hand. "What you got there?" I said. It seemed like all of a sudden the problems with the Ford were what I'd come out there for. All of a sudden I wanted nothing more than to fix Kenny's truck.

"Same ol'," Kenny said.

The Holstein's bell clanged behind us.

"Carburetor?" I said.

He shrugged. "I guess." The smell of gas was so strong it was a wonder the whole thing hadn't blown up in his face.

"Smells like flooding."

"All it's getting is gas," he said.

I leaned under the hood with him. There was no air cleaner. It had probably been tossed a century ago. He shook his head and some of his hair fell near the engine block. "You can't tell about a carburetor," I said. "You done anything with the carburetor, yet?"

"Was just going to try it."

"Temperamental," I said. "Probably want to leave it alone if you can." I was stalling, finding it harder and harder to bring the conversation around to what I came for.

Kenny leaned closer to see what I was doing. Everything about Kenny was fast, *swift*, I guess the word really was, like maybe the force of the wind was the thing that moved him. He hadn't asked why I was out there, hadn't intruded on me like I was intruding on him. I'd always known him as a gentle kid, and a kind one, and it still puzzled me that he had done what Molly said he did—led Edie and Patty astray. It didn't add up, but I believed it because really I didn't know what *did* add up anymore about those kids.

The choke cable had worked loose from the clamp so the choke was on when it shouldn't be. It was so obvious that this was probably the trouble, but he hadn't thought of it. I realized that Kenny never had a dad to show him this kind of stuff, that he'd had to figure everything out on his own.

"Got something to screw this on with?" I said. He swung his hair out of his face. "Got a screwdriver?"

"Don't think so," he said.

Where was Elsie? Maybe she had died. Everybody knew she'd been sick. Right then, the front door of the house squealed open. I looked up as Elsie shuffled out, stood in her slippers in the doorway. I nodded at her and found myself relieved she was still alive. She held a shawl over her shoulders, gripping it around her middle. Kenny looked around for something to work for a screwdriver. The cows, with their big heads, their horns swinging side to side, were eating that hay two feet from Elsie's legs. I could only concentrate on Elsie, the changes I saw in her. If I looked at where her hands held the shawl, it appeared she had gained weight. But her face had sunk in, her neck gotten as scrawny and loose as our old turkey's. She was almost all Cayuse, and last time I saw her she'd had a face round as good frybread.

Her face was so thin now the cheekbones poked at her skin, which had turned the color of wet cement. The wind whipped at the skirt of her dress, blew it against her thighs. She caught the material, held it away from herself like she didn't want me to see her shape under it. But she was too late, I saw she'd been hiding a huge growth hanging between her legs, big as a watermelon. It made me want to gag. She was holding onto that doorjamb like she would fall over if she let go of it. She raised her hand my way again and gave what appeared to be a little smile, and then she turned around and shuffled back into the house. Except for that tumor, or whatever it was hanging on her front, Elsie was as thin as Kenny.

I went over to where Kenny was squatting, still looking for something to tighten a screw and I squatted down beside him. "I think I have a screwdriver in the box in my truck," I said. I pulled myself up, went to the truck and fumbled for a phillips head.

I bent down beside him again, held the screwdriver toward him. "Did Patty come out here today?" I said.

There was the smallest pause before he took up the tool. Blackie, the white shepherd, came over and sniffed at my thigh, whiffing the scent of our dogs. I patted his head and shook his ears. The dog padded away, squeezed himself and his white tail back into the hole under the house.

In one easy move, Kenny stood up, went over to the truck. I had to brace my knuckles on the ground to unfold myself from the squat. We bent under the hood again, as if it could shelter us from some storm.

"Patty came out," he said, "before dawn."

"Tighten it good," I said.

He tightened, gave it a jiggle. "Try it," he said.

I gave it a twist or two. "Looks good. But you can't tell 'til it's running."

I stood back as he bent into the cab, touched the two ignition wires together, and held my breath as the Ford coughed and began to do no more than choke and rattle. Kenny was looking dark and serious behind the scum of bugs on the windshield. He loosened the ignition wires and the truck went quiet. "One more time," I said. I wanted it to start in the worst way, for him, for Elsie, for myself.

He turned the engine again and as if a miracle, the engine caught and started to run. It coughed again once, and spewed a little smoke, and the whole valley smelled like the raw gas Kenny had washed the parts in, but the truck was starting to run almost smooth. He set one leg up on the seat, left the other braced through the open door, and let the engine run a couple of minutes. I knew his feeling of pleasure, the way it was when something you did was finally going the way you wanted it to.

He shut off the engine. "You want to come in a minute? Elsie's got some coffee she's only had on the stove a couple of months."

I chuckled, more out of courtesy than at his stupid joke. "I got to get back to the house pretty soon."

Kenny got up, stood in front of me, not looking at me, but concentrating on wiping his hands on one of the rags that had been thrown over the fender. Then he looked up and he looked straight at me with his black eyes and with a little swipe of grease near his mouth. "Patty said she had to leave."

"Where to?"

He shook his head. "She said she had to."

"Where was she going?"

His mouth puckered in and I thought he must be tasting grease, but he was concentrating so hard, he didn't acknowledge it. "Pendleton. She was going to Pendleton to see about selling that bike." And then he gave out a little grunt-type chuckle. "And his rifle."

"Rifle."

"She stole his rifle."

"Whose rifle?" I said.

He pulled a face that made him look fifty years old. "Bill Murcheson's. She said she was going to get lost until her sixteenth birthday, when it was legal for her to work."

"Her birthday isn't for some months," I said.

"Yeah," he said.

"Pendleton?"

He shook his head. "Not for long, I don't think. It's not far enough away from Sweet William." He wiped his hands on his pants. "She had to stay away from him." He was looking me straight in the eyes in a way he never really did before. "I thought you'd know all this stuff. I thought she was out there living with you." It was probably what she had told him. "She thought she could get a work permit."

It wasn't making any kind of sense. "She left home because of her mother?"

"Her mother's why she *didn't* leave." He shook his head and frowned like I was asking some very dumb questions. "Him. Big Bill. That's why she finally had to."

chapter 20

I DROVE TO town for the mail, then had to sit in my rig in front
of the post office waiting and watching through the window as
George Plaugher and Rick Hendry finished up their postal business.
George was handing Sissy Miscek three boxes over the counter, and
Sissy was taking them, one by one to the back of the little sorting
room. I didn't have the strength for conversation. It took George
and Rick nearly ten minutes to finally quit standing there in front
of the counter talking, laughing with Sissy about something—what
I couldn't tell—for them to come out so I could go in.

Sissy was scooting George's boxes toward the back door with
her foot. It was quiet in there, but for the sound of her shuffling.
The back of her shoulders were broad, her gray hair held up off her
face with a couple of brown clips, unevenly placed. I went to our
box, took out an envelope from Publisher's Clearinghouse, the electric bill, and November's *Farm Journal*. Sissy heard me then, said
"'Lo, Jack," though she couldn't see me through the pigeon holes.

That was it, "'Lo, Jack." I could count on her not to press for more. "Sissy," I said. Sissy turned, nodded, then went back to fiddling with her boxes. I liked Sissy.

Two blocks down Main, a Dodge Ram pickup painted purple sat in front of the Masonic Hall. That truck was taking on some aspect, some representation I didn't understand. Could a truck look like something evil? It was nosed toward the curb but sitting two feet away from it consuming space, parked a half-length farther into the street. It took up a good part of that side of Main. The Dodge was new, less than a year old. It was painted with a metallic tint and sat on four racing slicks. A rifle rack crossed the back window. The rack was empty. The truck was polished, arrogant, sitting high on those tires like it owned the whole street.

The Masonic Hall was a homely, flat-faced building two stories tall. Wood stairs, covered over with a handmade roof, ran up the side. Masons did their ceremonies in half the upstairs hall; the other half had been turned into the only apartment in all of Philpott.

When Jackie sold the house on Maple, she'd moved up to the apartment on the second floor and had lived for a while off the bit of money she got from the house and from the sale of the stuff from Larry's store. Murcheson had driven a Chevy with no bumper and no lights when he'd moved in with Jackie. A week after the sale of Jackie's house, the Dodge Ram showed up, a rig rich enough to pay off a good piece of Molly's and my debt.

chapter 21

I BEGAN GOING into town several times a day, hoping to be there when the Dodge was not. But each time it sat in its spot. I did not know, exactly, what Patty's note meant but did not want my daughter to see it, did not want her going to the sort of place Patty had needed to leave. I had asked Edie if she knew where Patty went, and she started to cry and shook her head. Whatever went on at Jackie's place was something I could not understand. The miseries about the farm were bad enough, but they were not sinister. This, whatever it was about Patty, seemed evil.

It was, in the end, the situation with the farm that gave me a bit of relief.

Our Vancycle quarter section, the section we had agreed to put up for sale, covered three hills, rising up over the Walla Walla valley. I drove out one day hoping we could somehow hang onto the land, and the drive allowed me to forget Patty, at least for a while.

Since eternity, the wind had whipped the hills out there, had stripped the tops of iron, nitrogen, and potassium, and had blasted all the good topsoil east toward the Blue Mountains. But as poor as the tops of those hills were, the gullies and ravines held some of the best soil we farmed. It was these hills where I used to come when I was a kid. We had bought the land from Grandpa, who had bought it from the Hansels during the Depression. It had been one of my proudest days when Molly and I handed him the check for the final payment. All his life, Granddad had chucked away savings, and when the Depression hit, he took advantage, had money when the time came to buy.

The hills caught the view of the valley and a meandering curve of the Columbia River. As a kid, I'd thought God lived there. It was the place Jane, our old sorrel, knew to go even without me having to prod her. Our collie, Spike, would run ahead as Jane trotted up through the canyons and her back would be wet with sweat and my crotch chafing from the slivers of her quarter horse hair. We'd finally pull up and stand, the three of us, gazing out over the reach of the Columbia less than twenty miles away. And I would think that was the place, right there, where Roy Rogers and Trigger should be buried, a brave place where they could watch over the West forever and ever and make sure nothing unjust ever happened.

The real estate people were listing the land for sale that day. My pickup clicked cool as I sat in the seat of it, looking over the silver Columbia worming through the valley, maybe seeing that view for the last time.

I'd given the real estate agent directions, but in truth, I would have liked it a lot if she never found the place, if she ended up the rest of her life wandering around somewhere in the Blue Mountains. Unfortunately, a tail of dust rose out of the gullies, from the direction of the road. A white Cadillac pulled up, then disappeared in a cloud of grit. The engine went quiet. Connie Latrell, the agent, leaned over, began fiddling with papers on the seat beside her. After Molly's proposal to list the land, the bank recommended Latrell

Realty. If, in a few months, there wasn't an offer on the place, the bank would start to foreclose on every acre we farmed, including the house, barn, and everything else.

Connie and I shook hands. A skim of dust was beginning to settle on the shoulders of her blue suit, and dirt and clods buried her business shoes. The wind whipped her skirt and jacket, revealing the outline of her behind and the round of her stomach. She had brought a coat and was struggling to get it on in the blow. As she fiddled with the sleeve of the coat, she handed me the papers she'd brought. They whipped in my hand like they were alive. Reports, she called them, listing the tax values of land around there and the statistics from the most recent sale. The last piece of land to be sold anywhere between there and Walla Walla sold in 1952, twenty-four years before.

We were shouting into the wind to each other, "What was the average yield again, Jack?" In spite of the poor soil along the tops of the hills, the Vancycle canyons gave us our top yields nearly every year. It was why the bank went along with Molly's idea; they thought they could make a dime on it.

"Seventy-eighty bushels," I shouted back. Last year, the crop from these gullies brought in nearly forty-five thousand dollars. I couldn't see how selling the Vancycle quarter was going to do anything but delay losing the farm altogether, only making it a slow death, like losing an arm, then a leg, then pieces of yourself until there was nothing left but the heart and that would die without the rest. Farmers have to have something to farm, and the more wheat or oats or barley or grass you got from the farm, the more you could pay the bills. But if it sold, how were we going to make enough to live on the next year, and the year after that? I couldn't see an end to meetings with the bank and begging extensions year after year.

chapter 22

I PARKED NEXT to the purple Dodge, sat there with my hands on my thighs, listening to town. Steve Henderson drove by with his five-year-old son beside him. His eye went to the Dodge, then to me, and he gave me a two-finger greeting. I had started sneaking little bits of leftovers Molly had in the refrigerator, thinking any day now the truck would not be sitting at the curb and I could take them to Jackie, see how she was doing. And each day I went home with the sack still on the seat, and tossed it into the garbage, undelivered.

Patty's note was folded in eighths, in the dollar pocket of my wallet. I had read and reread it so many times the creases were going soft. Each time, I hoped maybe it would bring some kind of answers, but it didn't. I wanted to excuse her behavior, to convince myself everything she did was the dream of some spoiled girl who was still crying out for her dad. But every time, the answers seemed to go further into the dark.

Up the street, at the high school, the football team was running the track, and from behind the school came the thin yells of girls going through cheerleading practice. There had been a time when Edie and Patty worked up yells and kicks on the patio together. But that was a couple of years ago. There hadn't been a cheer on our place since.

Since I'd found the girls in the barn, Edie had been living mostly shut up in her room, coming down only when I called her to help with chores or when her mother made her set the table or sit at it to do homework and Bible lessons. Unless we found Patty, unless she came out for the Saturday sleepover like usual, Molly would figure something was wrong and dig for answers I didn't have.

Before I left the house, Molly had taken Edie in to the orthodontist's in Pendleton. Edie was getting her braces off that day, and the doctor was taking an impression for a retainer. Edie should have been ecstatic, or at least happy, but she wasn't acting that way. She was pale, her face dull like it had been dusted with flour. She didn't speak unless one of us spoke to her first.

The rich clean of the Dodge pickup stuck out, cold as winter in the amber light of the fall afternoon. Silver dust gleamed in its paint, a color of purple so deep you felt you could reach right into it. A new set of chrome-plated running boards had been added since last time I saw it. I had been keeping an eye on pickup for a week and a half, and had finally worked up the guts to climb up the stairs and knock on the door. I picked up the sack of leftovers, slammed the door to my rig, and started up. The steps were long and went straight up through a dark tube attached on the outside of the temple. At the top there was a landing that looked out onto the weed patch in back. The railing leaned away from the steps and was peeling a dandruff of white paint.

I rapped on the door, heard a guy shout, "Whoozzit?" I stood there, listening.

There was clomping from inside, boots on a wood floor. "Who is it?" he said again, closer to the door this time.

"Jack McIntyre," I said.

"Jack who?" he shouted.

"McIntyre," I said a little louder. "I've come to see Jackie."

I thought he said, "Shit," but couldn't tell for sure.

The door blasted open. Bill Murcheson stood there in an undershirt cut low under a damp fuzz of chest hair. He had on Levi's that were tight in the legs and not quite all the way zipped up. He didn't make a move to zip. His face was red, and he smelled like enough Aqua Velva to fumigate the whole hall. He'd combed his hair back off his forehead, and it was dripping from the curls along his neck.

"Jackie doesn't get visitors," he said.

I couldn't tell if he meant visitors never came or if they weren't allowed.

"Only take a minute," I said, and something made me stick my foot in the door.

From what Molly knew, nobody had seen much of Jackie for a long time. I didn't know if anybody had seen her at all for at least six months. When she took up with Murcheson, she seemed to disappear. Nobody paid attention at all until Patty started dressing loose and taking up with boys from Walla Walla and Weston and Pendleton and then started skipping school. Patty gave Philpott something to talk about—in fact people talked about all *three* of the kids, Patty, Kenny, and our Edie.

Standing there with the sack of leftovers in my hand, I was beginning to think Murcheson wasn't going to let me in. I put my knee in the doorway and he saw it. He made his voice high and sugary.

"Sweetie pie," he said over his shoulder, "it's Jack McIntyre." He didn't take his eyes off me.

People in town knew Murcheson had gone through every penny Larry's insurance had left Jackie, and, without shame, advertised where the money went with the Dodge and the damned radials sitting out at the curb.

"Jackie," I said again like I needed to remind him what I was here for. And then I added, "I've come to ask about Patty."

Murcheson's head whirled around, looked behind himself liked he was checking to see if Jackie was going to say something. He turned back to me, snorted. "What do you want from Jackie?" I held up the sack. "I brought something for her." Seeing the sack, he took on a curious look, like maybe he would like to see what was in it.

He grabbed the sack from me and stepped away from the door. "Jackie?" I said, "It's Jack McIntyre."

It was dark in the apartment. I couldn't see much but the blur of cigarette smoke, but I heard the sound of grunting from inside, like somebody hurt. The sound triggered something in Murcheson and he swung his arm away from himself, like all of a sudden he'd gone grand and was showing me in. The expression on his new-shaved face gathered up like he'd rather let in snakes.

Jackie was sitting at a card table in the kitchen. I didn't think I would have recognized her if I'd seen her on the street. She was thin as a stick, her blond hair slimy with oil and hanging over her face so only her nose showed. She'd never looked this bad before.

She was leaning forward, her elbows on the card table. As I walked over to her, her arms pulled tighter into herself. Besides her elbows there were only two things on the table: an ashtray and a photo in a frame. I came around to stand by her. The photo was of Patty, a school picture, taken about two weeks after the start of school. Someone had taken a marker and drawn an X right over the face. The image of Patty was looking straight at the camera with her blaring blue eyes and with an expression on her face like a dare.

A smell came off Jackie, dirty, like the smell of a basketball jersey worn too long. Her smell rose even over the aroma of Murcheson's aftershave.

Jackie and I had dated for a while in high school, before Molly and I went steady and before Jackie and Larry became an item.

Many times, I'd sent up a little thanks that, no matter what happened between Jackie and me, it ended up *Jack and Molly*, not *Jack and Jackie*.

Murcheson rattled open the sack, poked his hand in, started pawing through the wax paper I'd wrapped around the meatloaf, fingering the two apples, and the cup of cherry cobbler, the only food in the fridge that was red. I'd also stuck in three slices of bread.

Murcheson pulled out the bread, held the slices fanned out like playing cards. "We're not into fucking bread, are we, Jackie?" he said, his tone mean and accusing.

The ash dropped off Jackie's cigarette.

He threw the bread onto the table beside Patty's picture. He leaned into Jackie, made crawly movements with his fingers. "Bread," he said. "Yeast."

She leaned back in her chair, away from him.

He turned to me. "She fucking thinks it's going to kill her." He took out some of the cobbler, started eating it out of the paper cup.

The apartment was full of smoke and only half-furnished. Stuff you'd expect to be there wasn't. A table lamp sat on the floor without a table, a footstool but no chair, a bunch of 78 albums but no stereo. I guessed a lot of stuff had been sold.

An open can of chili sat on the counter with a spoon stuck in it, and I wondered if Jackie had eaten any of it. The counter was littered with dishes, the stove gritty with the crusts of dried food, and the kitchen was running with ants everywhere—on the oven, lined up along the sink, under the counter, a black string of them making it up over the fridge. Mice track peppered the baseboards. The apartment stank like a baby's diaper.

"Her bitch daughter," Murcheson said, "stole my rifle and the bike I loaned her."

Jackie made that grunting sound again and I was beginning to wonder if her mind even let her talk anymore. It was then that I saw a patch of discolored skin along her cheek through a crack in her hair. At first, I thought it was dirt, from the filth all around her. But there was a cut on her eye.

I folded my hands in front of myself and took a step closer to her. "Jackie," I said, "have you heard anything from Patty?"

Jackie didn't move, and she didn't make a sound.

Murcheson put his thumbs into the pockets of his jeans, pulled them lower on his hips. You could see the opening of his shorts. He smiled at me with half his mouth. "What do *you* want with Patty?"

I shook Jackie's elbow. "Jackie." I shook it again, there was only bone to it, no meat at all. "Have you reported anything to anybody?"

"You mean the cops?" Murcheson said.

Jackie made a noise, a rumbling sound, low, quiet like a roar from a cow before she bellows.

"What?" I said.

Jackie smacked open her mouth and then said, clear as anyone would say, "We're having a birthday party." Her voice was thick, her words sticky with phlegm. "Patty is five years old tomorrow."

I cleared my throat, made my voice soft. "Patty was fifteen last birthday."

Murcheson held his arm up in front of Jackie, put his flat hand in front of her face, as if to tell her to shut up or he'd pop her. Jackie didn't say anything more, sat there barely taking a breath.

"Fucking little twat," he said.

chapter 23

FOR A WEEK, Patty didn't show, even on Saturday. I had not shared Patty's letter to anyone. I considered showing it to Edie and had wavered because I did not want her to worry. I was thankful now. What Patty's note implied, and the feeling I got from Murcheson, was not something any girl should know.

I didn't breathe anything to Molly, but I did climb the ladder every morning to check the hayloft. There was no sign of her. Nothing. Edie made an excuse to her mother as to why Patty wasn't coming out, said Patty had a cold and wasn't feeling good. Yet all morning that Saturday I expected to hear the dogs bark and to see Patty come whipping down the drive on the bike, everything back to usual.

In the evenings after dinner, I started to take note of everything Molly was wrapping up for leftovers after supper, and I realized that I'd seen Edie doing the same thing, but I hadn't paid attention. I'd seen Edie's eyes slip over the dishes, the bowls, the platters of meats, and I hadn't known, hadn't even registered the gesture until I found myself doing it. I found myself figuring how I could nip a little here, pare a little there, snitch an apple or a slice of cherry pie without Molly noticing.

About midnight, when Molly was soundest asleep, I'd sneak down to the kitchen, and I'd open the leftover mashed potatoes sealed in the Tupperware bowl, or take out the leftover chop she'd wrapped in tinfoil, and I'd rummage through the leavings of green beans and the ear of corn on the cob. And I'd cover my theft as much as possible by spreading the potatoes to cover the dip of the spoon, or shaking the beans level again in the bowl. I'd wash the spoon and dry it and put it back into the drawer, like I'd seen Edie do. And I'd take the sack of food out into the cold of the night, and stuff it, hidden, under the seat of my pickup, ready to take into town the next day.

And all the time I was doing it, I wondered if Edie was lying awake in her bed.

I HAD BEGUN to make it a habit to go to town for the mail around three o'clock in the afternoon, the time Patty's note said Bill Murcheson would most likely be gone. School didn't let out until four. What had Patty done every day? Had she slipped out of class to take her mother the food Edie brought? Had she ridden her bike out to our place after dark every night? When had she had time to study? I finally understood why sometimes she was so dirty and others she seemed pretty clean. I suspected she showered in the girls' locker room, when she was attending school, but when school was out, God, I didn't know. And where was Murcheson? The Dodge hadn't been parked at the curb the last few days, since the day I first came to check up on Jackie.

Every day, when I walked into Jackie's apartment, without exception, she was smoking at that card table in the kitchen. Sometimes the sack of food I'd brought the day before would still be sitting there in front of her; sometimes there'd be crumbs on the table. The door was never locked. I'd announce myself, say something like, "Jackie, it's Jack." And she would not respond except to reach down and slip a cigarette from the pack that was always there on the table. She would light the cigarette and smoke would curl into her eyes and she never even blinked.

Sometimes I rinsed out a dish or two. Sometimes I wiped up the table a little, but I didn't do more for fear Murcheson would come back and see the place cleaned up and wonder who'd been there. I had no idea what he would do about someone messing with his place, no matter how filthy it was. He'd know, for sure, that Jackie hadn't done it. She was in no shape to do much of anything but sit there in the same sweater and filthy hair every day, smoking her cigarettes.

THE WEATHER WAS starting to get down into the 20s at night. One of Molly's garden hoses had leaked onto the cement pad we called a patio, then frozen in a puddle the color of the cement. One midnight, going out to the pickup with the sack of food in my hand, my foot hit the ice and I went down hard on the concrete. For a minute, I lay there, trying not to scream out. My ankle hurt like hell. I wanted to shout against the darkness, but I only lay there on the cement, the night air reamed frigid by the wind, and I closed my eyes against stars so close they sat on my chest.

IT WOULD NOT be long before the women would start getting ready for the holidays. Thanksgiving was just a few weeks away. The holidays were always the time of year for farmers to wait, waiting for spring, waiting for the cows to calve, waiting for the thaw that finally came and shouted "grow" and "live" time that thinned our blood and scooped us up into a fever that took the breath from us all the rest of the year. Winter was the time of year most farmers lived for, a time when you'd done your job, you'd worked like a jackass, and it was your time to be still, to put on a pound or two and catch up with bowl games and basketball standings, learn how choosy mothers choose Jif, or keep up with Julie and Barbara on *One Day at a Time*. It was the time of year you were supposed to spend afternoons hanging out at Haymire's, where you could sit beside the woodstove and listen to George Plaugher or Jim Elliott carry on about hunting, about the bucks they'd taken down and had in the freezer. Then you'd go home again and snooze through David Brinkley. Winter was a farmer's time to claim. That winter, though, I had nothing to claim, and I hadn't been to Haymire's once. I went directly to the post office or in to check on Jackie, then back home.

One afternoon George Plaugher came into the post office after I did. The purple Dodge, I'd noted, was still gone.

Patty had been gone nearly a month. I had stopped by the high school one morning, had asked Mr. Norton if Patty's records had been sent somewhere else. Jackie had family in Kansas, maybe she was there. He said no without looking at files, and I knew he had been checking. But like everyone else, he was probably certain Patty was carousing again with her band of no-goods from Walla Walla.

As he came out the post office door, George looked up from under the bill of his baseball cap at me. "We been missing you over at Haymire's."

"Yeah," I said.

"What's keeping you?" Without the baseball cap, he was totally bald.

"Busy, I guess." The sack of food for Jackie was sitting on the seat in the pickup. I would stop by the Masonic Hall on my way out.

George started to toe some invisible thing on the floor. "Everything OK between you and Molly?" The bill of the cap covered his face. It was a personal question, not the kind you expected from anybody but Boone Ellis. It didn't feel mean though, like it would from Boone, but I could see George was uncomfortable asking it. I couldn't think how to answer it.

George kept digging the floor with his foot, looking at his boot, hiding behind the bill of his cap. I wanted to say, *what're you aiming at, George?*

Then finally he did look up at me. He gave me a straight-on eyeball. "You still sweet on Jackie Pugh?" He didn't ask about Patty, but I didn't think he would. No one was asking about her. Everyone assumed she was holed up with some kid from Walla Walla, and everyone clicked their tongues.

Sweet on Jackie? "What?" I blurted out. What was he thinking?

"I remember you and Jackie was sort of a thing back in school," he said. "A few of us have seen you going up to her place when Murcheson's not there." He shuffled out of the post office before I could come up with something to say. The way he left was his way of sparing me having to say something to cover my ass, but it left the question hanging, thick as the smoke in Jackie's apartment.

IT WAS ONE o'clock in the morning, and I was limping back into the house after tucking half a steak, an apple, a plastic margarine tub of berry cobbler, and a banana under the seat of the truck. The swelling had gone down from my fall but my ankle still got stiff in the cold. I took off my coat, hung it on the hook, shivered through the cotton of my pajamas. I snuck up the stairs, heard the slurping noises Molly made in her sleep. She was sleeping longer and longer, going to bed some nights before eight o'clock and barely being able to drag herself out when I shook her in the morning.

Edie's door was open about a finger as if she hadn't quite gotten it closed when she went to bed. I reached to pull the door closed. A sliver of light from the hall lay across her face, gave into shadow at the pale curve of her cheeks, her nose, the shape of her mouth. Her mouth was in its sleeping position. Without braces, it was a young woman's mouth. She did not stir as I stood there. Her cheek lay on the pillow, her face calm and open. In her sleep, her expression was not clamped down like it was when she was awake. As she lay there,

I imagined she was little again, five, or ten, open and clean, bursting into one of her old gapped-tooth grins, though er grins weren't gapped-tooth anymore. The braces had taken care of that.

For a moment, in the quiet, I had a little hunch of the woman Edie would grow into. In spite of her straight, even white teeth, she was not going to be a beauty. In spite of her quiet ways, the secrets she'd learned to hold so tight, she would make a good wife, a good mother. Like mine, her skin would wrinkle early in life and, by the time she got out of high school, she'd be wearing glasses. She got all of that from me. She would be a blender, someone who caused no trouble, someone people pretty much liked because they could expect her to keep things calm, to keep things nice. She would never speak out, never be one to take things into her own hands.

The clock radio, with its green underwater face, sat on the orange-crate table between Edie's bed and the other bed where Patty had slept so often. The closet was still nearly half full of Patty's clothes, clothes that Molly had washed and ironed and folded along with our own.

Edie smacked her lips at some dream and rolled over to her other side. Her stringy hair whisped onto her pillow. Her shoulders poked up at the sheet, dipped away at her waist, then rose up again in the high-boned curve of her hips.

chapter 24

THE TELEPHONE WAS Molly's utensil, like a spatula was, or the oven, or the washing machine. I could probably count on two hands the times I'd used it to call anyone. Bad stuff happened on the phone; the electric company called for back payment, Molly phoned from Hansels' to say her car had slid off into their ditch, Edie's teacher called to say Edie had thrown up in the gym and somebody needed to come get her and take her home, inspectors called wanting to schedule appointments to check for tuberculosis in the milk cows, the doctor called to say Molly's pregnancy test came up negative again, the Health Department called to say the test on the well showed arsenic. And here it was, *me*, dialing the phone.

It was Wednesday. Edie was in school. In another week, or two, she would be out of school for the four days of Thanksgiving vacation. Molly was in town for a Ladies' Aid meeting, getting ready for the annual fundraising bazaar. I had the house to myself. It had been weeks since Patty was in school. No one had seen her, and some were whispering *good riddance.*

I hadn't told anybody, not Molly, not Lee, nobody that I was going to do this. Mom was still in Europe. There was a growing stack of postcards from her lying beside the bills on Molly's desk, the last one from Rome, with a picture of the Spanish Steps covered in flowers. She had marked a spot at the foot of the steps with a ballpoint pen. "Ethel and I are sitting at a little table where I put the dot. We're having a *tosta* and Cinzano. Weather good. Lots of pigeons and dark handsome men. Thinking of you. Love, Mom." I convinced myself she was teasing about the men.

On the other end, the phone rang three times. By the fourth ring, I was beginning to think I'd worked up a sweat for nothing, that nobody was there to pick up. Most people worked during the day, but I thought I'd remembered Raunch saying he worked swing. I'd had so little experience with employment, I didn't know what swing was. I knew it wasn't regular days. I was about to hang up when he answered.

"'Lo," he said. His voice was thick like he'd been asleep. It was nearly nine thirty in the morning. Last summer at the picnic Raunch had mentioned he was going into his ninth year at the cannery in Weston. I remembered then feeling sorry for him, having to work for someone other than himself.

"Raunch, it's Jack."

I heard a woman mumble something in the background. "McIntyre?" he said, like he couldn't believe who I was.

"Yeah," I said. I didn't think I'd ever called him before, even in all those years we were tight growing up.

The woman was mumbling something again. I could feel my face heat up, "I'm, I'll, um, I'll call back."

There was some rustling on the phone, like maybe he was sitting up. "What the hell, Mackie," he said. He sounded more awake and happy to hear it was me. "'S happenin'?"

"Maybe I better call back," I said. "You got company."

"No. No. I was getting up."

It was a lie, I thought, to make me feel a little more comfortable.

"We didn't get in until pretty late last night," he added. I heard a match strike, then him sucking in a deep breath.

The woman muttered, "I'm getting a shower," and then there was the sound of a door closing in the background.

I wiped my hands on my pants.

"What the hell, man?" he said.

"You sure you don't want me to call back?"

"Hell, no," he said. "I'm up. 'S up, Mackie?"

I didn't think he really wanted an answer, and I wasn't going to bother him with a real one. "I wonder," I had to clear my throat, "if maybe the cannery's hiring."

Raunch was quiet a minute, like he was giving it some thought. "A driver quit yesterday. They might be looking for somebody."

I was so thankful for Raunch right then, not because he said there might be a job, but because he had the decency not to ask me to explain anything.

"Can you meet me over at the cannery about three o'clock?" he said.

"Today?"

"Yeah."

Three o'clock was when I usually took food to Jackie.

"The crew chief and me are pretty good friends," he said. "I'll introduce you before I go to work. But, Mackie, I can't promise anything."

"I know."

IT WAS TWO thirty when I pulled into the parking lot of the cannery. I couldn't help thinking about Jackie. I had been taking stuff in to her long enough with no sight of Murcheson I'd let down my guard, had started leaving food with her rather than picking up what she didn't eat. She probably wasn't going to get anything to eat that day, unless I could take it to her, after I talked to the crew chief. I'd shoved last night's sack of chicken, an apple, and some rolls and jelly under the seat, in case.

The Lamb Weston cannery filled a good part of the draw on the north edge of the town of Weston. The road went past the plant where they processed potatoes, then wound on up the canyon to Walla Walla fifteen miles away. Sitting there in the clear afternoon, I started to wonder what I was doing and started to think about turning around and going home, or driving right on with the road up to Walla Walla, or Spokane or wherever the road would take me. But there I was, sitting in the dust of my truck, dressed in my one pair of slacks and jacket like for a wedding, or a funeral.

A few minutes later, Raunch pulled up in his blue Datsun, parked a few spaces down. He got out of his pickup, started to come over. He was tall and slim and wore a Stetson. And he walked bow-legged as if years ago his rodeoing had turned his knees out permanently. We nodded to each other.

"Sheesh," he said, "dressed like that, you'd get a job with the *president*." He still wore the belt with the trophy buckle from winning the saddle bronc competition one year at Cheyenne. He grinned, the dark bristle of his Fu Manchu bleaching all those white teeth. I could see why he never had trouble picking up women and I was glad he wasn't the same age as my daughter.

He led me up the dock and into the building. The plant smelled like disinfectant and raw potatoes. Conveyors bled potatoes into huge vats of water, and another took them in and they came out peeled, naked white.

He fingered hello to some of the people we passed, though it was too noisy in there to hear. Some were Mexicans, some Indians, some white men and women, everybody wearing white nets on their heads. I didn't recognize anyone.

The foreman's office was glassed in. He was sitting at a desk, his back to the door, flipping through punch cards. Raunch opened the door and leaned in. "Lyle?" he said.

The guy turned around and when he did, I had the impulse to run out of there, but instead I stood there in the doorway planted like a rock. Lyle Whitty. Raunch pulled me into the office. I'd forgotten Lyle worked at Lamb Weston, had no idea he'd be the foreman I'd be talking to. Lyle looked up from the paperwork on his desk. I stood in the doorway not knowing what to do with my hands. Raunch said, "I heard Stan Jenson quit yesterday."

I could see Lyle was beginning to put two and two together, that Raunch was bringing me in for the job. Raunch knew I would know Lyle but had said nothing. We were all the same age. Lyle went to school in Athena, about ten miles from Philpott. We'd played basketball against each other, some baseball. His folks ran a leather goods factory up toward Adams. Their business got so big ten years ago, they moved it to Spokane. The Whittys were the upper crust of all of the county, shaking hands with politicians, getting their names in the paper, leading lives that excluded the rest of us.

Lyle in his heyday, back when we were in school, would slide through Philpott in his brand-new Ford Victoria—black and red, cruising Main with Molly—*my* Molly—in the front seat beside him. For almost a year he had his clutches on her. Back then, Jackie and I were dating. In a town as small as Philpott, there never was much of a pool of people to date, particularly if you subtracted relatives. It turned out Molly dumped Lyle for me. But for months he came around and worked on her, pestered her to come back. I never knew why she didn't.

It didn't make for feeling real comfortable about asking Lyle for anything. And here I was, coming to him for a job.

"Hello, Jack," he said.

"Hello, Lyle." I wasn't wearing a hat, but if I had been, it would have been in my hand like a beggar.

"How's tricks?"

Did he mean Molly? "OK, I guess," I said, not knowing what I was saying OK to.

Raunch stepped back behind me. "I got to get to work. See you, Lyle. Jack." And when he closed the door, I was standing in Lyle Whitty's office hardly able to talk, let alone keep my feet from turning around and following Raunch right back out.

Lyle leaned back in his chair, twiddled a pen. He was looking at me through the bottoms of his eyeglasses, totally in charge. He had gained weight since school and was wearing sideburns on the hams of his cheeks. "I heard you got storm damage out your way.

"Yeah," I said.

"Bad, huh?"

Was he happy about it? I couldn't really tell. "Raunch said somebody quit," I said, to get this over as soon as possible.

Lyle wouldn't give up. "I mean I heard the Albertsons lost a quarter of their crop because of it." He shrugged, then grinned. I could tell he was taking some pleasure in it.

I didn't say anything.

"Farming's always give and take," he said. "It's why I never did it."

"Been driving for over thirty years," I said, hoping he'd take the hint. I didn't know how to keep a conversation going, even when I wasn't trying to get a job, but I couldn't make anything else come out of my mouth, couldn't do more than let the noise of the conveyor belts and the hum of motors fill the room.

Lyle was smiling. "I hear you didn't have insurance."

I shook my head.

"That's bad. What's your Molly say about that?"

My Molly. I knew he was still sore about Molly and me. He'd held onto it twenty years, and now he was getting me back. He had his own wife, some kids, too, I thought, but he still wanted the pleasure of seeing me squirm. I didn't think his question about Molly needed an answer so I didn't make one.

Finally he said, "Need a job, huh, Jack?"

I shrugged like I could give or take a job. It was a lie to shrug like that. "Raunch said you'd be looking for a driver," I said.

"Could be," he said. And then he let another hundred years go by without saying a word. I stood there in my slacks and tie wondering what to do with my hands.

He finally leaned up. "You got a current license?"

I nodded.

"Had any tickets lately? Speeding? DUIs?" He laughed. "DUIs," he said, "Right. Molly's a teetotaler these days, isn't she?" He shook his head slowly, like he didn't really believe how Molly had changed since the old days when she used to be open to a drink or two, when she was someone a guy could look at and want for his own.

"No tickets," I said. I wasn't going to talk about Molly with him.

"Handled a semi?"

Semi. I'd never even touched the wheel of one. He'd probably guess it, too. Two ton, double axles was all I'd ever driven, never a semi in my life. I shook my head no.

He leaned back in his chair again, looked down at me through the bottoms of his eyeglasses again, like he was winning.

It was the end, I knew. I'd come here for nothing but humiliation and defeat. I almost felt happy at the thought of giving up, like I wouldn't have to struggle one minute more, like the weight of it would just blow away. Giving up meant I could let go the knot in my chest, and knowing it I felt the heaviness melt like butter in a fry pan.

"No semis," I said. "But I can handle something on a hitch." It was final. I came all the way, talked to Lyle Whitty this afternoon, all for nothing.

He put his arms behind his head, spread his gut for full view. For some reason, it did me good to know he had a gut and I didn't.

"The job pays three dollars an hour, fifty cents more than minimum wage."

For a moment, I couldn't understand why he was telling me this.

"There's a load needs to get out in fifteen minutes."

I USED A pay phone out by the loading dock to call Molly. She answered after two rings. "Honey," my voice was shaking so hard I could hardly say it. "It's me."

"Jack?" she said. "Where you calling from?"

I didn't know how many years it had been since my wife and I had talked on the phone.

"You hurt? Where are you?"

"I'm OK, Mol. I'm in Weston."

"Weston?" she said.

"At the cannery."

"Cannery," she said quiet, like it made more sense coming from her own mouth.

"I got a job."

"You got a job?"

"Yeah."

"A job," she said, letting it settle.

"Yeah. I start work in ten minutes." I was supposed to take the first load to Washington, where Lamb Weston was putting up a new plant.

"Doing what?"

"Driving a load to Quincy."

"Washington?"

"Yeah."

"That's a day's drive," she said. "Why didn't you tell me you were doing this?"

I didn't have an answer for her. I didn't know why I couldn't tell her, but I couldn't. "I have to stay up there in Quincy overnight

while they load the truck with stuff I'm supposed to drive to Hermiston tomorrow," I said.

"You have to stay the night?"

It was the first time in twenty-one years, except when she had
Edie, that Molly and I would be sleeping in different places.

"I'll be in Hermiston tomorrow night," I said.

"Jack, I can't believe this."

"Me neither, Mol," I said. "But they're paying three dollars an
hour." It sounded like a fortune. "And they pay for my motel." At
the time, I didn't think to tell her about the eight dollars a day
extra I was going to get paid, something they called per diem.

"I don't know, Jack," she said.

"I can't let you do everything, Molly. You've been the only one
who could deal with the bank." For the first time in a long time, I
didn't feel about as useful as teats on a boar.

"I'll say my prayers," she said.

"I'll count on it."

"Jack," she said, but she didn't say anything more.

"Mol, I got to talk to Edie."

"She's in her room, doing her homework."

"I need to talk with her."

I heard Molly lay the phone down on the hallway table, heard
her slow steps as she went up the stairs to our daughter's room. A
semi was backing in to the cannery dock and I lost the sounds of
home to the hiss of brakes. It turned out I would not be driving
a semi after all, but a double-axle truck with a box on back, a six-
teen-foot bed the size of our big-bedded wheat truck. All along,
Lyle had been aware that I wouldn't be at the wheel of a semi.

"Hello," Edie said. Her voice was thick and dreary.

"Hi, Ede. I need to ask you a real big favor."

"What?"

"I'm going to be gone awhile."

"Gone?"

"I need you to do chores while I'm gone."

"Where you going, Dad?"

Lord, her voice could sound so sweet.

"I have a job."

"You got a job?"

"Your mother can tell you all about it. I won't be home for a couple nights," I said. "The farm is in your hands."

chapter 25

SOME PEOPLE SAY a door doesn't close but another one opens, but it seems they always say it when they've given up any other hope. My door closed right in my face, tore me away from my wife, my daughter, the only life I knew. Open? What door? The minutes dragged into hours, the hours dragged into days, and the days dragged into a week. The route Lyle Whitty hired me for meant I spent every day on the road, every night in motels that reeked of toilet deodorant, stale booze, and cigarette breath.

Five days on the job felt like five months. I thought about Jackie, but couldn't do anything; she would have to wait until I was home again to see about her. The Lamb Weston plant was closing for Thanksgiving, and I'd be sleeping in my own bed for the first time since I started the job. I'd only been home but once, for fifteen minutes, to pick up some work clothes and clean underwear. The first couple of days on the job, Lyle had me scheduled so tight that

I'd had nothing more with me to wear than what I'd worn to the interview—one set of underwear and the good slacks and shirt and tie. In Hermiston, I splurged on a toothbrush and a razor and shaving foam at a market. I'd finally dared to turn off my route, dared to risk I might not get the load up to Quincy when Lyle told me it had to be there. I'd only had time to pick up the clothes and kiss Molly on the cheek and leave again.

Every night, lumpers loaded the truck with office machines, parts for the plants—bearings, conveyors, hoists—equipment for the new plants Lamb Weston was setting up in Connell and Quincy, Washington, and in Hermiston. The next morning I'd take out. Driving the circuit was over a five hundred mile round trip and I did it every two days. It gave me time to think.

I was worried about everything—what was happening to the farm, the cows, the weather, Jackie. I don't think I ever sat so much in my life. My back was screaming to do something more than bang around in that truck. I knew for certain Lyle was keeping me on this schedule so Molly and I never had time to see each other. But with what Lamb Weston was paying, and the per diem and overtime, it looked like I'd clear about $880 a month. A fortune. I kept a tally sheet of the money I earned each day, stuck it in the pocket of my coat. Every night, in the lonesome motel room, I'd get the sheet out, pencil in another day's pay, and total it in my head. Thanksgiving was going to mean four days off without pay.

The afternoon before Thanksgiving, I dropped the truck at the plant, drove the last ten sweet miles home. As I pulled into our drive, I couldn't get over how strange it was seeing the farm after being gone. How could I have forgotten how much the house needed paint, or how the barn roof was beginning to sag, or how the corral fences weren't white like I still pictured them but were smeared with old cow dung? As I pulled up, the wind whistled through the shop in the barn. It felt like I'd plunked myself down on some strange planet. It didn't feel real. When had the milkweed taken over the yard? Had so much of the roof blown off the house since I got the job? The place was poor, unkempt. I guessed I'd never really noticed it before. I was supposed to be back at work in Weston after midnight Sunday. How could I? There was so much to do here. The light was on in the barn. Edie. Chores.

I stomped my feet on the back door mat, opened the screen, "Mol?" I said. It was near twilight, the world had gone dim, purple.

"Mol," I said again. I could smell a roast cooking in the oven, the sharp tinge of pepper and of fat crisped brown. God, it smelled good. I had been eating on the road, hamburgers for fifty-nine cents and, in the mornings, breakfast specials of greased eggs and bacon that set me back over a dollar. Eating that way meant I could pocket six dollars of per diem.

Water was running in the basement. I hung my jacket on the nail, clomped down the basement stairs. Molly was standing at the dryer, folding Levi's, her back to me. Over the washer, she hadn't heard me coming. The little bow of her apron fluttered as she laid a pair of my jeans on the stack of clothes she'd already folded. The backs of her arms were bare, soft and rolling, pressing against the layers of flesh over her ribs, soft and warm. I had an impulse to plant a smacker on both of her arms, and on the round white skin at the back of her neck.

I slipped behind, put my arms around her.

"*Awk*," she said and she dropped the jeans. She turned around, stood looking at me, her eyes shifting around my face, wary, assessing. It broke my heart. "Jack," she finally said. And she took me up into her warm arms. "Jack," she said again.

We stood there in the heat of the dryer, smelling the Fab in the air, and letting the churn of the drying clothes begin to make up for the time we'd been separated. Molly brought my face down to hers, put a kiss on my cheek.

"Lyle Whitty's my boss," I said and watched to see how she'd take the news.

"Edie's still out doing chores," she said, like hearing Lyle Whitty's name didn't mean anything at all.

chapter 26

HELEN AND LEE's place in Milton-Freewater was set in a neighborhood of fat maple trees, locusts, and oaks. The trees were bare that time of the year, their trimmed lawn and Helen's flowerbeds dull and dormant. The street meandered up to their house, which sat on the top of a small hill. Their neighbors, professors who taught at Whitman College and doctors who practiced at the hospital in Walla Walla, lived in trim houses like Lee's. Three years ago, Helen and Lee had painted the house a light yellow and white that should have showed the dust that blew nine months out of the year. But Lee pressure-washed every year, and the house sat there bright as the sun, even in the dim light of Thanksgiving Day.

Molly had spent Thanksgiving morning cooking in the kitchen, fixing her contributions to the dinner. We had loaded the car with her cinnamon rolls and her creamed potatoes and her pineapple-and-whipped-cream salad. Edie sat in the back as we drove the twenty minutes to College Place, outside Walla Walla.

Molly believed Helen and Lee's opulent style was sinful, somehow against what Jesus wanted. As we pulled into the driveway and parked, Molly had even more fodder for complaint: Helen's real estate business was picking up, and she and Lee were about finished with an addition to the house, twenty feet for closet space and a Jacuzzi in the bathroom.

I missed Mother, missed that she wouldn't be at the dinner, missed the way she loosened us all up, the way she laughed, coddled a glass of wine or two, kicked off her pump shoes, relaxed in Helen's white living room with its carpet the color of cream and its white sofa and the white-and-gold coffee tables. Mother never seemed to relax with Molly like she did with Helen, never seemed to giggle as much, or flirt with Lee or me when we were in our house, even though it was the house she'd lived in for so many years. It was tradition that Molly and I had Christmas at our place, and Christmases always seemed cloudier, murkier, quiet even though Mother brought a couple of bottles of wine that she and Helen and Lee drank from Molly's jelly glasses.

At the Thanksgiving potluck dinner, we talked about a couple of students in Lee's classes at school, about the way their own two boys were outgrowing everything, about the creamed potatoes Molly fixed, the chestnuts Helen had put in the dressing. We talked about nothing that really counted. After dinner, Molly scraped half a dozen uneaten cinnamon rolls from the pan, put them in plastic. "For your boys," she told Helen.

Helen objected that they shouldn't eat so many sweets. "Their teeth," she said, "cavities."

But Molly insisted. "Just once," she said.

"But what about you?" Helen said.

"We have another pan at home," Molly said, with some pride. I had my doubts Helen would let her boys eat any of the rolls Molly left.

By the time we left for home, the only thing remaining of the food we'd brought was a serving or two of pineapple-and-whipped-cream salad—Molly's yum-yum salad. I had managed to put the Tupperware bowl with the yum-yum salad under the old army blanket in the back of Molly's car.

Before I took the Lamb Weston job, Molly had begun mentioning food was missing from the fridge. She'd gotten up from the table to get some jam from the icebox, had poked around the shelves on the door, then inside where she kept the milk and the cheese and the lumps of things she wrapped in tinfoil. Finally she came back to the table. "What happened to the jam?" My stomach had gripped tight; I'd taken the jam to Jackie. I hadn't formulated an answer before Edie spoke up. "I get hungry sometimes," she said, "at night."

It sufficed to put Molly's suspicions away and she sat down, pleased. "I don't understand where you put all that food." And she smiled as if she had done something good in marrying a man who could produce a daughter who could eat so much and stay so slim.

Thanksgiving afternoon, as Edie and Molly took the Tupperware and washed dishes into the house, I waited outside, transferred the salad from Molly's car to my truck. I hid it behind the seat. I went back the house, leaned in the back door. "I'm going to go check on Tammy." Tammy was one of our heifers and that year she was due to calve out of season. I planned to use her as an excuse to get away to check on Jackie.

Edie peeked around the corner of the kitchen. "Can I come?"

"Sure."

Edie scuffed out of the house still wearing the limp dress she'd worn for dinner at Helen and Lee's.

As if remembering times past, when Edie and I used to make checking the cows a regular habit, she climbed into the driver's seat of the pickup. I opened the gate into the pasture. Edie drove through. We bumped down the rutted lane, Edie holding the wheel with both hands. She sat forward, on the edge of the seat, her

JEANNIE BURT

face puckered in concentration. At the end of the lane, she stopped, turned off the motor. Our whole herd, the three milk cows, fifteen whiteface cows, and a bull were strewn out at the north end of the pasture. All of them looked up as if wondering why we were sitting there in their pasture. I was so hopeful when she first asked to come with me, but as we went, her silence made me think coming along was only an excuse to get away from her mother.

We got out. As we stood watching, the cows went back to cropping bits of grass left from summer. Side by side, my daughter and I stood there, the bull rubbing his chin on the barbs of the fence, slicking his nose with his tongue. Tammy was lying in the middle of the pasture chewing her cud, her huge gut with the calf in it rolled high and full. How many years had it been since Edie and I had come out to the pasture to "check on the cattle?" It had once been our code to slip away and sit together in the pickup and talk about whatever came up—Bethany's snubbing Edie at school, or how much Edie hated arithmetic, or how a bull made a cow pregnant, news about things she did with Patty. It seemed like forever ago.

Edie followed me down the rutted path toward Tammy. As we got nearer, the heifer grunted, pulled herself and her heavy gut up. She stretched a small stretch as Edie and I came to her, mumbling in our versions of cow language. The heifer was small, and we were going to have to watch her. A small, first-time cow often had troubles at calving time. "She due?" Edie said, her voice clipped, dull.

Tammy stepped one step away before Edie laid her hand on the head of her tail and started scratching. It was the magic spot, the one place that could put a cow into cow ecstasy. As Edie's fingernails worked up and over the crest of Tammy's tail, the heifer started to moan. "What if she has trouble?" Edie said. Tammy's tail lifted, her eyes went white all around, blissful and unfocused. "What if you're not home when her calf comes?"

The heifer's tail came up higher, her head curved around and her behind began wagging side to side, in a cow's foolish dance. Edie

174

smiled a faint smile, as her fingernails loaded up with grime. Faint as it was, it was a smile, and for a moment I held onto the feeling my daughter had not grown so dark, so pinched and old, so hopeless.

I made an effort to look like I was inspecting the heifer, ran my hand along the tight skin of her stomach, poked gently here and there like I knew what I was doing. There was nothing wrong with the heifer. I didn't think there would be.

"I think she looks OK," I said. "I guess it was my imagination she might have trouble." I set my hand on my daughter's shoulder. She pulled away from me, and I wanted to put my arm around her and hold her like I used to. It seemed like I was lost to her anymore, lost, gone, dead. We stood there, still wearing our good Thanksgiving clothes, me in my jacket and wedding slacks, her in her dull, covered-up dress. There was manure on her shoes, the first shoes Molly had allowed her to wear that had heels. Pumps. The wind blew Edie's dress against her legs. She started to shiver. I opened my jacket, nodded for her to come in and be warm, but she grabbed her arms around herself and turned away.

THE YUM-YUM SALAD bumped around behind the seat as I turned the corner into Philpott. The three streetlights flickered on over Main Street. As town manager, Rusty Cousins saw to it the lights went on minutes before dark, no matter the weather, no matter the season.

I'd never been into Philpott on a Thanksgiving afternoon. A small town had its own pace, its own way of beating out its rhythm. It was still now, totally bare of movement, nobody coming out of the post office, no slap of the screen door at Haymire's, no car, no truck, no*body* anywhere. Here and there a light shone through a house window. Campbell's Oldsmobile was parked in front of his house, but the town was dead, strange, clamped shut.

I checked for the purple truck, slipped my own pickup in the space where it would have been. The two windows in the apartment over the Masonic Hall were dark. They seemed to stare out on the street as sightless as two blind eyes. I pried the Tupperware bowl from behind the seat, I wished I'd been able to find something more, a wing from the turkey, maybe, or a piece of pie, or something red, but there hadn't been a chance.

It had been a week since I was there last. The stairs were buried in shadows so dark I couldn't see. Even the streetlight couldn't keep the dark away. I pulled myself up the steps, holding the bowl with one hand, fingering my way up the wall. It hit me: what would become of Edie and Molly if something happened to me, like it had to Larry? What would they do? God. But thinking it, I knew Molly would take care of things, Molly would see to everything like she'd always done. Edie would be all right, just like she was at that moment, her mother taking care of her.

I put my ear on the door. I couldn't hear anything, not a sound. I gave the door a knock and waited, looking down the steps at the curb, expecting headlights.

"Jackie?" I said, "It's Jack."

I shifted the salad, waited another couple of minutes. Finally I turned the doorknob. The door creaked, then ground open. The room was lit only by the streetlight through the window, a haunted highlighting of the shapes of the couch, the table lamp without a table, the scatter of trash on the floor.

"Jackie?"

Every time I had come, Jackie had been sitting in that one spot at the kitchen table. But she wasn't there, the table was empty.

I slipped farther into the apartment. It was as cold inside as it was outside in the wind. For about one breath I let myself believe that maybe Jackie wasn't there, maybe she was gone. Maybe her family in Kansas had all of a sudden shown up to care for her. Her parents had moved away not long after we'd finished high school, and as far as I knew, they'd never been back. Until maybe now.

I patted the wall for the light switch, flipped it up. Nothing. I felt my way into the kitchen, tried another light. It stayed dark. Off the kitchen was a hallway. I knew from Patty's note that the bedrooms were down the hall and Patty's was way in the back. The hall was totally dark, even the streetlight didn't make it there. I felt my way, patting the walls for a door. Finally I came to a jamb, felt along for the knob. The only sound I could hear was the blood pumping through my ears. What would I do if Murcheson came home and caught me in there? I considered it. Would I face him in his own house or leap out the window out onto the shed in back, like Patty did? Surely he'd know it was me up there. My truck was parked in his space at the curb.

The door began to swing open and with it came a terrible stench, rancid as dog's breath. The streetlight showed onto a bed rumpled with bedding. It was a moment before I could make out that someone was in the bed, lying still, not moving, not turning over, not looking up. I patted the wall, found the switch, but the switch was already on.

"Jackie?" I was afraid to go to whoever was lying there in the shadows, afraid to find her dead. I backed up and patted my way back through the apartment, ran down the stairs to my truck, still holding onto Molly's yum-yum salad. I wanted light. A flashlight had been rattling around under the seat for ten years, along with tire chains, ropes, tire irons, screwdrivers, and an assortment of wrenches.

The flashlight was stuck under an arm of the tire iron. I pried it out, carried it back up the stairs, praying it still worked. I thumped into the apartment. I'd seen death before, had seen the carcasses of calves that coyotes had taken down in the night, had seen the popped-eye skull of Dad's shepherd, Boots, after Lee ran over her with the duals of a wheat truck; I'd seen Grandpa and Grandma and Dad in their caskets, the skin of their faces settled smooth, peaceful. But I'd never seen death I felt accountable for.

I toed myself through the door. God, the smell.

"Jackie?" I didn't expect an answer. Then, in the quiet, there came the faintest rustle of covers.

"Jackie?" I said again. "It's Jack." I stepped through the door.

I could see the faint outline of shoulders, a head, the thin neck. I stood there, wondering what I was going to do next. "Jackie?"

"Jack," she said.

I tiptoed closer. "I went and got a flashlight."

She took a breath, phlegm rattling in her throat. She coughed, swallowed something that came up from her cough. "Do you have a cigarette?" she said. Her voice was brought up from the same deep place in her chest she'd brought up the phlegm. She grabbed my arm and pulled herself out of the bed. Her fingers were stiff and sharp. Holding her hand was like taking hold of a bunch of drinking straws. Every move she made brought up more of the smell that was on her, a smell like a sump needing bleach. With the flashlight, I could see there wasn't anything of Murcheson's around, no clothes, no boots, nothing but a scatter of reeking clothes on the floor, more flung over the foot of the bed. There was nothing but the bed in the room, everything bare, no dresser, no bureau, no bedside tables.

"Cigarettes?" she said.

"I brought something to eat," I answered.

She shivered.

"You cold?" I said.

She didn't answer. I held onto her hand as she pulled her robe tighter around her waist. "Here," I said, "let me tie it."

"Thirsty," she said.

"I'll get you some water." I was relieved to have something to do. I started to leave, to walk out to the kitchen and leave her standing there in the light by her bed. Then realized I should do something with her. "Why don't you come on out to the kitchen while I get you a glass of water," I said.

She followed along after me like Inkie, our dog, would when he followed the cows in for chores. The kitchen floor was littered. I stepped on something glass, a plate maybe, that crushed under my shoes. I swept the glass away with my foot, cleared a path to the place Jackie had been sitting the times I'd been there before. Something alive and furry brushed against my foot. I jumped. "Jesus," I said.

Jackie took her place at the table. I made my way to the sink. The counters, the sink, the stove were all totally dark. I felt through the dry clutter inside the sink, found a glass that was crusty with something. I turned on the faucet. Nothing, not even a drip, ran from it.

"I want a cigarette," Jackie said.

Looking back, I didn't know why her asking for a cigarette made me angry. "Jackie," I yelled, "I . . . don't . . . have . . ."

And I could see her shrivel into herself.

"I'm sorry," I said. "Stay right there." I started out the door. For years, a canteen had hung from the front grill of my truck. I couldn't remember the last time I'd filled it, but it was years ago. I didn't know if there would be anything left in it. The canteen had lodged in a crack behind the bumper. I worked it free, heard the slosh of some water inside it. Back in the apartment, I unscrewed the top, then I steadied it as Jackie drank long gulps, her throat making noises like a horse's does when it drinks.

I WIPED MY shoes on the welcome mat. Molly came out from the kitchen, stood with her hands shoved into the sides of her waistline. "Where have you been?" she said.

I cleared my throat, took my eyes off the power of her stance. "Honey," my voice cracked. "We've got to talk."

MOLLY LISTENED, AND as she did, her face twisted in recognition, like a bunch of things she'd been wondering were beginning to settle—the food missing from the refrigerator, the daily trips I'd been making at three o'clock every afternoon with the excuse to pick up the mail.

We were sitting in the kitchen where bits of us always seemed to play out. For some reason I hadn't dropped into my place at the table, but in the chair face to face with my wife.

Molly hovered high on her chair, and as I went on, I took strength from the width of the oak table separating us. The house was quiet except Edie upstairs and for the murmur of the television set in the living room where nobody was watching.

I took in air and spilled out portions of my story. When the story was finally out and sitting there between us, Molly said, "So, I still wouldn't know any of this was going on if you didn't have the job."

I could only look down at my hands. "I would have told you."

"When?" she said. She sat there, her face reddening with what I could only hope was compassion for Jackie's wretchedness.

I leaned back, away, spent as a three-day clock. No matter Molly's reaction, I was relieved to have it said. I'd only held back a little. I hadn't revealed about the night I caught the girls in the barn, nor seeing Kenny, or anything Edie knew about any of it.

"Jackie Pugh is an adulteress," Molly said, her voice low as a dog's growl. I thought she really wanted to spill out "whore."

"Molly," I said.

"How long have you been seeing her?"

"A few weeks," I said.

Molly dropped forward, laid her head in her hands.

"It's not what you think," I said.

She looked up then, the flesh of her cheeks falling forward, crowding her mouth. "She's been living in sin ever since Larry died. Jackie has a history," she squinted, "as you know." The accusation that had been floating silently between us for twelve years began banging around the kitchen walls.

"I've been taking *food* to her," I said.

"She's got Bill Murcheson to take care of her."

"He's gone," I said, and as soon as I'd said it, I knew it was a mistake.

"Oh," Molly said, "so you were alone." She dropped her head into her hands again.

I sat there, remembering Molly's Tupperware bowl. I'd left it at Jackie's.

"Jesus help me," Molly said, "give me strength." She mumbled the words into her hand.

"Nothing's happened," I said, "between Jackie and me."

I put my hand on her arm.

She pulled her arm back. "I wish I could believe you."

It had been twelve years since Molly had uttered Jackie's name, since then only referring to Jackie as "Patty's mother," or simply, "her." It was a dozen years ago Molly and I had hit the rough spot. We were still living in the house we rented from the Hendersons then.

Things happened that year, Edie turned three, Molly and I bought a television and I'd spent a good part of spring putting up a tower for the signal that couldn't make it down the draw to the house without it. Lee was home from OSU for the summer, staying in his old bedroom at Mom and Dad's. Fall term, he'd met someone named Helen and made a rush trip to Astoria to meet her folks before the start of harvest.

The world in those years was either fuller of happenings than ever before, or the television brought the world into our house in a way no magazine or newspaper ever had. Leonid Brezhnev became president of the USSR. Over a couple of years we felt like we knew Jack Kennedy after he debated Richard Nixon, then got elected president, then as we watched the horse pull his hearse when he was shot. We watched Illinois beat Washington 17 to 7 in the Rose Bowl. The night Clark Gable died, Mom called the house in tears because Dad was gone to a meeting at the Masons and she needed somebody to talk to about the tragedy.

That year, harvest had gone pretty well. We still ran on the tradition Molly loved. "Our time," Molly called harvest, "when we're all together," Dad and I taking the two combines, Lee and Molly the trucks. Molly would get up when it was still dark, would fix all of us lunches, make sure the canteens and thermoses were full of iced tea, and would drive all of us out to the fields. Three-year-old Edie would sit in the seat next to her all day as she pulled up for a load of grain, drove to the elevator in town, then back in the field again, to wait for Dad or me to fill her truck with another bulker of grain. Edie would color in the books Molly brought or nap or play on the floorboards with her doll. Sometimes I'd catch Edie leaning against her mother as Molly read stories, in the lulls, and Molly would look up and blow me a kiss before she returned to the pages of the book.

It all went so well that year. Two days before we thought we'd be done, Dad knuckled the racks on one of the trucks and said, "We might get the crop in this year in record time." He should have knocked harder or said nothing at all. The next day, as we were finishing the last half-section, both threshers broke down. The International went first, when the reel sucked up a jack I'd forgotten to take up from a tire change, and then a bearing went out in the Deere. The bearing meant the Deere was out of action until next year, if we could get it to run again at all.

After a couple of hours' working, the three of us together—Dad, Lee, and me—got the International going again. But before Dad got into the Deere to drive it the five miles back to the barn, he said, "You and Lee take it from here." His face was burned brown-red and dry, his eyebrows needed a trim.

Molly climbed up onto the seat of the International beside me. She planted a kiss on my cheek. "Don't worry about chores tonight," she said, "I'll take care of them." Then she headed off behind Dad's Deere, the flag of a red handkerchief flapping as the truck heaved over the furrows.

With Dad and Molly gone, the field felt forsaken, the weight of responsibility hot and prickling on my shoulders. Lee and I ran long into dark. It was nearly nine o'clock when Lee pulled up beside me and I started the auger for the last load of the summer. We finished by the lights of the truck.

Molly was in the kitchen getting Edie a cup of Ovaltine when I shuffled into the house. I passed Edie lying on the couch dressed in her bathrobe. Her face was white, the color of paste. She looked up at me, said in a weak voice, "Hi, Daddy."

"What's wrong with her?" I asked Molly.

"She's got the flu." The pasty color wrapped around Edie's mouth and along her hairline, her cheeks were yellow under the color of her summer tan. She was drawn up, holding her stomach.

While I washed my face and shook the chaff out of my hair, Molly carried Edie upstairs to her bed.

The dinner table was laid out for just the two of us, Edie's high-chair scooted away. As Molly poured me some milk, she said, "Maybe you want something else." I saw then that Molly's face was red and puffy.

I thought she was worried about Edie. "Edie will get well. Kids that age always do."

But Molly's expression stayed dire. She wasn't buying my prediction. She filled my glass only half full of milk. "Maybe you want something stronger," she said.

I had no idea what she was talking about. I always had a glass of milk, milk from our cows. I looked up to her red face. She set the jug on the table and went to the cupboard by the stove. She returned with a bottle, held it out. Smirnoff. And then I tumbled. With me finishing harvest up late, with Molly doing the chores, she'd found the barrel with the Smirnoff in the barn, the barrel I never thought she'd see. I kept three barrels in the barn, one for beet pulp to sweeten feed for the cows, one for the grain I fed them, and another one that didn't have anything in it but bottles. She'd opened the wrong barrel.

"It was Dad's," I'd said.

"Why would your dad keep whiskey in *our* barn?"

JEANNIE BURT

"Vodka," I blurted as if it would make things OK again.

From the door into the room, a little cough stopped us. Together, Molly and I turned, saw our daughter standing there in her nightie.

"Edie," Molly said, "it's time for you to get to bed."

Edie stumbled to her mother, leaned against her Molly's hip. She was holding onto her stomach. "I can't sleep," she said. Edie looked like she was about to throw up. Molly picked her up and stood there with our daughter on her hip.

"I wish you'd tell me the truth, Jack." She was tired, we all were, after the long day. She swung around. Edie's fevered eyes glanced over Molly's shoulder at me. "I have to get her back in her bed."

In a rage at the injustice of Molly's accusations, I flew out of the house. I had never drunk to the point I'd passed out, never had to be driven home by my wife. I wasn't like my dad. Even with Molly's Baptist upbringing, she couldn't accuse me of excess.

I got into the pickup, peeled out of the driveway. The injustice rode with me all the way into Pendleton. It hadn't cooled by the time I went into Cimmyottis' tavern to do the real celebrating I felt I deserved for the end of the season.

Patsy Cline's sad voice was playing on the juke when I walked in. A thousand times later I would wonder how different things would have been if Raunch and Larry and Jackie hadn't been in that tavern that night, but they were. Raunch and Larry were sitting at the bar with Jackie between them. I pulled a stool up beside Raunch, ordered a beer and sat there dowsing self-pity over my harping wife.

Jackie wore a dress with red-and-yellow flowers that fit tight to her narrow ribs and was bare in the back. I wouldn't remember that their daughter, Patty, was staying with her grandmother in Milton-Freewater. I would remember that Patty's grandmother moved to Kansas a couple of years later, and I would recall it was the last year before it became obvious that there was something nobody understood cooking in Jackie's mind.

That night, as the music played Brenda Lee and Chubby Checker, Larry and Jackie danced, then Raunch grabbed Jackie and swung her around. We laughed and I forgot the pit in my gut.

Larry passed out around midnight. He stumbled across the dance floor, dropped himself beside one of the little tables, and started cracking out snores. I ordered another beer. I don't think I could have been held to an accounting of how many beers I'd put down by the time Larry blacked out. Raunch began hustling a woman ten years older who was wearing bright green pants and cowboy boots, and Jackie was getting pied, moving her hips against me, slipping her hand down my thigh.

God, she was beautiful, laughing at my jokes like she used to in school, leaning on my arm with her waving red hair. We were free that night, back in school, neither of us parents, neither of us saddled with life.

For the rest of my life I would remember only clouds of what happened at the end. I woke up at dawn in the backseat of Raunch's car, Larry shaking me awake. Jackie was slumped out cold on top of me, her dress unbuttoned and her underpants wadded on the floor. Larry started pulling her off me. "Get the fuck away from my wife," he shouted through the gap in his front teeth.

That morning, as the sun was beginning to rise, and as the headache drummed in my ears, I drove home. Raunch tried to cover for me with Larry. He came up with how he'd walk-carried Jackie out to the car when she passed out, how her dress must have come loose as he pulled her along and how her underpants must have come down. He told how dark it was when he put Jackie in the back of his car, how he hadn't seen me stretched out drunk and he was real sorry, too, because if he had replaced the damned dome light like he should have when it burned out two weeks ago, he'd have seen me in there and none of this misunderstanding would have happened.

I let Raunch give Molly a version of the same story. He was always a good friend that way. But everything changed afterward.

Molly grew quiet and took up a relationship with her Bible that never let me back into her life the same way again.

The ghost of the old Jackie shimmered in our kitchen as Molly and I sat across from each other at the table. I heard Edie opening, closing her door, then the door snap shut in the bathroom. Pretty soon she'd be changed out of her Thanksgiving dress and she'd come down wearing jeans and the faded brown sweatshirt that made her look top-heavy over her spindly legs, like a Tootsie Pop.

Molly's head was still laid on her arms. She started rolling it slowly back and forth. The vertebrae popped in her neck. Mention of Jackie was bringing everything up again.

"Molly," I said, and let the rest of it lie there. I never knew for certain what Molly really knew about that night after harvest years ago, but I lost her then. I lost Larry, too, that night. He barely ever spoke to me again.

I could hear the thump of Edie's feet in her stretched-out bedroom slippers coming down the stairs. I leaned toward Molly. "Jackie's not getting enough to eat," I whispered. "She's almost dead."

Molly looked up from her hands, straight at me like she was assessing if I was telling another lie. I had to offer up some kind of proof. "I took her the leftover yum-yum salad." I could see the recognition in her eyes that she hadn't accounted for the Tupperware bowl when we got back from Helen and Lee's. I could see her relax a little. "There's nobody to take care of her since Patty ran away," I said.

The upstairs steps were crackling under Edie's slippers. Molly's face grew dark again. "Does Edie know about this?" she mouthed.

I shook my head. It was not a lie, really, Edie didn't know everything. I was sure Edie hadn't mentioned any of the last few weeks to her mother.

"How do you know Patty's not just skipping school again and is just going to show up? You know how she is," Molly said fast.

She had a point. I had to come up with something. I'd never been quick enough for Molly. I couldn't tell her about the note, I couldn't even tell Edie about it. "I talked to Kenny," I said.

"Muffin?" She rose up out of her chair. "You saw Kenny Muffin?" she shout-whispered. Though she'd let Patty back into our lives, she'd still outlawed Kenny. "*He* caused all the trouble."

"He told me Patty's gone. Disappeared."

Edie appeared in the doorway, her eyes searching me.

Molly said out loud, "It's the will of the Lord that Patty be punished for her sins."

The conversation went no further. Molly stood up and I followed after her into the livingroom. I wondered how much Edie had heard.

Edie was draped on the front couch, her leg slung over the arm, her finger in her mouth, chewing at a fingernail that had already been chewed to the quick.

Molly took her thick wool coat from the hall tree. "Your father and I," she said, "are going into town to check on Jackie Pugh."

Edie's eyes widened, then shifted to me. Her eyes jittered back and forth across my face, like she was searching me for answers. Finally she looked back at her mother. "Can I go?" she said, her voice weak, pleading.

"No," Molly said. *Barney Miller* was on the television. "We won't be long," she added.

Before we left the house, Molly's face was set as if she had made some kind of decision that I knew must have come from so many years with her Bible, not quite acceptance, not quite forgiving, more like a turning of the other cheek. And she placed four phone calls—to Mildred Coxen, Rena Olmstead, May Rae Birnbaum, and Sissy Misczek, the women of the First Christian Fellowship Ladies' Aid.

chapter 27

I HAD TO be in Hermiston before dawn on Monday morning. The weather had changed for the worse since Thanksgiving. The wind between Pendleton and Hermiston on I-84 where it runs along the Columbia River posed a challenge when I deadheaded back with the truck empty. *Deadheading.* There was a term I'd learned on the job. I was learning a lot of terms I'd never even heard before this job: *paid overtime, swing shift, grievance,* words you never hear in relationship to work on a farm. *Deadheading* meant the empty truck was so light, the wind did what it wanted with it. It meant it wrenched you one way and another. It meant you needed to watch the road, pay attention to where the truck took you because you had nothing to hold you down.

The cannery job was taking over my life. Five nights a week I would be on the road, get someplace then wait, standing around while the grunt-labor end of the union people emptied my load and loaded me up again with whatever was supposed to go out the next day if there was anything. My shift ended in Washington on Fridays, the farthest point in the whole route from home.

A week before Christmas, the weather went tropical and warm somewhere in the upper skies but stayed frozen on the ground and we had our first silver thaw in a decade. The roads were, as Raunch put it, slick as snot. He and I were getting together every Thursday after work. His job took him to Hermiston two times a week. Thus, Thursdays were "Hermiston" days for both of us. We'd have a steak in town, then go to the Lotsa Luck and watch basketball on the TV hung high over the bar while we threw back a few beers.

Ice had closed down the plant for almost two days, and ice had closed down truck traffic on I-84 until the wind died down some. I had to hole up in the motel in Hermiston for an extra night.

I found out Raunch hated Lyle nearly as much as I did, though he worked for Jim Renfrew in the flash-freeze department. "Whitty's a jerk," Raunch said one night in the middle of December as we sat at the bar. Bart, a guy in his seventies, ran the tavern. Over the weeks, I'd gotten to know him a little. He'd owned the tavern since he came home from the First World War.

Five of us were taking up room at the bar, drinking, watching the television, talking now and then. The Trail Blazers were winning. Bill Walton was carrying the team to a record that was sweeping up the whole state, pulling us all together with its wins. That night they were playing Sacramento.

Bart had turned the volume down a little at the start of halftime. He looked at Raunch and me, held up two fingers in a question. Raunch nodded yes. Bart clinked another pitcher under the Oly tap, bled out the head like Raunch liked it.

"Whitty's jerking you around," Raunch said. Raunch took the glass up, let it swing between his fingers. "Jerking you around, *big time*, Mack," he said.

"Yeah," I said.

"Whitty never jerked Stan's route around the way he's doing now that you're on it," he said.

I shrugged. Bart set the pitcher on the bar between us.

Raunch swung his face my way. "Don't that bother you?"

I shrugged again. "Yeah," I said. Stan Jenson was scheduled to be back from medical leave in a couple of months. I'd had the job nearly a month. I was beginning to mark the days until the doctors released Stan to come back to work and, in the same breath, I was beginning to resent that he would take my job out from under me. When the job went away, there wouldn't be any more nights like this leaning over the bar at the Lotsa Luck, no more days where I could leave the worry, the bills, the house, the responsibility of home to Molly, no more weeks of leaving the care of the cows, the pigs, the rooster, and hens up to my daughter. And no more turning away from whatever happened to Patty Pugh. There was a day or two, since I'd been gone, I hadn't thought of her. But she laid there in the background like a tune you couldn't get out of your mind.

I-84 was closed another day because of ice. I passed two whole days cooped up at the Bluebell Motel watching the *Partridge Family* and *Welcome Back, Kotter*. It looked like it would be another night; ice covered the parking lot, the street, it rolled down the sidewalks, smoothed out the curbs, rippled down the stop sign across the street. The only business that managed to open its doors was the Quick Stop grocery on Ridgeway. I'd slipped the two blocks to the grocer to buy a *Playboy* and a *True Detective* magazine. I read them both the first night.

I was stretched out on the bed watching Walter Cronkite through the gap between my boots. The motel phone jangled, startled me stupid.

"Ciao, Jack," Mom said. It was five thirty and pitch dark outside. I'd pulled the curtains shut two hours ago when the skies had grown dark as oil.

"Chow?" I said.

"Buon soir," she said.

I pulled myself up, leaned against the headboard. "Mom," I said.

"Hi, sweetie." She sounded sleepy.

"When did you get home?" I said.

"A couple of hours ago." She yawned. "It's three thirty in the morning in Paris," she said.

I heard her shuffle the telephone from one ear to the other. "Molly said you have a job," she said. There was the clink of ice in a glass. I pictured her sitting in her warm living room having a toddy. I wished I was there.

I wadded the pillow behind me. "Well, how's the world traveler?" I said.

"She wants to turn right around and go back," she said.

"So, did you find the hunk of lust you and Ethel were looking for over there among all those Eye-talians?" It was dull, I knew, but the best I could do for something light.

"I'll never tell," she said, flirty. Then she said, "How are you and Molly getting along?"

I stood, went to the TV, and snapped off the news. "Oh . . . ," I said.

"Oh, what, honey?" she said.

"Pretty good, I guess," I said.

"Edie?" she asked.

"She's running the place now," I said, and saying it made me feel how useless I was at home.

I heard her take another drink and shake the ice down in the glass. "Jack," she said. Her tone was low, like she meant business. "How are things? Really?"

She had done this ever since Lee and I were little, put her voice low, asked questions we didn't want to think about, let alone answer, yet put in such a way that we confessed. "Could be better," I said.

192

"I see," she said. Then, without even a pause to acknowledge she thought anything more about it, she said, "Stay warm, honey. Kiss Molly for me when you see her. I'll see you soon for Christmas. God," she said, "I can't believe we're already into Christmas."

TWO DAYS BEFORE Christmas, the wind died, the highway crews sanded I-84 and traffic started to move. I followed a string of semis into Pendleton. Just after noon I pulled off at the exit to City Center. It was not a stop Whitty would have scheduled. I parked in a spot in front of the long steps that led up and into the offices of the Pendleton police station.

Santa Claus banners fluttered from the light poles. Store windows were lit with electric candles and snowmen, and blinking Christmas lights. Molly would say Christmas was the time to celebrate the Savior's birth and our salvation through the blood of Jesus. But to me Christmas had always been a time to back your daughter up to the grow door and make that year's mark over her head. It was a time to chain up one of the trucks, take your wife and your kid and her friend bumping up Strickland Road into the Blue Mountains to cut a long-needled pine to put in the living room window. That was Christmas. For me that was all I'd ever wanted or believed Christmas to be. Only this year there would be no time for any trip into the mountains to choose our long-needled pine. And there would be no time to see how much Edie had grown.

The only experience I'd had with police was tickets, tickets when I'd got caught speeding, a ticket a couple of years ago when they'd nabbed me for hauling a disc without a warning flag. I did have a red flag, when I started out, but by the time I was stopped, it had blown off. The officer didn't seem to appreciate my excuse. It cost fifty-two bucks. And there I was, sitting in front of the police station, feeling the weight of being seen in the truck with Lamb Weston written all over it, wondering if stopping was worth the chance of being caught doing personal business in a company truck.

Tomorrow was Christmas Eve day. I hadn't been home for over a week. I could have been on my way home, on my way to wrapping up the sheep's leather slippers I got for Molly and the portable radio I bought for Edie. Christmas Eve would be the only time we'd have together. Sunday, when Christmas came, there would be the fracas of Lee and Helen and their kids at the house, and of Mother showing her pictures from the trip, the noise of carols on the radio, the opening of more presents, Molly's tight thank-yous over the impractical doodads from Mom and Helen.

I wasn't eager for it. It was like I was growing further and further away from all of it, the farm, the barn, Molly even. The history I'd always thought was in my blood had thinned and flowed away to some horizon more distant every day. The one draw that tied my gut into the biggest knot of all was the thought of my daughter. That thought squeezed like a vice grip against my ribs. What if, God, what if it wasn't Patty at all who was gone but it was *Edie*?

I opened the truck's door, stepped out into the blast of wind, and began the trek up the station steps.

It was getting near dark. Inside the station, two posts stained dark and cut thick as tree trunks bracketed a stairway that sliced the lobby in half. To the right were doors labeled Chief and Prosecutor. To the left, a pair of glass doors let into a reception counter and beyond that to open desks.

A woman about thirty years old—a clerk, I thought—was shrugging into her coat, picking up a poinsettia wrapped in wrinkled Christmas paper, and saying, "Thank you" to a younger woman standing at a bank of file drawers. She grasped the poinsettia in one arm and looped her purse strap over her shoulder. As I held the door open, she came out, then turned around, and said back into the office, "Merry Christmas, everybody. See you next year."

The place had the feel of people wanting to leave, wanting to get home to start the holidays. Most of the desks behind the reception counter were empty. There was only one coat on the coat rack.

The station smelled like floor wax and papers. I stood at the desk while a girl not much into her twenties, and probably having to be the one to stay until closing because of seniority, stood with her back to me, fingering through a file drawer. She was chewing gum. The hoops of her earrings flickered every time she chewed. She snapped the gum so loud it sounded like a shot. I almost jumped. A couple of officers in uniform were sitting at desks farther into the office. A policeman in uniform always made me want to comb back my hair and have a fresh shave and clean clothes. I needed a shave and was wearing jeans and a shirt I'd worn for three days that was getting so gamey I pulled in my arms.

I made a little cough back in my throat to get her attention. The girl kept on fingering the file drawer. She was dressed in a short, tight skirt like the waitress at the Lotsa Luck in Hermiston. She wore her hair long and kept swinging it back over her shoulder. She must have been standing at the file for a while, because she was barefoot, and a pair of high-heeled shoes were lying beside her feet. She snapped her gum once more, shoved the file drawer closed, and twisted her feet back into her shoes. She pulled down her skirt, which was about a foot above her knees. The shortness of it would have sent Molly to clearing her throat. She clicked over to where I was standing. "Can I help you?" she said.

"I'd like to check on someone missing," I said.

She made a bubble with her gum, sucked it back into her mouth. "Who?"

"Patty . . . Patricia Jacqueline Pugh."

"Birthdate?" She took out a piece of scrap paper, started to jot on it.

"June, uh," It was always Molly who remembered these things, anniversaries, birthdays, the day Easter came year to year, when to call for appointments with Edie's orthodontist. "I think June," I said.

"How old is she?" she said.

"Fifteen," I said, "now."

"When?"

"When?" I repeated.

"When would the report have been filed?" She started to tick her fingernails on the counter.

Maybe the school called the police when Patty first went missing. Maybe Murcheson reported that she had stolen his rifle. "The end of October," I said, "probably."

The young woman turned, tapped away to another section of files. She pulled out one drawer, took a few minutes looking through it, closed it and went to another drawer. This was taking longer than I thought it would. I was supposed to be on the road to return the truck to the plant in less than half an hour. Even after spending three days at the motel in Hermiston, I didn't know what I was hauling and I knew Lyle Whitty would probably be pissed because the storm screwed up his schedule.

Finally the girl came back. She licked two fingers, took the gum out of her mouth, and threw it into a waste basket behind the counter. "There's nothing on a Patricia Jacqueline Pugh. Do you want to file a report?"

No one had reported Patty missing? I felt like somebody was holding my head underwater, that I'd never be able to take another breath. I thought the clerk must be mistaken, that the teachers in school, or the principal, or even one of Molly's church women surely would have called and reported Patty gone. After all, the LA had taken over everything else, cleaning Jackie's apartment, cooking, ministering to Jackie with the vengeance of good Samaritans. The ladies had stocked the cupboards with peaches and tomatoes they'd canned from summer and brought her bread they baked every day, and roasts they roasted. They had gone into Jackie's apartment with buckets and ammonia and bleach. They'd held the biggest bake sale in the history of the church, and with the proceeds, they had paid to have Jackie's lights and water turned back on. They'd even persuaded the Masons to donate the space for Jackie to live. Jackie had become their project, their Christian goodness. Why hadn't they thought about Patty?

Why hadn't I?

"Could you check one more time?" I said. She shook her head, sent her earrings flailing. There was no file on Patricia Jacqueline Pugh.

OFFICER AL TOOK me back to his desk. He was one of the Als from the reservation. Dad used to know Clarence Al, from when Dad rented pastureland from Clarence years before. Officer Al had crow-black hair and an Indian's wide chest. He was younger than I was by ten years.

He pointed for me to sit down in the chair beside the desk. I tucked my feet under the chair. He got out an empty form from one of the drawers, plopped it on his desk. The Als lived near Mission, a town the size of Philpott in the canyons east of Pendleton. He patted some of the papers, finally picked up a pen, made a whirl with it on a scratch pad. He took down Patty's whole name, her birthday, which I'd finally remembered, and then sat there writing while I told him a little about Larry and Jackie.

"What's your relationship with Miss Pugh?" he finally said. His voice was so soft, I had to lean into him to hear. In the Indian custom, he didn't look me in the face but down and away, a sign of respect for my privacy. Kenny did this, too, and Elsie Standinghorse.

"I'm a friend," I said. "I know her mother."

"Do you have a relationship with her or her mother?" And for a second he looked up at me straight on with his two black eyes.

"I guess so," I said. "Yes, you could say that."

Something about what I'd said made him sit back in his chair, his manner changed. He wasn't humble, courteous, looking away

197

now but squint-eyed, head tilted back looking at me straight on. I didn't have any idea what had happened. "You have a relationship with the girl?"

"I did."

"But you don't *now?*" His mouth pulled in.

"No, not since she disappeared." I wanted to cover myself up from the intensity of his black-eyed stare. The skin at the back of my neck began to go squirrelly, like I had done something wrong. I had an urge to get back into my truck and race home.

"Who else knows the girl's gone?" he said.

I thought about who might know. "Everybody, pretty much, I guess."

"Her mother knows?"

"I'm not sure," I said.

"Not sure?" he repeated. "So Patricia Pugh's mother doesn't know her daughter's gone, but *you* know," he threw up his hands. "She told you she was going and then she ran away."

"No." I swallowed and sat there with my heels whapping together under my chair. Finally I thought to show him Patty's note. I pulled out my wallet, unfolded the tablet paper. "I found this." I scooted it toward him over the desk. I had read it so many times holes had worn in the creases. I sat there while he read it.

"Who's E?" he said.

"My daughter."

"It says, 'Don't let the son of a bitch get his hands on you.' What does that mean to you?"

Was I supposed to give him Bill Murcheson's name? Officer Al sat there quiet, not blinking, not looking away, like for some reason he was letting me stew. It appeared he was looking for me to say something, but I didn't know what. I couldn't tell him what I thought Murcheson was doing to Patty because I'd barely been able to think of it myself.

Finally he laid the note down, flattened it on his desk. As uncomfortable as I was, I was relieved that someone else had read what was on it.

"Who else knows Patricia Pugh is gone?"

"The school," I said.

"Why didn't they report this?"

"Patty has been gone from school before."

"Skipped?"

I nodded. "My wife," I said, and I lost what else I was going to say.

He started to slowly shake his head.

"My daughter is—was—friends with Patricia Pugh," I said. Officer Al held himself stiff. I had an urge to blurt anything to make whatever was wrong right again. "My wife and I are friends with her mother."

Officer Al's face loosened up a little. "You have not been in a relationship with Miss Pugh?"

"Yes," I said, "I *have* been in a relationship with her. I've known her since, well, since before she was born."

And Officer Al started to laugh, and he shook his head. Then it hit me what he'd been thinking, and I wanted to throw up.

"So," he said.

"So," I interrupted, "it's not funny. She's disappeared and I want to know what happened to her."

He clamped down on his laugh but I could see, in the shine of his eyes, how stupid and naïve he thought I really was, and it felt a hell of a lot better having him think I was stupid than what he had been thinking.

chapter 28

I PULLED INTO the drive before chore time. It was dusk already, and the lights in the house broke the gloom like signs on a dark highway. Officer Al said he would put out word on Patty, but that was the best he could do. The kitchen window was steamed up, Molly's smeared image moving back and forth from the sink to the counter. It was intimate seeing her there and her not seeing me. I stayed in the truck awhile and just watched the warmth of my wife in her kitchen.

I went inside, kissed her on top of the head, smelled her shampoo. Her hands were powdered with flour from the breadboard where she'd rolled out dough in a fleshy stretch to be cut for biscuits. She turned, holding her hands up high, and clamped me in with her elbows. I sank into the damp warmth of her. "Edie's out doing chores," she said, and she resumed cutting dough rounds with an old jelly glass.

I went out to the barn, took up a stool, and squatted on it beside High Pockets. But High Pockets' bag was loose, flaccid. Edie was done with her and had already progressed to Henrietta. The radio was on, playing "A Horse with No Name," a tune Molly would have objected to, not for any reason she could name, but that it was about something that the Bible was surely against. Neither Edie nor I spoke, but we went on with the milking as though it had not been days since we'd seen each other. And when the milking was done and the cows had clomped out, Edie got the shovel and scooped up a pile Henrietta had left.

She had grown the past couple of months, her shoulders wider, her arms shaped with muscles, even under the sleeves of her barn coat. She was getting a young woman's shape in her hips. Her middle was small, nipped in like a wasp's, like her grandmother's, her legs long and thick at the calves like mine. She was still thin but no longer what anyone would call skinny.

Edie had carved out her own order to chores while I'd been gone. The hogs lined up at the pen fence and waited for my daughter— not me—to feed them. They grunted for her attention as she took out a bale of hay and heaved it over the hayrack for the Hereford bull and the twelve beef cows we still had. The bull and the cows hummed as Edie forked in sheets of dried alfalfa, and she dodged their horns as they turned their heads toward her when their turns came. When she had thrown the last of the hay, she patted the bull's head, leaned out of the rack, done. "You can take the milk in for separating, Dad," she said to me.

I saluted and she squeezed out a smile. I took the buckets into the house as she closed up the barn for the night.

CHRISTMAS MORNING, IT was quiet in the barn. It should have felt like home, but the sense that I was a stranger hung around the pens and hovered over the mangers. Even the cows eyed me sideways as I milked. The barn seemed like it was no longer *mine,* like it was no longer part of my life. Working for the cannery was getting to be my routine any more, the solitary hours in the truck, the nights sleeping solo at motels, the Thursday nights meeting Raunch at the Lotsa Luck, beginning to count on the two of us sitting there, drinking our beers with no one to account for, watching Blazer basketball. The freedom.

There was something uncluttered about the way Raunch lived in a rented house in Pendleton, his kids living with his first wife in Idaho. He had sold the Datsun and was driving a new Ford truck. He came when he wanted, he went when it suited him. Nothing in life tied him down.

Every Friday night, I handed my paychecks over to Molly, but the per diems I kept. I still hadn't told her about the per diems.

MOLLY MANAGED CHRISTMAS in the same competent way she managed the rest of us, and she dealt Edie and me pieces of it with lists she wrote on the backs of envelopes and by ticking duties off on her fingers. Instructions gave the hoo-hah of Christmas a sort of sense.

Molly had gone upstairs to change into the dress she wanted to wear to church that morning, then for the dinner. In the kitchen heat with the turkey cooking, Edie was setting the table for the ten of us. Before Molly went upstairs, she asked me to help her hang the Christmas quilt. I'd missed every other bit of the holidays—missed going for the tree, missed stringing up the lights over the front porch. Molly and Edie had done all of it themselves. A tree stood in the corner of the living room decorated with lights and tinsel. Molly said she bought it from the Boy Scouts in the Safeway parking lot the day before I came home. Hanging the quilt was the one Christmas tradition I'd made it home in time for. I stood there holding one edge of it as Molly thumbed up or down until it was level.

Molly had made the quilt a few years after we moved into the house. Without plan, the quilt had come to symbolize us as a family that included not only Edie but Patty. Molly had cut the pieces to show the image of the Nativity. And Mary, Joseph, and the baby Jesus were clustered together in a place that looked very much like our own barn. There were three cows near our manger, some pigs milling about in a pen, a dog that looked an awful lot like Inkie, and a couple of calico cats. The quilt was six or seven years old now. Each year since, it had hung on the wall at Christmastime.

Patty had been staying with us a lot the year Molly sewed the quilt. The girls were still in grade school. I'd found books at a bookstore in Pendleton to give them. One of the books told the story of a pig named Wilbur and a spider named Charlotte. To the girls, one of the pigs in the quilt looked like the pig in the book.

Now, after all those days on the road, it felt good to be part of the habit of the holidays and I turned myself over to the fracas. I gave every decision over to Molly, I showered and shaved, according to her instructions, I dressed in the new brown sweater she'd knitted for me while I was on the road, and I put on the same brown slacks I'd worn to the interview with Lyle Whitty. When she and Edie got back from services, I'd be on call for last-minute duties, but until then, my time was mine.

I waited until Molly's car disappeared, went outside, got in the pickup and headed into town.

chapter 29

MAYBE IT WAS legend that strung us all together, maybe tradition, or maybe plain routine. Whatever it was, everyone in Philpott hung onto it all the long decades since Ignacious Philpott gave name to the place we lived out our lives. We studied Ignacious in school, wrote English assignments about him, about the way he founded our town, about the way everybody lived in the time of Ignacious Philpott, how they built their houses, what they ate and how they cooked it, how they kept food cool in the summer. And we teased and were teased by his ugly name. The opportunity to misspell Philpott gave people outside our community a great deal of pleasure at times. Now and then somebody would want to change the name of the town, to give where we lived a little more flair, a little more *umph*, and for a while we'd throw around the name Stonebrook, or Waterton, or Fieldstone, anything but Philpott, but it never stuck.

Our history went something like this. Twenty years after the Cayuse tribe wiped out Marcus Whitman, Ignacious Philpott ventured down the draws of Sandhollow in the Oregon Territory. Ignacious liked what he saw, and he ambled on a bit farther and proclaimed the juncture of Spring and Juniper creeks the center of town. And there he staked his claim. It was March when Ignacious first came over the hills. Fresh streams of melt ran through the creeks. He envisioned a populace racing to settle in the beauty of the green canyons. He carved the name *Philpott* on a wood slab and pounded it into the ground, and he hammered up a shack for a trading post on the same spot in front of the store where Haymire keeps the gas pump. And when the trading post was done, Ignacious built on a room for a school and sat back to wait for the rush. Three years later, he left after Millicent, his wife of one year, died from consumption. By then, the town had collected two more homes and Ignacious's schoolroom saw to the teaching of seven students. No one knew what became of Ignacious. He never saw the completion of his dream, was never around to see when farmers began working the hills or to take pride in the tall shiplap church at the end of Main Street that the community built a dozen years after he left. By the time they'd finally put the roof on the church, Philpott boasted thirty-six people.

For a hundred and twenty-five years, the First Christian Fellowship Church sat there, minding the souls of north Umatilla County, its bell clanging every Sunday morning at nine and again at eleven. It had been added to three times over, and the foundation repaired in the late eighteen hundreds, after a siege of termites had eaten a corner of it away.

Decades ago, the hitching posts rotted down to stubs. Curbs and sidewalks replaced the mud walks and the ghosts of horses and wagons that once clattered into town bringing families in for services and socials once a week. Now, through the arched windows bled the same plunk of the upright piano and the same hum of voices singing the doxology. And there, in one of the original pews, sat my wife and daughter singing their greetings to Christmas morning.

I drove into town, past the closed doors of the church, pulled off Main to a place where, when the doors opened, parishioners coming out of the church could not see me.

The Masonic Hall had taken on a whole different feeling since the first time I'd wandered in to check on Jackie. With a new coat of paint, gone was the ugliness of the bare stairway no one cared for. Gone was the bleak feel of poverty. A knee-high potted Christmas tree squatted at the foot of the stairs now, lights on another tree blinked from the upstairs window.

I bumped the pickup into the vacant lot behind the temple where I knew I could stow it out of sight and jounced over the clumps of dried foxtails behind the building. I had, before turning off, taken note of the curb. The purple truck was still gone, just a memory I hoped.

Going there posed more problems than I cared to think about. Jackie was Molly's now. I couldn't say why I needed to see her again, maybe to settle for myself the idea she would be all right. But as I crept up the steps, I began to realize it was Patty I was coming for. I wanted her there in the worst way. I wanted her eyes to snap at me like they used to and I wanted her to come back into our lives, to set the light in my daughter again and for her to fire up the temper in Molly.

I knew what it felt like wanting to disappear. I had spent my whole life disappearing. It was what Jackie and I had in common, the thing I could understand about her. But neither Jackie nor I were Patty. Even in what must have been the worst of it, since Larry died, disappearing didn't seem to be something Patty would do. But where was she?

I tapped the back of my knuckles on Jackie's door, afraid someone might hear a knock three blocks away at the church. On its own, the door swung open.

Jackie was sitting, smoking, at her usual place at the kitchen table. The hair hanging in her face was clean, and her mouth was colored with lipstick the shade of tomato. She was dressed in a sweater I recognized, one Molly had worn years ago. A tooled-leather Western purse sat on the table by Jackie's elbow. She looked up when I came into the room, and she blinked.

The Aid ladies had refurnished the place. Tables, a chair with an afghan sat beside the tree in the window, a sofa, even a footstool. No two pieces of furniture matched. A couple of pieces I recognized from our own attic. The kitchen floor gleamed in the glare of winter sun and the apartment smelled like Pine-Sol. The ruffled curtains were white and ironed stiff as paper. And there was Molly's red and yellow quilt.

"It's Jack," I said.

"I know," she said.

I knew from Molly that Jackie refused to leave the apartment. She had not been out of it at all for four months. I didn't know what her voices told her to keep her there when Murcheson was with her, but I thought she felt safe there now. The Ladies' Aid had seen to that.

A plate sat in front of her, with a half-eaten roast beef sandwich. I scooted out a chair, pulled across the table from her. The photograph of Patty was still on the table, but there was another one as well, one I recognized of Patty and Edie together, both holding piglets in their arms. They were seven or eight years old.

"How are you doing?" I said.

She blinked, took a drag off her cigarette.

"They feeding you enough?" With anyone else, it would have been a joke. The Ladies' Aid always made sure there was food, lots of it, with the least excuse. Jackie sat there still as a stick. "Getting enough to eat?" I said again, not knowing what else to say.

"Fine," she finally said, but her voice was flat, without any kind of feeling at all.

It was then, sitting there grappling for words, that I noticed the book that lay open beside her elbow. It was a child's book with pictures of a train, *The Little Engine That Could.* It was the same book Mom read to Lee and me when we were kids and that Molly had read to the girls when they were little. It brought all the last year up to my throat in a way that made it hard to take a breath.

chapter 30

THE DOCTORS TOLD Stan Jenson he was ready to come back to work. My job was up. By the time Whitty called me in to say he'd be cutting my last paycheck, I knew the routine as if it were mine, and I could have stayed in it forever.

After nearly four months on the road, it was getting harder and harder to face going back home each weekend. The place was leaping downhill now. You would think a farm would stay put during the winter, and it did during the worst of the weather, but come the first hint of a warm day, the first sniff of a shorter night, the seedpod of every weed sprouted, a post of every fence flopped over, the battery in every piece of equipment went stone cold dead. And I'd touched none of it for months.

Molly was beginning to get telephone calls about the Vancycle section we'd listed for sale. The bank was beginning to send letters again, reminding us they couldn't wait forever, as if we needed reminding. It seemed cruel, something to keep us on our toes, telling us time was running out, like we didn't know that already.

Spring was still a way off, but with the promise of it, it seemed our property might look like something worth buying. The realtor called the first week of March, saying she had shown the land to three people. With my job, and with a few days of overtime, Molly had managed to put nearly four thousand dollars in the bank. I had thought we would be rich when I started the job, but I knew we were going to need to spend three times that for fertilizer, seed, hay and feed for the cows, and diesel to run the Cat.

I stopped at the police station my last day on the job. It was a little strange how the station seemed like it had shrunk since the last time I was in it. In fact, it was sort of amazing how all the world seemed like it had become a bigger place since I had been working for Lamb Weston. Now that the job wasn't mine anymore, I wished my world was small again, wished I could go back to when it was still the size of something I understood.

There was a different clerk at the counter when I walked in, smaller, rounder, a woman in her thirties with short, fuzzy brown hair. She wore rubber-soled shoes and slacks that made whipping sounds as she walked.

"I wonder," I said, "if I could speak with Officer Al." I could see him in the back, leaning over another officer in uniform, pointing out something on papers spread out on the desk. I gave the clerk my name.

She checked a schedule posted on a board on the wall. "He's about to go out on patrol."

"I just need a minute."

"I'll tell him," she said.

Officer Al reached out to shake my hand. His hand was broad as mine and his shake firm.

"I came to check," I said, "on whether you have heard anything about Patty, Patricia, Pugh."

He shook his head. "It's not too good, the longer it gets."

"So," I said, "are there any hints?"

"We sent out a bulletin." He shook his head again. "When it's been this long, there's a good chance we'll never hear from her."

"You mean ever ever again?" I said.

He must have had a sense of my panic, for he looked down at his dark hands, cleared his throat.

"What do you think *happened* to her?"

I knew that question was stupid. He was courteous enough not to answer it. "You're not the only one checking on her," he said.

"Who else?" I said. Maybe Molly had called in, maybe the school principal, maybe the four ladies of the Aid had finally come around to it, maybe they had felt it was their Christian duty to check on her. But Molly had not said a word about it and I thought she was still thinking the Lord was punishing Patty for all her sins.

Standing there in front of Officer Al, I felt like someone wanting communion, wanting the blessing of him telling me that it was my wife who had been checking on Patty Pugh.

"Kenny Muffin," he said.

chapter 31

A WEAK LIGHT with no warmth began to edge into the days.
Pigweed, knapweed, thistle, even the first sprouts of morning glory
were taking over the best piece of ground I farmed. I'd turned away
from it, had no plans for planting, or weeding or anything else,
because I didn't feel there was anything I could do about it. It was
like the Vancycle quarter section was already gone, out of my hands.
It felt like death, like I was losing a friend, something precious and
loyal that had taken care of us all those years. I had not gone up
there for months. I couldn't face it, so it lay there dry, helpless, vulnerable to anything, weed or person, that came along.

We had nothing at all in the bank now. The money the job had
brought was already spent on seed, which I couldn't put in yet, until
the weather let up. The crops, I knew, would come up thin, patchy,
starving for fertilizer we couldn't afford. We ate, however, we still
had a few head of cows in the pasture and could butcher, though
I'd sold all the feeder calves. And we still had the pigs, we still had

milk morning and night, though Henrietta's old udder had gone permanently dry, her hormones finally given up. She had not asked for the bull at all that fall. I couldn't make myself tell Molly about the old cow, because I knew Molly would insist we sell the rickety Jersey with the black watery eyes and get what we could from it.

It seemed Molly had seized onto Jackie Pugh. Jackie had become her project. Molly threw herself into her good works, though the other ladies had lost some interest, were begging of more and more, so it was mostly just Molly, now, taking care of Jackie's needs. She kept Jackie fed and the apartment cleaned. It was almost like Jackie became one of the children Molly always wanted, now that Edie wasn't needing her so much anymore.

Edie was spending more and more time in her room. Marybeth Hobbs, one of the four girls in Edie's class, called a couple of times, asking if Edie wanted to stay the night or ride into town to shop. I'd heard Edie drone, "I don't think so," and then shuffle back up the stairs to do whatever she always did alone in her room.

Meanwhile, every morning, I got up and did chores, and while I worked out in the fields, Edie did the evening chores. We still sat at the same table noon and night, we still watched the same TV shows, Molly still worked with Edie on her homework, but to me it seemed like that hailstorm, and the rift between us over Patty, had broken our family to pieces.

Molly was planting seed starts for her biggest garden ever. She had managed to lose some weight. One day, while she was fixing dinner, she threw out her hands and displayed herself. "Haven't you noticed, Jack?" She turned around, the caftan's sleeves draping like angels' wings. "I'm losing weight."

I scrambled for something to say. "I was going to say that." And it wasn't a lie, maybe she did look a little smaller.

She came over to the table, smacked me on the cheek. "It's the answer to my prayers."

chapter 32

IT WAS WEEKS since I had been into the police station, and I did
not have time right then, although I could not stop worrying. I
worked by myself in the shop, robbing parts from one machine to
use on another, hoping a valve would hold or a bearing wouldn't
give out. I had to shove away thoughts about how it had been this
time last year when the seeds were beginning to pucker the soil and
to send tender white shoots up looking for sun, and they had been
feeding on the chemical buffet I'd spread for them, fertilizer I'd
foregone this year.

The bull was scheduled to go to auction in a week. The rest, three
hogs and a half dozen steers, would also go into town with the bull,
and we'd be down to the three milk cows and two hogs. Bit by
bit, we were chipping away, selling whatever we could do without.
Sometime soon, I knew, there would be nothing left to chip. Molly
and I were sending whatever money we could to the bank. One

month it was $22.59. Every few days I drove into Pendleton to sell cream to the creamery. And I'd keep feeding dried up old Henrietta, because I couldn't make myself live with her stall being bare. It would happen some day on its own, but that was some day, not now. I was hoping against hope that something—weather, prices, even Molly's connection to Jesus—would pull us out.

Edie had started to sprout in ways that made me uncomfortable. Molly had bought her her first bra and had announced it at dinner one night. Edie's face had turned the color of one of Molly's tomatoes. "Mo-o-o-m," she whispered.

That night Edie stayed over with Marybeth Hobbs. It was Molly who'd arranged it. I was beginning to think that if chores or mealtimes or Bible studies or school didn't force her, Edie would never leave her room and one day her mother or I would open the door and see just the dust of what had once been our daughter.

It worried me, all these changes in Edie. It was awful. Marybeth was new to town. The Hobbses had lived in Philpott only a few months, moving into town when Fred, Marybeth's dad, took the principal's job at the high school, after Mr. Norton took a job in Portland. The Hobbses were Episcopalian, and I figured Molly would have trouble swallowing that. But because Edie didn't seem to have anybody else, now that Patty and Kenny were out of her life, Molly made do. To her, Episcopals were suspect for their tolerances of all kinds of things, like playing cards, dancing, and stylish dressing. For so many years, Edie and Patty hadn't needed other girls and had made their own little universe together; I didn't care whether Marybeth went to church or not. I was just thankful Edie might have someone to call friend again.

THE PHONE RANG. It was late, after eleven at night. The house had already given up most of the heat from the day. I knew if I turned on the light, I'd be able to see my breath. Molly was lying on her back in bed, gargling out snores. I had been dozing but hadn't been able to get into real sleep. Over her snores I could barely hear the phone downstairs. If it had not rung so many times, I think I would have missed it.

I sat up, found one slipper, and as the phone kept ringing, I couldn't find the other. Molly did not stir. Barefoot, I stumbled downstairs, picked up the phone. "Hello."

"Jack?" It was a voice I didn't recognize, thick with mucous as if the person had a cold. "It's Kenny." His nose was all stuffed, his throat swollen. "Is Edie there?"

When I didn't say anything right away, he said, "Something has happened."

"Is it about Patty?" I said. "If it is, you can tell me."

"My grandma," he said, and he had to stop talking. I waited a moment while he collected himself, then blew his nose. "My grandma died."

Death always seemed to put things where they belonged. My misery, my crop, the state of my life withered into the background. "I'm sorry," I said. "When did she die?"

"A couple hours ago," he said, sniffing, his voice still thick, hoarse. We let the words lie between us.

"Where is she?" I said finally.

"Back," he was quiet, like for a minute words were taken away from him. "At the house," he finally managed.

"Where are you?"

"I walked to the Olsons." The Olsons lived two miles from Elsie's place. "They have a phone," he said.

"Stay there," I said. "I'll come get you."

"I'm going back to the house. I don't want to leave her alone."

"Wait there. I'll be there in a few minutes." I said, but the phone had gone dead.

I took my clothes downstairs where Molly wouldn't hear me dress and I drove out of our place, not turning on the lights of the truck until I was out of the drive.

THE NIGHT WAS black as tar, the sky clear, the light from the stars cold, blue. It was still, that night, frost sparkled in the headlights. Kenny had not yet reached Elsie's, and his figure drew up in the pickup's lights. His black hair rippled down his back. He turned as I pulled up beside him, opened the door, got into the warmth of the truck. We parked at their place and went in without saying a word.

His face was the color of ash, his eyes hollow but tearless now. He'd laid her out on the narrow kitchen table, covered to the chin with a blanket. It was hot in there, the woodstove crackling. It was like Kenny didn't want her to get cold. We stood silently beside her, the skin of her dark face the color of tanned hide that pooled like cow pies around her ears.

Kenny tugged the blanket tighter under her chin, then dropped himself into a chair, and began to hum a low note that came from someplace deep in his chest.

THE LIGHT WAS on in our kitchen as I pulled in the drive. I stomped my feet on the back mat, let myself into the house. Molly looked up from the pan of bacon sizzling and she gripped onto her spatula like a weapon. I stood in the doorway looking down. "Elsie Standinghorse died last night," I said.

She came over, put each of her hands on my shoulders. "I'll call the Aid ladies," she said. Her eyes welled up with tears. She didn't ask how I knew, she didn't accuse. I guess it was the tender glow in her face that brought everything down on me, and I broke down and I bawled.

chapter 33

AND THEN THE Vancycle quarter sold.

It happened in what seemed like the snap of a finger. A check for $58,000 sat on Molly's desk beside the colored envelopes for the electric bills and the Texaco payments for the diesel. It looked grand, that $58,000, but the bank would swallow almost every cent of it, and in six months we would need that much again for fertilizer. Molly called the Grain Growers, and she called Freewater Fertilizer and Chemical and she asked if there was some way we could pay $25,000 *ahead* on next year's bills.

I was standing beside her as she made the call. I leaned down, mouthed, "Pay *ahead*?" She turned away, concentrating on the call.

I could tell that whoever she was talking to at Freewater Fertilizer was checking. Molly didn't look up or anywhere but at the check, intent on whatever she had in her head. "Yes?' she said. "That would be fine. What about interest for the time you're holding it?" She sat quiet. "Well, I guess, if that's the way it has to be," she said.

She put the phone down so slowly it made no noise as it settled in the cradle. And she picked up a pen, opened our checkbook, and wrote out a check for $25,000. Then she drove to Milton-Freewater herself and delivered it to Freewater Fertilizer. She made a swing by Pendleton to deposit what was left of the check for the sale of the Vancycle land.

Even before she returned from town, Mr. Sturgis, the bank manager, was on the telephone. Like a fool, I answered it.

"Well, Jack," he said, like we were the chummiest friends ever. Of course, he knew the sale had gone through. "I see you made a deposit which covers part of your loan." Did he sit around all day watching our account to see if he was going to get his money from us? "The sale was for considerably more."

I cleared my throat, wished I hadn't picked up the phone. This was Molly's territory. What should I say? "Molly has written some checks to pay some bills."

"Certainly. I understand," he said, in a way that indicated he thought the bank was going to get more of the money. And it was then that I could see what Molly was thinking, it was then I could see why she'd done it. She paid for the fertilizer before the bank could get their hands on the money. She knew this would confuse the bank, would not settle things. We still had a few weeks before the bank's deadline; she hoped this payment would hold Mr. Sturgis off, when the deadline came. Her ability, her intelligence, scared me sometimes, she was so quick. The bank couldn't take what was already spent. I could have laughed right then. Wasn't that stealing from the bank, in a way? And I wondered where in the scriptures she could come up with the Lord's blessing on paying money before it was owed.

THAT NIGHT MOLLY gave the longest grace she had given for a long, long time. It was like she was fortifying her prayers, thanking the Lord for everything from the blessing of the sale, to thanking him for Edie's friend, Marybeth, who was staying over for the night and who was sitting in the place at the table where Patty used to sit, and she thanked the Lord for the thirty pounds she had lost.

THE DAY AFTER we sold the Vancycle quarter, I drove up through the canyons of Sandhollow, winding the truck up the track we had used for a road over thirty years. And when I got to the top of Vancycle Hill, I shut off the engine and sat there looking over the Columbia River, shining twenty miles away like one of my mother's silver platters. And I listened to the wind whip around the fenders of the truck, and I got out and let it whistle in my own ears, and I knew that would be the last time I would do it, because in a few more days the Vancycle quarter wouldn't be in the hands of a McIntyre, where it had been for three decades. And I was the one who had lost it.

chapter 34

IT HAD TURNED colder. For three days the thermometer outside
the back door didn't get above thirty. And it blew a dry wind that
took every spit of moisture from anything it touched. The cows'
teats were a mess of cracks and oozing blood and they stomped,
foot to foot, while Edie and I milked. We spread Bag Balm on
them morning and night. Even old Henrietta's teats were suffering,
though she hadn't produced a drop of milk for a year.

The equipment was in for the year, parked around back of the
barn, I had taken apart the Deere's header and pieces of it were
strewn around the floor of the shop. The weight from worry about
money had lifted, if only a bit, but left a place in my gut to think
about Patty. I had gone in to see Jackie a time or two, and each time
she told me Patty had called. It was, I was certain, her delusions
that had called, but just hearing her say Patty's name seemed to
weld Patty into my head. She had been gone nearly five and a half

months. I could not imagine how she could be alive. We did not talk about her in the house. Edie never brought up her name, but I thought Patty was like an infection that continued to fester in Edie. Edie was half a year older, now, but still undeveloped for her age. She still had not gotten her period, and her mother was planning to take her in for a checkup. It was as if my daughter were being eaten up since Patty disappeared. She went about her days, she followed her mother's orders, went to school, studied the Bible, set the table, did her homework. And she had a friend now, but there seemed to be no fire in their friendship, no long talks with the telephone cord stretched from the hall plug to the crack under her door. No exchanges of ribbons and bracelets made of string as there had once been with Patty.

Edie rarely spoke to me, though when I pushed her, she was courteous. Behind her manner I could read her thinking *my dad doesn't care about what happened to Patty anymore than anyone else.* And it tore me up. I went into Pendleton one day again, and talked with Officer Al, and tried to think that was enough. Sometimes Edie asked her mother for permission for a sleepover at Marybeth's, and she would pack her overnight case and ask me for a ride into town, but we spoke only in blurts without meaning. School would let out again in a few months, and we hoped summer would revive some spark in her, but she seemed to grow quieter and quieter every week.

IT WAS SATURDAY night and she had another sleepover with Marybeth. After lunch, I drove Edie into town. She carried her overnight case in her lap as I drove her into Philpott. The Hobbses' Buick was not in the drive when we got there, but I gave it no thought. They had a garage, though Tom Hobbs usually filled it with a mess of his woodworking projects. I thought they might have finally cleaned out the garage and had parked the car in it. Edie waved me off and I waved back.

I couldn't bring myself to head back home yet. The dull depression of the cold was bothering me, so I drove. Sometimes driving helped, and I headed out of town going nowhere. Smoke rose from some of the houses, the low sun bleached things and gave barns, hills, the road, a peace I did not feel.

I'd been driving a couple of hours, running the gas needle down, spending money on it I shouldn't have.

I saw him then, Kenny in the driver's seat of his old beater, parked in a draw; the same truck we had worked on together last fall. Off and on, he must have been able to keep it running, at least so far. It was cold, clear, the air dry and the sun low that time of day.

Only five families lived out that way and it was not the time of year for wheat trucks or tractors or anything else to be on that road. I saw the heads of two people in Kenny's truck, facing into the sun. I drove nearer, then saw the face of my daughter. I could see Kenny's expression, a "caught" sort of sick. He lifted his hand out the doorless truck as I pulled up. "Jack," he said.

Edie was busy trying to get her window down, but I knew it was rusted shut. Cigarette smoke billowed out Kenny's window, made a reek.

"You're supposed to be at the Hobbses'," I said. Neither of them questioned who I meant was supposed to be at the Hobbses'.

"We needed to talk," Edie said, "Kenny and me." Her lips were purple, her teeth chattered with cold.

"Talk about what?" I said.

Kenny leaned forward, hugged his arms around the steering wheel.

"Patty," she said.

"What about Patty? Has someone seen her?"

Kenny gave a minute shake to his head.

Edie pulled forward, leaned over Kenny, her face red but her mouth pursed tight and bleached angry white. She began to spit out works, then, a sound I had never heard from her. "Who cares, anyway . . . ," she said, "Dad?" How could someone spit the word "dad" as she did then? "Patty doesn't matter, does she? Nobody cares about Patty, do they?"

"I care," I said. "Your mother cares."

Kenny was staying out of this. "Puh," she said, an expression Patty often made. "Mom doesn't care about anyone but her Lord."

"Edie!" I said.

"Well, she *doesn't.*"

"We all could use some of your mother's faith."

"Yeah, Mom says Patty deserved what she got."

"Edie, I don't think . . ."

"She says it's the Lord that does everything." She picked up a pack of Lucky Strikes sitting on Kenny's dash, and she flicked open a lighter and lit it. And she looked at me in a dare as she blew out smoke she did not breathe in. A part of me credited her with more grit than I'd seen in her for a long time.

I opened the passenger door on my truck. "Get in," I said.

She sat for a moment.

Kenny said, "Better go."

And she snapped the cigarette out the window and picked up her overnight case. She came around, got into my truck. "You going to tell Mom?"

"Let's talk," I said, "while you get the stink of smoke off you."

WHAT CLOUDS THERE were pulled closed and left only a smear of light. The forecast said moisture, meaning snow, was coming in the next twenty-four hours. It was like someone had drawn a curtain over the world.

I hated this time of year, the distraction of the holidays was behind us, and cold would keep us holed up for weeks yet. Molly would have said how can you hate anything the Lord gave us? Still, I hated that winter.

I bumped along with my silent daughter. We finally began to talk and when we did we talked of her mother and why her mother was so mean about Patty. It was a relief, somehow, to have Patty's name said. I defended Molly, told Edie her mom loved her and did whatever she could to make sure the same things never happened to her that had happened to Patty. I told her it was her mother's sternness was her way to protect her.

Of course I did not tell her I knew Molly still carried resentment for my screw-up with Jackie and that I knew she put some kind of burden and judgment on Patty for it. And I could not tell her what I suspected life was like for Patty with that bastard Murcheson. That was not something a naïve girl like my daughter should know.

When we got back to the house, Edie made an excuse she wasn't feeling good and had seen me in town and asked me to bring her home.

And Molly flapped her hands and said, "Whew, Jack. Have you been hanging around Haymire's? You smell awful, like cigarettes."

She didn't give me time to answer, and I whispered thanks inside my head. Neither Edie nor I mentioned it again.

chapter 35

MOLLY WAS SEWING a new set of curtains for the community room at the church. The Ladies' Aid was painting and redecorating in time for Easter in another six weeks. A few miles of tan fabric were piled on the dining-room table. Since the day we rode together in the truck a couple of weeks ago, Edie had opened up a little and had even improved her grades, particularly in science classes. Off and on, Marybeth would call and ask Edie to stay the night or go to a basketball game with her at the school. Only once had Edie had Marybeth out to our house. I suspected it was because she didn't want to open Marybeth up to Molly's judgment.

I had managed to busy myself in the barn until I got too cold and had to go into the house and warm up. I let myself envision— pretend really—that any threat of cold would break pretty soon and the rains would come again and we'd have one of those record-breaker years Dad seemed to have most of the time.

Molly and I didn't talk except about little stuff, her asking me to bring up some string beans from the cellar, or some of last year's peaches, or maybe about the crop, or a few bookkeeping details she had to have, or gossip she brought home from the Ladies' Aid, or how good Edie looked now that she didn't need either the braces or retainers. The past few days we'd been discussing who was going to take Edie in for her driver's permit. At bedtime, Molly and I had worked into a routine of quiet smacks on the cheek that were no more intimate than the squeaks of kisses between sisters and aunties, then nothing again but the sounds of our covers pulled up and the eventual rasps of her snores.

One morning, I left the house a little before ten o'clock. The wind moaned through the shed like someone with a secret. As I got into the truck, the moaning got louder, like it was trying to shout something, but the meaning was as veiled and fuzzed over as the clouds that covered the sun.

Looking back on that day, I don't think I could have told a soul why I did what I did. Boredom, maybe, the waiting, waiting, waiting for the day when the weather finally broke and I could get on with what I was meant to do.

The road into Pendleton was dry, the ground blowing dirt from the fields that had lain fallow last summer. The stubble from last year's crop was bent, but holding. I probably couldn't have said where I was going. I only knew I found myself parking in front of the police station steps. I'd been in the building half a dozen times again since I'd taken Patty's last school photo into it, but Al had been out each time. I was beginning to think we'd never see or hear about Patty again. It had been so long since she disappeared, and there was only Kenny and me, I was certain, who were checking, though Kenny had never brought it up. He was still living on his grandmother's place, but I'd heard he got a job somewhere.

I had never told Molly about these visits to the police station. I didn't think it would do any good. Telling Molly wouldn't make

Patty come back. Everybody in Philpott was going on with their lives. Jackie was still living in the Masonic Hall. Molly was taking her food and cleaning for her, the Ladies' Aid was still running bazaars and bake sales, now and then, to keep the lights and water on for her, but no one ever mentioned Patty. It was like her disappearance, and her behavior before she left, was too much of a threat to remember.

I opened the door to the station, wiped my feet on the mat a little longer than necessary. Al must have seen me come in the door because he came over to the counter as soon as I got to it. The clerk smiled at me. She was beginning to know me, though I always had to remind her of Patty's name.

Al shoved his hair back from his face, reached out to shake my hand. "Jack," he said. There were some stripes on his shoulder, bright gold and new.

"Sergeant," I said.

He grinned. "Yeah," he said, "every so often they find some new sucker."

"You the sucker this time?" I'd grown to like him, like the quiet in his manner.

"Yeah." He shook his head. "I had to tell that same joke to somebody else."

"Nobody who counts, I hope."

"Kenny Muffin," he said.

Kenny.

"You know him very well?" Al said.

"He's a friend," I said, and then I added, "of my daughter's."

"Nice kid," he said. He stepped out from behind the counter. He seemed to walk straighter now that he had that stripe on his shoulder. "I want to show you something," he said. "You ever looked at the bulletin board?"

I had looked at the pictures on the posters every time I walked into the station, pictures of wanted felons, faces scarred, dark eyes half-closed, men who looked like they could leap right off the cork board and grab you around the neck. Here and there the board was pinned with the image of a woman who looked as hard and used up as Jackie Pugh did, like someone whipped her with a belt or lit into her with an eggbeater. Off to the right of the board, there was a section labeled "Missing" and there was the school photograph of Patty.

"You heard something?" I said.

He shrugged. "Don't get your hopes up."

We stood at the bulletin board together. Al didn't say anything, only pointed at a piece of newspaper with no picture on it, a clipping pinned there. "I found this in the paper yesterday."

It was some kind of advertisement, or column, or something else I couldn't really make out. It had been cut square and precise and tacked up in a bottom corner, underneath the Wanteds.

"From the *East Oregonian*?"

"Yeah," he said. He braced his arm over the clipping while I leaned in to read it.

> *Cavalerie dans la Rue*, a foundation providing services to runaway youth and the homeless in Montreal Canada is seeking someone who knows about Umatilla Indian goods.
>
> *Cavalerie dans la Rue* was founded in 1973 and is funded by its founder, Major Dalrymple, and by the proceeds from trade and sale of Indian goods. *Cavalerie dans la Rue* is interested in talking with anyone who may want to participate in a lucrative business opportunity as well as helping youth and the poor. If you are interested in this important and financially successful endeavor, please call Major Dalrymple at (514) 555-0154. ABSOLUTELY NO POLICE

"What is this?" I said.

"I don't really know."

"What's it have to do with Patty?"

"I don't that either. What I do know is that no other paper in any other county in Oregon has run this. Pendleton's not the only place with Indian stuff. Why is it only in the Pendleton paper? Why Umatilla Indians? Why not Cayuse, or Nez Perce, or Walla Walla? And why no police?"

"You're asking me?"

"Rhetorical," he said and laughed. "My wife threw that word at me last night, and I had to look it up in the dictionary." He shook his head then. "It doesn't feel right. A foundation for runaways in Montreal putting an ad in the Pendleton paper."

"So, why *do* they say 'no police'?"

He looked at me from under his eyebrows, a look that said there was probably some good reason not to go to the police.

"Muffin said you went to his place to check on the Pugh girl after she disappeared."

"Yeah," I said.

"Did you know his grandmother died?"

I nodded.

"She was my aunt," he said.

"I'm sorry."

"A week ago he got a job at Hamley's." He nodded in the direction of Hamley's Western store. "Kenny and I have coffee sometimes, before he goes to work."

"He driving to work?"

"When his rig runs," Al threw his head back, laughed. "Hitches," he said, "when it's on the blink. I told him that was illegal. He told me to arrest him, at least he'd get a good meal."

We walked together back toward the reception desk, away from the bulletin board. He stepped through the swinging gate into the office area. "I'll keep an eye out. You never know about this stuff."

chapter 36

SNOW WAS BLOWING everywhere, the wind whipping the ground bare and brittle, heaping the dry powder in the cache of foxtails along the fence lines where it piled up in white scallops. The school had called a snow day. Edie was home helping Molly clean the upstairs. They had been working all morning at it, the vacuum going in our bedroom, then Edie's, then whining down the hall, over the walls, the woodwork, even into the upstairs bathroom.

I couldn't put the poster in Al's office out of my mind. Why would they want Indian goods from *Pendleton* when you could find Indian goods all over the state? Why would that major whatever-his-name-was not want police? Why would somebody who ran a foundation for youth in *Montreal* put something in *our* paper? That was the real question and it wouldn't leave me alone. Montreal. I doubted I would have really known where Montreal was if someone pulled out a map, except it had been in the news last year because of the Olympics. From what I could remember of what

we saw on television it looked like a busy, confusing place I would never choose to go to.

I fled the noise of the vacuum, went outside to the shop, lit a fire to blaze in the old oil drum I'd tricked up to use as a stove one year. A half dozen cats and the two dogs settled themselves into the heat, fanning out far enough not to burn, but strewn around the shop floor like dead bodies. Now and then one of them would get up and stretch, then curl around again and plop back in the same staked-out space it claimed every day of the winter. I went over to stand by the drum, holding my hands out to it, but inside I still felt cold.

Around ten o'clock I went into the house to see if somebody would maybe whip me up something hot. A cup of hot chocolate might take away the cold. I would ask Edie to make it.

The little hallway inside the back door was stacked with boxes full of old clothes and a couple of pairs of shoes Edie had out-grown. I went in, yelled "Edie," up the stairs. The wheeze of the vacuum didn't stop. "Edie?" I called out, but the machine still wheezed. Neither Molly nor Edie could hear. I picked over the bills on Molly's desk, waited for the noise to shut off. The stack of bills had gone down, the envelopes were mostly colored white now and without the red stamps proclaiming "urgent" or "overdue."

The kitchen was clean and still but for the noise upstairs. Molly kept a busy kitchen, rarely did it not have a pot simmering on the back burner, or the dishwasher roaring, or a timer ticking for something in the oven. But that day, the lights were off and it was dim, the counters were clear, except for her canisters of flour and sugar and for the recent issue of the *Daily Word,* which was lying open by the stove. Light from the snow lit the inside of the house with a glare that never happened any other time but in the winter. It was a clean light, bare and clear.

A cardboard box was sitting on the kitchen table, open. There was a little pile of folded clothes in it, a coat Patty had grown out of, pants, some T-shirts. There was also a stack of books on top,

Charlotte's Web, that I had given Edie years ago. It was worn, read many times, and the hard cover had been torn nearly off. One year, some time before their pet-show phase, the girls had named one of the new batch of pigs Wilbur and they brought him into the house and bathed him, squealing, in the tub where I washed the milk separator. How they sorted that particular pig out from all the others in his litter and made him such a pet, I'll never know.

They spoiled him, giving him special treats of fried potatoes and fruit, the meat of oranges, bowls full of bread sopped up in whole milk. He grew fatter and fatter, and he followed them everywhere like one of the dogs.

And then came the day for me to take the hogs into town to auction.

It was fall. The girls were in school. I put the stock racks on the truck, loaded all the hogs except for our two good sows and the boar into it and took them all to the sale. I used the money to bid on another impregnated sow.

That night at chores Edie saw the empty pen, the new sow standing, nervous and suspicious against the far fence. Edie climbed up on the pen's fence and screamed, "Wilbur!" over and over until she sank down on her knees in the dirt and cried. I said I was sorry. I said I'd try to see about finding out about getting Wilbur back.

Patty rode out on the school bus with Edie the next day. I knew Edie had told her about the pig, told her I was going find him and bring him back home. But by the time I went back into town to the sales yards, the lot with Wilbur was gone, trucked to Spokane and to the slaughterhouse. I thought the episode might teach Edie something about life, learning about death, learning how things went. But she never really seemed to trust things again, me, or any of the animals she raised. She never gave another animal one of her names, never named another cat Fluffy or Smitz. She called her 4-H calves by numbers after that, and she never cried again as they were sold and as she led them to the chutes to be trucked off to the plant.

There beside the box of clothes, lying by itself on the table as if someone had opened and read it, was that book with the picture of a girl, a spider, and a pig.

FINALLY THE NOISE upstairs died down, though Molly and Edie were still thumping around up there. I felt the draft of an open window, heard the snap of one of them shaking out dust from a rag. The thin old floors transmitted the sounds of every move they made, the rumble of water running, the whir and screech of the vacuum. I made myself useful, loaded the boxes near the back door into Molly's station wagon. I'd left the book where I found it on the kitchen table, but I thought about that book, the years the girls were still together, the years when Edie was still happy. And I thought about that damned pig.

MOLLY SET A plate with a roast beef sandwich at my place, then settled the bulk of herself and her plaid dress into her chair. I was still distracted by the dim sadness left behind by the book. I fingered the thick sandwich from my plate, took a bite of it.

Molly's foot nudged my shin. "Jack," she said, "grace."

And I held the meat and the slick oil of mayonnaise and butter in my mouth as we bowed our heads and Molly said grace.

When she was done, when she had patted her napkin into the neck of her dress, and when Edie had drunk a half glass of milk, I ventured to say what I'd planned to do most of the morning. "Where are you taking the boxes?"

"To the church sale," she said. "For the bazaar for Jackie."

"I'll take them in."

She mumbled "thanks" around her bite of sandwich.

"I need to go into town anyway," I said. "Your tires are low."

She tucked the bite into her cheek "Today? The roads aren't good. I can have Haymire's check the tires tomorrow, or whenever the weather clears."

"I think you're going to need a new battery. I don't want you getting stuck in weather like this." It was an excuse. I wanted some way to talk to Edie alone before the rest of the day was gone. Taking the car in for a checkup was the best I could come up with.

Molly nodded, reached for a slice of mincemeat pie.

"EDIE," I SAID, "help me take these boxes into the church." The lunch dishes were drying in the strainer, the leavings of pie and sandwiches put away. Molly was in the basement running a load of wash. The machine had started to run and I could hear it all the way upstairs.

Edie was in her room, pulling up the quilt on her bed. The room sparkled from the cleaning; every book, every stuffed bear, every piece of clothing, was in its place. Her pink slippers sat in a perfect perpendicular beside her bed. The closet door wasn't open to a pile of thrown clothes and messed shoes. Now, the closet was closed, the mirror on the door gleamed.

She straightened up, flicked a glance my way. Her cheeks glowed peachy from all the housework, her mouth was open slightly in surprise. She was lovely, standing there, and I wanted to reach out, but as soon as I thought it, she turned away.

"I thought you might like to ride along with me into town," I said. It seemed like forever since we'd bundled up in the winter or rolled down the windows in the summer and bounced along in the dust of the truck.

Edie patted the pillow on her bed. She started to open her mouth and I thought she was going to come up with some reason she had to stay home, some reason not to go.

"We can check on Jackie while we're at it," I said.

EDIE THUDDED UP the wooden stairs behind me, carrying a box of clothes Molly had labeled "Jackie." We'd had to step around the pile of snow blown over the first step. The snow had stopped falling,

241

but the roads were drifted over with it, here and there, and slick in open places where the little bit of sun had melted, then iced over again as the afternoon went on. The rest of the stuff, four boxes labeled "Aid Bazaar" were still in the truck. The box in Edie's arms was full of clothes she'd outgrown but still "had some wear in them," Molly had said.

I rapped on the door, hesitated, knocked again. Edie stood beside me. Her eyes glittered, scared. She had not been here before.

Slowly I pushed open the door. "Jackie?" I said, "it's Jack and Edie."

Jackie was sitting at her usual spot at the table. Edie stood in the archway, the box clutched in front of her like a shield, her eyes jittering around the apartment. Jackie looked up. Her hair had been cut in an awful, homemade way, short, uneven over her ears. It was practical, no matter how pathetic it was. She was clean, the apartment gleamed like our house back home, the little tables beside the couch had neat doilies on them, the kitchen smelled of bleach, its counters free of clutter. Aside from the stench of smoke from Jackie's cigarette, the apartment no longer reeked.

Jackie was wearing moccasins and slacks and a flannel shirt that was too big, one of Larry's, I thought. "Edie and I brought you some stuff," I said.

Jackie mumbled. Her voice was thick with mucous. "Yes," she said. And then, slow as a mummy, she took the cigarette out of her mouth, laid it in the ashtray. And she braced her two hands on the table and pulled herself out of the chair.

I stepped back, but Edie stood her ground as Jackie shuffled over to stand in front of her. Jackie reached up and pushed Edie's hair off her forehead and said, "I'm glad you're home."

AFTER WE LEFT Jackie's apartment, we deposited the rest of the boxes on the back steps of the church where the wind couldn't whip them open. Neither of us spoke as we worked. Neither of us spoke as we drove to Haymire's on the edge of town or as I pumped up the tires on Molly's car.

When that was done, I opened Edie's door, stood there, and said, "You want to drive?"

She looked up at me surprised. "It's snowing," she said. A skiff of snow was beginning to come down again.

"I'll be here."

Three miles out of town, she signaled to turn toward our place.

"Let's go on," I said, "into Pendleton."

She turned toward me, and the car started to skid. "Look where you're going," I said.

The glare was blinding. White hills blended into sky, sky into horizon, road into ditch. I wondered if letting my daughter drive was another of my stupidities, one that might get the both of us killed. She had pulled herself toward the window. On the steering wheel, her hands gripped nearly as white as the snow. Her eyes were squinted against the glare, almost closed.

I got the dark glasses Molly kept from the jockey box, flipped them open, handed them to Edie. The car swerved as she took them. Molly kept such tight control on her, reined her in, kept her in sight, safe, buffered from danger, that I doubted Molly had ever let Edie drive, other than in the safety of the fields. My daughter could drive a half-ton truck but didn't know how to handle a car.

The road was empty. Here and there a fence line poked from a snowdrift, like a line of dark slivers. It was almost impossible to tell where the edge of the road dropped into the ditch.

A couple of miles ahead, a truck lumbered over the crest of a hill, disappeared into the hollow at the turnoff to Holman. Edie pulled herself even closer to the windshield. "I can't see the center line," she said.

"Take it slow. You'll do fine." But I wasn't so sure. God. By the time I thought to tell her to pull over, the truck was on us. A plume of black diesel dirtied the white like a bruise. It must have braked because it started to skid as it came down the hill toward us. Edie let off the gas, picked up her foot like she was about to hit the brakes, then must have thought better of it, because she held her foot frozen over the brake as the truck slowed. I grabbed for the dash. She pulled to the side. I could feel the car beginning to lurch into the ditch, and she held it there, kept it on the shoulder as the truck sidled by.

We came to a stop. She wiped a fringe of hair from her forehead. "Maybe you better drive, Dad."

And I said, "Honey, you're doing a better job than I could." And she put her soft foot on the gas and the car spun a moment, then went on.

WE MADE OUR way down through the Holman Hills into Pendleton. Edie had not released either of her hands from the wheel the whole time into town. She sat with her thin fingers pulling herself forward like she was inspecting the glass of the window. At one point, I said, "You might want to relax a little, Ede."

She puffed out her cheeks and let out her breath. "Why are we going into Pendleton, anyway?" she managed to say as we made it to the sanded streets in town. "Didn't you check the tires back at Haymire's?"

"I think we might want to check prices on a battery for your mother," I said. She looked at me, puzzled.

I directed her to the Napa store. She crept through green lights, started to brake two blocks before a light turned red. Only once did I feel I was any help at all, when I reminded her to blinker as she turned into the Napa lot.

And she stood beside me as I priced batteries like I told her mother we'd do; another of my excuses. We left the store.

I said, "I have one little errand to do before we leave town."

THEY HAD SHOVELED the steps of the police station and had tossed some sand in the middle. There was just enough room in the sanded path for Edie and me to walk up the steps side by side. I wanted to show off, to show her how they all knew me, by now. And I hoped Sergeant Al would not be out on a wreck with this weather. I wanted her to know he knew me.

It was quiet in there and a blast of hot furnace air pumped out as the glass doors opened.

"Why are we *here?*' Edie whispered.

"Hi, Jack," Cathy said right away when she saw me. She was wearing a sleeveless blouse and had died her hair. It was a frizzy black now. She walked over to the reception counter, leaned on her elbows, flapped her hand toward her face. "Whew," she said. "You'd think this day in age they could make a thermostat that worked."

"Maybe," I said, "you could do like the Finns."

"Fins?" she said.

"Finnish." I said, thinking I'd screwed up what you were supposed to call someone from Finland. "Or Swedes. They get too hot in the sauna, they go out and roll in the snow."

She fanned her face again. "It *is* hot in here, and it's not my age."

Edie looked up at me with an expression that said she was thinking, *you know this lady?*

"Wasn't it yesterday you were in checking, or is my brain gone as well?" the clerk said.

"Yeah," I said.

Edie blinked.

Cathy quit fanning herself. "You have something new on the Pugh girl?"

Edie's face went the color of paper. I couldn't imagine what she was thinking, and I couldn't imagine why I hadn't been able to tell her why we were coming. "Is Sergeant Al in?"

The clerk turned. "I'll get him."

"Jack," Al said. He reached out for a handshake, then stood back and put his hands on his hips, looking at Edie. "Who's this?" he said.

I put my hand on her shoulder. "My daughter," I said, "Edie." I felt the bones of her shoulder under her parka, the straight stick of her collarbone. She was stiff as a timber. "This is Sergeant Al, Ede."

He loomed in front of us, his slick brown police uniform, his crow-colored hair, his badge. His posture made him big, his badge, his holster, the thick of his blue-black hair. I felt her shoulder press against my side.

He reached out to shake her hand. She gave him the tips of her fingers. He took them and shook, like it was a real shake. "Edie," he said.

"Edie and Patty Pugh were friends," I said. "I thought we might look at the posters again," I said, "and the newspaper clipping you showed me yesterday."

He nodded. His face had gone serious, as though he thought my daughter would bring him some sort of clue.

He let himself through the swinging door.

Edie looked at me with an expression I'd never seen her give. Her face was old, crumpled in. "Patty is dead," she said. It wasn't a question. "He's going to show us a picture of her body."

She was not crying, she did not appear to be surprised. What did my daughter know? How could she come to this? I could only shake my head. There was not a word I could say because, who knew? It might be true.

Since yesterday, the faces on the bulletin board had changed. There were more of them now, pinned one over the other. But the memo was still where it had been, still in the lower right corner of the board, off to the side by itself.

Al and I chatted a moment. Edie slid quietly toward the bulletin board. She looked up at the faces, her eyes sweeping the posters. When she had taken them in, I heard her blow out a breath of relief, like she had been holding it since the moment we came in. "I don't see Patty," she said.

I turned back to Al and that was when I heard my daughter scream, "Daddy!" so loud I think every person in the station jumped. It was awful to hear, like a dog hit by a car. I ran to her. Sergeant Al came from around the counter. Edie touched the paper, stood there, still, unmoving, then she began petting the paper like it was an animal, something alive. "Patty's *there*," she said, and as she said it, her chin puckered up like she was about to cry. She touched her own mouth with the hand that had pet the paper. "She *is*," she said.

It was Al's turn to put his hand on my daughter's bright pink parka. It was a coat with no shape her mother had made her. It revealed none of the young woman underneath. Al's dark hand sunk into the seam of that pink, and I knew he could feel the lift of Edie's shoulder as she breathed, knew his hand could tell that under her coat there was the bud of a woman, no matter how hidden.

"Edie," Al said, "could you let your father and me talk?"

chapter 37

I'D SPENT A good part of my life wanting to turn away, to wipe out what was coming. What Was Coming. What Was Coming. I was never up to what was coming, never prepared, never smart enough, never man enough. What was coming was always bigger than me. Sergeant Al took me behind the counter, into his office. "Have a seat," he said.

We left Edie in front, slumped in a pink fluff on one of the benches in the hallway. Officer Al had slipped the article off the bulletin board, brought it to his desk. His chair squawked like a hen when his weight hit it. He picked up a yellow pencil, tapped the eraser on the column of newspaper. "I hope your daughter is mistaken about this," he said.

He looked out the glass to where Edie was slumped against the wall. "I looked into it a little after you left yesterday," he said. "Made a call."

"To Montreal?" I said. "Police?"

He nodded. "If she's there, it's probably not good."

"She can't be. That's halfway around the world," I said.

"Kids who run can end up in God knows where. If she's there, she's got herself into something you probably don't want to know about, is what I'm saying."

"Like what?" I said.

I thought he was stalling, trying to avoid telling me what it was he brought me in to tell me. "The Montreal police know about this guy. They don't have anything on him, don't get me wrong, but they are watching him." He sat back, didn't say anything for a second. "Jack," he said, "do you know what the term 'dating' means?"

I frowned, saying "*Of course.*"

"I doubt the kind of dating I mean," he said. "Some dude calling himself a Major sent this announcement—or this advertisement, or whatever it is—*here*, not to Montreal." He slapped the column. "Why? That's what I want to know. Why?"

"What's the difference?"

"You tell me," he said. "It's weird, that all. Some stuff's the same everywhere, been going on since cavemen. The only difference with this guy is it's weird. I don't know what to make of it, that's what I'm saying."

"Who *is* he?" I said.

"You're asking me?" Al said. "Montreal police *do* know somebody who calls himself the Major. Sounds like he presents himself as some kind of mucky-muck up there who doesn't want to get his fingers dirty. He appears, or tries to appear, to be doing good with kids. Well, if he *is* doing good with kids, why are Montreal authorities watching him. They wouldn't say anything more for fear of lawsuits. This guy has bucks, apparently."

"How would he know *Patty*?"

"If he does, you probably don't want to know," he said.

chapter 38

A BLAST OF warm air from the car pushed against my face. While I was wrapping it up with Sergeant Al in the station, Edie had left to sit in the car. She was slumped, wadded up, knees braced on the door of the glove box, and angry in the passenger seat as if our bond during the drive had snapped. The radio was turned on high, blaring a loud thumping song, someone singing in a voice that scratched like nails on a chalkboard, "Tonight's the Night." It was the type of music her mother would never allow in the house.

As I slid behind the wheel, she crossed her arms in front of herself and buried her chin in the neck of the parka.

I snapped off the radio.

She turned to me with a bitter face. "You're not going to do anything, are you?"

"I don't know what I'm going to do," I said.

"You'll do what you always do. Nothing."

I turned the key in the ignition "Let's go."

HAL'S HAMBURGERS SQUATTED at the edge of Pendleton, near the turnoff toward the road to Philpott. As long as I remembered, Hal's had been there, the fading sign saying "Burgers, Fries, Shakes." The sign was on, blinking against the white of the horizon. I was driving now, Edie sitting there, biting the nail of her thumb. As we neared Hal's and the turnoff, I slowed. I wanted time to think about what had happened in the station, needed time to come up with how I was going to tell Molly, and more than that, *what* I would tell her.

Hal's was familiar, comforting. Hal's was memories. Hal's was there when Dad and Mother stopped on hot summer days and bought us burgers and Coke floats. And later, when Molly and I were just becoming a thing, we pulled in after a movie at the drive-in theater on a hot summer night. It was unchanged but for the little area of outside seating they'd put in a few years ago.

I said, "Let's get a bite before we head home."

Edie sat there, silent.

I turned in. Only then did she let her chin out of the neck of the parka and turn her head slightly. But she didn't say a word.

WE SLID INTO a booth across the table from each other, didn't talk. A girl not much older than Edie put our two plastic baskets in front of us. Grease from the fries was bleeding into the paper.

We sat there, silent, still bundled in winter coats. Edie fiddled with her burger, would not look up at me. Anyone looking on would know we belonged to each other, a forty-year-old guy sitting there with his teenaged daughter, both with the same dull brown hair, the same long, thin arms, the same hands, strong from milking, muscular from pitching hay, dry and cracked around the nails, the same big knuckles. One day the daughter would have trouble getting her wedding ring over her knuckle, and when she finally did, it would fit loose as a dog's collar. She would never be able to gain weight. People would comment on it all her life.

She would envy others who entered a room with their shoulders squared, confident they could handle whatever was thrown at them. She would take herself to one quiet corner, observing, watching as everyone, but her, knew the right thing to say or caught the gist of some current joke. The world would see her as someone who came along, someone who followed, but in keeping to herself, she would go her own way, and her way might not be something she ever let anyone know.

"Did you turn her in or something?" she finally said. Her voice was accusing.

"Turn her in?"

"Rat on her."

"I," I said, "reported her missing is all." I felt like I had to apologize somehow.

"So, you going to do anything?"

"I don't know what I'm going to do."

She fingered one of her fries.

I took a bite from my burger, dipped a fry into a pool of ketchup. "If this is Patty."

She laid her own fry back in the grease of the basket. "It is."

"Eat your burger," I said.

She took a bite of a fry, and sat there with it in her mouth, not chewing, not making any move at all. She tongued the bite into her cheek. "Dad," she said, her voice tired.

"Don't talk with your mouth full," I said and hung on the words like they were going to take away the pit in my stomach.

She continued as if I hadn't interrupted what she'd started to tell me. "I don't think you know anything."

"That's flattering," I said, and felt silly afterward.

"I mean, like why she was staying in the barn."

I could see the fry lying whole in the trough of her tongue. "I think there was trouble at home," I said.

After I said that, it was like a dam broke loose. She began shoving food into her mouth, smacking at bites, wolfing her burger. It was like in the span of a breath, she had become starved.

"She had to," she said as she slammed a fry into a puddle of ketchup, pushed it into her mouth. "It was the only place she had." She swallowed almost without chewing. And, between bites, she started to talk, words about Patty that should never come out of anyone's mouth, let alone my daughter's. "Pants down . . . tongue . . . chain . . . fists . . . weiner . . ." Her words came fast, crumbs flying, little mists of her spit spewing. Between each utterance, she ate like a dog gone out of control.

Finally, she sputtered to a stop. "She made Kenny and me promise not to tell." A drip of mustard smeared the side of her mouth like an infection.

"Some people," I managed to say, "embellish. It doesn't mean it's true."

She ignored my excuse. "Nobody *helped* her. She didn't have anybody but Kenny and me."

"For what?" I said.

"To stop him."

"Why didn't you *tell* us?"

"Puh" she said.

"You could have."

"Tell *Mom*? What's she going to do, go up there and read scriptures?"

"Then me," I said.

"Yeah," she said, her voice full of doubt. "Yeah, sure." She sat low, like some weight pushed down on her head. Mother—her *grandmother*—had more youth than my daughter right then. Someone had to step in. Someone needed to take away some of her hurt. But who? Me? God?

Edie fingered the mustard off her mouth. "You always do what Mom says." She thrust her hands belligerently into the pockets of her coat. "If we'd told you, you'd get all *superior*, and say she was making it all up."

"You could have given us a chance."

"Yeah, and have Mom ground me for the rest of my life."

A Chevy pickup with chains on the tires clattered up. Two men got out, stomped their feet at the door, then came in. Their presence, the clomp of their boots, the taking off of their coats, their raised hellos to the bald guy working the grill ended our talk. A string of lettuce had caught in Edie's hair and trembled there.

chapter 39

IT HAD BEEN two weeks since Edie and I visited the police station. We hadn't spoken of our trip to Pendleton again. I'd made some excuse to her mother when she wondered why we'd been gone so long and was thankful she didn't seem to suspect or want to pry more out of me, or out of Edie.

Molly's work at the church preparing for Easter took up a good part of her time. Besides sewing new curtains, she was in charge of the LA Easter bazaar again that year. The proceeds were earmarked for Jackie, to pay her utilities and for an upcoming doctor's appointment. Molly had pulled her car out of the garage, parked it in the drive. Inside the garage she'd set up a couple of tables she'd brought out from the church, and she was beginning to sort stuff coming in for donation.

"Why don't you sort in the church basement?" I said.

"I want it done right," she said.

Sundays, people were beginning to bring boxes of whatever they found in their attics, some of it was familiar, some of the stuff that had floated through the bazaars more than once. The garage was becoming crowded with bassinets, bedspreads, curtains, toys, hair curlers, glassware, kitchen utensils, even one brand-new truck tire. All of it Molly sorted, some of it she patched, and she took some of the paint left over from when we painted the living room and slathered a set of four kitchen chairs green.

More than ever Edie hid out in her room. She seemed to be dodging me. I only saw her for chores and for the fifteen minutes it took her to eat her dinner. She slogged through her meals, her limp hand bringing the fork to her mouth, the milk glass to her lips. Now and then Marybeth would call. Edie would spend a minute, or two, muttering to her over the phone, and when the call was done, would traipse upstairs and shut herself into her room again. Her friendships with the kids at school were short-lived or irregular. For a couple of weeks she and Suzie Haymire were thick. I didn't know when the friendship ended, suspected that Suzie had been taken up by a boyfriend. At dinner, if we hadn't said grace, or if Molly hadn't had the bazaar to chatter about, I didn't think one word would have been said.

If it had rained, maybe things would have looked up a little for me. But it didn't rain. Our lips grew so dry they bled, the quick around Molly's nails split and one nail got infected. Leaves left from fall heaved up in dust devils, foxtails whistled in the wind along the edges of the pasture. The newspaper said we'd had less than eight hundredths of an inch of moisture for the past couple of weeks. The late snow had dampened us a little, but not enough. A farm couldn't survive on twice the moisture we'd had. The forecast showed nothing that held any hope. I had no idea when I could begin to seed.

Three weeks to the day after Edie and I drove into Pendleton, the telephone rang. Molly had come home from town seeing Jackie and packing another box or two into the garage that had come in for the bazaar. She was washing up in the kitchen, opening the refrigerator, running water, getting ready to fix dinner. Edie had been home from school an hour or so and was sitting at the kitchen table doing homework.

I was watching David Brinkley on the early news from Spokane, but was having a hard time keeping a lot of it straight. The news the past few weeks was filled with stuff that caused me to stay awake at night. The Hillside Strangler had killed his tenth girl, Roman Polanski fled after raping a thirteen-year-old. Somebody was killing people in California, somebody else in Florida. The only news that gave me a little lift was they had caught that murderer Ted Bundy. All this was going on in the world, and I couldn't keep my mind around any piece of it but murders.

I heard Edie say, "Hello," her voice dull, uninterested even though this was the time Marybeth often called. The telephone, when it hung on the wall in the hallway, gave nobody any privacy at all. Edie held the receiver out to me like an accusation. "It's for you."

"Who is it?"

She shrugged. "Some guy."

Her eyes shifted toward the kitchen. The aroma of ketchup, and pepper, and meatloaf beginning to bake wafted into the living room. I thunked back the footrest, pulled myself out of the recliner. I took the phone from Edie's hand, motioned for her to turn down the TV. "Hello," I said.

"It's Ben Al."

Molly called from the kitchen, "Jack, did the telephone ring?"

"Yes, officer," I said.

Edie stiffened, listening closer now.

"Jack?" Molly said from the kitchen.

I held my hand over the phone. "I've got it."

I heard the water run, thought Molly was probably going to wash up to come see who was on the phone.

"This nut," Al said, "sent another notice to the *East Oregonian*.

He left the phone number again, but I don't think you should do anything about it. Jack, I just wanted you to know."

Edie's accusation that I wouldn't do anything, the implication that I never did anything her mother didn't approve, sat heavy in my gut. I patted under four issues of *Guideposts* Molly kept on the little telephone table, searching for a pen. "You got the number?" I said.

Al hesitated for a long moment, then read it off to me.

DINNER WOULD NOT be ready for forty-five minutes. The scrap with the number was shoved in my pocket, scribbled on a page torn from the back cover of one of Molly's *Guideposts*. I couldn't make the call from home and risk questions from Molly, so I went into town.

The only pay phone in Philpott hung from the cinderblock building that served as the telephone exchange. Lester Pate, who ran the exchange, had put up a wood cabinet on the side of the building to house the phone and protect it from the weather. He'd designed the cabinet door to open bottom up so you had to balance it on your head, or hold it up with one hand, while you talked. It was supposed to keep you a little bit out of the rain and the heat of sun in the summer. The telephone and cabinet looked brand new, like it had never been put to much use.

I punched in the number. An operator told me I had to insert nearly three dollars. I started feeding the phone coins I'd taken from the change jar we kept on the bedroom bureau. Four thousand miles away, the telephone rang while I huddled under Lester's cupboard door. I wiped my hands on my jeans. It was cold and the wind bit. I turned my back to it, but it didn't help. Now and then, I gawked around like a thief standing in the dark, hoping no one would catch me making a call. I didn't want Molly, or anybody else to know about it, or to see me holding the telephone door over my head like some kind of nut.

The phone rang twice, then twice more. Breathing became easier with every ring. I began to feel safe in my virtue. Al said he thought the guy was a kook, or worse, and wouldn't put a whole lot of stock in anything.

The phone clicked. The ringing stopped. "Alloo," a voice said. It was a soft, flowing woman's voice. Foreign.

"Hello," I said.

"Alloo," she said again. "Who eez thees?"

"Someone gave me this number," I said.

"Who?" Her voice was full of breath.

"I am calling from Pendleton, Oregon," I held Al's note up, "to speak to the Major?" I didn't sound certain, even to me.

"Pen-del-*tone*?" she said. I heard a man's voice in the background and her saying something in a foreign language, French.

There was a rustling on the other end of the line. "Who is this?" It was a man now, and he spoke English without an accent.

"I got this number from the paper," I said.

"Who is this?" he said again.

"Jack McIntyre. I'm calling to ask about . . ."

"Where you calling from?"

"America," I said, then remembered Canada was in America, too. "United States," I said. "Oregon."

"Oregon," he said, "You calling from the Umatilla Reservation?"

"No."

"I don't know anybody in Oregon," he said.

"You didn't put your number in the Pendleton paper?"

"You from the *police*?" His voice got higher, like a kid in a whine.

"No."

"Then *who are you*?" he said.

"I guess there's some mistake," I said, "I got your number from the paper in Pendleton, Oregon."

"Not Umatilla?" he said.

"Well," I paused, "sort of."

"Sort of *what*? Is this another one of those crank calls? If it is, buddy, fuck the hell off."

I could feel my stupidity, the heat on my face.

"Are you in Umatilla or not?" he said, like he was in charge of the call, not me.

"County," I said, "not town."

"So, you *are* in Umatilla?" he said.

"Yes," I said, and the operator cut in, asked for another two dollars and thirty-five cents for five minutes. I told her I thought the call was done.

"No, no," he said, in a voice raised almost into a shout. "Give me the number."

I was stuck between words. I wanted off the telephone worse than I'd pretty much wanted anything in my life.

"I met a girl," he said.

The operator said to put in more coins. I wavered, a quarter pinched in my fingers.

"She's . . . ," he said, and the line clicked.

I let the quarter drop into the slot, then another. The guy mumbled in the background as the phone dinged a count of my coins.

When the money had finally dropped into the bin, I said, "You help runaways?"

"Yes," he said with a tone that sounded suspicious.

"I'm looking for the whereabouts of a girl." Whereabouts. Where did I come up with *that*?

I could hear the woman's voice in the background. He must have turned to her. "Be quiet," he said. Then he came back on to me. "You aren't with the police?"

"No."

"You know anything about Umatilla Indian goods?" he said. "Umatilla princesses' dresses?"

"I guess I do," I said.

"You know Charlotte La Force?" he said. Now his tone changed again, got all quiet and low, intimate like he was talking to someone in the next room.

"No."

"She says she knows about Umatilla Indian goods."

"Goods?" I said. I couldn't keep track of this guy.

"Art, leather goods, beaded maidens' gowns, headdresses, that sort of thing."

"Not much," I said. "There must be people who know more, experts or something. You try them?"

"I'm the expert," he said. "Besides, I like to do things my own way, buddy."

"I guess I know a little bit," I said. Everybody in the county knew something about Indian goods.

"Listen, buddy," he said, "I'm in that business." I couldn't guess what kind of business that might be. "What was your name again? Jack?" he said, "McTavish?"

"McIntyre," I said.

"Scotch or Irish?" he said.

"Scotch," I said.

"I knew it," he said, "I knew it," all excited and friendly now.

"I'm looking for Patty," I said, "Patricia Pugh."

"Pew?" he said. "How do you spell it?"

I spelled out Pugh for him.

"Give me your number," he said. "I have ways to check. If she's here, the *Cavalerie* will find her."

Cavalerie?

"I'll let you know what I find. I need," he said, "some way to reach you when I locate this Patricia Pugh." There was a pause as if he was waiting for me to rattle off my telephone number. "Are you still there?" he said. "Where can I reach you?"

And I rolled out Raunch's telephone number in Pendleton.

chapter 40

MARCH MARKED THE last of the season of waiting. But for the freak snow, and the lack of moisture, that March would have been pretty normal. In a normal year, March was when you got off the recliner and went into action. That year, by the middle of the month a thousand ants were crawling up the nerves in my neck, leaving a track of hot, fired-up hives. Nothing, I knew, would salve the jitters but the first day the weather let go and field work began again. When the middle of the month began warm, I dragged equipment out of the shed, hitched the drill to the tractor. Work had begun. I had a reason again.

But then my back gave out. I was wrestling with the hitch, lining it up to the back of the tractor, and my back went out in a bomb of pain that made me yell out so loud Molly heard it from the house. It was a school day, and Molly and I were on the place alone.

She came high-stepping out the back door, yelling my name as she headed toward the shed. She managed to get me into the car and she drove me into the emergency room at St. Joseph's in Pendleton. It took nearly three hours for the doctor to poke and x-ray and write out a prescription for painkillers and muscle relaxers.

The pills knocked me out even before we had gotten to the Pendleton city limits. The next thing I remembered was Molly shaking me awake, saying, "Jack, we're home."

I had no power to move my arms or my legs. The relaxer pills had even ruined my eyes and I saw things in a sort of one and a half, not double, really, but almost.

Molly push-pulled me into the house, made up the couch for a bed and laid me down.

And for three days I lay there in a mess of sheets, flat, my knees raised over the roll of a blanket and with one of Molly's green, quilted pillows under my back. I was useless.

RAUNCH CALLED. I'D been up but limping around for two days, the spasm gone, but my back so sore I couldn't stand even the pressure from the waistband of my pants. Edie and her mother had been back from church for nearly an hour. The house was warm from the furnace and smelling of chicken dressed with sage that Molly had baking in the oven. I was stumbling around with my shirts hanging out to cover the fact I had to leave the button undone at my fly. Once again, Edie had taken over the milking, slopping the three pigs and haying three feeder calves I'd picked up in January.

Edie answered the phone. She listened a minute, then held it out toward me "Dad," she said, "it's Raunch." She stood there with the receiver clutched in her fist, blinking at me like she suspected the call was something important.

I hadn't told her I'd talked to the fellow in Montreal, hadn't mentioned to anyone—even Raunch—that I'd left his number. I didn't think anything would come out of the call.

"'Lo," I said.

"You know somebody named *the Major*?" He chuffed out a laugh like it was some kind of joke. "In *Montreal, Canada?*"

"Sort of," I said.

"Sort of?" he said. "He called here, said you gave him my number."

"Yeah," I said, "I didn't think he'd ever use it."

"Jesus, Mack," he said, "what's going on?" I could envision him, his face open with his brand of humor, a white-tooth grin spread across his face.

Molly was working on dinner in the kitchen, but Edie still hovered. I lowered my voice. "Later," I said.

"I mean this guy asked you to call but says you better not go to the cops. I mean like, what's going on, Mackie?"

Molly yelled for Edie to come help her with some of the dinner. At first, Edie stood planted like she wasn't going to move. "Edie?" her mother shouted, "come set the table." Edie turned and went into the kitchen.

Raunch said, "Man, what the fuck's up is what I want to know." His voice wasn't worried so much as curious. "You in trouble again?" he said.

And I wasn't real sure if I was or not.

"I can't talk now."

I could trust him to keep this to himself. He'd tried to cover for me so many years ago, but I don't think Larry would ever have spoken to me again if it hadn't have been for the girls. For them— his daughter and mine—Larry kept lines open, but we never did the things we used to do together again, never played town team baseball again, never slapped one another on the shoulder again, nor took ourselves in to the Slammer in town, or to Cimmyottis for a quick beer or two.

chapter 41

I DIALED THE numbers Raunch gave me. It was not the same telephone number I had called from the pay phone a few days before.
The phone rang twice. "Alloo," a woman's voice said, lower than the
first one but soft.

"Hello," I said, "is the Major there?"

"Who ees calling, please?" Like the other woman, this one's voice
was foreign and sweet and girlish, somehow.

"Jack," I said.

She muffled the phone, said something I couldn't make out.
There was some shuffling on the other end, then he came on. "Hello,
Jack. I take it the number I have been calling is a friend of yours out
there."

"Yes," I said.

"Is this fellow someone I should meet?"

"Just a friend," I said.

"He know anything about the Umatillas or the Nez Perce or the Cayuse? Maybe he can turn me onto some stuff," he said, his tone cute, almost flirty, like he was talking for the benefit of some audience. "You cowboys got history out there, man. Sacajawea," he smacked his lips, "Jesus, what a woman, the Whitman massacre, Chief Joseph." He seemed to know more about our history than I did. "Maybe I should meet your friend."

"I don't think so," I said.

I was beginning to think this guy had a screw loose, as Sergeant Al had said, and I was wasting my time, as well as a whole lot of change, calling him. What were the chances he knew anything about Patty after all this?

"After we hung up the other day," he said, "I thought of something else about the La Force girl. God, Jack, she could be the same age as Josette, my little granddaughter, you know. Pretty, too, like my Josette. I mean Josette is going to be a knockout, a *knock OUT.* The girls could be sisters," he said, "The blue eyes run in my family. But of course my Josette wouldn't . . . ," he paused.

"What?" I said.

"Wouldn't be a," he giggled, "dancer." The woman giggled behind him, as if they shared in some kind of joke.

"Is she there?" I said. "We'd like to talk to her."

"Here? Hell no. Who's 'we'? You haven't told the police you and I have been talking, have you?"

"No," I said.

"Who's 'we'?"

Cornered, I said, "My wife and me."

"Oh, you're married?"

"Yes," I said. Why did I feel I didn't want to admit it to him? "Why did you want me to call?" I said.

"You don't need to get mad." He was flirty again, "Silly man." He paused like maybe he was switching the phone from one ear to the other. "I forgot to tell you that she had an unattractive tattoo on her left hand, one I'm sure she did herself."

Tattoo? Patty didn't have a tattoo. I was starting to breathe again, starting to think this was finally the end of this guy.

"It's a P," he said, "a letter P like for Patty."

chapter 42

SERVICES FROM THE Church of the Redeemer in Boise were playing on the kitchen radio, the choir beginning to swing into "All Hail the Power of Jesus's Name." Edie was making her way around the table to our three places, laying the forks around. Once the forks were done, she concentrated on folding three napkins into paper triangles, settling them to the left sides of our places. Molly was stirring gravy on the stove.

As I walked in, Molly stopped stirring, took the pan off the stove. "Raunch called," I said.

She turned around to face me, holding the wooden spoon up like a weapon she was aiming to whack. "Mol, I need to tell you something."

Something in my tone made Molly's eyes flicker to Edie. "Edith, go up to your room and change out of your church clothes."

I cleared my throat. "No," I said. "She should hear what I have to say."

The radio choir sang, "*. . . every tribe on this terrestrial ball . . .*"
Molly set the spoon down on a saucer smeared with gravy goo. She
turned down the element under the green beans. I took my chair at
the table, waited. Edie sidled into hers, slipping her narrow waist
into the space without bothering to pull out the chair. "*. . . and
crown him Lord of all . . .*"

Molly sat, her breath coming from the back of her throat ragged
as if she had run a mile rather than walked the few feet from the
stove. She laced her fingers together in front of herself, waiting for
me to spew out what I had to say while her chicken roasted in the
oven. Under her apron, Molly was wearing a dress she hadn't been
able to get into for years. It had a wide belt. It was knit, black, tight
across her chest so the shimmer of her white slip showed through.

I looked at my own hands lying where Molly would soon set my
plate. They gave me something besides my wife and daughter to
look at. "A man," I said, "says he knows a woman who he thinks is
from around here."

Molly's face was blank. Edie's temples throbbed with blue veins.
I didn't know what Molly expected, but it couldn't make much
sense from what I'd said, so far. It left her without words. She
couldn't even counter with a question. "Sergeant Al says it's reaching for straws, but there's a tiny," I measured a quarter inch with my
fingers, "chance it might be Patty." My back hurt, and I straightened up. I eased the muscle a little.

"Sergeant Al," Molly said.

"Yeah," I said, "with the Pendleton police."

"Have you got us in some kind of trouble, Jack?"

I shook my head. "No," I said, "honest."

Edie sat quiet but straight. She wasn't slumping any longer.

"I met him when I reported Patty missing," I added, like that
might clear it up.

"You reported Patty missing," she said, a statement, not a question. Molly sat there, her breasts peaking like headlights from each side of her apron, her damp hands laid on the table.

"Yes."

"Why you?"

"Nobody else did," I said.

I told her again there was a woman in Montreal who might be from around here and someone had reported her to the police in Pendleton. It was not true, there was no reporting to police, but I didn't know how else to put it.

"Montreal is four thousand miles away."

"She knows about Umatilla Indians."

"Oh," she said, "*that's* proof."

"They are checking," I said.

Edie had stuck a finger in her mouth and was going at one of her nails.

"Well," Molly said. "It can't be Patty."

"I don't know," I said.

Edie pitched herself down into her chair, sat buckled in half like an empty pop can, her teeth thunking on an edge of her nail.

A DAY LATER Raunch got another call from Canada.

chapter 43

RAIN CAME IN a whip of wind, thin, prickly stuff, not worth more than misery. The drill I'd worked on the day my back spasmed was now attached to the tractor, though I'd not used it. But for the rain, I could have begun fieldwork as my back was slowly getting better, though bending, or twisting in certain ways still held the threat of another spasm. By afternoon, the storm blew serious. The dogs' dishes filled with water, waterfalls streamed off the barn roof, the bare patches of siding where paint had given up on the house were dark, nearly black.

I'd told Raunch to hang up on the guy the next time he called. The guy wanted Raunch to tell him my home number, which Molly had made unlisted, when the creditors were all calling. Raunch refused. But the guy told him it was urgent, an emergency. I dialed the number Raunch passed on. This time, I was calling from home, from the phone in the living room, with Molly around the corner, sewing. The Major said he would be waiting for my call at six o'clock their time in Montreal. He added, as if I couldn't figure it out, that would be three o'clock our time.

It was nearly dark outside, and fierce. Black clouds blew by the windows, then tumbled on toward the east. Every lamp in the house was on. Molly was at the Singer under the chandelier in the sewing room. Mother had not taken the chandelier when she moved, said she didn't have room for it. It was the last thing to suggest Mother had ever lived in the house. Molly was working on yards of brown and yellow flowered material she'd ordered from the Sears catalog. She had finished the church curtains and bought more for herself, enough to cover the two windows in our room and the tiny window in the upstairs bathroom.

I took the receiver from the little niche, strung the cord across the braided rug to the recliner. The sewing machine stopped when I dialed. Molly was going to overhear whatever I had to say to the guy in Canada.

It was three o'clock exactly.

It was as if he was waiting there for the phone to ring. "Jack?" he said.

"Yeah."

"I've been thinking," he said, before I got anything else out. "What if Charlotte *is* Patty? You'd want to find that out, wouldn't you?"

I didn't answer.

"You'd want to know for sure," he said, "wouldn't you?"

When I didn't say anything, he said, "Wouldn't you?"

"Yeah," I said.

Fabric *shisshed* quietly, but the sewing machine remained silent.

"I'd pay your way up here," he said.

"What?" I said.

"I need to develop contacts in your neck of the woods."

"I don't think . . ."

"Call it business," he said. "You come up, spend a few hours, maybe we put something together, you win, and I win."

"No," I said.

"You don't care about Charlotte, then?" he said. "Patty?"

I listened to his breathing up there in Montreal, him waiting for some kind of reply from me. When I didn't make one, he said, "I care about Charlotte," with no speck of sincerity in his voice. "Patty," he said.

"I don't think so." Go to Montreal? God, if I never went anywhere the rest of my life, I would die happy.

"I saw her again," he said, "last night." He paused, as if remembering the night. "The more I see of her, the more I think she could be your girl." There was another small pause, the hushing noise of the long-distance telephone lines, familiar in a way they hadn't been a few days ago. He said, "I mean, I'm serious, buddy. You get your bones up here. See for yourself. Let me call my travel agent, set you up with a ticket."

"It couldn't be her."

"Why not come on up here and find out?" he said. "Listen, Jack. I'm in business, Indian goods, Civil War items. It's how I know Charlotte . . . Patty."

"I don't know anything about the Civil War," I said. Molly's fabric lay quiet as if it, not Molly, was the one listening to my side of the call.

"Uh-uh," he said, scolding. "I think you are sitting on a gold mine of Indian goods out there. Beadwork vests, gowns, parfleche bags, baskets. I want to talk with you, Jack. I need a contact out there. Right now the market for Northwest Indian goods is wild, wild, I tell you, buddy, wild. I don't want somebody else capturing a market that could make you and me a hell of a lot of money. Hear what I'm saying, *Jackie*?"

I still didn't get why he didn't find some legitimate expert. This all seemed so roundabout. How did anybody keep up with this guy?

"I need you," he said, "now."

"I don't think so."

"A couple days of your time," he said. "*Jackie.*" I was beginning to despise this guy.

"There is no way."

"I'll call the airlines right now, have them wire you a ticket."

Wire me a ticket? He was going to wire me a ticket?

"For the cost of a freaking airline ticket, I'm not going to miss a chance."

"I said no."

The foot of the sewing machine clicked down. I waited for the machine to start up, to cover my end of the conversation, but it didn't.

"Why not?"

"Work," I said.

But something in my voice must have clued him that work was not too much of a choice right then with the rain.

"Three days," he said, "I wire you a ticket tonight, you fly up here tomorrow, we talk, you check out our girl, fly home the next day, and you're back to work."

"I can't come to Canada," I said.

Molly's shadow appeared in the archway.

"Why not?" he said. "If nothing comes of it, I'm out a few measly hundred dollars US, and you've got a little vacation to show for it."

"My wife," I said.

His voice went wary. "I'll send a ticket for her, too, what the hey. There's big money to be made, Jackie, *big* money." Then he cleared his throat. "Is she cool?" He paused, then said, "A progressive type? Listen, Jack, I know—and you know—that most women, my wife included ..."

WHEN PATTY WENT AWAY

Wife? He'd said he had a granddaughter, but even then I'd assumed he wasn't married.

"Most women don't want to see some of the more interesting sides of human nature, and Charlotte *is* an interesting side of human nature." He paused. "I can send you a ticket for your wife, what the hell. But think about it. You, me, we can check out the scene, you settle for yourself if Charlotte isn't your Patty. I suggest you come up here alone, you know what I mean."

I was beginning to get a hint at what he could mean.

"The way I see it, it's a win-win. You find out about the girl, and maybe I get a business partner that makes the both of us richer. You think about it. Give me your number." He waited like he was waiting for me to fill in the blank. When I didn't, he said, "Call me, then, and if you tell me no, you'll never hear from me again." He paused, and I thought we were done. "And, you'll never know for sure if it's your Patty up here."

MOLLY WAS STANDING in the doorway, holding the wad of brown and yellow material.

"He wants me to come to Canada," I said.

"I heard."

Outside the front room window, the school bus ground to a stop at our corner. The bus was slick yellow in the rain, the same shade as the daisies in Molly's curtain fabric. We both turned to watch it, as if it was the first time it was letting out our daughter from school. Molly's expression was empty, unfocused, waiting for me to give direction, but open in a way I hadn't seen on her for years. The school bus door whapped shut and the bus wheezed on down the road.

Molly said, "We will talk about this later" and turned with her wad of fabric toward the sewing table.

"I think we need to talk about it now," I said.

"You started this, and you're the one who has to put an end to it." Her face had drawn in again, closed up, she seemed certain again, convinced I would go along with her like I always did. She dropped into the sewing chair, laid some of the material under the sewing foot, and lined it up to set the machine to chattering, closing off further discussion.

Edie came in the back door, stomped her feet clean on the mat.

"I think we need to talk about this now," I said.

Molly looked up from the seam she'd begun to sew, her hands dangerously close to the needle. "As soon as our daughter goes up to her room," she said and laid her foot on the electrical feed. The machine whirred into action.

Edie clomped up the back porch steps and came into the living room, her arms full of books.

Over the noise of the sewing machine I said, "Edie, sit down for a minute. You, and your mother and I need to have another talk."

Molly stopped the machine. Edie's eyes shifted toward her mother as if she was looking for confirmation from *The Parent Who Decided*. I went to my daughter, set my hand on her shoulder.

MOLLY SAT IN her rocker. Propped against her bosom was the Bible, a warning of black leather and worn gold lettering. I had started to blurt a word or two about how was your day at school, Ede? You get wet coming home? but hadn't uttered anything truly coherent. Molly set the chair to rocking, the floor to groaning. Edie eased into the couch at the far end of the living room. We all sat as if pitted against one another, each in our own corner. I finally managed to get out, "Raunch got another call from Canada."

Edie jumped up. "They found Patty," she said.

"Probably not, honey," I said. "It's a long shot."

Molly rocked faster.

"But maybe," Edie said.

Molly rocked on, shaking her head, now, to the beat of the chair.

"I think we have to at least consider me going up to see, Molly."

"Daddy," Edie said.

Molly patted the Bible. "You're taking after your mother, Jack," she said. It was an accusation.

I said. "I haven't left the place since we've been married."

"Don't exaggerate. You were gone for months."

"That was work."

"You always wanted to," she said, her nose beginning to redden. Edie pressed herself into the couch. She had never seen her mother cry. I'd once heard Patty proclaim Molly was tough as John Wayne. John Wayne never cried. "You can't leave now," Molly said.

"I'm not saying I'm going," I said.

"What *are* you saying then, Jack?"

What was I saying? I was getting confused again, like I always did when it came to confronting her. Raunch would call and tell me when the Major had called again. He was supposed to take the Major's number. "All I'm saying is that the fellow from Canada is going to call back in a few minutes and I have to know what to tell him."

"Tell him no," Molly said.

Edie nearly disappeared into the pillows and the clutter of school books and pink parka. Only her knees jutted up sharp. "I knew you wouldn't do anything." Her knees began to flap. "You never do."

Molly's rocking slowed. "Your father has things to do here at home."

"What if it was *Edie* who was gone?" I said, "instead of Patty."

"It isn't," Molly said.

"What if it *was?*"

Molly squeezed her slab of Bible.

"I'm afraid for Edie," I said.

"Trust in the Lord. What's to be afraid of?"

"The way nobody cares," I said.

Molly bolted forward. "Nobody cares? Nobody cares?"

"About Patty," I said. "What if it was someone else? What if it was *Edie*?"

"Edith has the faith. The Lord Jesus Christ will take care of her."

"Why?" I said.

"Why, what?" Molly said.

Edie stuck a finger in her mouth, chomped on a nail.

"How can anyone sit in judgment of a girl?" I said. "Patty is only a child."

"No one is sitting in judgment," Molly said.

"You are," I said.

She patted her chest. "'The angels will come and separate the wicked from the righteous,'" she said in a helpless way, as if she wasn't part of it at all.

"We've been waiting a long time for these angels," I said.

She thrust the palm of her hand at me. "Stop it."

"Well, we have."

"You don't hear the word of the Lord, Jack. You never have."

I ducked my head, swallowed the urge to do what I always did: back down.

"Traipsing off to the edge of the continent," she said, "on some harebrained hunt is not the work of the angels, and it isn't doing right by your daughter."

Edie sat there, her finger buried in her mouth.

"I'm saying that's exactly what this *is* all about. The world's changed, Molly, you see it every day, kids grown up before they are supposed to, wars being fought for no reason anybody understands, machines, televisions, radios blaring things—ugly things—telling us stuff none of us should even have to know. I don't know if I can understand where the world is going anymore."

"Patty's made her bed," Molly said.

"Is that in your scriptures, too, Molly?"

She brought the Bible up to her eyes, rifled through some of the pages. "Psalm 1:1," she said, "'Blessed is the man that walketh not in the counsel of the ungodly, nor standeth in the way of sinners, nor sitteth in the seat of the scornful.'"

"So who," I said, "is the judge?"

She slapped the Bible down onto her thighs. "What have I been reading to you, Jack?"

"I don't hear the Lord in this," I said. "I hear *you* in it, Molly."

Molly gasped. I'd never spoken to her like this.

Edie pulled the parka into her lap, crumpled herself behind it, but she kept her eyes on me. They were filled with something awake I hadn't seen in them for a long time.

The telephone rang. I jumped. Molly set the rocker into wild sweeps. The phone rang again and again. Edie coughed. I heard the whish of her parka as she pulled herself up off the couch. She picked up the receiver, pressed it against my ear. "Hello," I said.

It was Raunch. "Well, buddy," he said. "I just got off with your Major."

I wanted to puke, but said, "Thanks." I dialed the number. The phone answered on the second ring. "Jack," he said, "are you sure that fellow is not with authorities?" I told him no. "I made reservations. Your ticket is at the airport in Pendleton. I'll see you tomorrow evening." He didn't even ask if I was coming.

chapter 44

IT WAS LIKE a dike broke between Molly and me. The stream of words we'd kept inside for so many years busted out, flooding the room. We sat up way past the time Molly usually went to bed. Each of us was planted in our own place, me in the recliner, Molly in the rocker, the stretch of braided rug the size of a football field between us.

Wind moaned, humming in through the windows where the sashes didn't meet the sill, the notes moaning high, then low and high again. Molly had sent Edie to bed two hours before and she had left the room looking back over her shoulder at me, doubting, as she disappeared into the dark of the hallway.

"She's like her *mother,*" Molly said.

"Edie?"

"Patty," she said, implying Patty was loose, immoral. "It still hurts, after all these years. I try to forgive her. I try not to think her crazy mind is God's punishment. I try to see that she is a child in God's eye. It's why . . . ," she said, then stopped and blew into a tissue.

I went to her, put my hand on her shoulder.

She didn't wince but hiccupped twice. "So," she said, her face glowing red, "you're going on this wild goose chase."

I squeezed her shoulder.

Her mouth turned down, sour. "It's foolish," she said.

"It's not the first time I've been called a fool." I chuffed a bitter laugh. Outside, iced rain peppered the windows. The gusts had lost their harmonious voices, sounded more like screams now.

Molly looked up at me standing over her, the dark of her eyes swimming. "Does our daughter have a sister?"

"A sister? I'd never thought of it exactly like that," I added. "I guess the girls were close enough."

She swung the chair forward, getting ready to bolt out of it. *Never thought of it?*" She blew her nose on a wadded paper napkin she took from her pocket. She mumbled something into it that sounded like "The wild *mumscum yurcide.*"

The rocker hit the instep of my boot, jerked to a stop. "Guess I never did think of them like sisters exactly," I said.

"But is that why you're doing all this?" The rocker kicked back, taking her shoulder out from under my hand.

"I guess so."

She rocked forward again, took another whack at my instep. "I knew it," she said. She pulled in her lips, rocked back like she was going to have another go at my foot. But she braced the rocker back on her heels. "Larry was a saint, to take care of her all those years."

The only movement then, the only life in the room was the whip of the windowpanes. "Why wouldn't he take care of her?" I said.

"Would *you?*"

"Would I what?"

"Take care of her."

A gust of wind billowed the windows, warped the reflection of the lamp, torqued the glow from the woodstove into a grimace. What had happened? What was Molly talking about? Edie has a sister? Jesus. "You think Patty . . . ?" I said.

"Is she?"

My heart jerked the snap on my shirt. I stumbled over to the recliner, put my head in my hands. "Jesus, Mol," I said.

"Well?"

There was no way anybody could add up the months or the years to make Patty my daughter. Jackie and I had dated in high school, but there had never been anything more between us until that one fucking night when everything went wrong, one fucking night when Patty was already three years old. Was Molly saying for years Jackie and I had . . . "Of course not," I said.

She drew both arms over the Bible. Her face went solid as a brick. "The Lord knows if that is the truth," she said.

"Of course it's the truth," I said.

This. *This* was what had eaten on Molly all these years. I stared at the rounds of braids on the rug. "Molly," I said, "I'm a stupid jerk farmer. All I ever wanted was my family and a place to feel at home. I never wanted to hurt anybody, never wanted anything more than to make you and Edie happy. But I never figured out how to do it. I look around and wonder how everybody else knows what they're doing, where they're going. You particularly, Molly, you knew, I always thought you had it right. But I can see you got things wrong, too. Big things. Awful things." It was then that I understood the words she'd mumbled earlier, that I hadn't understood. "The wild comes from your side," she'd said. She thought Patty's wildness came from me.

"How can you keep track of all the things you do, Molly, the bank figures, the budget, and still think there is some way Patty could be my daughter?"

She didn't answer, but I could see that she was beginning to believe me and seeing it made me feel stronger. "All I ever wanted was us, you, Edie, me, and whoever else might come along. It's all I wanted, Mol, a family, food on the table, somebody to count on day after day. What's happening to us?"

"We're here," she said.

"I mean *everybody*, Mol. Stuff's changing. When Patty went away and there was nobody to look for her, I finally saw that the world's going somewhere I don't understand, somewhere I don't want it to go, somewhere I can't hold onto. I don't want my daughter growing up in a world where she can't trust somebody's going to be there if something happens to her."

"As far as I can see, *we're* here for her," she said.

"But what's she seeing? She's seeing nobody's taking care of a friend she loves, a girl who's like her."

"They aren't alike in any way, Jack." She was angry now, bitter.

"But they *are*," I said. "They're too young, too dumb to know which way's up, and Edie sees her best friend cut loose and nobody's standing there for her. How's Edie ever going to trust in anybody? What kind of world is Edie seeing?"

"So, you're going," she said, but now she wasn't sniffling, only tipping her head to the side like she was the one who was confused.

"I have to," I said.

THE NEXT MORNING as I did chores, Molly laid out slacks and socks and shirts on the bed. We ate in silence, the three of us, Edie sitting quiet at her place, her mother fussing with pans and toast, and pouring more than necessary of our milk and cocoa.

After breakfast, I went upstairs. Molly was still in the kitchen, cleaning up from breakfast. As I shoved the tail of my white shirt into the slacks Molly had ironed, I heard Edie clomp up the stairs. There were still ten minutes before the school bus came to pick her up, an hour before I had to leave for Pendleton for the flight.

Edie rounded the bedroom door, stood there holding onto her school books as tight as her mother clung to her Bible. She had on a plaid skirt that was out of fashion and heavy socks and rubber, knee-high boots. Even I knew girls Edie's age were not dressing that way those days. They were wearing tight jeans and sweaters, and plastic earrings that dangled almost to their shoulders.

I sat on the bed to tie my shoes. She came over, sat down next to me. Her face had a little color, for a change, her eyes snapped with a little life. She began toeing a tan-colored flower on the rug.

I put my arm around her shoulder, pulled her against me. "I hope you are right."

"I am," she said, and she pecked a sharp kiss on my cheek, then stood up and walked out of the room.

chapter 45

MOLLY'S HONEYMOON SUITCASE pressed against my leg. I was standing in the baggage claim at the airport in Montreal with Molly's suitcase, the only thing anchoring me. It was small and beige. Molly's parents had given it to her to take on our honeymoon to Coeur d'Alene nineteen years before. She'd had little use for it since.

I stood on the hard pavement of the Montreal airport listening to voices on the loudspeaker speaking languages that I'd never heard before. I was so nervous I belched one puff after the other. It was too hot in the terminal for my jacket. The flight had come in early, and the Major wouldn't be meeting me for another fifteen minutes.

Through the glass doors, cars pulled up, people hugged, picked up their luggage and drove away. I squinted every time a car drove up. The Major said he would be wearing a Pendleton coat and described himself as a little past his fighting weight. The terminal was dizzy with movement. Hundreds of people were going places, up the escalators, milling around the conveyors that clattered round and round. I had been in airports when I was a kid. Every other summer Mom would pack Lee and me off with her to Minneapolis to see her folks. Given a choice, I'd never have gone with them. I appreciated that Molly never wanted to go places any more than I did. For Molly, the tighter she made her world, never venturing farther from the house than to go to Philpott or Pendleton, the happier she was.

And there I was, an impediment among all these people and all this noise. I didn't dare move. How did anyone carve out peace in a place like this where nothing stood still, where there was always somebody shouting or whistling and grappling clothes bags hung over their shoulders, or hauling around their crying babies, or lugging their suitcases, the loudspeakers blaring a garble of babbling languages?

My back was screaming. I lowered myself into one of the chrome and plastic seats, leaned forward. There was no one sound in the mess, yet all was sound. I'd spent so much of my life out where the warble of sparrows or the caw of a crow seemed loud enough to plug your ears, and where there was no more movement than the breath of a breeze over the hills. I closed my eyes against the acid glare of the fluorescent lights.

The last time the Major and I talked, I had tried to describe myself, my mud-colored hair, my skinny, six-foot frame. "Cowboy boots?' he'd said in a hopeful sort of way. At one time, I'd had a pair of cowboy boots but rarely wore anything but the lace-ups with steel toes Molly bought. I told him I was past forty and he didn't answer with his own age.

I felt a tap on my elbow. "Jack McIntyre?"

I STOOD UP. My back threatened. He held out his hand. I took it. His hand was damp and soft. Mine, I knew, was dry and crusted with calluses. After we'd shaken, I wanted to wipe may hand on my slacks but didn't.

He was fat. His Pendleton coat gapped open over the feed-sack expanse of his gut. The Pendleton coat was an expensive blue-and-black plaid, the kind of coat outsiders—dudes—wore when they crowded into town for the Round-Up.

"My car is out front," he said.

I stumbled after him with the honeymoon bag. If this Charlotte wasn't Patty, I was getting out of there as fast as I could.

Sergeant Al had warned me he didn't trust this guy any farther than he could throw him. He was dressed downright weird. He was wearing tight black pants with a yellow stripe down the sides and black knee-high boots with spurs that jangled when he walked. People gaped when he went by, stepped back to clear the way. He made small talk as we walked out the front doors, commented that they had had snow most of the day.

A blast of cold air hit me in the face like a wall. People ran to their taxis grasping their coats closed in their free hands. I hadn't planned on this much cold or the exhausts from the running cars spewing clouds.

"Over here," he said, and he led me to a yellow 1937 Cord 810, a car nobody I knew had ever seen except on calendars or the centerfold of *Car and Driver*. He gave a wad of bills to a traffic cop standing with his arms folded beside the car, and he opened the trunk, said, "You can put your suitcase in here."

WE SAT IN the heat of the Cord as he wound it through the afternoon traffic. I had never been in such traffic, cars jutting in and out, trucks farting Jake brakes. Nothing had prepared me for this. I hung on as he bolted in and out of the crowds risking that Cord like it was nothing but a half-dead farm truck.

"So how long have you lived in Oregon?" he said.

"All my life."

He held onto the steering wheel like a woman, with both hands. "Beautiful country." Every finger was covered with silver and turquoise rings. The Cord made a turn and set me off balance. My back began to cramp.

"You go often?" I said, "to Oregon?"

"I've been everywhere," he said, "Montana, New Mexico, Texas, California, but I never got the chance to get to your neck of the woods. Always wanted to, no time to do it." He whacked my thigh with the back of his hand. "It's why I was so glad to meet you, partner."

Through the windows I could hear tire chains rattling, studs popping on the street. The curbs were piled high with filthy snow, people running on the sidewalks, cupping gloves over their ears, ducking into stores. He handled the Cord like it was a sports car in a race, careless. I could only guess at what the car might be worth: sixty, seventy thousand, maybe a hundred.

"Do you mind," he said, "if I stop a minute?"

I shook my head.

He pulled into a narrow alley behind a shop with a broad brown awning. "Major Dalrymple's Trading Post," the sign said. "Western and Native Collections, Civil War Regalia." He parked the Cord behind the store in a lot with only two car spaces. The other space was occupied by a Jaguar XKE. "I'll be back in a moment."

So I sat there watching the blank of a brick wall and an unmarked back door in Montreal, sitting in an automobile so rich it could have paid off everything I owed.

He wasn't gone five minutes before he came back with a package the size of a seat cushion wrapped in brown paper. He handed the package to me, said, "I thought you might be interested in this." He looked at me like he was assessing something. "Later," he said.

I looked around that car. It was a thing designed for no more than two people to get somewhere. There was no backseat, there was no space but the floor to settle the package. The package was heavy and smelled of leather tannin.

HE WOUND THE Cord through traffic without any regard to the grit of the sanded streets that kicked up and peppered the windshield and the car's perfect grill. He turned onto small streets where the traffic was lighter, then edged too close to the tail of the car ahead. "I'm putting you up at the Bonaventure," he said.

It had turned dark, the lights from the city reflecting on a white sky getting ready to dump more snow.

"We'll get you checked in, then grab a bite at a little place I know." He checked his watch. It was thick gold, rimmed with diamonds, and it glittered in the streetlights. "The show won't start for another three hours," he said.

The Bonaventure turned out to be the Hilton. It rose seventeen stories. The carpet swallowed your feet. The Major pressed the elevator button marked "Lobby" and up we went. When the elevator stopped, he ushered me out. The lobby was filled with leather sofas gathered around heavy coffee tables where people sat and looked out the broad window onto a rooftop garden. The carpet was so thick it muffled noise in the same way Helen and Lee's white shag muffled Thanksgiving dinners.

The Major left his hand on my shoulder as he led me to the front desk. The clerks, there were three of them in black suits, nodded and said, "Major," as if they practiced it every night.

"My secretary called," he said.

One of the clerks, a fellow in his thirties, stepped up. A string of thinning blond hair was combed over his scalp. The clerk looked at me. "Mr. McIntyre?"

The Major pressed me into the counter. I set Molly's honeymoon suitcase by my feet.

The clerk reached under the counter, pulled out a key. "The Suite?"

he said. His blond sideburns were thick as patches of tumbleweed, like he kept them that way to make up for the loss on top.

"Naturally," the Major said.

The clerk held up one finger. "*Une nuit?*" he said.

The Major held up two fingers. "*Deux,*" he said.

I handed the suitcase over to a bellman that the Major tipped with a ten-dollar Canadian bill.

chapter 46

AS WE LEFT the hotel, the Major said, "Hungry?"

I didn't think I was hungry in a way the Major would under-stand. I was hungry in a meatloaf way, burger-and-fries way, a way I could afford. I shrugged, maybe yes, maybe no.

We drove down streets lined with stone buildings, some with turrets. They must have been there for a couple of centuries, dark, huddled behind snow drifts, doors closed, shop lights dimmed for the night. It had started to snow again, tiny cold flecks that the wind gave no chance to stick or stay put.

We drove out of the area by the St. Lawrence River, away from the old stone buildings heading toward a newer part of town. The Major turned onto a street called Maisonneuve. It cut a swath into the glass and granite canyons. The Major muttered, "the Financial District." The Cord swept up to the front of a restaurant tucked into a narrow street, near a sign that said McGill University.

The Major stopped, and a valet opened the Major's door, then stood back, rigid. He was dressed in a short red jacket and a squared-off cap like a French legionnaire. The Major got out without saying a word, started toward the restaurant, then he turned and threw the valet the keys.

The *Beouf et Biere* had a small bar where a piano player fingered out a mushy version of "Heart of Gold." It was quiet in there, hushed like whispers, dim light, dark, the feeling of brown. The mahogany bar was backed by about a thousand beveled mirrors that sparkled like a wall full of diamonds. An assortment of people, men mostly, sat at the tray-sized tables. In fact, there were only a couple of women, dressed in long legs and low-cut blouses, sitting alone with guys, highballs sweating on the tables. The men wore dark suits, and you could almost smell the money. They were laughing, their ties loosened, collars pulled open. A couple of them looked at us as we walked by, nodded. I heard them mumble something—the Major's name maybe—as we passed them. I felt important following along in the Major's updraft.

The Major's spurs clanked as he sauntered over to a table marked *Reserved*. Our coming in set the bartender, the waiters, and the waitresses into motion. The Major held up one finger toward nobody in particular. A door behind the bar, covered in mirrors, opened up and set the bevels in the mirrors alive. A guy exited the door, swung it shut, and set the mirrors blazing again. He came toward our table. He wasn't one of the waiters, and he wasn't the bartender.

As he came through the room toward us, he was smiling, white, even teeth that looked like they had been sculpted in the dentist's office. "Major," he said a little too loud. He was a slick sort of guy, somebody you'd never see in Philpott or Pendleton, a type you could find only in a city. His hair was shaved on the sides, and curling to his shoulders in back. He wore a silk shirt, and he had a diamond ring on his little finger that glittered like one of the beveled mirrors. He shook the Major's hand and said, "Let me take your coats."

The Major said, "Sharl," then, "Jack McIntyre."

Sharl shook my hand. His shake was strong, unlike the Major's. He took my jacket and the Major's coat, held them pinched in his fingers.

"A friend of the Major's," Sharl said, "is a friend of mine." He had a Frenchy kind of accent. "You must be new to Montreal." His eyes slipped over me like he was assessing my JC Penney's shirt and the scarred face of my Timex watch. He didn't seem to pay much attention to the garb the Major had on. Under the Pendleton coat, the Major was wearing a dark shirt with epaulets, and there were brass buttons and tan-colored gauntlets folded over his belt. It was, I realized, an old Union cavalry uniform.

"Jack's from *Oregon*," the Major said, in a way that seemed a challenge to Sharl to guess where Oregon was. The Major chuffed a hearty laugh. "Oregon," he said, like coming from Oregon was the dearest thing in the world.

Sharl dropped the coats over one arm. "The States," he said, his voice maybe a little on the sarcastic side. "Let me hang your coats." As he walked away, he was turning the Major's Pendleton coat inside out. One of the waiters took the coats from Sharl and disappeared through the diamond door behind the bar. Sharl came back. "A couple sours?" he said.

The Major laid both hands on the table, fingers splayed to show all of his rings. "Sour OK with you?" he said.

I nodded. "Just one," I said.

Sharl went off snapping his fingers at one of the waiters.

The Major fingered one of his rings, a huge turquoise the size of a dollar coin and surrounded by diamonds.

"So," he said, "tell me about yourself. How did you come to live in Oregon?"

I told him a little about my dad and granddad and so on. He asked more questions, then sat back and let me ramble on as if what I had to say meant something to him. The waiter brought our sours, and as he set them on the table, the Major ordered two more.

It was warm in there, stuffy with the soft notes of the piano, the shuffling of feet, the muttering of voices talking low, laughing. My back was easing up; the sour, the low dark tone to the room were soothing as a cat's purr. The Major asked me a couple of more questions, listened as I spoke, then said, "So, what's your association with," he paused and gave me a sideways glance, "Charlotte?"

This was, I thought, what he was really after. I shook my head. "Probably nothing." I was glad to get that out. Now that I was here, I was thinking there was no way Patty would have come all the way up here. There was no way I could imagine it, no way at all.

"You know," he said, "there was a time when I thought she might have been young." His eyes popped open, a freaky kind of open. "*Real, real* young," he said. "Young enough she could have caused me a hell of a lot of trouble."

I wondered how young he thought this Charlotte was. As if he got a sense of my question he said, "Like maybe fifteen, sixteen." He took a drink of his sour, flashed four knuckles of his rings at me. "The same age as my little Josette." He downed the rest of his sour, then said, "My granddaughter."

At that moment my back began to cramp up again. I sat back in the chair.

He must have sensed some kind of disapproval coming from me. "Shit, man," he said, "don't get the wrong idea."

"Josette?" I said.

"My daughter's girl." He looked right and left like he was winding up to share a secret. "I might like them young—don't we all—but I make them legal, if I have to. You know I've seen her a couple times since I talked to you on the telephone."

"Josette?" I said.

"Charlotte, fucker," he said. He shook his head as if to say, you wouldn't believe this Charlotte. "All woman," he said.

The blond waiter set another couple of sours on the table, went away without asking for money. The Major held his glass up in a silent toast, took a long drink, then laid the glass on the table and began to spin it with the tips of his fingers. "She really doesn't look like my Josette at all," he said. He raised up his behind from the chair, dug under the gauntlet gloves into the pocket of his cavalry pants, pulled out a snake-skin wallet. He flapped it open, unfurled a line of plastic credit cards nearly two feet long.

I took another drink of my sour, thought how easy life must be for him.

He pulled a snapshot from somewhere in the wallet, flipped it in my face. It was a picture of a young girl about eleven or twelve years old. She had brown hair and bright, staring blue eyes. "My Josette," he said. He turned the picture back to look at it himself. "This was a couple of years ago. She's grown some since."

He turned the picture so I could see it again. His granddaughter was pretty, had the same reddish round face as he did, and a string of freckles lying over the bridge of her nose. She also had his cracking blue eyes. I had to admit, they were kind of like Patty's eyes.

"Her mother," the Major said, "is my wife's and my only girl."

"You have sons?" I said.

He held up two fingers. "Two," he said, in a way that said he'd rather not admit this. He took another drink of his sour but made no effort to find pictures of his sons, or anybody else, in his wallet. "I almost called and told you I was sure Charlotte couldn't be our girl, after all." He put the wallet back in his pocket. "I thought about it some, but the gown gave me the idea we should get our heads together anyway."

"Gown," I said.

"The Umatilla." He must have seen my confusion. "Her dress," he said, "the gown she wears when we see each other."

He said it was the Umatilla Indian gown that made him write the note in the Pendleton paper in the first place. "You got an untapped market down there," he said. "I can use it, in the wife's business. See," he leaned forward like he didn't want anybody in the bar to hear what he was about to say, "we've done Arizona, we've done New Mexico, we've done Montana. It's all been done—Navajo silver, pawn, trade, blankets, parfleche bags, papooses, Iroquois beads, peace pipes. The market's saturated. Don't get me wrong, we're still selling stuff like a son of a bitch. But I need a new line.

"A few years back, I put my wife into this collecting business. She was getting on my case about this and that. I thought hey, get her into something, keep her busy, now that the kids are out of the house.

"Well, let me tell you, buddy, I did good. That business of mine is panning out. Shit, six months ago, I bought the building for her."

He elbowed me.

"And she's into something that keeps her busy enough to give me a little elbow room, time to myself." He took another drink from the sour, drained it. "You know what I mean."

He pushed his broad face toward me like he wanted to whisper. I leaned closer.

"I can use you, Jack." He said. "Wasco baskets, cradleboards, even some pretty good beaded stuff comes from out your way."

The more he spoke, the less I understood.

He cleared his throat, let his eyes slide one way, then the other as if the people at the next table were listening in. "I thought," he said, "a cowboy like you could do some, uh, scouting."

"Scouting?" I said.

The waiter came over, took up our glasses, set two more sours in front of us.

"Seeing what's out there." He took the sour glass in his fingers. "For a fee, of course. A finder's fee." He took a swallow, breathed into the glass loud, like a horse. "You believe in past lives? You ever think about your past lives?"

I shrugged. I never thought about it. We lived, we died, and we either went to heaven or hell.

"I know all about mine," he said. At that moment, Sharl came over, laid his hand on the epaulet of The Major's cavalry shirt. "Your table," he said, "is ready."

The Major threw his napkin on the table and stood up. There was still half a drink left in his glass. I had drunk two. One more, untouched, sat in front of me. We left the drinks there. Sharl led us to a table off in one of the corners through a double-wide door. It was as dark as the bar, chandeliers made of elk horns and fitted with candles, red carpet as thick as the Hilton's. The tables were crafted out of myrtle burls and surrounded by high-wing chairs covered in leather. It swallowed you, that place, it took you into it the same way a down comforter would, settled you into the mumble of talking, leaning back, relaxing like the other men in their wing chairs, ankles crossed over their knees. Even their socks looked expensive. It was mostly men in there, forking up their steaks, drinking wine poured from dark bottles, leaning back in their chairs smoking cigars. What women were in there looked as expensive as the men, their bracelets with stones that sparked in the light and earrings they wore under blond beauty-parlor hairdos. As odd as it was, the Major in his cavalry uniform settled in as though he belonged there.

I HID BEHIND the menu. Even with a couple of sours down the hatch, I nearly fainted at the prices. The Major said he was going for the chateaubriand, the most expensive thing on the list. Then he clapped the menu shut and a waiter came over, stood by the Major's wingback. I was still stuck on the prices when the Major said, "Two briands."

"Your usual accompaniments, sir?"

The Major circled his fingers over the table. "A couple of Coronas with the dinner."

The steaks came. I'd never sunk my teeth into anything as fine as that steak in the *Beouf et Biere* that night. The meat was tender as custard. The beef was, the Major said, raised in Japan, fed special grains fermented in beer. Juices from it ran down the corners of his mouth and he patted them dry with the white linen napkin. Then he said, "Do you know the core of your being, Jack?"

I must have looked lost or something because he said, "I know." He hit his own chest with a closed fist. "*This* is the core of my being."

"The steak?"

"Funny man," he said. "Seriously, I do not belong here, in this time, this place, never did, never will. It's a hunger," he said, his fleshy face glistened, "a longing to be a man, the man I was meant to be. It *eats* at me, Jack. Eats at me. You, Jack, what is the core of you?"

Sharl returned to our table, rescuing me. I had never wondered who I was. Who I was, was something I had always known. I was my family. I was Molly. I was Edie. And, I realized, I was Patty Pugh.

As the waiter cleared the table, Sharl sat down. He said something to the waiter in French and held up three fingers. The waiter nodded, then went away. The Major and Sharl talked about the weather, in English. Tomorrow, they said, it was supposed to turn cold.

"Cold?" I said. "This isn't cold?"

They laughed. The Major clapped his hand on my shoulder. "You'll learn," he said.

The waiter brought a tray with a votive candle and three brandies. He swirled the brandies over the votive before he set them in front of us. There was also a leather humidor on the tray. The waiter opened the box, held it out for the Major. The Major looked up, his face shining. "Cubans," he said. "Habanos."

The waiter pulled a clip from his pocket, snapped the end off the cigar, handed it to the Major, then did the same for Sharl and me. The Major and Sharl poked their smokes into their mouths and pulled them out wet. I followed their lead. Sharl lit us up with the flame from a gold lighter. I sucked in the smooth wonder of that stogie, let the soft blue of it waft up and into my eye. The closest thing I'd ever had to a cigar was one of Dad's Tiparillos before I married Molly.

Sharl tapped the side of his head. "The Major is a very smart man."

The Major tipped his head, fake humble.

"This place," Sharl drew his arm in a broad gesture that took in the room, "would never be if it was not for the Major."

The Major drew on his own Cuban.

"Oh?" I said.

"Like me," he patted his chest, "you would be smart to have the Major be your partner. Like me, he will help make you rich."

"You own part of the," I started to say the name of the establishment, then realized I had no idea how to pronounce it, "restaurant?"

Sharl answered. "The Major owns half of Montreal," he said.

"Sharl," the Major said, "you do exaggerate." He was looking modest, but false-modest, like what Sharl said was true.

And as if to back up what he said, Sharl ticked off some items with his fingers, "Hotels, Indian antiques shops. Even, part of *Beouf et Biere*." Sharl pulled a cardholder, made of some rich-colored animal skin, from his pocket. He set a business card beside me. Charles Renaud, it read, restaurateur. He laid his hand on my shoulder and said, "Welcome to the brotherhood, Jack."

AS WE WAITED for the dessert, a flambé, the Major said, "So, Jack, you into anything interesting?"

"Into?" I said.

"What turns you on?" I guess he could see I wasn't tracking. "What twirls the tail of a man like you?" He laughed at what he'd said, dabbed at his eyes. "Hobbies, you must have some hobbies, a man like you."

I looked down at the table. Our plates had been neatly taken away, crumbs from the bread swept up with a little broom the waiter carried. The candle, half burned down, danced around in the movement of air stirred up by the staff. I thought, but couldn't come up with anything in my life I could label a hobby. The closest I could come was the town team baseball I used to play with Larry and Raunch and some of the other guys around town. So I said, "I used to pitch a pretty mean game of baseball."

He laughed, like I'd said something funny. He circled his fingers around the rim of his brandy snifter, set the glitter of his rings to life. Then, under the awning of his eyebrows, he looked up at me and straight into my eyes, and he left his gaze there long enough that it made me look away. "Come on, Jack," he said. "Don't be coy. You must have some good times where you come from."

"I guess so," I said.

"A lot of squaws out your way?" He had that look again, dipping his head, putting his chin on his knuckles.

"The last time we played ball," I said, "before the team folded, we played with only seven guys."

The Major blinked.

"Against Milton," I added.

He took a sip from his glass of water. The ice clinked. He held the glass dangling in his fingers from a limp wrist. "A squaw," he said, "knows what a man wants. It's the way they're brought up," he said. "Cultural."

"I wouldn't know," I said.

"Charlotte and I can show you some fun," he said.

"Fun," I said.

"It's a trip," he said.

"I don't know," I said.

He lifted his rear end off the chair, began fishing around in his back pocket. He brought out his wallet, opened it. It was thick with twenty-dollar bills and the corner of an American Express card. He poked a finger into one of the pockets, brought out a photo ripped from the page of a magazine. It was a picture of a black-haired woman looking over her bare shoulder, smiling at the camera. It was worn at the creases as much as I'd worn out my note from Patty. He set the photo in the candlelight at the table, patted it with his fingers. "There she is. There is Charlotte, my Morning Dove."

I drew closer to the picture, saw the cloud of black hair, the worn-out flirt in her smile, and knew for positive I wasn't going to find Patty in Montreal. "It can't be her," I said, "this one is too old. The one I'm looking for is only a *girl.*"

He looked me straight in the eye, then, as if measuring what more I had to say about the photo. He wiped the napkin on his forehead. I could tell he was nervous. I shook my head.

"Oh, Jaysus," he said. "Fuck, man, I mean." He folded the photo into the tight little pocket of his wallet. "You can't imagine the trouble the Major would be in if my Charlotte was your Patty, only a girl. My name wouldn't be worth shit around here, everything I worked for down the tube." He slapped the table. "The worst," he was gleeful now, "the worst would be that I would have to give up the best piece of ass in the province.

"Ah," he said, cozy now. He leaned forward. "Let me tell you all about my girl," he said, and he whispered, "my hobby." And he started to tell me about a scene he'd played out with her, a dream, or something, about how he was a cavalryman, captured and staked out in the desert sun to die a horrible death. "A squaw comes to me," he said, "and she offers water. Her name is Morning Dove." His knee was beginning to jump up and down under the table and he was starting to make some sound way back in his throat. It sounded painful.

I squinted at my watch. "Do we need to think about the time?"

He shook his head. "There's time," and the soft skin of his face fell back into his dream. "You wait," he clicked his tongue like what he was about to say was incredible, "just wait 'til you see her."

I relaxed into the booze, into the way his kind of talk was beginning to seem OK. "How did you meet Charlotte?" I said.

"Morning Dove? Princess?" He shoved himself up closer to the table, his gut squeezed over it. "It was her who met *me*."

I flipped my eyebrows at him.

"You ever hear the legend of Jim Little?" he said. He pushed even closer until the fat of his gut rose into his chest like breasts. He cupped one hand to the side of his mouth. "The Second Cavalry," he said. "Ambushed by Pawnee." He leaned back to assess the impact that had on me.

I slugged another gulp of my brandy, thought about what Molly would make of him, then shoved that thought out of my head.

"The whole regiment," he swept his hands away from himself, "killed. Braves counting coup. All except Major Dunne, the leader of the unit. With him they didn't count coup, didn't give him the mercy. Him they kept alive for more. He was shot, one arm useless. But he kept up the fight, shooting with his good arm until every shell was spent."

The Major's eyes gleamed in the candlelight. "At which point he began attacking those braves with his saber. The braves finally felled him with an arrow to his leg. For hours they let him lie there, circled him on their horses, the stain of his blood darkening the land. And still they did not count coup. The prairie was marked by the bitter battle, the convergence of the blood of his men, and Major Dunne's helpless form lying among their corpses.

"The braves robbed him and his men of everything, knives, swords, guns, everything. And when they had gathered what they wanted, they pounded four stakes into the hardest ground and dragged Major Dunne toward the stakes, through the blazing heat, his feet tracing two useless trenches. He could not move, could not but understand that he was the leader of the enemy and the braves would test the measure of his courage.

"The Pawnee braves tethered his hands and his feet at the stakes with rawhide."

The Major was getting excited, his words coming faster and faster. More and more the story was beginning to sound like a movie.

"From an outcropping of rock," he said, "a Pawnee maiden watched as the braves beat Major Dunne again and again, and she watched as he bore the agony yet made no sound. And more and more of his life bled into the dry earth. She watched as the braves circled the beaten form of Major Dunne one last time, and finally they left. For two days she watched as he lay there, day and night. For two days she waited until he began to moan the tremulous sounds of dying. Only then did she come out from hiding in the rocks, only then did she kneel beside him, and offer cool water to his raw lips. He was nearly out of his head. But, in spite of his condition, he did manage to whisper, 'Acchhtahh,' in her tongue."

Maybe the story was true, maybe it wasn't a movie.

"The third day," he said, "the Pawnee princess came again. This time with a whip. She knelt by him, but she gave him no water. She stood and began whipping him and between whip lashes measured his bravery. And when his blood once again flowed and when he still had said nothing but that one Pawnee thank-you, she unbound his hands and his legs and took him in her travois back to her village."

I had an urge to ask what happened next but didn't.

The Major wiped his forehead on his napkin, sweat running down his cheeks in rivulets. He dabbed his face dry. "She was," he said, "some woman, Jack." He shook his head. The sweat had already shined up his face again. "Some woman."

He leaned himself over his drink, set his round elbows on the table. He held up his two index fingers a shoulder's width apart, then brought them together in front of himself, "Charlotte," he said, "the Pawnee princess, one and the same."

311

IT WAS AFTER ten o'clock when we left the restaurant. "Don't be a stranger," Charles said. It was the same thing Kenny Muffin had said the last time I'd seen him.

There must have been a million people who came up to Montreal for the Olympics not long ago. Some must have seen Sainte Catherine and Saint Denis streets. Or maybe they didn't see them at all. Maybe the tour buses missed that dirty part of the city, maybe the Chamber of Commerce kept everyone away. It wasn't the type of place you'd see in a brochure.

The Major drove the Cord past dark windows boarded up with plywood and written all over with paint. The streets were lit by the blinks of lights. "Danseuses," "Foxy Ladies," "Nues," "Films Erotiques," "Films Peeps."

A couple of blocks from the main corner, on a street named Sanguinet, rode two guys on horseback. Men on horseback were something you might see around Round-Up time in Pendleton. But *Montreal*? One of them was swinging his leg off the saddle as we pulled up. Snow swirled in drifts at the curbs, the panes of what few windows were not boarded up whipped in the gusts of the wind.

The fellows on horseback were both dressed in black leather coats that buffered the wind and shed the snow and draped over the haunches of the quarter horses. Panniers hung from their saddles.

The Major pulled up, cut the engine. The guy who was still up on his horse rode over. "Sergeant," the Major said.

"Sir," the rider said.

From my seat, I could hear him, but could see only the brisket of the horse and the tie-down and the rider's legs. The horse was a gelding.

The Major looked up at the rider through his open window. A bitter cold blew in. "What are the numbers tonight, Sergeant?" he said.

The horse stomped, the saddle groaned. "We counted fifty-sixty, sir."

The Major shook his head, clicked his tongue. "In this weather."

Snow whipped through the legs of the gelding. "There's one girl's been beat up, maybe a jaw broken," the rider said. The gelding stomped again, turned sideways, close enough its haunch touched the Cord. I could see the rider's thigh then, and the pannier filled with bread and a huge Thermos. As the horse moved, I could hear the liquid slosh in the Thermos.

"Bad?" the Major said.

"Looks like it," the sergeant said. "Corporal Higgins is looking her over." Up the street ten to fifteen yards the other rider knelt down on the sidewalk. He huddled among a dark group of kids, teens mostly, standing beside someone lying, unmoving, on the concrete. He said something to one of the teens and the kid went to the fellow's horse and untied a bedroll from the cantle. For a moment the wind whipped up even worse and a drift of snow obscured my view. When it cleared, Corporal Higgins was settling the blanket over the person on the sidewalk.

"How many meals have we given out tonight?" the Major said.

"About three dozen," the sergeant said.

"That one," the Major bobbed his head toward the body on the sidewalk, "need medical?"

"Looks like she's got something internal going on," the sergeant said.

"Get her help," the Major said.

"Yes, sir," the rider said, then bent down to shake the Major's hand and I could see part of his face. He was young, maybe thirty, with a wool scarf wrapped under the leather collar and over his mouth. His forehead was smooth, reddened from the cold. The Major turned to me then and said, "Sergeant La Croix, this is Jack McIntyre."

"Pleased to meet you," the sergeant said.

"Same here," I said.

"You joining the regiment?" he said to me.

"He's visiting," the Major said, "from the States."

"Getting a glimpse of the good the Major does?" Sergeant La Croix said in a tone that sounded like he might be talking about a saint.

"You bet," I said.

"Because of the Major, the Regiment is saving kids' lives every day."

"Sergeant," the Major said in a warning tailored to sound modest. It was clear a lot of people in Montreal thought the Major was some kind of god. "Get her to the hospital," he said.

Sergeant La Croix nodded to me. Then the saddle groaned again as his face disappeared from view. I heard him say, "Sir," again and he must have saluted, because the Major's hand rose part way up. The gelding turned and clopped away.

The Major put the Cord in gear, and as we drove away from the dim sadness of the neon lights, I said, "How long has the regiment been out here?"

"Just over a year," he said. I started to ask why there were so many hungry kids but he went on. "The Olympics brought them. Thousands of them, tenfold more than there ever were before. All young." His voice grew soft and it looked like his eyes were tearing up. "I guess," he said, "they all have different stories, but after a while they start to blend into one. They come from places no one should ever call 'home.' Places," he hissed, "so bad they have to leave. And they come up here, broke, no place to stay. They shoot up to be able to face another day, another night, and they get sick, and they starve."

I was beginning to wonder why these kids held such a soft spot for him and then he said, "My little Josette got involved." His foot let up from the gas, the car slowed as if allowing him to think. "Don't get me wrong, she had—has—a wonderful home. She just got in with the wrong set of kids. I shipped her off to Arizona, a place that straightens out what goes on in kids' lives. Every time I

WHEN PATTY WENT AWAY

see one of them, I see my little Josette. And it keeps you from sleeping at night. Keeps you from sleeping."

And the story he was telling could have been straight from the mouth of Patty Pugh, only Patty didn't have anybody to send her to Arizona. Patty didn't have anybody in the world but a mother whose mind went wrong somewhere along the line, and she had Edie. Patty had Edie.

chapter 47

THE CLUB SAT like a black-sheep relative on Crescent Street among fancy shops with furs and expensive clothes. The place was called *Le Club Perroquet*. Two huge parrots perched on swings behind the glass of the front windows. A sign with the image of a parrot and the words "Danse Revue" blinked red, yellow, blue over the front door.

The Major threw the keys of the Cord to yet one more fellow, this one standing in front of the club wearing a fur coat and white shoes. The car, for all the care the Major seemed to take of it, might as well have been our old Chevy truck. In the course of our dinner, he had made an offhand mention that the Cord had once been Tom Mix's. I knew the actor rode horses in the movies, and every kid in high school knew he had driven a Cord. We also knew Tom Mix died in it. The Major said he had bought the wreck from someone in Arizona and paid a mechanic thirty thousand dollars to restore it. If that was true—and I was beginning to think everything he said when it came to money was true—I had been riding around Montreal in Tom Mix's car.

A guy with a low forehead and black oiled-back hair greeted us at the door of the Club *Perroquet*. The Major handed him thirty dollars. Inside, the place smelled like stale whisky and dead cigars. We followed the shine of that guy's hair into the bar, which was nothing more than a small room half the size of our kitchen at home. They wanted you to pass on through the bar, because there wasn't room for tables, only the bar and a few stools, and dozens of bottles lined up on plain shelves behind the counter.

The bartender eyed us as we came in, nodded at the Major, then went back to drying shot glasses with a towel. The bartender was thick as a tree stump, muscled meat, no fat to him. And the bouncer looked like nobody you'd want to get on the wrong side of, his shoulders rolling high into his neck, arms rippling like the hills at home.

We went through the bar to a long narrow room lit at the opposite end by red and blue swirling lights. On the stage, a negro woman in red high heels and a red G-string wiggled her backside toward the audience. The Major squinted at his watch. "We've got half an hour or so," he said.

Rows of black speakers lined the ceiling like houseflies. The music thumped in my bones. A waiter in a white shirt that glowed like the Milky Way in the blacklight led us to a table right in front of the stage. As soon as we sat, he said, "Major, what can I get you?" He had black hair and a huge sideways crook for a nose that made him fearsome, in a way a crow can be fearsome. The scum of old smoke and the oil of hands filmed the table, made it sticky, and I didn't want to touch it. The place wasn't the *Beouf et Biere*, that was for sure, but I wondered if the Major owned a part of it, too.

The Major said, "Scotch?" He looked at me for approval.

I nodded my head.

"Doubles," he said and the crow and his white shirt disappeared.

I couldn't keep from watching the woman on the stage. She'd turned partway toward us and was swiping her hands up and down her stomach, smoothing them over her breasts, her skin so brown, so soft. Her hands cupped under the fullness of her breasts, held there a moment as she slid us a tempting, sideways tease. Then she put both thumbs under the strips of her G-string and danced her way out of it. She blew me a kiss. I felt a heat inside. Like a coward, I looked away.

The floor was filled with round tables about big enough for one person. No one but a handful of men up front were paying much attention to the naked woman. It appeared she'd been there awhile. A sheen of sweat glistened all along the sway of her back and down her legs. The music, some piece with a loud saxophone, was winding down, and as the drums thumped to a stop, she stooped over, picked up a pile of clothes on the floor and swung them over her shoulder. She walked off the stage naked with no more concern than if she were walking down Main Street, full-dressed, going to the post office to pick up her mail.

As I watched her wiggle off the stage, the Major elbowed me in the ribs, the kind of nudge that said, "What do you think of *this*, bucko?"

I dipped my head, hoped it seemed appreciative, but in truth I was winding up to a heap of guilt and fear that somehow Molly and her Lord Jesus were in the room right there with us and they would know everything, know that I wanted to be here, even that I could see some fun—some future—in living the kind of life the Major lived.

The waiter's white shirt floated over to the table. He set down our doubles. As the music started to blare again—reveille now—another girl pranced onto the stage. She was blonde, her skin white as cream, and she wore boots that came to her knees and that had heels so high she teetered sometimes. She wore a Girl Scout uniform cut short and high as a swimsuit. She sashayed out onto the stage and saluted like a soldier. Then, as the music bled into a jazzy piece, she started to shed her uniform. It took about five minutes for her to be standing there in nothing but an army-green G-string.

We downed the doubles, and the Major snapped his fingers for two more. The girl scout finished her dance and all the pain, the worry, the failures of my life, rippled away, down to the floor of the club as if worry was nothing more than a stain on the carpet. I felt wonderful, never surer of anything in my life. I had found my true brother in the Major, my partner. I clapped a hand on his shoulder as a dark-skinned guy climbed up on the stage. He had thick, black Elvis hair and said something in French in a thick, bored voice. The Major gave me a little nod, and a salute. The music was beginning to play, thumping drums, tom-toms. "My girl," the Major said, and his knee began to hammer under the table.

Elvis put down the mike. A black-haired woman dressed in a doe-colored Indian dress as short and fake as the Girl Scout uniform stepped out onto the stage. Her hair was dyed so black it looked like a solid thing on her head, and it bushed out from under her sequined Indian headband like a storm. She pranced out onto the stage in her "Indian" squaw's dress, fringe rippling high on her thighs, more fringe fluttering off the sides of her boots. She held a whip in one hand and a rubbery knife in the other.

The Major gave out a huge moan, cupped his hands on the rise in his lap. She strutted from one side of the stage to the other, pulling back that whip, snapping it over our heads. This, I knew, was Charlotte. I was beginning to feel dizzy. All the muscle drained out of me. Drunk with the Major's booze, drunk with relief. It was not Patty.

It was not Patty.

It was a woman with heavy eyes loaded down with black pencil and pasted on eyelashes. It was a woman with a set, hard mouth. It was a woman with tawny-colored grease paint smeared over every bit of her to make her look Indian. But she wasn't Indian, and there was no way she could be considered a girl either. The Major had trumped up some way to get me here, some way to make business for himself, and I was the lucky one who'd answered the call.

The tom-toms slowed, and as they did, she strutted one way across the stage, then the other, then back again, standing right in front of the Major with her legs a yard apart, letting those of us in the front glimpse the shadow at the top of her legs. She paid attention to nobody but the Major. It was like, for her, no one else was in the room. She heaved back on that whip, whirled it to a snap as loud as a bullet over his head. The Major groaned, "Save me." Chairs behind us were shuffling, legs crossing, men grabbing themselves. Sweat ran down my own ribs.

She lashed the whip near the Major's ear one more time. She was not looking at me, she was not looking at anyone else in the audience, her attention was only for him. She snapped the whip again. I was beginning to feel the room start to move, was beginning to see everything from some place high in one corner of the ceiling up by the speakers. I saw the Major raise his hands as if in surrender. I saw her wind the whip around his wrists and draw them together. I saw her pull him up to lay on the stage, the butt of his cavalry pants rising toward the audience. I heard her say in a low growling voice, "The Major will die," and she drew back the whip and snapped it again, so it missed the fat of his buttocks.

I couldn't remember anything after that.

chapter 48

FOR A MOMENT, I thought it was the terrible scum in my mouth that woke me, the taste of a pigpen. My gut was sick, my head exploding.

A knock came, again, sound that pulled away sleep. I didn't know where it came from, didn't know where I was except in a bed that wasn't mine, in a room that had no cracks on the ceiling, no windows with a moon bleeding in light.

The knock came again and a voice said, "Mr. McIntyre?"

I peered toward the noise and another shot of lightning split my head. A thin strip of light shown under the door. "Mr. McIntyre, it's Sergeant La Croix. The Major wants to know if you would come with me."

The Major? Ah yes, I was in the Hilton in Montreal.

I rose up and sat there for a moment, my head in my hands.

There came another knock, louder this time.

I stood, waited for the nausea to pass, stumbled toward the door.

I was still dressed. The smell of the club and the dead odor came from *me*. The reek was everywhere on me, in my nose, on my hands, in the jacket I hadn't taken off since I left home a thousand years ago.

Standing in the doorway, with his hand raised like he was about to knock again was Sergeant La Croix. "The Major has asked me to see if you would like to join him."

"Join him?" I said.

"Yes, sir."

"Where?"

"Upstairs," he said in a secretive tone that implied I shouldn't ask any more. I still didn't know how I'd gotten back to the hotel.

"What time is it?" I said.

He looked at his watch. "Three thirty, sir."

The hotel was so quiet, he could only mean three thirty in the morning. He reached beyond me, pulled closed the door as if he assumed I would follow him upstairs as the Major had requested.

THE ELEVATOR LET us off on the top floor. At one end of the hall was a room with two double-wide doors. Standing like a sentry was another of the Major's men, dressed like Sergeant La Croix, in a Union uniform. Sergeant La Croix pulled a key from the tunic of his coat, unlocked one of the doors. He motioned me to go in but remained in the hall as he closed the door behind me.

The room was dark. I stood in the entry blinking, not quite sure where forward was. I put out an arm to feel for a wall, and as I did I heard someone—a man, mumble, "Have mercy." I thought I hadn't heard right, thought it was the liquor that was making me hear things, turning this night into the strangest night of my life. The top-floor room at the Hilton seemed to torque, bend, and go crazier than anything I'd ever encountered, even at Jackie's.

A man, not the Major, said, "McIntyre?" and I felt the touch from a hand coming from somewhere out of the dark.

"Yes," I said.

The hand gave a gentle pull. "This way." I followed along, blind. Drapes rustled, and a sliver of dim light showed through the opening. I was in a large room, a living room with a heavy leather couch, two wingback chairs, and a small table with four more of the wingbacks. There was only one light on in the room, a dim nightlight that sent shadows so deep they could have been in a child's nightmare.

Off to the right, through another door, I could see the foot of a bed, the covers rumpled, the spread draped sloppily on the floor. I heard thumping, moaning as if somebody was in pain in there. "Mercy," and there was the sound of thrashing as if somebody was hurt.

There was a third man in the room, sitting on a couch. "Go on in," he said. I hesitated. "Go," he said. It wasn't something I really wanted to do, but he stood and gave a firm push on my back and I went.

The bedroom was even dimmer than the living room. A small candle flickered from somewhere beyond the bed. Two more of the sergeant's men stood, nearly in the dark, against one wall. They were looking down at something on the floor, something I could not see from where I was. One of them had the fly of his pants open and was jacking off.

"What is this?" I said, but no one answered.

Another fellow, dressed in civilian clothes, was sitting on the bed, leaning over a small mirror. He had rolled a paper bill and held it to his nose as he snuffed from a row of white powder. I didn't know what it was, for sure, but I had a hunch.

I heard the groaning again from beyond the bed, saw then the backs of two women, kneeling there. Their hair was arranged in braids, each of them were dressed squaw-style in soft leather dresses. They were working on someone down there, someone in pain. If somebody was hurt, why were those guys standing there doing nothing? Why were the women the only ones doing anything?

Then all of a sudden, one of the women rose up with a whip in her hand and made a mighty show of bringing it down on whoever was lying there. But at the last moment, she slowed the whip and merely laid it on him.

"God," he screamed, "the pain."

She was dressed in a white Indian dress. The dress was soft, the leather fine, and the fringe lying along the yoke of the back a foot long. A Umatilla Indian princess's dress.

I could see then that his boot was strapped to the leg of the bed. The boot moved violently as he screamed. I leaned over the bed, as she pulled back the whip one more time. The boot belonged to the Major. Both of his feet were tied to the bed, his wrists tethered in rawhide to the legs of a high chest. He was hard, the buttons of his fly rising in a row like a regiment, his hips flailing left and right, and his stomach stretched so that his fat lay in folds around his belt.

"Mercy," he said. "Have mercy on an old soldier."

One of the women stood up then, shook out her knee, as if she'd been kneeling there too long. She wore a tan Indian dress with beads along the shoulders. As she stood, she muffled a yawn.

The other woman, the "princess," still kneeled by the Major. She had not looked up since I came in, but I could see by her black hair that it was the woman from the club, the one the Major called Charlotte La Force. Her braids were interwoven with strips of rabbit fur now. The skin at the back of her head where the hair parted was white. The braids were thick enough to tether a ship and the ends of them flew out in puffs like black cotton. She drew back the whip.

"Water," the Major whispered, like his throat was parched dry enough to die.

"Get him some water," she said, her voice sleepy.

I could see, then, that the other Indian girl was not very old, her cheeks were round and young. I wasn't sure, but I thought she was the girl who had danced at the club, the fake Girl Scout. Her face was scrubbed clean of makeup now, so I wasn't real sure. Without the makeup, she looked a lot younger, like she wasn't much older than Edie. But her coloring was sickly, yellow as a newspaper that had been lying around for months. She moved sluggishly as she sauntered to a bar at the end of the room, dumped ice from an ice bucket, filled the bucket with water from the little sink. It was like she had spent the whole of her life in this dim place with the Major writhing on the floor. She pushed by the guy with the open fly. He was whimpering now, making a chorus with the Major that had no tune. He was about to come. The Indian girl didn't even take notice of him keening a high "jeh, jeh, jeh," sound.

The Major's Indian princess was tapping him again with her whip. He writhed back and forth as if it gave him a huge lot of pain. The other girl brought over the ice bucket. The Major's Indian princess reached up to take it. I could see then that she was missing the tip of her ring finger. She had washed her face and wore no makeup now. I could see the side of her face, her profile scrubbed clean as she turned my way, and I saw the dark spot of a mole over her lip, the burst of freckles on her cheek.

There was some philosopher, or somebody we read about in school, a writer who said you could sometimes see eternity in the bottom of a teacup. A teacup. I hadn't even tried to guess what he'd meant when he wrote it. Why did it come clear now? Why did that particular thing—a teacup for Christ's sake—make sense? What that writer saw in his teacup was loss. He saw losing everything in the crack of one moment. He saw the scold in his wife's eyes at one more of his stupidities. He saw his daughter lost in a world neither she—nor anyone—could ever, ever, ever understand. He saw the beauty temptation could be wrapped in. He saw the rich glow of sterling in a belt buckle, he saw the silky burn of brandy when it rolled down your throat, he saw the rich tangle of colors in a coat made from an old Pendleton blanket, he saw the cat's curve of a car once owned by Tom Mix.

In the spark of a moment, I saw that eternity. "Edie," I whispered.

The Major jerked on, hearing nothing, feeling nothing but that fantasy of his.

Edie. Edie. It was like the Lord shouted her name at me. I'd come to Montreal for the life and the future I thought my daughter should have. If life had been different, if Edie had been Jackie and Larry's, it would be *her* kneeling there beside the Major's gross gut.

"Patty!" I shouted.

She jumped, heaved the ice bucket. It hit a wall, and water ran down onto a light plug. The plug sparked, then poofed black. She fell against the bed, her legs and her moccasins pedaling back, away. Her hand flew to her mouth, startled.

"Jack!" she shouted, and for a moment her face went soft and round and she was eight years old again, the girl I used to know.

"Fuck," the Major yelled. He was writhing now, for real, pulling against the bindings. He bellowed, "Get the fuckhead."

All of a sudden, a flurry of blue uniforms grabbed me, knotted my hands behind me, wrenched my head back.

Patty's mouth went tight then, her eyes squinting, once again the used-up eyes of the dancer on the stage. The eight-year-old flashed away, replaced in a bitter pinch as if she thought somehow I was part of the Major's sinister notions. Someone jerked back on my neck, held it there so all I had a view of was the ceiling.

"Patty?" I got out again before somebody shoved his fingers in my mouth and pulled down my jaw with such force that I couldn't close it.

I heard the Major flopping this way and that in his bindings.

"I thought you didn't know her. Fuck. Fuck. Get him out of here," he shouted. "Get him out of here."

I managed to bite down on the fingers. The soldier grimaced, jerked them out of my mouth. "*Merde,*" he said.

Somehow Patty pulled herself up off the floor and was standing there with the whip dragging.

I blurted out, "What are you *doing*?" And I heard the way it sounded, like scolding, like a schoolteacher, like Molly when she found the girls into something they shouldn't be. How, in all of this, could I be so calm?

"Untie me," the Major shouted. One of the soldiers kneeled in the spot Patty had been. He started to cut the bindings with a knife.

"Get this prick out of my sight," the Major ordered. "Get him the fuck out of here."

"Where?" One of the men said, "The dump?"

"Fuck," the Major said. "What do you think?"

The soldier turned, muttered something in French. Another of them was not having any luck undoing the Major's bindings, with him thrashing around like he was.

"Jesus," the Major said, in English now, "He's got a fucking trail. Not the dump. Get him out of fucking town." And the Major started shouting in French and I couldn't understand anything more.

I managed to say, "She has to come too."

And the Major bellowed, "She's not going anywhere, fuck-o. She's mine."

I FELT THE scrape of the fellow's nails on my neck, the clasp of someone's hands grabbing at my arm, but I kicked, my feet got a purchase on the floor, and I bolted, free. I was in the air jumping over the bed.

Over the yells of his men, the Major screamed, "Cut me the fuck loose. Cut me loose."

Patty was pulling herself up, looking one way then the other, her braids flinging from her head, the fringe of the dress flailing. It was taking years to reach her, years. I flew through the air, and yet saw everything: men with knives, and swords, others likely had guns.

"Patty!" I shouted.

She was backing toward the wall, holding her hands up in front of her face, the fringe swinging from her arms. I landed half on the bed. The men started to scramble, blue uniforms coming at me. Two more of them were trying to free the Major, another one taking aim at me with the butt of a pistol. I felt the gun slam on the side of my head. I didn't dodge, didn't reach up, didn't do anything but grab the back of Patty's princess dress and one of her braids. I yanked her up and over the bed. She was so light, had no more substance than a blade of dry grass.

There was a flurry of cavalry uniforms, a squall of men yelling, the Major screaming. One of the Major's legs was untied now and he kicked around and landed a blow on the thigh of one of his men. A strange silence came from the room. I could still see movement, could see the gapes of the mouths of the men, their jaws swinging open and closing in yells and screams. But I couldn't hear one bit of sound. Nothing. Only the voice inside me saying I had to get Patty out of there.

In the awful scramble, I knew Molly and her Bible and her Lord were hitting me with one more of their tests. All my life I had failed, had come up short in every test Molly and her rightness tossed my way. I wasn't up to it, and for a moment I wavered. All our lives, I'd let Molly bear the doubt, the isolation of decisions mounted on her one after the other. Had she felt as alone as I did then, frozen to the edges of her bones?

The neck of the princess's dress, the rope of Patty's black braid were locked in my fist. My hand shivered as I yanked, pulled her up, over the bed. She yipped in pain, but I couldn't let go. I ran toward a cold place I didn't know, pulling her along after me. I pushed by two of the Major's men too stunned to do anything but yell.

Patty had no choice but to come along. I felt her resist, pull back like she always did as a kid. Then in one sudden step I felt her push into my hand as if she was part of me now, going with me.

We pressed toward the door, and the force of our motion

slammed me into it. It would not open. I felt, right then, on the cusp of getting away that the hotel door was going to do us in.

The men were yelling, the Major screaming, the force of Patty's body shoved against me. I turned the doorknob, but the press of us kept it shut tight.

Then I felt Patty pull away and I thought she'd decided to stay, but she yipped again. Someone was grabbing her, pulling her back. I held tight to her dress and her hair, felt the skin of her scalp yield a little, couldn't think how much it hurt. It was a tug of war, me on one end of Patty, the soldier on the other. He gave a fierce yank on her waist, the force of it pulled her and me back. The door yielded, flew open in my hand. I threw my weight forward. The fellow lost his grip and Patty and I bolted out into the hall, her head, her hair still locked in my grip.

He grabbed her again, and, from the side of my eye, I saw her moccasin fly back. The Major's man yelled with more urgency than the Major, and, as he grabbed at his groin, he let go and Patty was free.

We were out in the hall together, the back of her dress, her black braid still gathered in my fist. Her head was bent, her hands gripping my wrist as if she never wanted to let it go.

We ran. At the end of the hallway a green sign said "Stairs." I thought to let her go, it must have hurt her the way I clutched onto her, but I couldn't. Behind us, the men were beginning to pour out of the room, swords clattering, boots thumping. They were yell-whispering, as if keeping their voices down would not alert anyone staying in the hotel. So far, all doors in the hall remained shut.

I dragged Patty toward the stairway sign. The door opened outward. I pushed with all my might and whipped her through it, let go my grip. "Run," I screamed. "Run," I said again, as she stumbled against the railing.

"But," she said.

I pushed her hard on the collarbone, sent the fringe and her arms flapping. I said, "Call Molly."

Finally she started down the stairs. The Major's men were coming, silently, saying nothing. I braced myself in the doorway, locked my arms, my ankles tight as I could in the opening. First there were two men, then there were three, faces squinted up, red. One of them had his hand on his sword like any moment he was going to pull it out and run me through with it. I heard a little whisper of something behind me moving down the stairwell, the hiss of moccasin leather, the feathery sound of fringe as Patty disappeared.

One of the men bent over, rammed me with his head. It threw me back onto the landing where Patty had stood a second before. But she was gone. There was no sight of her, or the dress, no more sound of her moccasin.

Just as the men ran past, I threw out my foot. The first one tripped, rolled down the flight of steps. I heard the dull sound of something breaking, the crack of a bone, and he yelled out a hoot of pain. The other one drew out his knife, was coming at me with it. I made a fist with the same hand that had gripped onto the black braid of Patty Pugh. I aimed it between those two brilliant rows of his brass buttons and let go. The sharpest edge of my knuckles landed in the soft of his gut. He gave out a "whooof," and the knife flew out of his hand, hit the railing, and banged down the stairs. The rest of the men were almost to me. I turned to look down the stairs, saw the feather of fringe and a hand throbbing down the rail three stories below.

chapter 49

YEARS AGO, WHEN I was young—early teens maybe, Dad shook me awake in the night. It was summer, my upstairs room in the house was still warm. "Jack," he said, "I need you to get up." It should have been scary being woken up like that, but it wasn't. Something about the firm pat of his hand on my shoulder, the dim light of the moon from the window made it all right.

I started to put on my jeans.

"Just come," Dad said, then waited as I slipped on my boots without socks. Through the open window I could hear the high yip of a coyote, the call one of them makes when it's made a kill. And then came the bellow of a cow, an urgent sound, high, gargly, back in her throat. Dad was wearing only his pajamas, and, like me, nothing but boots on his feet.

I followed him to the back closet, waited as he grabbed the rifle and checked it for shells. As we left the house, the voice of the one coyote was joined by several more. The cow was silent then, but the coyotes were beginning to pick up their song. They were not very far away, out somewhere behind the corral in the near pasture where Trixie, one of the Hereford cows, had calved a day before.

In the moonlight, Dad held up his finger to tell me to be quiet and we stepped gingerly through the gate as the cow groaned and there was a horrible rustling of feet, yips from the coyotes, a scramble of movement we could barely see. Dad put the rifle on his shoulder, took aim, but couldn't see well enough to fire. I followed him closer, could make out now the still form of the calf on the ground, the cow stamping back and forth as the coyotes parried and dodged her horns. She kept at her hopeless task of defending her dead calf from the attack. She was alone, the far corner of the pasture darkened by the rest of our frightened herd, yet she didn't give up. Finally Dad yelled and frantically waved his arms. He took a shot at the dark form of one of the coyotes who had started to run. There was a scramble of movement and in an instant all the canines were gone.

The cow was what I thought of, helpless yet still protecting her calf.

I braced myself in the doorway again. The soldier on the landing was holding onto his knee, rolling back and forth groaning. The other, the one I'd punched, was still holding his gut, winded, but his breath coming easier. He'd be on me in a minute, or he'd be chasing after Patty, but there was nothing I could do about that.

I stood there, braced in the jamb, open as Christ on the cross when the Major, all veined red face of him, came out of the room. He walked slowly, like he had all the time he wanted at his command. He was tucking in the tails of his cavalry shirt. Two of his soldiers bracketed him. Their spurs, their knives in their sheaths, clattering toward me in a blue-shirted swath.

As the Major stepped up, the jowls of his face three inches from mine, I crammed my elbows harder into the jamb. His red eyes did not blink but stared into mine as if with a dare.

And there was an explosion of the Major's fist in my gut. From some miles away I heard the whoof of my own breath. I saw worms. I could not breathe.

Under his breath, the Major said, "Get the bitch, Sergeant."

From some other history I heard the clink of spurs, the rattle of a scabbard, and then I was lost to the buzz, and the worms, and the dark.

chapter 50

I WOKE WITH my head banging against the metal floor. I was being taken somewhere in the same van the Major's men used to pick up kids from the street, marked with *Cavalerie dans la Rue*. I smelled of vomit, of stale cigarettes, and of the reek of sweat. I pulled myself up. One of the two soldiers in the front seat saw me, then muttered something to the driver in French. In the flicker of the headlights, the piles of snow along the curbs were old, used, filthy.

We pulled up in front of the airport. The driver gave a wad of money to one of the porters and left the van at the curb. The two men took me by the elbows, paid for a ticket, and pushed me down the concourse. I had no idea what had become of Patty, and I could not bring myself to think about it.

For two hours we sat in the Montreal airport, waiting for the six thirty flight to Chicago, me sandwiched between the soldiers in the plastic seats. How different the crowds, the gates, looked now, darker somehow, as if harm resided in the very downward slant of the gate. Now and then a traveler with bleary eyes would flop by carrying a heavy coat and suitcase or a baby. Once in a while someone's attention riveted on the two strange men in their uniforms. But most of them passed on by without a hint of curiosity.

The men chattered between themselves in French, kept me out of the code of their talk. I understood none of it except the word "Mah-jhur," the Major.

My head still hammered, but the pain of it seemed almost friendly, deserved. I had blown it. And what would happen to Patty? That was the question: What would happen to Patty? It sure wasn't going to be *me* to take care of things, Molly's Lord had seen to that.

The PA system announced our flight, first in French, then English. The two men stood, yanked my elbows for me to stand, as if I were a cripple. One of them, the taller one, mumbled something to the desk attendant.

I thought they would leave me there and let me make my way down the ramp and on out of town, but it didn't happen that way. One of them said, *"Adieu."* The other escorted me down the ramp and took a seat next to me in the plane.

We spoke not one word between us as the plane made its way to Chicago. It was a breakfast flight. I couldn't eat. The stewardess served beverages. I couldn't drink, but the soldier did both.

After we landed, he escorted me to my next flight. I wondered if he was coming with me all the way home. I swallowed the thought; honestly I had no idea what to expect of anything. But when we reached the gate for the next flight, he gave me a nod and said, "The Mah-jhur has been forgiving thees time. Eef he sees you in Quebec ever again, he cannot promise what will happen." He patted the holster I knew was under his jacket. He squared his shoulders in a way meant to threaten, then he turned, and he and his shoulders and his tunic and his knee-high boots made their way through the crowd. This was not Montreal, people were staring at him, and I found a good deal of comfort in that.

MY FLIGHT DIDN'T leave for another fifteen minutes. The second hand of a clock on the wall chunked away the seconds. The clock and I had counted away ten minutes. All my life I'd believed other people, the Boone Ellises, the Lyle Whittys, whose cruel voices were the ones I heard. They told me over and over again how I came up short.

I held my breath, listened. And I heard nothing, no one. Nothing. God, to have Molly there right then. God.

THE HAND ON the clock leapt to 6:01. I stood up, went to the desk, and said, "I need to change my reservation."

The agent looked at me as if there was nothing unusual canceling a flight minutes before it left. She took the ticket, opened the paper folder. "It's prepaid," she said.

"Yes," I said, as if I understood what she meant.

"It can't be changed."

When I didn't answer, she said, "There are restrictions." She put the ticket neatly back into the paper folder, held it toward me. When I didn't take it back, she said, as if I were an idiot, "You . . . can't . . . change this kind of ticket."

Here was a ticket home, and I wanted to grab it from her and run down the ramp. I wanted to get back to Molly. "What's the price of a ticket back to Montreal?" I said.

She flipped through a book the size of the pope's Bible. "Coach or first class?" she said.

"The cheapest," I said. I pulled out my wallet, set it on the counter. I was so used to leaving it in its back pocket to shaped to my backside, of no more use than a place to put my driver's license and Edie's school picture. The agent told me that would be coach. As far as I knew, Molly had never hidden a cent from me, had never thought of it, or been as dishonest as I felt right then. I did have the money—sneak money—I'd hidden from her. In my wallet, under a thin flap of leather, was what was left of my per diem, money Molly had no knowledge of. It had given me some sense of strength, of being a man. Three worn one hundred dollar bills. "Coach," I said.

chapter 51

A STRETCH OF ten pay phones lined one wall of the concourse. Three dollars and forty-five cents, half the money I had left, bought me a call across three thousand miles. It would be about eight in the morning at home. I wondered if it was still raining. Had it only been two days since I left?

"Police," the voice said. Cathy, the reception clerk.

"It's Jack McIntyre," I said. "Is Ben Al in yet?" Lord, what if he wasn't?

"I think he's here," she said, and the phone clicked on hold.

He came on right away, "'Lo, Jack," he said, his tone low, maybe worried. He knew I was going to Canada, I'd called, told him the day I left. He'd warned me to be careful.

"I've got to ask you something," I said.

"Where are you? You home?"

"Chicago," I said, and I started in on the story, told him I'd seen

Patty and it wasn't good, like he'd said it might be. When I finished, the only thing he said was, "Geez, man."

"I'm out of my league, Ben," I said.

"You got that right," he said. "You get yourself home."

"I have to go back there."

"Then what?"

"Bring her home."

He said, "Wait there, buddy. I gotta make a call." He sounded rushed.

"I only got half an hour before my flight," I said.

"What's the number there?"

I gave him the number on the pay phone.

"Wait there," he said.

I waited, leaning on the little shelf, taking some kind of fortification from the phone book. American. Something I could understand. I never wanted to see Canada again. But Patty was in Canada, and she was in awful, awful trouble. It wasn't only for Edie, now, that I had to go back.

The phone rang. I jumped. "The Montreal Police will meet you at the airport. Apparently they've been trying to get something concrete on this Major for a while. He's a piece of work, Jack. You be careful, man."

TWO UNIFORMED POLICE were waiting for me at the gate. As we strode back up the same ramp I'd stumbled down a few hours before, they asked me questions, and I gave them answers that made it hard not to gag. But as we drove farther into the city, it got harder and harder to talk. I felt like passing out, breathless like I might never take a whole breath again in my life.

They stopped in front of the Parrot Club. It was just before noon. Behind the grease of the club's windows, a black-haired guy—one of the gypsies from last night—wearing a wild Hawaiian shirt was feeding the two birds, heaping food onto small shelves near the perches. The birds' eager squawks came through the windows and onto the street.

I followed the two police through the door. The gypsy looked up at us, then went back to putting food onto the shelves, oranges cut up in chunks, collard greens, cottage cheese, sweet potatoes, and some whole slices of bread. The guy finished then wiped his hands on a towel he had draped over his arm. "Yes?" he said.

The taller of the two cops said, "Your dancer named Charlotte . . . ,"

"Not *my* dancer," the gypsy said, "no more."

"Where is she?"

"Gone," he said.

"Where?"

"Where go?" the gypsy said, and then he added, "Where the Major takes them." And, for a moment his eyes widened and he looked startled, as if he had said something he shouldn't.

"I see," said the cop.

We left then, and as I followed them out, I said, "The Hilton."

"I'm very sorry, Mr. McIntyre, Sergeant Al in Pendleton, Oregon, already suggested we check the hotel. We stopped there before we came to get you. They will tell us nothing. They said the Major had not been in the hotel for some time."

"He was there last night," I said, "I saw him. He checked in with me. He paid for my room."

Both policemen folded their arms over their chests and stood there like they had suddenly realized something about me, and it wasn't good, and now they were both braced against me. "He brought me up here to see if we could do some business together."

And then one of the men said, "You might want to get back to where you came from." His voice was still, smooth, now, as if I was too small an item, too stupid, to be involved with him.

I'd come back to Montreal for nothing.

chapter 52

EACH DAY STRETCHED longer than the day before, growing into a string of warming days that once made a season I thought blessed like a hand on my back. The whisper of spring in the breezes almost made me forget.

I'd been running the springtooth, working the section closest to the house, pulling the harrow with the Cat where the gullies near the house were too steep for the tractor. The weather had dried in the two weeks since my trip; the sections I'd gotten planted in the fall had begun to sprout from the bit of rain that had come down when I was gone. The crops looked thin but alive, and, as I worked that morning, I searched for a word to describe a crop like that. Somehow courageous came to mind. Our hard-pressed crop might make it after all, in spite of everything. I forced that thought to take over the day, forced the search for a weed or a bare patch of ground to push away everything I'd seen in Montreal.

I'd told Molly some, but not all of it. Once again, I dodged what was truth, told her—and Edie—I'd found someone who looked a lot like Patty, and I let that lie as truth. She had asked how I got the cuts on my face and the bruises on my back and I told her I'd taken a tumble. She didn't ask if I had been drinking, but her expression told me she thought so. But what was real, what was true, kept me up at night, wondering where Patty was and if she had ended up in a dump somewhere.

At the end of that day, still dressed in field clothes, I put up the harrow a little bit early and went into Pendleton to talk with Sergeant Al, for probably the final time. He didn't know anything more, and I hadn't expected him to. On my way home, I stopped at Hal's. I bought a strawberry shake and sucked at it as I drove out of town, and the cream of it put out the fire in my gut, for a few minutes anyway.

Some nights, on a couple of doses of Nytol, I could sleep. But on others, even Nytol didn't take away the images of rich yellow cars and cities and horses and black-haired gypsies. They left an ache in my gut that took me to the bathroom for a handful of Rolaids.

Then, one night in mid-April, not long after dinner, the telephone rang. Edie was upstairs in her room listening to the radio and doing homework. *The Six Million Dollar Man* was on the television, Molly was crocheting in the rocker. I was trying to doze in the recliner, a crick already starting up in my neck. By the second ring, I heard Edie's expectant feet hit the floor upstairs. But Molly was already up and out of the chair, going to get it.

The phone didn't make it to the third ring. "Hello," Molly said.

Edie appeared in the hall archway. "Yes," Molly said, shaking her head to Edie that the call wasn't for her. Edie turned and went back up the stairs.

"I'll get him." Molly held her hand over the receiver. "It's for you, Jack."

"Who is it?"

"Didn't say."

I cleared my throat, took the receiver, cleared my throat again. "'Lo," I said.

"Jack?" It was a woman. Her voice was hoarse, not a voice I recognized.

"Yes."

She cleared her own throat. "This is Patty."

chapter 53

LIFE DID NOT start up the first day of January that year. It started that day, April 17, with no celebration, no fanfare, no rockets, just a quiet voice on the end of the phone.

The living room tilted as I stood there with the handle of the telephone stuck to my ear. I was grabbing it so tight my hand cramped, but I had to hold on or I feared it would start to slither out of my hand and slide on down to the floor.

Molly was standing behind me, her empty rocker still making little dips.

"Patty," I said. As soon as I'd said it, I felt Molly's hand on my shoulder, the warmth of it set the room straighter somewhat. "You home?"

"It was you, wasn't it, at the Bonaventure?"

"Yes." Didn't she know?

"I thought so," she said as if she had to convince herself.

"Patty," I said. And for a century neither Patty nor I spoke a word. I finally said, "Are you OK?"

"It wasn't a head trip, then."

"Are you OK?" I said again.

"I guess so." Her voice was dull, all the old dare and life gone out of it.

"Where are you?" I expected her to say Montreal.

I heard her muffle the phone, turn to someone, "Where are we?"

A female voice answered in the background. The phone came clear again. "Philadelphia," she said.

Molly's hand stayed on my shoulder.

"How's Mom?"

"Fine," I said.

"Really?" she said, wary.

"The LA is taking care of her."

"The *LA*?"

"Yes."

"Sure," she said like she didn't believe it.

"Murcheson isn't there anymore."

There was a pause, a silence, maybe the faint sound of her breathing. "Son of a bitch," she said.

"Molly's taking meals up to your mom every day."

There was a shuffling of the phone, like for a moment she couldn't talk. "*Molly's* taking care of Mom?"

"Yeah," I said.

She blew again. "Mom eating OK?"

"Fine," I said, "I think she's gained a pound or two." I looked at Molly for confirmation. Molly nodded. "They've cleaned up the place, got her some furniture and stuff." The line was quiet but for Patty's breathing. "Molly takes her supper every day and groceries every week. When you coming home?" I said.

"How's Edie?"

"Good," I said, "Edie and Marybeth are getting pretty thick." I realized that might not be something Patty wanted to hear. "But she misses you awful."

"Kenny?" she said.

"Doing good. Has a job at Hamley's."

"Yeah?" she said and the phone went quiet as if she had to have a moment to make sense of what I was telling her. "Elsie still OK?"

"No."

"Died," she said and her voice sounded ancient like dead was something she truly understood. Even *I* didn't understand dead.

"We want you to come home," I said.

"Does Molly know?"

I waffled, waited for an answer. "Yes," I said.

"All of it?"

"Not really," I said.

"She's there," Patty said, "isn't she?"

"She knows," I said and turned to look at Molly. She was looking away, out the back window, but there was no doubt she was listening.

"Prove it," Patty.

I said nothing.

"I thought so," she said.

"She wants you to come home," I said, "too."

"I bet," Patty said, an accusation. "Why did you leave?"

What I said now was going to unravel all that I hadn't told Molly, all that had kept me awake these couple of weeks. "The Major," I said. "The Major's men escorted me out of town. I went back, talked with the police, but you were gone." Molly's hand dropped from my shoulder. I hadn't told Molly about the police, hadn't told her I'd spent my per diem money to go back to Montreal after the Major had evicted me from Canada.

I heard Patty whisper something—"Fuck"—I thought.

"When are you coming home?" I said.

"Mom have a phone?"

I turned to Molly. "Jackie have a phone, yet?" Molly shook her head no. "No," I told Patty.

"Would you tell her," she paused as if she didn't know what to have me tell her mother, "to eat."

"I will," I said.

"And tell her I will see her one of these days."

"When?"

"Tell her," she said, then didn't say anything more.

I said, "You have a phone number I can call?"

"Maybe when we find a place."

"We?"

"Me and Aphrodite and Sheba."

"You taking care of yourself?" I said.

"Yeah, yeah."

"When you coming home?" I said again.

"I need to think."

There was quiet on the line again. I stood there looking at my feet.

She didn't say anything for a long while, then she said, "Daddy would have come up there, too." She sounded young then, and small.

"I know," I said.

"I didn't know anybody but Edie and Kenny gave a fuck."

And I could tell she was crying now, as much as she was trying to hide it.

"I got to go," she said.

"When are you coming home?"

"Lay off."

"When?" I said.

She laughed but her nose was all stuffed up.

We waited there for a year and a half, and then she said, "I don't know. I've got to think about everything."

chapter 54

FOR TWO YEARS after the call from Patty, we turned over the calendars: 1979. 1980. The Sandanistas made a mess in Nicaragua, Pope Paul died, Muhammad Ali took back his title, the Ayatollah Khomeini gave the boot to the shah in Iran, Patty Hearst got out of prison, Mount St. Helens blew her top. And still we didn't hear anything from Patty, not one word.

During those years, Molly and I did what we always did about things; we didn't talk about them. Every day, I shoved the thought away that something terrible had happened to Patty. I began to see her in all the murders in the news, all the faces of runaways they showed on the bulletin boards at Safeway and Gentry's markets, and on crime programs on TV. I grew certain Patty was lost to all of it, dead, hurt, or maybe her mind gone the way her mother's had.

Then one night, toward the end of summer, two years after the trip, Kenny called the house asking for Edie. Edie had been accepted to Oregon State by then. Her grandmother had bought her a gift certificate for books and a bunch of college clothes for her birthday. The clothes were of good woolens, cut slim, stylish. Molly's mouth turned in a little when Edie tried them on, but she didn't say anything. We'd be taking Edie to Corvallis to begin college as soon as harvest was done. I was already starting to get lonesome for her, even though I had enough to think about with harvest coming. In another week Edie, Lee, Molly, and I would start threshing.

Edie answered the phone that night. I was laid out snoozing in the recliner. Molly was knitting booties to sell at the church bazaar in the fall, getting up, now and then, to wander into the kitchen for ice for the glass of water she kept on the table beside her. Even though we'd pulled down the south and west blinds, the house was hot.

As soon as Edie answered the phone, she turned her back to us, her posture when she wanted privacy. Molly's needles quit clacking. I strained, along with Molly, to hear what was so secretive. Molly's needles only resumed when we couldn't make out the gist of the call.

Edie strung the cord of the phone as far down the hall as she could get it. She mumble-whispered, making sure neither her mother nor I could hear. For ten minutes her muttering went on to whoever was on the line. When she hung up, she appeared under the arch of the hallway. She waited a minute, crossed her hands in front of her waist, then she said, "That was Kenny."

Molly took off her reading glasses, laid them on the side table.

"Patty's coming home to get Jackie."

PATTY CAME ON a Sunday morning when Molly and Edie were in church. Only afterward did Edie confide that she knew what Patty had planned.

Kenny met Patty at the bus station in Pendleton. Without a word, Edie went with her mother to the nine o'clock service like they had every Sunday since forever and ever. At nine fifteen, Edie motioned to her mother she had to go to the bathroom. To make the bathroom excuse convincing, she tiptoed through the little side door leading to the restroom. But instead of going to the bathroom, she let herself out the back door of the church and, wearing the cotton dress she had made in 4-H, jogged four blocks down Main to the Masonic Hall.

Patty and Kenny were in Jackie's apartment waiting for her. By the time Edie got there, Kenny and Patty had already packed a small cardboard suitcase with Jackie's things in it. Edie hugged Patty, shook hands with Kenny, and said good bye to Jackie. Then they were gone.

Edie was away from church service for twenty minutes. The voices singing "Praise God from Whom All Blessings Flow" didn't waver as she took her place beside her mother, picked up the song with the rest of the congregation. No one but Edie and Kenny got to see her, and no one but Edie and Kenny got to tell Jackie goodbye.

chapter 55

1997

THERE'S KENNY AND Hanna and their kids, and there's Edie and Buster and their kids, and there's Molly and me. It's a clear day, with a low sun that promises, maybe, our first freeze tonight. When we left, the house was beginning to smell like the turkey Edie and Molly had put in the oven.

I take a Rolaids and it settles my stomach a little bit. Not much has changed at the Pendleton airport in the past twenty years. The floor of the lobby still clicks hard and cold under your feet, the murals over the counter still show scenes from the Round-Up and Happy Canyon.

Our lives have moved on, Molly's and mine and our daughter's. Mom died eight years ago while driving her Cadillac to a bridge game with "the girls" at Mildred's in town. A semi plowed into her on the west exit of I-84. I had finally managed to pay her all of what I owed her on the land. She left Lee and me what she still had, and mine was enough to pay off Edie's college. I still miss Mom's

357

high laugh, I still miss the way Molly used to cluck about the high-heeled shoes Mom wore until the day she died, and about the shock of blond wigs Mom took to the hairdresser and wore every day, even the day of her wreck. Molly never seemed to get over some kind of envy about the elegant ways of Mother, or of Helen and Lee, for that matter.

Molly and I hung onto the rest of the ranch. There were some bad years, years when rain gushered in flashes and washed gullies into some of the draws, years when prices went so far down it was hardly worth the effort to bring in the crop. Mr. Sturgis, the bank manager, was eventually promoted to a branch in Sacramento. The new manager was a woman with three kids. I guess she liked the way Molly approached things, and she pulled strings to cut us a little slack when things were tight. It still sits sour when I see Ingmar Steadman seed up on the Vancycle quarter he bought from us, or when I see the row of white towers where they put in wind generators. Those white towers are not ugly, but they don't belong up there on what I still feel is our place.

Through Kenny and Edie, we've kept up with Patty, though only in snatches that Edie thought we could swallow. A couple of years after her move to Philadelphia, Patty moved to Minnesota. It seemed like a curious place for Patty to end up until we learned she went to Minnesota because of her mother. The state of Minnesota had the kind of services Patty's mother needed, and they were available even if she was poor.

You think you put stuff behind you, but then something like this Thanksgiving brings back those years when everything in the world twisted up so it looked like it could never be right again. I would have imagined life meandering along its way altogether different from what it did. I would have imagined Patty growing up with us. I would have imagined her standing with Edie in the receiving line dressed in her green robe and mortarboard after high school graduation. I would have imagined getting letters from her every week, imagined them coming on Tuesdays, like the college letters came from Edie. I would have imagined her becoming a veterinarian, like Edie and her husband, or whatever she wanted to become. I never would have imagined any of what all happened.

Edie told us some of Patty's recent life, in preparation for today, I think. She told us that Patty has been sick with hepatitis for a few years. Edie says she is on a "vacation" from her meds—she calls them meds—for a while because they make her sick. She is feeling better, so she and her husband, Enrique, are coming for a Thanksgiving visit. Patty never had any kids.

I hardly think about Montreal anymore. It's like another century or something. I haven't spoken with Sergeant Al since a few months after I got back, though I heard through Kenny that he and his third wife moved to the Willamette Valley. He's chief of police now, in Salem.

The week I got back, the Montreal police were in touch with Al most every day, trying to get something to pin on the Major. Al even had the police in Philadelphia try to find Patty, but Patty hadn't given me enough information to find her there.

It turns out that the Montreal police had broken up a prostitution ring along the east coast of Canada. And guess who was the head of it. The Major and his *Cavalerie* were picking up kids from the street and "saving" them in the same way they'd saved Patty. The Major wanted to expand part of his business to the west coast of Canada and the US, so he paid for advertisements in some small-town papers, looking for hard-up chumps like me who were ripe for the plucking. He also wanted to see if I was a threat. Some of the facts could be funny, if you saw them in a movie, but this was no movie.

The notice the Major sent the *East Oregonian* was a pig in a poke, a way for him to get a rise out of whoever might know Patty up here. Apparently, before he had advertised in the Pendleton paper, Patty had stolen the genuine Indian dress one night. The Major's men caught her trying to exchange it for a bus ticket to Pendleton. She tussled with the men and got mouthy with the Major, telling him she knew authorities in Oregon and they knew where she was and who to look for, if anything ever happened to her.

At the Major's trial, one of his men testified that they could never get Charlotte La Force's real name from her, or the names of anybody else she knew. The Major had locked her up in the Hilton hotel room and had given her as much dope as she wanted, as long as she "pleased" him with her dancing and acting out their little "scenes."

If I had recognized Patty that night at the club, I know things wouldn't have worked out like they did. Who knows what would have happened to her? Who knows what would have happened to either of us? I probably would not be waiting for her at the airport right now. I do know I am a weak man, and I don't let myself think how close the Major came to winning me over. It still keeps me awake some nights.

I know now he wanted me to help him move drugs. His Indian goods business was apparently legitimate, and his wife continued to run it after he landed in prison. He'd been using her and her business as a cover. His prostitution business was huge, arms of it reaching down into Florida and west to British Columbia and Washington state.

A plane drones into view. All of us start craning our necks toward the west. "Here she comes," Kenny says. Kenny's big now, has a little bit of a gut. Gone are the days when he could run like the wind with his hair flying back like a mane. He wears a crew cut and a baseball cap.

It's Molly who's gotten thin, since her stroke six years ago. And she's changed in other ways, too. A stroke will choose its injury, will select the part of a brain it wants to work on. It left her a little bit weak on one side and it worked on the area of her brain that let her make lists and plans and set out goals for us and herself. And it worked on the part that used to make her worry and fret and grab up her *Word* and Bible. She still believes in the Lord, she still goes to church, and she still can recite the Psalms, and a lot more of the Bible. But she's no good at lists. Edie draws up her mother's menu now for dinners and every month takes inventory of the cupboards and writes out what her mother needs to get at the grocery. I keep track of the finances and write on the calendar the first of every month what bills need to be paid. And, instead of invoking the name of the Lord in her frustrations, Molly often throws up her strong arm and says, "What the hey." What the hey. Who would have ever thought it?

As for Edie, she married Buster while they were still in college at OSU. They have a veterinary practice together in Walla Walla. She seems happy with her life, her kids, and with Buster.

Funny that there are so many kids in our lives these days—eight, if you count Edie's, and Kenny's, and Lee and Helen's grandkids— two more than what Molly always wanted.

The plane puts down on the runway, lets out a little smoke from the brakes. We put our hands over our ears and take them away when the engines wheeze and then go quiet. There's a moment of anticipation. Edie's kids quit jabbing each other and running around, and they push up against the fence. We're all still, now, but for a few wisps of hair in the wind. At this moment we're all—every one of us—waiting for the side door to open and for the stairway to come down. I don't know what to expect. Edie's excited, I can tell, by the way she's biting her nails, but I don't think she's wound as tight as I feel.

The plane's door cracks open, and a male attendant in a starched white shirt stands in the opening as the steps unfold.

Edie and Kenny stand shoulder to shoulder near the gate. The kids are all lined up together. I think they might be as nervous as I am, because they are quiet. They've never met Patty or her husband. We don't know much about Enrique, only that he drives truck for the state of Minnesota, where Patty worked as a clerk in the accounting office until the hepatitis made her quit. They met at a meeting a couple of years ago. At first, Edie called it a support group and let me and her mother think it was for hepatitis. But one night she admitted it was a group for people who were addicted to narcotics, and it brought home all the kinds of things we never learned about Patty. The meetings helped them along with their lives, helped them clean up, but they still go to meetings three times every week, even more often than Molly used to go to church. The meetings hold them together.

We press tighter into the fence. The wind whips at our coats. The flight attendant stands aside, looking up the aisle, motioning for passengers to come out. It's as if someone has blocked up the passage. He cups his fingers around his mouth, says something into the plane like he needs to hurry things along.

The pilot wipes a speck from the window with a piece of white cloth. I dry my palms on my thighs. And, all of a sudden, there's movement in the dark of the door. A bush of short, dull, red hair pushes like a tumbleweed out into the sunlight. And there stands Patty.

I don't know what I expected, the old strut of her, maybe, or the stuck set of her jaw. It isn't there now. There's no strut about her. But she stands straight, shoulders back, ready it seems. Her small frame is lost in a huge white sweater and baggy brown slacks. It's as if she's shrunk, like a grape shrinks into a raisin. With one hand, she holds a hank of hair out of her face, then reaches up as a fellow steps into the doorway with her. He smiles at Patty, nods his head a bit, and I know this is Enrique. Edie's told us some about him, how he has worked at his job for twenty years, how he was the oldest of five kids, how he never married until he met Patty. He wears a base-ball cap and is dressed in a Minnesota Timberwolves sweatshirt. He's black. Edie never mentioned that.

Molly clears her throat. There's a flicker of judgment behind the sound of it, a hint of the Molly before the stroke. I squeeze a look at her, but she's already put the old thoughts away. There's no judgment behind her smile now or in the eagerness in her eyes.

It seems to bolster Patty to have Enrique there, and she waves one short wave at all of us before she starts down the stairs.

Enrique has a carry-on bag and a purse that must be Patty's slung over one shoulder. Patty starts toward us, but Enrique stands back. I feel responsible for the wither in Patty's face. It carries all the ways I failed to bring her back, failed to bring her home where she was supposed to be all along. In a crowd, I don't think I would have recognized her. She looks both the same age as Edie and a hundred years older. Her face is crinkled with lines that don't come with laughing. Her coloring is not pink and expectant like Edie's but yellow, curdled somehow.

Enrique stands beside the bottom step, facing into the sun. It is as if he's waiting to be invited, after coming all this way to get here. I know from Edie that Enrique is a quiet type of fellow. I know he almost didn't come on the trip because he's a homebody. I know Patty almost didn't come either, but Enrique insisted, told her for her sobriety she had to come home and make amends. When she still balked, he paid for a ticket for himself, and he came with her, to get her here.

Patty makes her way toward us. She stumbles at first, then bursts into a run as she gets closer to Kenny and Edie. Once through the gate, she collapses onto Edie, then grabs at Kenny, losing her face into his chest. Enrique is watching, standing there so still, all that moves of him are his pant cuffs in the wind.

Patty stands back, sniffing, blowing her nose. Edie is blowing as well, and Kenny's making some movement with the back of his hand that looks like he's working on a bit of nose drip himself.

I look at Molly, expecting some of the old reaction Patty always used to conjure in her, but she's only smiling. Though there's no dearness in her eyes, no sentiment, there's no judgment in them either.

I hear Kenny say, "Who'd a thunk it. Who'd a thunk it."

Patty pats him on the gut. "Yeah," she says, "Who'd a thunk it." And all three of them laugh harder than the joke warrants.

Finally Patty turns our way. She starts past Edie and Kenny's kids lined up at the fence. They stand there quiet like all of a sudden they've seen the ghost they've heard about all their lives. I can see how tiny she is under that huge sweater, her legs thin as chopsticks. Though Molly's the one who's nearest to her, Patty's eyes stick on *me*. As she gets nearer, Molly reaches out, and, for the first time I see a little color come into Patty's face, a flare of anger. Molly says, "Hello, sweetheart," and takes Patty into her good arm.

When Molly doesn't let go, Patty gives in, relaxes, like she never used to do in her life. Molly continues her one-handed pat. "We're so glad you're home, honey," she says.

Patty leans back and nods. Then she comes to me, and it's *her* who takes *me* in her arms. She's sniffing and I am too.

Patty motions Enrique over to us. "Jack," she says, when he gets to us, her throat thick and constricted, "this is Enrique." It's me she's brought her husband to and I want to swallow the urge to apologize for everything I never did right.

"So this is the guy," Enrique says. His voice is low, quiet, vibrating like a stereo speaker that's seen better days.

I shrug. "Guess so."

"This is the guy I hear about every day of my life," he says. He is calm, solid.

Patty puts her hand on his shoulder and says, "You'll like him, Jack."

I say, "I can see that."

He reaches out to shake hands. His hand is thick, like mine, and dry with a heavy thumb that speaks of hard work. But for the dark color of it, it could be my own hand. "So," he says, "this is Jack." His gaze is steady. "The fellow who saved my wife's life."

I look at Molly, hoping she can make heads or tails of this, but she is only standing there looking at me with her grin that says she knows everything. All I can hear is the wind, and the rush of my own breath. I say, "Well, I don't know." And then I realize I *do* know. I know we're all here—all of us—and it's everything. It's everything.

acknowledgments

WE WRITERS FANCY the idea we work alone, that we tell our stories singularly and from our own walled-off and silent caves. It is pure romance. Like Fibber's Molly said, "'Taint so, McGee." Writers don't become good at it without help along the way.

I was lucky. For starters, I had Lisa Norberg who delivered my first writing class, one for abject beginners. Lisa hammered on one of the most liberating and important lessons ever: that a first draft is pretty much solely to give you something to edit.

Then, thanks to the heavens, came Craig Lesley. Year after year I sat at a desk in a class filled with seekers like me wanting to learn to write, and Craig had years of experience and success to throw our way. I think every word I write now has some Craig in it.

Our stories can never bloom without the help of readers who read and yawn through all our writes and rewrites. I have had the best: Carol Hirons, whose honesty and insistence on finding the real story has been a miracle; Lisa Alber, an incredible writer herself, who has given me so much intelligence and insight I can't imagine how I'd have managed without her; Holly Franko whose red-pen edits can make a flawed manuscript right; and Elizabeth Wales who hung in there so long with me.

Along the way, *When Patty Went Away* also grew under the generous guidance of Jane Sterrett, David Lytle, Dan Gibson, and Michael Bigham; some of whom are also amazing writers.

And last I want to thank both Pat Brogoitti, whose knowledge of farming and his generosity passing it on, were key to *When Patty Went Away*; and Chris Wilson who shared so much that became essential to Patty's history and her story.

about the author

JEANNIE BURT WAS raised on a farm in Oregon. There were six, counting her, in her high school graduating class. She was related to half of them, a situation that fostered neither romance, nor privacy or adventure, but it did tend to keep her in line.

Her career in business and human resources allowed her to escape the confines of small-town life; she lived in San Francisco, New York and Milano where she became passionate about art. She adores Paris and visits often.

Jeannie has had two non-fiction books published: *Lymphedema: A Breast Cancer Patient's Guide to Prevention and Healing* and *What You Need to Know to Show Your Dog*. In the last years, she has put the writing of non-fiction aside to eat, drink, and sleep her first love: fiction.

When Patty Went Away will be her first published novel. Two more of Jeannie's novels are in the hands of agents.

CPSIA information can be obtained at www.ICGtesting.com
Printed in the USA
LVOW08s0031160714

394545LV00001B/121/P